Time Waits for No One

by

M. W. Arnold

Broken Wings, Book 5

The Wild Rose Press, Inc.
PO Box 708
Adams Basin, NY 14410-0708
Visit us at www.thewildrosepress.com

Publishing History
First Edition, 2024
Trade Paperback ISBN 978-1-5092-5500-9
Digital ISBN 978-1-5092-5501-6

Broken Wings, Book 5
Published in the United States of America

Dedication

I'll go against type and keep this dedication short,
for which, I'm sure, you'll be truly thankful.

~

My thanks, as ever, to Nan, editor par excellence,
and to the rest of the team at the Wild Rose Press.

~

To the best writing team on the planet,
the Romantic Novelists Association,
you're always there and I'm sure, always will be.
Here's to many more years together.

~

To the family Winter, I'll always be here for you.
Wookie shall always be remembered.

~

Finally, to my longsuffering better-half.
You're my muse and my life…enough said.

~

Keep safe all!

Prologue

"And I can't tell my friends about any of this?"

Inspector Herbert Lawrence stifled another yawn. It wasn't being called up in the small hours of the morning to come into London which was the cause, it was being unable to sleep on the journey up; and whose fault was that? It didn't help his mood that he could clearly hear Sergeant Terry Banks snoring away on the chair he occupied outside the meeting room. Driving at night in wartime England was dangerous enough without trusting your life to a speed merchant. If he hadn't been a witness, he'd never have believed it was possible to do the journey from Dorset to London so quickly when you could barely see the road! The car had been Terry's personal one—very inconveniently, Lawrence's official car was in for a service, and Lawrence hadn't realized his colleague was so protective about the vehicle until he'd volunteered to drive his boss up, every offer to share the driving had been politely refused, and Terry had so obviously enjoyed himself he didn't notice he'd been scaring his friend out of his wits.

"Are we keeping you awake, Inspector?"

Lawrence turned his eyes and hoped the odious man from the War Office couldn't read his mind. It was all right for him. When all this malarkey was over, he'd undoubtedly be back in his own bed within the hour.

"Not at all, sir."

Without troubling to even acknowledge this, the man took off his half-moon spectacles, shook out a spotlessly clean white handkerchief, and polished the lenses before turning his attention back to the rather apprehensive young woman on the other side of the table.

"Miss Coates, I realize you must be tired too," he said, making certain Lawrence saw him flick his eyes his way as he spoke, "but time is of the essence, and we cannot lose any more. Yes, if you agree to our proposals, not a word must pass your lips of what we are speaking about."

To give herself some thinking time, Sharon picked up the letter before her once more whilst musing upon what he'd just said. She wasn't even certain she could remember the name of this little man across the desk from her. Come to think of it, had he even offered it? About all she knew was that she was holding a letter from her maternal grandmother in her hands. This alone was a minor miracle! The woman herself was currently residing in Guernsey, occupied by the Germans since 1940. She was dying to open it, not having heard from her since the very beginning of May 1940 when her last letter had arrived. Despite her advanced years— somewhere in her eighties, Sharon believed—she'd refused to be evacuated when the opportunity came, having pressed a short letter onto a friend who was leaving. The letter, which had found its way into Sharon's hands, explained she would never leave the island she so loved.

The ministry man reached forward and took the letter from her hands. He did this gently, but firmly enough so she had no choice but to comply. Huffing, she opened her mouth, only to catch an encouraging smile from Lawrence, and stopped to take a steadying breath, instead asking him, "Why can't I read it?"

"Because…"

Lawrence didn't give him a chance to get started, "Let her read the letter. It's from her grandmother, dammit. Don't try and coerce her into doing something for you just so she can read a letter. We're not Nazis!" he finished and was very satisfied to see that his last words had the desired effect.

The man slid the letter back across to her.

"Have you read this?" she asked, and when he failed to reply, harrumphed. "Rather two-faced of you," she commented as she re-opened it.

The man had no response to this, and Lawrence had to work hard to turn a laugh into a yawn. Though he believed there was little this officious man could do to the girl, Lawrence suspected he himself could be transferred to somewhere a lot worse than Portsmouth if he pushed too far.

Wiping away a tear or two as she read her letter through twice, Sharon finally put it down and turned her blue eyes upon the dark brown ones of her interrogator; that was how it was beginning to seem to her. "So my grandmother's seriously ill and the Germans will treat her, but only if I provide information on the coming invasion." She then stated, "All rather vague, and how am I to get this…information? I'm no spy!"

Lawrence nodded his approval of the girl's words. He'd met her briefly the year before at a hangar dance with his wife and her friends and thought her very young for her age. Now, he amended this assessment. Young in years she may be, not even twenty, he'd bet, but she had an old head upon her shoulders. Switching his attention to the ministry man, he was in time to notice his mouth open and close a couple of times without any words coming out. Clearly, he was expecting Sharon to simply go along with everything he uttered; his admiration went up another notch.

"Leave that to us. So far as your colleagues at Marham will be concerned, you're moving south to be nearer your mother. Homesickness, if you will."

"My mother's dead," Sharon informed him. "I'd have thought you'd know that."

The man flicked through the pages of a buff file before him before clearing his throat and looking a little sheepish. "So I see. My apologies, Miss Coates. Your," this time he checked before carrying on, "Aunt Mabel. From what I can see, your only other surviving relative?"

Sharon nodded, though she looked far from confident. "And the information?"

"Leave that to us."

"Then what, exactly, do you need me for?"

The man's eye flicked around the bare room, as if expecting someone to come and save him from what was turning out to be a rather awkward situation. Except for Lawrence, who could only think he'd been brought in because of his tentative association with Sharon, there was no one else, so he was on his own, and he clearly wasn't comfortable.

He ran his hand through what remained of his hair. "Simply this. We'll arrange for you to be transferred to RAF Hamble, to work in the Air Transport Auxiliary mess there. Essentially, you'll be doing the same job as you're presently doing at Marham. We'll provide you with the information to send…which will be either out of date or fake…and then you write back. We believe there's a new operative at work on the south coast, and this will be a great chance to flush out him or her, though not before we use them to our advantage. The Germans would be able to recognize your handwriting. Undoubtedly, they'd have found some examples at your grandmother's house, so it has to be you in person."

Lawrence felt compelled to ask, "Surely someone could fake Sharon's handwriting?"

This suggestion got a shake of the man's head. "It would be possible, in fact, likely, if time wasn't of the essence. Sorry, but for this to work, it has to be Miss Coates."

Sharon poked the letter. "And how am I to get a letter to my grandmother? I doubt if I put one in the post box it would get there."

"You won't be sending it to your grandmother. There's a name at a POW camp in Germany you're to send the reply to, though I can't go into the exact method, as obviously that would be too slow to be of any use."

"If all Sharon has to do is to send a letter, then why does she have to move to Hamble at all? Why not simply have her write out what you want passed on and let her stay at Marham?" Lawrence asked, earning himself another annoyed glance, which he ignored.

"Because, undoubtedly, she'll be under surveillance, so she will have to be local to Southampton to back up the information she'll send. She has to be seen, so it's got to look right."

Lawrence arched an eyebrow at Sharon, who immediately understood and nodded her permission for him to continue speaking for her on this point. "That makes sense. However, nobody who lives down there is blind, we all can see *things* are happening. There are a lot of places where civilians aren't allowed to enter now. So how's a young girl supposed to be seen where she shouldn't be, without being arrested?"

"And what about my grandmother? Doesn't she get a say in this? What happens to her when the Nazis find out the information isn't any good?"

Lawrence decided the running-the-hand-through-the-hair thing was a nervous tick.

"That's why you're here, Inspector," he told Lawrence. "We haven't had time to work out all the details, but we'll be arranging for our people…"

"Who, exactly, are your people?" Sharon asked.

The ministry man turned on her the coldest smile she'd ever seen. "All you need to know is that I work for the War Office."

He carried on as if Sharon hadn't spoken, his attention fully upon Lawrence. "We're aware of some of the…shenanigans which have occurred around RAF Hamble in the last year and a half, and of your part in them. We also know you are in a relationship with a Third Officer Mary Whitworth-Baines of the ATA at Hamble." He quickly held up a hand and waved for Lawrence to retake his seat. "Calm down, Inspector. We're not bothered about those. What we want you to do is to be our local point of contact—and yes, before you interrupt, I'm aware you're based at Portsmouth and not Southampton. It's not ideal, but we'll be speaking to the Southampton Constabulary and making them as aware as they need to be. They won't get in the way. We'll provide Miss Coates with paperwork which will, if challenged, allow her access to Southampton seafront so it will appear she is doing what the Germans wish. I know I said things are a little hurried, but we have to give this a couple of weeks, at the very least. I'll be in contact with the information when I deem the time is right."

Sharon repeated, "What about my grandmother?"

"I didn't really want to tell you this, but I can see I'll have to," the man began, only to be interrupted by Sharon getting to her feet, sending her chair flying backward.

"I suggest you do, or I'm out of here right now!"

The ministry man shouldn't have got to his feet, as it showed Sharon was a good six inches taller than he was. She noticed this and made a point of straightening up.

"The man who brought that letter, he was *allowed* to escape from Guernsey. He hasn't got any family and wasn't their original choice, only he somehow managed to persuade the Germans to let him take the place of that person. Undoubtedly they wanted to be able to blackmail the person of their choice, and I don't know what he said to change their minds, and he won't tell us. But that's not important," he hastily added, seeing Sharon balling her fists. "This," he reached into the inside pocket of his jacket, "is. Before he left, he was allowed to speak to your grandmother, and the Germans made the mistake of leaving them alone for a few minutes. She took advantage of that and passed on this other letter to him, which he smuggled out." He passed her another letter, which had obviously been folded up as small as possible to aid concealment.

Sharon reached out and took the missive. It was simply addressed to her by her first name. "And I suppose you've read this too?" She got a simple shrug by reply.

Not waiting for permission this time, Sharon opened and read it. Barely a few seconds later, tears began to flow, though she didn't stop reading. Eventually, she put the letter back down on top of the other one and retook her seat.

"Sharon?" Lawrence said, placing a hand over hers.

She turned to face Lawrence. "It's definitely from her. I'd recognize Ada's handwriting anywhere."

"What did it say?"

"She's told me not to trust the Nazis. She doesn't believe they'll help her, even if they could." Sharon took a deep breath and accepted the handkerchief Lawrence offered her. "It's not a long letter, but she told me she's got terminal liver cancer, and she knew this when she chose to remain when the evacuations took place. She didn't want to be a burden on anyone. There are some other personal words, though in a nutshell, she's told me to not give them anything as there's nothing they can do for her."

Lawrence shook his head, noting the ministry man did the same. "Brave girl," Lawrence could only say, knowing words couldn't reflect his feelings and thoughts enough.

Sharon wiped her tears away and smiled at him. "She always has been." She fell silent for a few minutes, both men knowing she needed some thinking time. When she turned her attention back to them, there was a steely look to her expression.

Unexpectedly, she slammed a flat palm down onto the table, startling both men. "Right. Let's see what tricks we can play on the Nazis! I'll teach them to mess with Ada Coates!"

Chapter One

Sunday 9th April 1944

"I wonder if Jane's having an easier time than we are—" Ruth Stone interrupted herself to swear, again. "Mary! Watch it, please? It's the bed frame you're supposed to be screwing together, not my finger!"

"Sorry," her friend and next-door neighbor, Mary Whitworth-Baines, muttered, rearranging her aim from where she lay stretched out under the two single beds she was endeavoring to fix together in the attic of Ruth's cottage. "Look," she said, poking her head around the leg, "are you sure it wouldn't be easier to ask either Lawrence or Sharon to swap places with this pair? We then could abandon this malarkey before one of us really gets hurt."

What had been a wonderful idea, to have Walter's room in the attic of Riverview Cottage ready for the newly married couple upon their return from honeymoon, had quite quickly turned into a minor nightmare. Being a Sunday and with nobody at work, Ruth had rushed around to Betty Palmer's place and, over a breakfast of porridge and tea, had put to everyone the idea she'd had upon waking that morning. Jane Howell had, naturally, been delighted and had immediately volunteered to pack up Doris's belongings. This came as no surprise to anyone, as she'd be moving into Doris's old room once the girl in question had moved in with her husband. So whilst Jane happily hummed a tune as she went upstairs, everyone else put on some old clothes and followed Ruth from The Old Lockkeepers Cottage around to Ruth's. Walter, Ruth's friend, assistant, and a reporter at the *Hamble Gazette*, lived in the windowless attic of her cottage, hardly the most scenic of places in which to begin married life.

Looking around the room, Ruth sighed and rubbed her forehead.

"She's got a point," Betty agreed, her head popping up through the hatch. "It's very dank up here."

"When's the last time Lawrence slept over?" Penny's voice asked from somewhere beneath Betty.

Ruth shrugged. "I can't remember. Maybe a few weeks?"

"A week last Tuesday, actually," Mary supplied. "He came over for the quiz night down the Victory."

"I remember, all right," Penny said. "I still say the quizmaster was wrong. Bela Lugosi's Hungarian, not Romanian."

"Let it go," Mary advised.

"That was the biggest lump of cheese I've seen in years, and it should have been mine!" Penny loudly complained.

Betty looked down at her friend. "Mary's right, Penny. Let it go."

"Suppose I'll have to," was the grumbled reply.

"Well?" Mary asked. "What about it? We've spent the best part of an hour trying to fix one single bed to another, after it took us another hour to get the damn thing up here in the first place! Wouldn't it be simpler just to have Doris and Walter downstairs? We could fix up a double bed in Shirley's room."

"Ruth?" Betty asked, reaching up and tapping her friend on the foot.

"Hmm?"

"What about it? Shirley's still in training, and what's the likelihood of her being posted back to Hamble? So how about we move the things Shirley left behind up here and set up Doris and Walter in her old room?"

Ruth took her spectacles off, rubbed her nose, and replaced them. "I suppose that makes sense. Have any of you heard Jane say anything about her?"

"Not me," Mary replied, having heaved herself up into leaning against the wall.

"Nor me," Penny shouted.

"Afraid not," Betty added. "So how about it, Ruth? Shall we leave Lawrence's room as it is and do as Mary suggested?"

Ruth slumped down next to Mary and took the screwdriver from her hand. Looking wryly at her waiting friends, she told them, "We'd better get a move on, then, or we'll be here all day."

Mary looked between the bed they'd been wrestling with and the attic and then back to where Ruth was waiting. "The only problem with this is that we've now got to get this bloody thing back down that hatch."

Ruth could only exhale stoically.

Mary sighed. "There go my remaining nails!"

****

"So has anyone heard from the happy couple?" Jane asked, coming down the stairs carrying a bagful of Doris's clothes, with her ATA uniform on a hanger.

She was greeted by the sight of four rather sweaty and tired girls, all in varying degrees of dishevelment as they came in through the front door of Betty's place. The incident with an ex-Blackshirt of Moseley's was still so recent in their memories that they'd only recently taken to leaving their front doors unlocked again, and only whilst they were local to the cottages. Lawrence had insisted upon having an extra lock installed on the front doors of both cottages, and he being the local police inspector and a close friend, no one had argued. The only one not affected was Bobby, Ruth's faithful Cocker Spaniel, who made one of his regular appearances from the kitchen, where he had his own dog flap in Betty's back door.

"Do you think that can wait until you've put the kettle on, please, Jane?" Ruth asked, wiping her brow as she bent down to fuss Bobby behind his left ear, being careful to avoid the new growth of skin.

Ironically, for all the shooting and disruption the girls had suffered last February, Bobby was the only one of the group who'd actually been hurt. He'd had the bad luck to run into the man who was trying to blackmail Betty and had taken a stone to his head for his trouble. Patched up, he'd made a good recovery and swiftly returned to his old self. Cadging food off all and sundry, he'd made good in no time the weight he'd lost whilst recovering.

Seeing all her friends were tired out, Jane dropped the bag and hurried past everyone and into the kitchen. "Anyone feel in need of one of Doris's coffees?" she asked, filling the kettle.

"Just tea," Penny and Mary said at the same time.

"Just tea it shall be," Jane replied, putting on the kettle and busying herself laying out the mugs.

"To answer your question," Penny said, her legs

12

stretched out before her and her head lolling over her shoulder, "I spoke to Walter yesterday."

"Walter. Where was Doris?" Jane asked, spooning tea into the pot and willing the kettle to boil a little quicker.

"Apparently, she was taking a turn around the gardens for a bit of exercise, pushing some guys who were in wheelchairs."

"Since when did our Doris do turns around the garden?"

Penny shrugged. "Search me, but that's what he told me. Seems like a lot of the wounded chaps like her accent, and she makes them laugh."

"That sounds like her," Mary said.

"Seems like they heard her moaning, in that subtle, dulcet tone she has, as they came into the manor, something about not being able fly up to Scotland and being forced to take the train. For his part, Walter confided he was glad they hadn't flown. Said he'd heard a little too much about her flying style to want to go aloft with her. He also said not to tell her he said that."

"I'll bet he did!" Ruth laughed, watching Bobby sniff around the pantry.

Jane didn't say anything until she'd made the tea and poured out. "Could someone remind me to put Doris on flying nothing but biplanes for a month, when she gets back?"

"And get on Doris's bad side?" Penny said. "Sorry, boss. I may be your number two now, but you're on your own with this one."

Jane stopped pouring and looked at Penny, her recently promoted Second Officer, and nodded. "I suppose that's fair. I'd say the same thing, in your place."

"When are they due back?" Betty asked.

"It's what, Sunday today? So long as nothing untoward happens, which is always a possibility with you lot, they're due back Wednesday evening."

Betty got to her feet and went to open the cold box. Shaking her head, she turned and announced, "I was going to ask if anyone fancied some toast, but I'm all out of butter."

"If you like, I'll pop along to see Ambrose on Monday, see if he's up for a swap. I could probably do with some more myself."

"You know where my rabbits are. Take your pick," Betty told Ruth.

"We should get a good deal for one of those and one of my chickens," Ruth replied.

"In the meantime, I'll pop out at lunchtime and see what I can get on the ration," Penny volunteered. She reached forward and wrapped her hands around her mug. "Thanks for the tea, Jane. You all moved in?"

Jane took a seat next to her. "I thought I may as well, plus you lot were taking longer than I thought, so it made sense."

"We had a change of plan," Mary told her.

"Mary convinced me to swap Shirley into the attic," Ruth put in. "It makes sense. We don't even know if Shirley's going to be posted back here, do we, Jane?"

Jane hesitated a little before telling them, "Not as such." At multiple raised eyebrows, she filled in the gaps. "This stays here, okay? I have asked if Shirley can be posted back here once she finishes training. I'd like her here as much as anyone, but nothing's a guarantee, so don't get your hopes up."

"Fair enough, thanks for letting us know," Ruth

replied. "Anyway, taking that into consideration, Mary's suggestion made sense. That's the reason we took so long. Who knew trying to fix two single beds together would be such a bugger to do!"

"But it's all done now?" Jane asked.

Mary held up her hands. "Only cost me a few nails."

"Well, I'm sure they'll both be very happy with the new arrangements," Jane said, after taking a long sip of tea. "I take it you're keeping Lawrence's room for him?"

Ruth nodded, wincing as Bobby decided there was nothing worthwhile going on that required him to be awake, so he dropped asleep on her foot. "I do wish he'd get out of that habit," she muttered, indicating his position. Nevertheless, she reached down and patted his back while replying to Jane's question, "Yes, even though he doesn't use it much."

"I've been meaning to ask," Penny put in. "What were those bods with all the survey gear doing at the end of the runway the other day?"

"Nothing too exciting," Jane began enigmatically. "They're looking at extending the runway so we can handle damaged bombers better than at the moment."

This statement brought silence to the group, eventually broken by Bobby's snores, making everyone chuckle. "Bobby doesn't seem very impressed," Mary commented with a grin.

"With everything that's been happening over the last year, I'm rather surprised we haven't had the odd bomber dropping in."

Everyone slowly nodded their heads. Not only were they now used to the sounds of the British bombers going over at night, but they could quite clearly see and hear the Americans as they passed over almost every day too.

Something was in the air, and though no one would say so, they all knew the tide of the war had changed for the better.

"Well, I guess all we can do is wait and see what happens," Betty said, putting her mug down with a thump before reaching into her back pocket and pulling out a letter.

Everyone leaned forward, with Ruth beaming at her friend and asking, "Is that what I think it is?"

Betty matched her friend's grin tooth for tooth. "It's Jim's first letter from the States!"

Chapter Two

"How's the head, husband of mine?" Doris asked, dramatically draping herself across the bed, her silk nightdress revealing a provocative amount of thigh. Turning onto her front, she kicked her feet up and back, heightening the allure and causing Walter's eyes to flick toward the door, even though he knew he'd locked it when they'd got in from dinner the night before.

Hauling himself up to sit with his head against the headboard, Walter tried not to show he had a splitting headache, especially when presented by such a vision of loveliness. The trouble was, his good left hand refused to obey his mind and went of its own accord to stroke the bandage he still wore around his skull. Thankful his headaches were becoming fewer so they'd at least managed to, ahem, consummate their marriage; he closed his eyes. Talk about bad timing, he mused, letting his head fall backwards again.

As vigilant as always, his new wife noticed and crawled up the bed to sit up on her knees. Resting her hand against his, she leant down and pressed her lips to his, thankful he responded despite how she knew he was feeling. Knowing he still needed his rest and not wishing to push things, she sashayed her nightdress, bought especially for their delayed honeymoon, back down over her hips, not wishing to be too much of a temptation to her wounded husband.

Walter managed to open an eye. "That doesn't help much, you know," he told her with a smile and a wink, for which she rewarded him with her most saucy grin.

"Good to know," Doris answered, not helping matters by running a hand up and down the side of her body, before looking slyly at Walter out of the corner of her eye. "How about I run you a nice hot bath and you take a long, relaxing soak, maybe read something. I'll get changed and go out for a walk for an hour or two. Who knows," she waggled her eyebrows in an unmistakably seductive manner, "maybe you'll feel up to continuing our own *adventures*, when I get back?"

Walter gathered her to his chest. Running his hands along her arms, he allowed them to stray onto her thighs, relishing the soft rustle of the silver-colored silk beneath his fingers. He buried his head at her neck and proceeded to gently nibble her soft skin, stimulating a long, deep moan of lust from her throat. As he heard this, Walter stopped, getting a different, frustrated groan from his wife instead.

"Don't stop," she pleaded.

Reluctantly, Walter held her by the shoulders. "I think if I don't stop now, we're liable to split my head open. Let me go take that bath and we'll see if we can carry on where we left off a little later."

It took Doris a good few seconds before she got her breathing under enough control so she was able to reply, "I think," she stopped to take another deep breath, "that I like this idea."

As Doris slid off the bed and bent over her suitcase on the chaise longue, Walter eyed her appreciatively. "You know, I think a cold bath may be more appropriate."

Glancing at him over her shoulder, Doris reminded him, "You do know that these headaches are a lot less frequent than even a few days ago?"

"I do," he reassured her. "Hopefully they'll be gone completely before too much longer."

Ten minutes later, dressed in a pair of jodhpurs, the favorite white sweater she wore under her flying suit, and a pair of army boots she'd picked up, Doris made her way down the stairs toward the entrance of Mary's manor.

She was passing one of the corridors which led toward the burns ward when there came a shout, "Is that you, Yank?"

Turning to her left, Doris pasted on her best smile and followed the sound of the voice which had yelled out the same question once more. "Is that you, Taffy?" she called back, knowing the reply she'd get back.

"Damn right it is! Now, where are you?"

Doris nodded a greeting to the nurse on duty at the desk as she entered the ward. "Hi, Sally. Is he causing trouble again?"

Before the young VAD nurse could reply, the same Welsh voice interrupted them. "I've never caused anyone any trouble in my life." The voice belonged to the young man in the last bed on the left.

Sally, the nurse, shook her head before retaking her seat. "Go on. Take him out for a spin around the gardens, give us all a rest. Honestly, you're both as bad as each other."

"I'll take that as a compliment," Doris told her, as she strode toward the soldier. "Now," she said, plonking herself down on the bed next to him, "what's all this hullabaloo? I thought this was supposed to be a military hospital."

"It is," he answered, stretching out his bandaged hands, searching blindly for his visitor, "but that also means it needs shaking up once in a while."

Doris gently grabbed hold of both the man's injured hands, and immediately he stopped waving and settled down, letting out a little murmur of pain at her touch. "I'm sorry!" she instantly said, having heard this. "Did I hurt you?"

Even though the man knew she could feel his hands trembling slightly at her touch, he still shook his head. "I'm all right. Believe me, just being able to feel makes me happy."

Doris had seen a lot in her short life; however, getting used to the sights of a military hospital wasn't something she'd wish to go through again. When she'd visited with Mary back in February, it had only been for a night, and because of the strange circumstances which occurred, neither had any time to investigate what the good medical folk did at the manor cum hospital. On this visit, as Walter had been rather worse for wear the morning after they'd arrived, Doris had decided to take a walk around or, in her exact words, "See what I can see, without getting into too much trouble."

Disappointingly, she'd not been able to find Captain Mark Wood. It was the one thing she'd promised her friends to tell them about once she got back. It had been less than two months since they'd tried to help the captain and his (strictly speaking) deserter brother and even knowing how slowly army bureaucracy took, she'd still hoped to find out how they'd got on. Curiously, when she'd asked about him upon arriving, nobody would tell her where he was! Suspicious, now everything must be out in the open, she'd stopped and, instead, opened her ears. She was still waiting to hear something useful.

Doris tried to let go of the injured man's hands, but he gripped her fingers, however lightly. "No, please," he gasped, laboring to get his breathing under control, "I've only been able to pick things up for the last few days. I'd like to see if can hold onto a pretty girl for a while. Um," his head went up turning in her general direction, "I take it you are a pretty girl?"

Doris barked out a laugh, letting his gentle grip relax until his hands fell back onto his lap, "I've been told so…especially by my new husband," she added, feeling very guilty her new friend couldn't see her blush through the bandages wrapped around his head.

Taffy held up one of his hands and Doris gently retook it. "Would he arm wrestle me for you?"

"I'll tell you what. You get better, and we'll see what we can fix up."

"If I had eyebrows, they'd be up around my hairline by now," her companion told her.

Sally appeared and touched Doris on a shoulder to get her attention. "I see you're practicing your gripping exercises, Major. I don't think that's quite how the doctor meant for you to exercise, but if it helps."

"It does, Nurse, it does," Taffy nodded as vigorously as he could.

"I don't mind," Doris assured the nurse, "if it helps him get better."

Nurse Sally looked around the ward, where everyone else was unashamedly listening to the conversation. Someone had even turned the wireless off. "Stop bothering her, Nurse!" one of the other patients jokingly shouted. "She's better than any therapy any of us have had!"

"You'd better be careful, Lieutenant, or I won't pop over later," Doris shot back, immediately getting a guffaw from him.

The nurse shook her head. "I don't know how you do it, but keep right on doing it. I've not seen this lot so happy, ever."

"Do you blame us?" Taffy answered. "We know where we are, but most of us haven't seen anything for ages. Doris, here, she's put a smile on our faces when we don't have much to smile about."

Doris choked back the tears threatening to burst forth. "Now you stop that, Taffy. I know you're going to be able to see again real soon," she finished, not being able to prevent herself from looking up at the nurse. To her dismay, the nurse merely shrugged. It wasn't the answer she wanted, but she supposed the girl had to be honest. Gulping down the stone in her throat, she prayed her voice would sound normal when she spoke. "Right, enough mushy talk. The good nurse has brought up your chariot, so I suggest we get you some fresh air before she changes her mind."

Ten minutes later, the two of them were taking a leisurely stroll around the gardens at the rear of the manor. The two were quiet, with the major wrapped up with two blankets covering his legs and another around his torso.

Reaching up one of his hands, he patted around until he found one of hers. "Are we alone?"

Doris went all, Doris, on him. "Why, Major, whatever are you suggesting?"

Naturally this got a laugh from her companion.

"Don't put ideas into my mind that my body can't do anything about."

"At the moment…" Doris amended.

"At the moment," he agreed, after a small pause.

"Good boy. A healthy mind, and all that rubbish." Doris laughed. "Anyway, why did you want to know? Yes, we are alone, though."

"You've been asking about Captain Mark Wood, and no one's been talking," he surprised her by saying.

Doris was so surprised she barely managed to stop the wheelchair before she pushed its contents down some steps. "I beg your pardon?"

"Wood, Captain Mark Wood," he repeated. "You've been asking about him."

"How did you know?" Doris asked.

She saw his shoulders shrug. "I listen. There's not much else I can do."

Doris managed to prevent herself from saying *I see that,* just in time. Glancing around, she made certain they were alone. "What've you heard? I've not been able to find hide or hair of him!"

"And you wouldn't."

"Going to need a little more information than that, Taffy."

"You know how the armed forces are," he began. "The more you try and keep something secret, the more people know about it. We all know about his brother and what he did. The rumor mill says you and a Mary, I can't remember her full name, had something to do with what went on, but as he's refused to confirm that, together with her family owning this place, that's the reason why you've still been allowed here." He waited, as if expecting Doris to confirm what he'd said, and when she didn't he eventually told her, "Whilst they figure out what to do with him, he's now in charge of the hospital's transport, with orders not to set foot in the hospital again. From what I understand, he even has to take his meals and sleep in his office! Everyone has been warned against talking about him."

"So how come you're telling me?" Doris asked.

Taffy waved a hand vaguely around. "What else can they do to me?"

After a moment's thought, Doris bent over and kissed the top of his head, "Thanks, Taffy."

"I don't suppose you'd want to fill in the blanks?"

"Sorry, but no," Doris told him. "Now, I'm sorry to cut your fun short, but I have to go and find Mark."

****

After taking two wrong turnings—deliberate attempts to mislead her, she felt, on behalf of the two army chaps she'd asked for directions—Doris finally found the transport section and, a few minutes after, the office where Captain Wood worked. Indeed, there was a camp bed tucked away in a corner, half-hidden by an army blanket acting as a curtain.

"I see you've been sent to Coventry, I think is the expression," Doris commented as she came through the door, without bothering to knock.

The face which looked up at her entrance was far from the animated one she'd last seen in the pub, after his brother had been examined by the doctor Doris had arranged. There were shadows under his eyes you could ladle soup from, his hair seemed ill kept and greasy, and it took him a few moments to realize who his visitor was. Then he seemed to transform before her eyes.

Leaping to his feet, with his seat flying backward,

before she could do anything he'd wrapped his arms around her and shouted, "Doris!" down her ear.

Eventually she managed to persuade him to release his grip and guided him back to his seat, whilst taking the only other one present. "You took some tracking down," she told him, shaking her head.

Before replying, Mark opened the bottom drawer of his desk and took out two small glasses and a bottle, "Whiskey?"

"Happy to," Doris nodded.

Raising their drinks in a toast, they both knocked back the shot, with Mark refilling them both immediately. "Well," he said, leaning back in his chair and regarding his visitor, "I'm very happy to see a friendly face."

Doris took in the rest of his office before answering. Apart from the half-hidden bed, the only furniture in the room was a trunk poking out from beneath the bed and the desk beside him. There wasn't even a threadbare carpet on the floor. "I can see you would be," she told him.

A smile cracked his weary face. "Yes, I don't get many visitors. Most people I see come in to get their orders and then leave as quickly as possible."

Doris sighed. "It's really that bad?"

Mark shrugged and took a sip from his glass. "Yes, but I really couldn't care less. John's welfare's all I care about. They could have busted me down to Private and it wouldn't have mattered," he said, tapping the two pips on his shoulder.

"You're a lieutenant now!" Doris said after working out his new rank.

"It could have been much worse," Mark replied.

"Care to share what happened?" Doris asked, over the top of her glass.

Mark placed his own glass down upon his desk and leant forward, elbows upon his knees, "There's not that much to tell, so far, anyway. You'll be pleased to hear your doctor honored his agreement and sent in his report. He didn't recommend that John should be discharged, worse luck, though he did strongly suggest he shouldn't be in a combat unit and in fact suggested he be transferred to the Catering Corps."

"Why didn't he recommend a discharge?" Doris asked.

"He didn't think John's intelligence was low enough for that to be a realistic option," Mark informed her. "The important thing is, though, the army's actually taken notice of his report and he's been transferred to a station near our parents."

Doris couldn't stop herself and clapped her hands together, "That's great! I suppose it could have worked out better, but not by much."

Mark nodded. "At least he should be safe now. Or as safe as it's possible to be during this mess," he amended.

"And you?" Doris asked after a short pause. "How are you doing?"

He let out a short, mirthless laugh. "Me? I'll survive. I'll keep my head down, do what the army wants me to do, and try to keep out of trouble. If I were a cat, I reckon I've used up a good number of lives recently."

"Well, if there's anything I can do…"

Mark reached toward her, and when she didn't move them away grasped both of Doris's hands and brought them up to plant a kiss on her knuckles. "You and your dear friend Mary have done more than I could ever have asked for, and you will both forever have my eternal gratitude."

Chapter Three

Ruth took a Sprats dog-cake out of her pocket, reached down, and waved it in front of Bobby's wet nose. As she'd expected, after a few sniffs, his mouth opened, his tongue lolled out, and within a split second, the treat disappeared. A few crunches later, he was back in the land of nod.

"That's…amazing!" Jane declared. "If I hadn't seen it with my own two eyes…"

Betty reached down, lifted one of the dog's ears, then watched it flop back down. "It's quite a trick. So much for radar ears, eh?"

"Don't listen to them," Ruth bent down and ruffled said ears. "You're still our early warning system!"

"Quite right," Jane said. "Only don't tell anyone on the station about this little trick of his or everyone'll be waiting for him to fall asleep, which doesn't take much, and feeding him even more than they are already."

"Look, enough talk. I want to hear what Betty's beau has to say!" Penny said.

"Beau? That's a bit posh." Ruth laughed.

Penny threw a cushion at her head. "I like a romance as well as a good Agatha Christie, so sue me."

"You haven't the money. I'll wait and sue Doris sometime," Ruth told her, promptly receiving a few more cushions for her trouble.

Ruth held up her hands to ward off the

bombardment. "I surrender! Can we hear what Jim's got to say? I'd rather my headstone didn't read, 'She died by cushion.' "

Betty took out the letter and smoothed it on her lap before looking around at her friends. "Give me a minute. I've only read it once, and there are parts which, ahem, I can't share, even with you lot. And the first person to make a sound gets to drink a cup of Doris's tea!"

"I think that's against the Geneva Convention," Jane mused, with a smile.

"Mm-hmm," Betty mumbled, engrossed in the letter. "Right," she said, looking up, "here's the bits you lot can hear."

"We're all sitting comfortably," Mary said, "so you may begin."

"Thank you, Mary," Betty said drily, holding the letter up before her eyes. "Well, he says hello to you all and hopes you're all keeping well. Er, he's told his folks, as he puts it, all about me and says they're looking forward to welcoming a limey into the family. There's some stuff about his sister looking forward to teaching me how to speak properly, which he goes on to say he's had to put her right on. Then he tells me he's put in the paperwork for obtaining permission to marry—" Whereupon she was interrupted by multiple whoops. "Yes, thank you. This bit may surprise you lot…he's also applied for service back in the UK."

"Bloody hell!" Jane couldn't help but say.

"I guess he must love you," Mary said, receiving one of the cushions Ruth had gathered for her trouble.

When Betty didn't speak up, Penny asked, "Is that all you can tell us?"

Betty made a show of flicking back and forth

through the pages before looking up and sheepishly shaking her head. "Nothing else really. He's missing me…"

Bobby gave a small *woof* without waking up.

"…and it goes without saying, he misses Bobby too. He doesn't miss warm beer, but strangely enough, he says he's found himself drinking tea instead of coffee now, whenever he can get it."

"Ha!" Ruth slapped her thigh. "That's one to the Brits!" she said before getting to her feet. "Right, thanks for the tea, Betty, but I'd better get off if I'm going to catch Ambrose before he disappears. Funny, he never seems to be around when I want to see him these days."

Betty saw her friend out, and when she got back into the lounge, everyone else had put their jackets on and was waiting for her.

"Ruth's right," Jane said, holding out Betty's jacket for her to pull on. "We'd better get to work too."

****

"Would you look at that?"

"Give me a second," Betty muttered over the intercom. "I'm a little busy avoiding these bloody barrage balloons at the moment," she added, jerking the control column hard to port and then back just as swiftly to starboard, before straightening up once again and resuming course. "Let's see what we've got this time."

Coming in over the Solent and up toward RAF Hamble, Betty banked the Anson slightly as she brought the air taxi around for a second pass. As they'd begun their first approach, the clouds had cleared and they'd been presented with a gloriously clear view of Southampton waterfront from out their port side. Both Mary and Betty had become distracted by the view before them, forcing the go-around. For a while now, everyone had noticed a significant increase in the military presence around the area, so visits to their favorite haunts of Portsmouth and Southampton had become fewer, as it simply wasn't worth the trouble it caused to get around, plus petrol was even harder to obtain. Everyone had their own thoughts as to why, though no one had voiced their thoughts out loud. However, the sight before their eyes this afternoon changed everything.

"Just what the heck are those things?" Mary asked, her gaze drawn to the huge gray, rectangular blocks taking shape.

"You've got me," Betty muttered. "Though something tells me we wouldn't be very popular if I did another flyby for a closer look."

"Shame," Mary said, as she craned her neck to watch the strange, obviously concrete masses slide from view.

The curious sight was all the pair could talk about as they changed in the flight line hut and it continued on the walk over to the operations hut.

"I can't see why anyone would want to build chunks of concrete that big," Mary was still complaining as they opened the door.

"What chunks of concrete?" Penny asked, looking up from her desk. Beside her, leaning over the desk, Jane also glanced over at Mary and raised an inquiring eyebrow.

Betty closed the door before hopping up beside the pair. She helped herself to the remains of Penny's cup before spluttering, coughing, and pulling a disgusted face, "Bovril! Oh, for a decent cup of tea," she informed the room, much to everyone's amusement.

Penny rescued her remaining drink before Betty had the chance to throw it out the window she'd opened. She sat back down and finished the dregs her friend had left, before asking her, "You do realize you sounded remarkably like Doris?"

Betty blanched as she closed the window, saying, "Oh, hell! Please shoot me if I ever say anything of the like again?"

Jane coughed. "Now I've got your attention, you lot," she said, "find yourselves somewhere to sit." Amongst much shuffling, the girls pulled out chairs and settled down to stare expectantly in Jane's direction. "Good, thank you. Now, listen very closely. I shall say this only once. No one's blind, so we all know something is going on at the moment, especially around here. I'd imagine we've all made a pretty good guess as to why, as well. However, speculation won't get our job done, and careless talk won't help either. Yes, we've all been hearing that expression since the war started, and I believe it's more important now than ever. I'm not silly enough to ask you to stop talking about what you've seen today and will continue to see. However, I will implore you all to *not* talk about this subject around anyone but yourselves and certainly not anywhere but on this station and at home. This means no talking at any other station you may go to for the foreseeable future. If it helps, pretend we're back in the dark days of nineteen-forty."

Pausing to look around the group, Jane finally asked, "Do you all understand me?"

All three either nodded or said, "Yes."

Nodding her satisfaction, Jane let out a breath she hadn't realized she'd been holding. "Thank you. Right, that's the official spiel out of the way. If everyone's got their gear, let's get home. Oh, and someone please remind me to give the same speech to Doris when she gets back?"

****

Sharon buried her face in her hands as Lawrence drove her out of RAF Marham. He turned right and pulled over as soon as they were out of view of the camp gate. Pulling out what he hoped was a clean handkerchief he tapped the distraught girl on the shoulder and offered it to her.

After dabbing her eyes, she blew her nose on the cloth before holding it out to her policeman friend.

He shook his head. "Keep it, please," he added, knowing what she'd just been through hadn't been easy on her, and it was only the tip of what was to come.

Sharon blew her nose once more, dabbed the end of her nose, and let out a deep sigh. She turned her head toward where Lawrence was staring at her, not troubling to keep the concern from his expression. "I guess that could have gone better," she said, turning a watery smile upon him.

Before replying, Lawrence reached behind him and picked up a flask from off the back seat. "A cup of pick-me-up?"

"Please tell me there's some alcohol in there." She put out her hands to accept the cup he held out to her before filling it to the brim.

"Sip it," he advised, with a grin.

Sharon did, but nevertheless immediately dissolved into a coughing fit. Recovering her breath, she took a somewhat more sensitive sip and this time only let out a smaller cough. Settling back, she looked sideways at where Lawrence was drinking from his own considerably smaller cup. Taking a slow, deep, breath, she closed her eyes. "Do you think he'll forgive me?"

"Stan?"

"Of course Stan!"

Lawrence swept a hand through his hair and went a little red. "Of course, sorry. I suppose," he ventured, "it all comes down to this—do you love him?"

For a long few minutes, Sharon sat staring into space. A low-loader exited from the RAF station behind them, a pair of Mosquito wings on its back. Rumbling past them, the passenger leaned out and waved at them. Lawrence raised a hand in greeting.

Only when it had disappeared into the distance, did she answer, "I think I do."

"You think?" Lawrence asked.

She nodded. "I think I love him, but I also think what I've just done could be unforgivable. I mean, he knows I'm not someone who makes decisions out of the blue, and declaring I'm homesick and am moving down to be with my Aunt Mabel… Well, it doesn't come more out of the blue than that! I didn't believe the words I said, and they came out of my mouth. How can we be sure Stan does?"

Taking a sip of his supposed tea, and stifling a cough, Lawrence contemplated the question. "You're quite right, we can't, but I don't think we're going to be totally alone on this venture, and to be completely honest, what Stan thinks is the least of our worries."

Sharon raised an inquisitive eyebrow. "What makes you say that?"

Without looking behind them, he jerked a thumb behind them. "I take it that means you didn't notice the car that's parked about a hundred yards behind us. Don't look!" he blurted out at the same time as Sharon's head began to automatically swivel around.

Turning back to face him, she belched loudly. She'd gone slightly red around the cheeks, and it didn't have anything to do with the alcoholic content of the tea. "Sorry about that," she said, somewhat sheepishly. "Couldn't help myself. So you reckon they're from the same people I'm supposed to be working for now?" Lawrence nodded. "Honestly," Sharon huffed, folding her arms, "talk about a lack of trust!"

"If it makes you feel any better, I doubt they trust their own mothers," Lawrence suggested.

This thought, more than anything else, seemed to help Sharon to relax a little. With a last, slightly less obvious glance over her shoulder, she let out a sigh. "I suppose we'd better get going. It's a long way to Brockenhurst."

"Especially as we have to go via Hamble first," Lawrence added, turning the car's engine back on.

Sharon pulled her coat tighter around her shoulders before asking, "Hamble. Why?"

Glancing over his shoulder to make certain the way was clear, he pulled out onto the road, noticing with a wry smile their shadow doing exactly the same thing a few seconds later, before replying, "Because I have to fill in Jane Howell, the lady in charge of the station," he added, in case Sharon didn't remember the name, "as to what's going on. I've a letter to give her which orders her to co-operate, but things will go so much more smoothly for everyone if I tell her face to face."

****

A few tiring hours later and Lawrence was

regretting the optimism of his words.

After giving Flight Captain Jane Howell the sealed letter he'd been carrying, Lawrence had settled back to enjoy a semi-warm cup of the tea Penny had made the pair when they stumbled through the door of the Ops Hut, teeth chattering with cold. His enjoyment of the welcome beverage quickly disappeared as he watched Jane reading, her frown deepening and her lips pursing together in annoyance. Finally, she refolded the letter and carefully placed it back in the envelope before suddenly slamming it down on her desk.

"Jane?"

It took a good minute before the station commander found her voice, and when she did, it was only the fact he already had his chair back against the wall which prevented Lawrence from tipping over backward.

"Is this a joke?"

Lawrence frowned and placed his cup carefully on the edge of Jane's desk. "I…beg your pardon?"

Jane prodded the envelope before her with disgust. "Do they, whoever *they* actually are, think that we've got the time to play around here? It's even busier than normal right now, and we're expected to become part of some…some…" Jane actually flapped her hands around before her as she sought for the right words, "some spy game!"

Lawrence picked his words very carefully. "I'm sure," he began, doing his best to ignore the skeptical eyebrows raised before him, "they do appreciate everything you and the girls are doing, Jane…"

He got no further, as Jane's chair shot back at a rate of knots, and before he knew it, she had both hands planted upon her desk and was fixing him with a glare which would have had Hitler quaking in his jackboots. "You agree with…this?" She stabbed the envelope with a finger. "You're in agreement with putting Sharon into danger? Does she know what she's doing?"

Before Lawrence could reply, Sharon herself put her head around the open door of the office. "I know what I'm doing, Miss Howell," she began, rather timidly. "I'm not going to pretend that I'm happy about it, but I have to do what I can to try and help my grandmother. I wouldn't be able to live with myself if I didn't, and from what I understand, all I have to do is to wander around so I can be seen and copy out and send some letters."

"As simple as that?" Jane muttered, shaking her head.

Sharon allowed a small smile to grace her lips. "That's the theory."

Noticing that Penny, Mary, and Betty were unashamedly listening in, Jane shook her head. "You do realize that with this lot"—she waved a nonchalant hand toward her friends—"it's very unlikely to go as smoothly as all that?"

"Hey! Not fair, boss," Penny protested. "Trouble finds us, not the other way around."

Slowly, Jane nodded her head before stating, "This had better not come back to bite us, or"—Jane treated everyone to a flinty glare—"I'll be having words with whoever came up with this scheme, and I can promise you this…they won't like them!"

Chapter Four

Everyone gathered around Betty's on Wednesday evening, awaiting the return of the happy couple. Fred, the owner of the local fish-and-chip shop, upon being told that Doris and Walter were expected back later, had happily waved away Betty and Mary's attempts to pay, telling them it was his Welcome Back present. Realizing there was no point in arguing and also that, with Doris now back in situ, his weekly takings would soon go back to normal and easily cover the cost of the supper, the girls thanked him for his generosity and hurried back home, knowing that wartime train timetables were to be taken with a pinch of salt.

"Put that nose away," Betty was telling Bobby. The Cocker Spaniel raised his head and, for the fourth time in as many minutes, inhaled deeply from the steaming pile of newspaper-wrapped temptation upon the kitchen table.

With a rather pathetic whine, Bobby let his head flop back onto his outstretched paws and resumed his vigil.

"You know, I don't think I've seen him so awake for a while," Jane mused, reaching down to give the dog a scratch behind the ears.

"Who's awake?"

"Doris!" everyone shouted in unison at the voice which came from the open kitchen door.

Penny was the first to reach their American friend

and had her arms wrapped around her by the time everyone else joined them. "We didn't hear you come in!"

Doris had to wait for everyone to let go before she could catch her breath to speak, "Blame my Walter," she said, still keeping hold of Penny's hand as she turned to look down the hall to where her new husband was putting down their cases. "He's been teaching me some 'silent-skills'!"

"Walter! What've you been up to?" Ruth asked, whilst at the same time hurrying along to the man and giving him a hug. "Your hair's starting to grow back!" she added, ruffling the downy covering. "Excellent. You don't suit being bald."

"I've missed you too, Boss," he told her, smiling.

By now, Doris's nose was in the air and matching exactly what Bobby had been doing a few moments back. Penny made a half-hearted effort to prevent her friend from making her way toward the table. "Unless I'm much mistaken, do I smell the delectable scent of Fred's fish 'n' chips?"

Bobby promptly *woofed* in agreement.

Doris bent down, placed her hands either side of the dog's head and kissed the top of his furry head. "Don't worry, you'll get your share."

'Not too much, mind," Ruth warned.

"Aw, but it's my first night back!" Doris replied, batting her eyelids unashamedly.

"Stop teasing, love," Walter said, as Ruth helped him into a seat, whereupon he nodded his head gratefully at her.

Whilst his wife helped Mary and Penny set the table, "I see my timing was spot on," Doris remarked as she nearly dropped a plate trying to point at the still-steaming pile of goodness. Ruth took the seat next to her reporter.

After a few seconds, Walter stopped watching proceedings and told her, "I know I'm not handsome, Ruth, but why the scrutiny? Do I look that bad?"

Ruth hurried to shake her head. "No, not at all. In fact, you look a lot better than I expected to find you."

Walter raised a curious eyebrow. "A strange thing to say. How so?"

By now, all activity in the room had ceased as everyone was unashamedly listening in on their conversation.

Ruth coughed to clear her throat before saying, "Well, to be honest, I thought that with the state you were in when you went off on honeymoon, Doris might finish you off."

As Walter went red to the tips of his ears, his lady wife merely went back to laying out cutlery before taking a seat next to Ruth, laying a hand upon her arm and confessing, "Don't think I didn't try. He's tougher than he looks!"

Ruth went the same color as Walter, whilst everyone else burst into laughter.

Doris banged the handle of a fork on the table. "Now I've managed to embarrass my dear husband, can we eat? I'm starving."

On the way to a chair, Jane pinched Doris's cheek. "Ah, I've missed your quiet, self-defacing demeanor."

A slightly puzzled expression graced Doris's features for a moment before swiftly being shrugged away. "As I haven't a clue what you mean, I won't let it worry me. Now, are we finally ready to tuck in?"

Penny couldn't help shaking her head as Doris

warmed her face over the rising steam from her package. "I've missed you, too."

Doris's mouth was too full to reply, so she only nodded and filled a minute space with another chip.

"As your lady wife is busy, I'll ask you, Walter. How was your honeymoon?" Mary balanced the chip on the end of her fork as it tried to make a bid for freedom.

Laying his utensils back on the table, Walter grabbed Doris's hand, the one wielding her own fork, so that she had to stop eating. "Huh?" she got out.

"Mary was asking if we enjoyed ourselves," he repeated.

Thoughts of fish 'n' chips momentarily forgotten, Doris gave her friend her full attention to the extent she nearly leant an elbow in her bread and butter. "Oh, hon! How can we ever thank you? A honeymoon in a real-life castle! We had a great time, and I'll never ever be able to stop thanking you."

Mary beamed back at her. "Just seeing how happy the two of you are right now is more than enough for me. Absolutely no thanks needed. I'm so happy I was able to help."

The beautiful silence was broken by an exuberant pounding upon the front door.

"What the heck?" Betty exclaimed, rising to her feet and hurrying out into the hall. "It's open! Come in before you break the door down!" she added.

As she reached the door, it opened and in tumbled the local builder and sergeant in the local section of the Home Guard, Matt Green. Fortunately, he didn't quite lose his feet, as Betty was able to grab him by the arm just in time. Hauling him upright, she asked, "Where on earth's the fire?"

By now, everyone in the kitchen was on their feet.

Before anyone else could speak, the man himself, though slightly out of breath, said, "Ah, good, you're here."

As he had his hands upon his knees to get his breath back, everyone looked at everyone else before Ruth asked her boyfriend, "And, you're speaking to whom, love?"

Looking up, Matt shook his head. "Sorry. I was on about Walter here."

"Me?" Walter asked. "Why? I've not been passed fit to come back to the section yet. Though I hope that won't be before too long," he added.

Before anyone else could speak, Doris was on her feet, wagging the largest chip anyone had ever seen under her husband's nose. "Oh, no, you don't! You're not going anywhere near a rifle until I say so, never mind the doctors!"

Fortunately, Matt had been around everyone long enough to know that Doris's bark was worse than her bite. It also helped that he knew exactly what everyone else around the room did, and that it was unlikely Walter would be fit enough to resume Home Guard duties for at least another week or so.

Preceding Betty into the kitchen, Matt leant up against the butler's sink and shook his head. "Don't fret, Doris, it's not that." He pulled a piece of paper from his back pocket and waved it in the air. "I've some good news to tell him, and everyone else," he added.

When he didn't immediately elaborate, Ruth and Mary both demanded at the same time, "Well?"

"Sorry," he muttered, shaking the paper in his hand and holding it up. "Ahem." He dramatically cleared his throat. "By the King's order, the name of Walter—"

He got no further, as Walter had jumped to his feet and, at the same time, Doris had leaped from her seat, for once ignorant of the chips she sent flying, and had grabbed the paper from Matt's unyielding fingers. She was already reading it when Walter joined her. Together, and oblivious to the stares of everyone but Matt (who was grinning ear to ear), the pair read through the letter, turned to face each other, read the letter once more and then, as one, collapsed onto the chair behind them. Whether by luck or design, it was the one Betty had vacated and hadn't yet reclaimed.

Neither said a word, but simply continued to stare off into the distance with identical expressions of disbelief upon their faces, until Penny had to ask, "Will someone please tell us what that means?"

Matt looked down at the pair and gently took the letter from Doris's unprotesting fingers. "This..." he held the letter up once more, though a little more reverently this time, "is the official notice, though there's a commemorative card back at HQ, that young Walter there has been awarded the King's Commendation for Bravery."

There was a moment's pause whilst everyone took this stunning news in before a wall of sound began bouncing off the walls of the kitchen, as everyone started yelling and cheering as one. Fish 'n' chips forgotten for once, everyone got to their feet and crowded around the still-stunned-into-silence duo, slapping them both on the back and congratulating Walter over and over again.

Displaying stealth no one would have credited him with, Bobby silently climbed onto Ruth's chair and helped himself to half his owner's fish before sliding back down under the table to enjoy his ill-gotten gains.

****

With Mary and Betty now back from buying some bottles of stout from the Victory pub, toasts were held to Walter's bravery—Doris added dire warnings to him at the end of each, happily embellishing what she would do to him if he tried anything similar ever again—which may have gone on all night if the hero himself hadn't had a yawning attack.

Noticing he was beginning to flag, Doris came and stood behind where he sat and wrapped her arms around his neck, kissing him on the cheek. "I think it's time I got someone up to bed," she announced.

Jane, Betty, and Ruth exchanged glances, something which didn't go unnoticed by the newly married couple.

"Something we need to know, Ruth?" Walter asked, accepting his wife's hand up.

Ruth ran a hand through her hair. "We haven't had the chance to tell you."

"Tell us what?" Doris asked, fixing the newspaper owner with a curious stare.

"Blame me," Mary hurriedly put in.

"For what?" Doris wanted to know.

"Well," Mary began somewhat hesitantly, "we were moving things, around the other day, especially beds, and it struck me that we don't actually know if Shirley will be posted back here once she finishes training…"

"And?" Doris prompted as Mary trailed off.

"And," Ruth picked up the tale, "we thought it would make more sense if the two of you took over her old room at my place. We've already put her stuff into Walter's old attic room."

"Oh, is that it? What were you worried about?"

44

Doris merely replied, her shoulders relaxing. "Just let me gather some of my things together for the night and for work tomorrow, and I'll get the rest tomorrow evening."

"No need," Jane told her, adding, to the American's enquiring look, "I may have packed all your belongings up and put them into your new room myself."

"Oh, right," Doris was able to say after a few moments. "Well, thanks, Jane."

"You're all right with this, then?" Betty asked.

With a suitcase in each hand, Doris turned around. "What's not to be all right with? Yes, I'll miss staying here. Betty, you've been so very kind to this Yank, but so long as I'm with my wonderful husband, that's all that matters." She was about to follow her husband out the door when she turned back around. "Penny! Have you finished *The Body in the Library* yet?"

Before she could reply, Jane said, "You said I could borrow it after you."

"Jane? What's all this? Do we have a new member of the ATA Mystery Club?"

Ignoring Doris's teasing, Jane was looking firmly at Penny who, looking somewhat flummoxed, eventually replied, "I may have promised Doris could have it first."

"Don't make me pull rank," Jane replied, though her relaxed posture and the grin upon her face showed she was only teasing. "Besides"—she turned to address Doris—"don't you married women have more important things on your mind, other than reading books?"

Doris picked her suitcases up and silently left the house, pulling the door closed with the tip of a foot.

Everyone was looking a little confusedly at each other as the letterbox in the door flipped open and Doris's dulcet tones issued forth. "Don't think this is over, Boss. We'll discuss over coffee tomorrow who reads that book next."

Chapter Five

"Jane Gertrude Howell! Where the hell have you been?"

Coming around the corner of the Ops Hut the next morning, Jane and Doris were ahead of their friends, who had quite rapidly grown tired of the continuation of last night's argument about the Miss Marple book, and so neither was prepared for the sight of the mess manager, Mavis. Standing at the top of the wooden steps, she had a rolling pin in one hand and a steaming teapot in the other. A tattered hairnet was half hanging off and together with the duffel coat she was wearing, she looked like she could take on the might of the Luftwaffe all on her own.

Behind her stood Sharon; incongruously, she was doing her best to hide behind the petite elderly woman and, unsurprisingly, failing. She looked as if she'd rather be anywhere than where she currently was.

Jane waited until she'd strode up the steps and stood beside Mavis before speaking, doing her best to ignore Doris's stage whisper of, "Gertrude? Really?" before the American hopped down to go and stand by the rest of the group. Jane couldn't help but notice that they were stood well within easy listening distance.

"Is there a problem, Mavis?"

"Problem?" Mavis parroted, whilst shooting a glare toward the other girls from beneath Jane's arm. They merely smiled, waved back, and stayed where they were.

"Good morning, Sharon. You're okay? Sleep well?" Jane took the opportunity of asking the younger girl.

Mavis's glare refocused upon the flight captain. "So you did know this lass was sleeping in your office! Which beggars the question, why did you leave her alone here? Why didn't you take her back to either Betty's or Ruth's to sleep? Why leave her with just a sleeping bag?"

"Not an unreasonable question," Jane replied before opening the door to the hut. "Shall we go in? A little privacy is called for."

Even though Mavis was quite obviously still hopping mad, she was also inquisitive enough to want to get to the bottom of things. So, with a quick glare up at her boss, she grabbed Sharon's hand and pulled her into the hut. Jane followed her, pulling the door closed behind her, saying to her waiting friends before she did, "Penny, give me five minutes, please, and as for the rest of you, don't you think you'd better go and get changed? There are planes to deliver."

The last thing Jane heard as she led Mavis and Sharon into her office was a loud chorus of, "Yes, Gertrude!" That was going to get annoying very, very quickly, she decided.

Waving the other two to the seats the other side of her desk, Jane took hers and looked across at her still very hostile-looking mess manager and what could only be described as a rather confused Sharon. She decided she'd be best off taking the lead.

Mavis, however, had other ideas. "How could you leave this poor girl on her own? Just what the hell's going on?"

Jane steepled her fingers. "What the *hell* is going on

is that you need to calm down and listen to me, Mavis. Understood?" She gathered up the special stare she kept for whenever Doris caused her issues; she'd had plenty of practice. To her satisfaction, Mavis closed her mouth, while Sharon continued to look embarrassed. "Good. To answer your question as to why Sharon had to sleep here, I had a meeting with *someone* yesterday, all to do with young Sharon here. I needed some time to think, and Sharon understood it would be best if she stayed here, though only for the one night," she hastened to add, Mavis appearing to be on the verge of blowing up again.

"A power-that-be? You mean, a hush-hush type of thing?" Mavis asked.

"Right down to signing the Official Secrets Act type of thing," Jane replied, getting a slow nod from the woman. "Which means that everything said here…*goes no further.*"

Mavis didn't say anything in return for a few minutes. Every now and then, her head would swivel back and forth between Sharon and Jane, her mouth would open, but no words would come out. Eventually, she asked, "So what's Sharon doing here?"

"So far as you and everyone else on this base are concerned, she's come from RAF Marham to be your new assistant and to do her best to look after her aunt Mabel, who lives in Lyndhurst, by the way."

This time, Mavis didn't wait. "Well, if she's going to be my assistant, I'm going to need a clean and fully awake one." She reached into a pocket, rummaged around, and came out with a key, which she pressed into Sharon's hand. "Here. This is the front door key to my house. Don't lose it, as you're going to be staying with me. Whoever this Aunt Mable is, she can like it or lump it," she told her firmly. "Walk down the High Street, second road on the right past the Priory Church of St. Andrew. You can stay in my rear room. Ask for directions at the guard post. Be back for eleven. Oh, and help yourself to some bread and margarine too. Unless Jane has any objections, that is?"

Jane smiled at her mess manager, who somewhat surprisingly still appeared annoyed with her.

Sharon looked up at Jane and asked, "Do you mind if I telephone my aunt and tell her of the change of plan?"

Jane showed her into her office and closed the door to give the girl some privacy. She'd barely walked back to where Mavis stood, before the door opened. "That was quick!"

Sharon shrugged as she bent down to pick up her suitcase. "We're not very close," she explained, before opening the ops hut door and leaving.

"From Marham, eh? Isn't this is bit unusual?" Mavis asked.

Jane let out a sigh and slumped back slightly into her seat. "You have no idea, and I wish I could tell you everything, Mavis, really I do, but I can't. All I can say is please trust me and keep an eye on Sharon. She's got a lot on her shoulders, and it's only going to get harder for her. I get the feeling she's going to need a shoulder to lean on, to cry on. Can I count on you?"

Mavis didn't hesitate. "Of course you can, and I won't ask you anything I don't need to know."

"That'd be perfect, thank you." Relieved, Jane let out a breath she hadn't known she'd been holding.

The roar of a Cheetah engine starting up made its way into the room, grabbing Jane's attention. "I think that's my signal to get to work too," she informed Mavis, standing up.

Following Mavis out of the office, she found Penny sitting on the steps outside the door. Waiting until the woman was well on her way toward the kitchen, she held out a hand and pulled Penny to her feet. "Ready to start work?"

Penny waited for Jane to precede her back into the hut. "Ready when you are, Gertrude."

****

"Ambrose! Ambrose!" Ruth cupped her hands around her mouth and yelled louder. Tightening her grip on the brown-paper-wrapped rabbit she had tucked under her arm, she kicked some mud off her wellies and decided to try around the back of the farm where the pigpens were.

Opening her coat, Ruth wished she hadn't worn a cardigan under her coat, as it was quite warm now it was approaching nine in the morning, and she could feel a bead of sweat begin its travels down her back. This was the third time she'd been up to try and see her old friend in the last two weeks, and she'd not managed to find him yet, despite plenty of evidence of work going on around the farm. In other words, all his pigs and cows seemed to be in fine health.

Opening the shed door, she peered into its dark depths and called out his name once more. The only answer was a cacophony of grunts from its porcine inhabitants. "For cripes' sake," she muttered, slamming the door shut and turning on her heel. She had to make a hasty grab for the handle when she slid in a lump of something she'd be washing off as soon as possible.

Jerking her head up, she peered curiously toward a door she knew led to the farmhouse kitchen. If she'd been a gambling person, she'd swear it had been open a few seconds ago.

Scraping her heel across the courtyard, Jane made her cautious way toward the door. Reaching out, she gripped the doorknob and twisted; it was locked. "Hmm, must have been my imagination," she muttered. "Ah, well, the ration will have to do for a few more days," she decided, turning her back on the farmhouse a second before the kitchen window curtain twitched.

****

As soon as she came to the lychgate leading up to the church, Sharon started to look out for the turning the young man on guard had told her to look out for. What neither Mavis nor he had mentioned was just how impressive St. Andrews was.

She'd liked her job at RAF Marham immensely, but one of its main drawbacks had been its isolation, there being very little to do when she wasn't on duty. Hence she'd discovered a love of old churches whilst cycling around the area's villages and hamlets. St. Andrews was right up there with the best she'd seen. One of those examples she liked to think of as a three-part church with a tall, flat-roofed tower at the end, coated in what always looked like flint to her. One of these days, she'd find out what its style was really called.

With a slightly weary sigh, and a silent promise to herself to make a proper visit as soon as she could, Sharon hefted her suitcase once more and continued down the road. Very shortly she found her turning, and after only five minutes more, she was standing open-mouthed in front of what was, according to her directions, Mavis's house. "House" was not the word Sharon would use, as what she stood before was a decent-sized thatched cottage with wooden beams built into its sides. If it wasn't at least a few hundred years old, she'd eat her hat!

She checked her shoes to make sure she didn't drag any dirt inside and went through the gateless entrance up to a front door studded with what could only be ancient nails. Taking the key out of her pocket, she inserted it into the door and slowly pushed the heavy door open.

As she closed the door behind her, she didn't notice a squat figure, which had followed her from a safe distance ever since she passed F. W. Woolworth's, detach itself from the shadows. If the face could have been seen, she would have shuddered at the satisfied sneer gracing the features.

Chapter Six

"Shh!" Mary hissed as Betty and Doris hefted the clinking box between them up and into the rear fuselage of the Anson taxi aircraft. "This is supposed to be a covert exercise."

Balancing the edge of the wooden box on her shoulder, Doris wiped the sweat from her brow and then gave one more push. With a louder-than-ever clunk, the box was wedged in place. "There we go. That's not coming loose."

"What's not coming loose?" asked a voice behind the three, causing them all to jump in panic.

"Nothing! Um, nothing's coming loose, Penny," Mary informed their friend, fooling no one.

"Uh-huh," Penny replied and went up on tiptoes to peer between Doris and Betty before taking a step back with a sly grin upon her face. "If you don't want any breakages, I'd pack some rags between them. I think," she added as she turned back toward the ops hut, "there's some on top of the lockers in the flight line hut. Jane doesn't need to see this. Safe flying, girls!"

Once Penny was out of sight, Mary asked, "How do you think she knew?"

Betty whipped her flying helmet off and ran a hand through her hair. "I wasn't sure, but now I am. When we were coming out of the flight hut, I'm sure I saw Penny looking out at us from ops."

"And you didn't think of saying anything?" Mary asked.

"I don't think she'd tell." Betty shrugged.

"Me either," Doris agreed. "A nice, cold, five-thousand-feet-high beer at the end of the day. Who'd pass that up?"

Replacing her helmet, Betty held open the Anson's door for her friends to enter the aircraft, followed them in, and shut the door before asking, "Do I want to know where you got this idea from, Doris?"

Doris's grin perfectly matched her mischievous character. "I used to bring up a few beers with me in my…" She gulped, and her friends let her take as much time as she needed, knowing she was dredging up painful memories. "In my previous husband's biplane. Of course"—she looked up and managed a smile—"seeing as we'll be able to get up quite a bit higher in this crate than I did before, I'm really looking forward to these at the end of the day."

****

Penny waited until the Anson had taken off to take the girls to their first deliveries of the day. Closing the door behind her, she called out to Jane, "Care for a brew?"

"Always!" came back the reply. "Thanks, Penny."

Five minutes later, Penny was poring over some of the delivery chits she'd need to hand out later when Jane came up, clapped a hand upon her shoulder, and sat down beside her.

"Looks like being another busy day," she commented, pointing at the chits with her mug. "Anything unusual?"

"Not really," Penny answered after a second or two.

"Mostly Spitfires, Mosquitos, there's a Hudson, and also a few Typhoons."

Jane grunted. "Better remind the girls to take it easy with those Tiffys. I know the boffins say they've fixed the issue with the tails dropping off, but I'd rather not have one of our lot finding out otherwise, the hard way."

"Got a note to remind myself to put that over the radio in a minute," Penny announced, waving a piece of paper from her notepad.

"Excellent." Jane nodded approvingly. "Now, speaking of types, how many girls are still to get their Class Fives?"

Penny looked up with a wry smile. "I'll give you one guess who, apart from yours truly, are the last ones?"

Jane let out a sigh and let her forehead flop dramatically onto the desk. "Of course, it could only be the ATA Mystery Club."

"Are you including yourself, Boss?" Penny asked with a mischievous twinkle in her eye.

"In the club, or to take the test?" Jane immediately shot back.

"I'd be careful with my choice of words," Penny replied cheekily, raising her own mug. "So, are you?"

"Am I what?" Jane asked, playing along.

"Part of the Mystery Club?"

Jane shook her head. "Just because I'm enjoying the books it doesn't mean I want to get involved in any mysteries with you lot."

Penny chuckled and shook her head. "Probably a little late for that. You've been pretty integral to our adventures since the beginning, and, as you keep telling us, it's not like we go out looking for trouble, so you're just as likely to get mixed up in something as anyone."

Jane waved her now-empty mug dramatically under Penny's nose. "Now, now, there's no need for that. Anyway, enough horsing about. We'll have words with them when they get back tonight. Mind you," she prodded some of the delivery chits on Penny's desk, "with the amount of work that's been coming our way lately, I don't think we'll be able to afford to lose them for a while, so maybe not."

"Do you think something's likely to happen soon?" Penny asked, glancing out the window as a number of planes sped over.

Jane's eyes too were drawn to the ceiling until the sounds had faded. "You've seen what's going on, how busy we are, what you've flown over."

"When you've allowed me to fly," Penny couldn't help but say.

"Until you're fully fit," Jane picked gently at the sling Penny still wore around the arm she'd been shot in, "you'll do as I say. Look, Penny," she said more gently, "we're both experienced enough as pilots to know you need to be fully fit to fly safely, especially in this job. You'd probably be all right if I restricted you to fighters and light aircraft, but we both know you'd soon grow frustrated not being able to fly something a bit more exotic. So until the doc gives you the all-clear, obey me, just on this one thing. Okay?"

Penny waited a few moments before nodding her head. "I'm sorry," she sighed. "Put it down to my frustration."

Jane patted her friend on her good arm. "No problem. Now, what did the doctor say at your last checkup?" Jane was being smart, knowing getting her friend talking about her last medical report would cheer

57

her up.

Sure enough. "So long as I don't do anything silly, his words, I can get rid of this sling in two or three weeks and go back onto full flying duties."

"See?" Jane said, happy her ploy had worked, though she couldn't help but let out a sigh, knowing what she also had to remind the girl. "I am sorry to have to remind you of something, though. You are still my second in command, Penny. This means, and I'm sure you know this as well as I do, that even after you've been passed fully fit, you're still going to find the majority of your time taken up helping with the planning of the deliveries."

It was Penny's turn to slump back, not troubling to hide the pain she felt when she knocked her wounded arm on the edge of her desk. "I know. I was hoping you'd forgot," she added, somewhat sheepishly.

"Nice try." Jane smiled back. "Now, how about you make that radio call about the Tiffys, and we can get back to work. Starting with, just how cold do you think those beers will get?"

****

Sergeant Terry Banks looked over at where his boss had been staring out the window of his office. Ever since they'd gotten back from their extremely late night—or early morning, depending upon how you thought of it— trip to London, he hadn't been the same. Things had only gotten worse after he'd brought that girl back from RAF Marham. Not that he'd imparted much of what had occurred in London nor between the girl and him, either. Oh, he'd tried, but Lawrence had clammed up tighter than a black marketer refusing to give up his sources.

Upon hearing Lawrence utter another mumble under

his breath, Terry threw down the pencil he'd nearly chewed down to a stub. "Come on, Boss. A trouble shared is a trouble...something or other. I can't remember what, but if you shared what you're thinking, I *am* a good listener."

Without turning around, Lawrence told him, "I wish I could, Terry, I wish I could." Lawrence shrugged his shoulders and sat back down behind his desk. Picking up one of the files which decorated it, he flicked it open before idly throwing it back down. "Can't concentrate," he muttered.

Pleased that he had a boss who encouraged open, honest speech, Terry went and shut the office door and took up a position on the edge of Lawrence's desk. "You're sure, one more time, that there's nothing I can do? Or that you could tell me?"

Lawrence let out a dry, humorless laugh. "There's nothing like the persistence of a copper, Terry. However, in this matter, no, and you're better off not knowing, to be honest."

Terry leant toward him and, as if he were a ham actor in an old movie, spread his arms wide and implored, "What if I don't want to be a good copper? Would you tell me then?"

"Nice try, Terry. You'll never make it on the stage, but you'll always be a good policeman." Coming to a decision, Lawrence heaved himself to his feet, grabbed his hat and picked up his car keys.

"Need me to drive you somewhere, Boss?"

Unable to suppress a shudder, Lawrence shook his head. "No, thanks, I don't think my nerves have recovered from the other night yet."

"It wasn't that bad, was it?" Terry asked seriously.

"Let's just say I'm still waiting for my appetite to come back."

"Oh, very funny," Terry mocked as Lawrence waved him a goodbye. "Where shall I say you've gone to, if anyone asks?" he quickly shouted before Lawrence had disappeared from sight down the corridor.

"Hamble!" came the reply as its owner disappeared down the stairwell.

"Might have known," Terry muttered, absently flicking the kettle on again.

Ten minutes later, Lawrence was behind the wheel of his car and heading out of Portsmouth toward the New Forest and RAF Hamble. Immediately he turned onto the road leading to Hamble village, he felt his somewhat frazzled nerves begin to settle. This was despite the realization that he'd be lucky if he got to see his girlfriend, Mary, as she'd likely be out on deliveries. Still, he thought, at least he could check in on how Sharon was doing. He could also make certain he gave her the papers which would allow her access to the area opposite Southampton that had been chosen as a good site they could view the activity toward the docks and which were normally out of bounds. He'd read and re-read the orders the *gentleman* in London had given him, as he'd wanted to make sure. If there was anything present which could put the girl in real danger, he'd never forgive himself. Not to mention what Stan Atkins would do to him if he allowed anything to happen to her.

He was coming up to the church when he spotted a girl strolling along in the direction of the airfield. Smiling despite the situation, he honked his horn to get her attention and, after a moment, her frown of curiosity turned into a smile of recognition and she waved at him until he pulled up next to her.

"Care for a lift?" he asked, flipping the passenger door open.

Clambering in beside him, Sharon inclined her head. "Very kind of you, Lawrence, I believe."

"Always," he said in return before putting the car back in gear and continuing on their way to the station.

"So what brings you here so soon?" she asked.

There was no point in beating around the bush, so Lawrence didn't. "I've got to give you your papers, so I'm pleased I ran into you, though I am a little curious as to why you're not on the station?"

Sharon smiled across at him. "Blame a little ball of fire called Mavis." Lawrence chuckled at hearing the name. "I assume you've met her?"

"You may say that," he answered, slowing down as he came to the turning which led toward both Betty's and Ruth's cottages, but keeping the car going straight ahead toward their destination.

"Well, she found me asleep in Jane's office and was waiting for her when she came in to work."

"Sounds like that may have proved interesting."

"That's one way of putting it," Sharon agreed.

Further conversation was curtailed as they arrived at the guard post. Fortunately, Jane's standing orders to allow Lawrence onto the station were well known, and once they'd seen his warrant card, something which both insisted be done, mainly to keep the guards' attention up, they were waved through and nothing more was said until he pulled up outside the ops hut.

As they got out of the car, Sharon noticed her companion taking a pointed look toward the airfield. "Penny for them?"

"Hmm?" He turned back to face the girl, "Sorry, just seeing if the taxi was in."

"Taxi? What taxi? I can't see any other cars," she said, obviously confused.

Glancing behind him, he saw their entrance had been noticed. "I mean the taxi aircraft." At seeing she was still confused, he quickly explained. "When they take the girls out to pick up the aircraft for delivery, they leave in an Anson. That's a small, twin-engined aircraft, and if it's not here around this time, then it usually means my girlfriend's out at work."

Coming around to his side of the car, Sharon snapped her fingers. "That's Mary, right?"

"Right," he agreed, before showing her up the steps to where Jane and Penny were waiting for the pair.

"Lawrence! This is a nice surprise," Jane began, before turning to address Sharon, "and Sharon. I take it you found Mavis's place?"

"Oh, yes!" Sharon enthused. "It's wonderful. I must thank her for being so kind."

At seeing the way Lawrence looked at the girl, Jane decided, "Niceties will have to wait, I'm afraid. It looks like Lawrence wants to talk to us, and then"—she glanced up at the clock on the wall when they'd gotten inside—"I'll ask Penny here to show you to the mess. I'm certain Mavis will want to put you to work."

Once all three were settled in Jane's office, Lawrence wasted no time. Taking an envelope out of his pocket, he laid it on the desk before Sharon. "Take very good care of these." He patted the envelope. "Seriously, these will allow you access to the Southampton waterfront. Feel free to read them, though if anyone in authority wants to see them, they say you're in MI5."

Both Sharon and Jane said, "No!" at the same time, and from the sound of it, something similar came from Penny, who wasn't actually in the room but was obviously listening in.

Chuckling, Lawrence shook his head and opened the office door. "You may as well hear everything clearly, Penny," he told her, "seeing as I trust you, and it's not like Jane wouldn't be telling you and your friends everything anyway. However," he warned, holding up a finger, "and I know I don't need to say this—no one other than the Mystery Club. Agreed?"

As Penny assured him that she would respect his orders, Sharon mouthed, *Mystery Club?* behind his back, to which Jane told her out loud, "I'll fill you in later."

"Right, Sharon, this is what I'd suggest. Take a few days to settle in. Then, on a Sunday, I'll come down and we'll take a drive out to Woolston. We'll have a little walk toward Southampton along the coast. That should be a nice start, and I know that we'll be seen. Just make sure to bring those papers with you. Without them, my warrant card won't be enough to stop them arresting us and probably throwing away the key. Once we're back, I'll have the first letter we'll need you to write and send off."

Once Lawrence had finished, Jane looked at the girl who, apart from a few more swallows than normal, appeared quite calm. "Sharon. How are you doing?"

"A lot to take in," she answered honestly.

"If it's too much to ask," Lawrence said, "it's not too late to pull out."

Determinedly, Sharon shook her head. "No, if we can make some trouble for the Nazis, I'm all for it."

"Good for you!" Penny butted in, slapping Sharon

on the back hard enough to make her cough.

"Well," Jane declared. "Seeing as we've now got a plan for scaring the life out of the Germans, it's time for your first real test."

Sharon gulped. "I hesitate to ask."

Jane couldn't keep the grin from her face as she answered, "Teaching Mavis how to make a decent cup of tea."

Chapter Seven

As the Anson taxied toward the flight line hut, Doris could see they had a reception committee. Leaning forward, she used a rag to try and clear the windscreen a little more, without discernible improvement.

"How did she know?" Doris muttered, shaking her head in wonder as she brought the plane to a halt.

Jane waited until the engines were turned off, the post-flight checks were completed, and the plane's wheels chocked, before strolling over to greet her girls and friends; all seemed to be in varying degrees of poor humor and most smelled of and looked like they'd been doused in beer. Finally, only Mary, Betty, and Doris were left. She peered in through the open door, the suspicion of a stifled laugh echoing around the fuselage, before she turned to face the three. Betty and Mary were looking at the ground, whilst Doris, rather typically, was attempting to whistle a tune.

"Had a good day?" Jane enquired. There was definitely more than a hint of an evil smirk upon her face, which none of her friends missed.

"I think so," Doris eventually replied, though only because neither of her friends looked like answering.

"Really?" Jane raised an eyebrow. "Nothing out of the…ordinary…you feel the need to report?" The eyebrow was joined by its twin.

Doris glanced over her shoulder at where the

Perspex of her plane was practically holding up a hand in disagreement. "I suppose there may have been one thing which made the last trip a little, unpleasant." A drop of beer was hanging from the end of her nose.

Jane made a point of letting the three watch how her eyes travelled back and forth down the fuselage, taking in every inch. "A little, unpleasant. How so?"

Doris cleared her throat. Lying didn't come easy to her, even for a good cause, and what had occurred could certainly not come under that banner. Jane was also a good friend and, in spite of perhaps enjoying herself a little too much, in the American's opinion, also wasn't blind.

"Maybe a little idea of mine didn't quite go according to plan," she began with.

"Do tell," Jane invited sweetly.

"If you don't need us…" Betty ventured, making as if to go into the flight line hut to change.

Jane reached out a hand to gently, but firmly, clasp her good friend's flying glove. "No, if you don't mind, Betty, please stay."

"Don't you think you're enjoying yourself a bit too much?" Doris asked, planting her hands upon her hips to clearly indicate that so far as she was concerned, Jane was.

Immediately, Jane's face broke into a wide, friendly smile and she clapped Doris heartily on the shoulder. "Perhaps a little. Mind you," she added, walking up and glancing inside the Anson once more before wiping her hand on the driest part of Doris's clothes she could find, "you can't blame me. I mean, talk about a mess! I'm actually quite impressed you managed to get her down without resorting to the kangaroo juice, Doris. Seriously,

66

well done!"

Doris beamed. "Really? Gee, thanks."

Jane's grin disappeared. "Now, you three clear up this mess before you clock off. I want those windows sparkling, the floor so clean I could eat my dinner off it, and not a whiff of beer."

"But…" Mary and Doris both started.

"But, nothing," Jane declared. "You three were responsible for the mess, so you three are cleaning it up. There's no way I'm having any ground crew doing anything to help."

Not giving them a chance for further protest, Jane turned on her heels and started back to the ops hut. "Oh." She stopped to ask, "Did anything survive intact?"

"Afraid not," Betty shouted back. "Casualties were a hundred percent."

****

"You wanted to see me, boss?"

Wing Commander Tom Alsop looked up from the letter he was writing and gladly laid his pen aside. "Your timings spot on, Stan. Take a seat."

Instead of sitting down as invited, Flight Sergeant Stan Atkins strode up and stood behind his pilot and friend. Looking over his shoulder at what Tom had been busy writing, he whistled, opened one of the desk's bottom drawers, and took out a half bottle of whiskey and two glasses. Going back around the other side, he poured two shots, pushed one into Tom's unprotesting hand, then took a seat.

"To Jack and Dobbo."

Tom chinked glasses, and they both knocked their drinks back.

"Lousy job," Stan remarked, flicking the letter.

Tom could only nod. "You'd think I'd be used to writing these damn things by now, but…"

Stan shared wisdom you wouldn't expect to hear come from a man whose idea of good reading material was the sports pages of a Sunday newspaper. "The day they do become easy is the day to get out of this business."

Nodding in agreement, Tom pushed the unfinished letter away from him and slumped back in his seat. "Very true. How many different ways are there to say, 'Your son never knew what hit him, he died instantly and could have felt no pain.' "

Stan looked grim as he recalled the circumstances which necessitated the letter Tom was attempting to write. "Too true. After all, who wants to hear, 'Your son was trapped in a Mosquito which spun in from six thousand feet after a wing had been blown off. He wouldn't have stood a chance of getting out and would have been conscious until he smashed into the ground.' "

"Grim," Tom said after a few seconds' silence. "Pour another couple, Stan."

This time both men took sips before settling back, lost in thought for a minute or two. Eventually Tom said, "I dare say you know why I wanted to see you, Stan. None of this is going on the record, by the way. This is strictly mate to mate."

Stan nodded in appreciation.

"So, what happened? That Junkers 88 should never have got that close to us. We're lucky the pilot couldn't hit the side of a barn door, or it'd be someone else writing letters to our loved ones. That's the kind of thing you'd normally spot in your sleep."

Shaking his head, Stan finished off his drink before,

with a huge sigh, he told his friend, "I'm sorry, Tom."

Tom slammed his glass down onto the table, smashing his pencil in two and startling the life out of his navigator. "To hell with 'sorry.' I know you're sorry. Tell me, why!"

"Sharon's called it off," he said and then, in response to Tom's silence, elaborated. "We had an understanding. When she turned eighteen, we were going to get engaged. Then she went and got transferred, to Hamble of all places, and called the whole thing off. Said she didn't think we could make a long distance relationship work." He snorted in disgust. "Long distance, my arse! It's hardly as if she's going to the States! It's not like she gave me much of a choice, either. No sooner than she'd had her say, she was off on her uppers."

"It is very strange," Tom agreed. "I've never known the like. No disrespect, but it's not like she's a spy. So, why the moonlight flit? She didn't give any hints about moving on at any time before, did she?"

"Never." Stan added a shake of his head. "And do you want to know something else that was strange? I followed her, from a distance, as she left the station. Not only did she leave her bicycle here, but she got into a car, which looked like it was waiting for her and, though I know the light was quite poor by then, I'd swear the bloke behind the wheel was Mary's boyfriend. You know? That copper. Inspector Lawrence, I think."

"Well," Tom remarked after allowing everything to sink in, "this is a bit of a do, and no denying it." He poured them both one last glass and put the bottle back in his drawer. "I suppose I can see how you would be distracted," he mused before, and in a much firmer voice, adding, "but that's it. If your head's not in the right place before tonight's sortie, you're not flying. Do we understand each other?"

Understanding there were times when Tom was his friend and times when he was his superior, Stan got to his feet, put his hat back on his head, stood to attention, and smartly saluted, "Yes, sir, completely understood."

Satisfied, Tom told him, "Good. Now, sit your bony ass down. What's the time?"

Stan glanced at his wristwatch, "Nearly half four. Why?"

Tom picked up the receiver and hovered a finger over the dialer. "What say we give Jane Howell at Hamble a call? I want to know why the best tea-maker I've ever known was taken away from us in such strange circumstances. Squadron morale needs to be taken into consideration."

Stan shuffled eagerly to the edge of his seat.

****

"Not the easiest conversation I've ever had," Jane declared, plonking herself down in the seat to Penny's left in the mess.

Penny looked up. "Cheer yourself up. Have a cup of tea."

Jane glanced at her number two, suspicion tracing her features. Traditionally, if they offered anyone a cup of tea here, it was only taken as a last resort, being something wet and occasionally warm, but never to enjoy. However, Penny's face possessed all the symptoms of actually enjoying the cup of whatever was in her hand. Reaching out, she took it from her friend's unprotesting fingers, brought it gingerly up to her nose and sniffed. She looked up, "Smells suspiciously like tea," she remarked, and upon getting an enthusiastic nod, brought the cup to her lips and took a tentative sip. Her eyes bolted wide open and her eyebrows shot up her brow. "Oh, my giddy aunt! I've never tasted anything like it!" She looked around and, for the first time, noticed a small queue of people at the tea urn, and they actually had smiles on their faces!

"This is Sharon's brew," Penny supplied, retrieving her cup from her boss's hand.

"I can see now why your Tom was so upset at losing her," Jane told her, with a shake of her head.

The cup was halfway to Penny's lips, but at the mention of her husband's name, it was forgotten. "That was Tom on the phone?" she asked somewhat unnecessarily.

At least Jane had the good grace to look a little embarrassed. "Sorry. Believe me when I tell you he didn't call up for a social. To say he's not happy about losing Sharon would be putting it mildly. Plus, his navigator is quite upset to lose his girlfriend."

This was news to Penny, who finally put her cup down, to look up and search out their mess manager's new lodger. When their eyes met, the blood seemed to drain from Sharon's face, as if she knew she were the subject of the conversation.

"That's a bit of a surprise. I wonder why? We're not that far from Marham," Penny mused.

After mulling this over for a minute, Jane decided, "Probably the least of our worries at the moment. He knew I wasn't telling him the real reason why she was transferred, and he wasn't happy."

Before Penny could reply, the mess door was flung open and in strode Doris, Mary and Betty. None appeared to be in the best of moods. Looking around the room, Betty pointed toward the pair. Betty strode over and very gingerly placed a rather sticky-looking brown bottle before Jane.

"We were wrong," Betty said, pulling up a seat from an unoccupied table so she could join the other four. "Meet the lone survivor. Enjoy."

Jane reached out a finger, touched the glass, then hurriedly withdrew the digit and quickly sucked it into her mouth. "That's bloody cold!" she said around the finger.

"Still," Doris agreed, glancing longingly at the bottle.

Penny picked up her hat and pushed her seat back. "If you'll excuse me, I'm going to give Tom a quick call."

Jane laid her hand upon Penny's and shook her head. "I shouldn't bother, if I were you. He couldn't say the exact words, but he strongly hunted they were going to be busy tonight."

Sitting back down, Penny looked out the windows. "I hadn't noticed it was getting dark," she remarked and then fell silent.

Chapter Eight

Lawrence turned up early Sunday morning; he had a small picnic basket in one hand.

Mary opened the door and waited for him to lean down to kiss her on the cheek before lightly slapping him around the back of his head.

"Oww," he uttered with a smile, pretending to be hurt. "'What was that for?"

"You've never taken me out for a picnic!" she pointed out, slapping him once more.

"Is that it?" Lawrence said and opened the lid.

"It's empty!" Mary remarked, peering into the wicker basket.

"Of course it's empty," he agreed, taking the opportunity to kiss her sweet lips this time. "For a start, I'm a man and can't bake an egg."

"Who can't bake an egg, apart from Doris, that is?" Betty asked, leaning over the banisters and looking down on the pair. "And it's boil, by the way."

Mary and Lawrence were taking advantage of actually having a few moments on their own, and it took Betty clearing her throat, loudly, for the pair to finally break apart.

"Maybe you two should follow Doris and Walter's lead? Ever given it any thought?" Betty asked, as she came down the stairs.

This probably didn't have the effect she'd intended,

73

as Lawrence and Mary sprang apart as if they'd been electrocuted.

What could have been a very awkward situation was saved by another rap on the front door. As neither looked like they even knew what a door was at that moment, Betty brushed past them and opened it to admit both Mavis and Sharon.

"Mavis!" Betty's eyes widened before she eventually stepped back to allow the unexpected visitor to enter, closely followed by Sharon, who shrugged an apology.

"Don't blame young Sharon here," Mavis said, as she took off a rather battered straw boater from her head and hung it up. "I realize I can't know everything that's going on, but that doesn't mean to say I can't keep as much of an eye on this one as I can."

Nodding her head at Penny, who'd appeared in the kitchen doorway, Sharon treated her landlady to a pointed look. "I think we're going to have problems if you keep referring to me as *young Sharon*."

"Well, you are," Mavis replied, frowning, before she asked, "Any chance of a cup of tea? Young Sharon here insisted we get here ten minutes early, so I haven't had my first cuppa of the day."

Having caught the conversation as she came out of the lounge, Jane rolled her eyes at Sharon as if to say, "You're fighting a losing battle there." Out loud, she took the girl by the hand and towed her into the kitchen after Mavis, along with Betty and Penny. "Come on. Those two don't get enough alone time as it is, let alone having to put up with everyone pulling their legs so early in the morning. Shut the door please, Penny, give them some privacy."

As the kettle came to a boil, there came a *woof* at the back door and in trotted Bobby, tugging Doris and Walter behind him.

"Sorry about this, Betty, everyone," Walter said, whipping off a flat cap and wiping a forearm across his brow. "We'd only planned on taking Trouble, here," he nudged the Cocker Spaniel lightly with a foot, "for an early morning trot along the riverbank, but as we passed your gate, he took it into his head to make a diversion, and, well…he's dogged when he gets an idea in his head."

Nobody said a thing.

Eventually, Walter couldn't stand the silence any longer. "Oh, come on!" he cried. "No one's got anything to say? That was a great pun!"

Jane nudged Doris in the arm. "Did you know your husband was so needy?"

Doris shook her head, playing along. "It's only occurred since he was awarded that honor. I think he's waiting for it to be upgraded to a knighthood."

All the girls, including Mavis, who was quite used to Doris's sense of humor, regularly jousting with her in the mess, turned to face the lone man in the room.

Without hesitation and keeping a wonderfully straight face, Walter replied, "Well, when they do, just remember to bow when I deign to speak to you."

Typically, Doris hooted with laughter and, flinging her arms around her husband's neck, planted a big, slobbery kiss on his lips. This caused him to lose hold of Bobby's leash., who promptly started sniffing the floor and then flopped to the ground with a disgusted grunt when he failed to sniff out any tempting morsels.

"Sorry, Bobby." Betty reached down to ruffle the

disgruntled dog's ears. "You'll have to wait. Let's get this pair out of the house, and then we'll see what we can come up with, eh?"

The kitchen door opened and in walked Mary, a little red around the ears, something Doris immediately picked up on. "I think the two of you should get going, Sharon. From the look of her, I don't think Mary could take being left alone with Laurence for much longer."

Mary let out a theatrical and long suffering sigh. "I do miss living under the same roof as you, Doris."

Without missing a beat, Doris replied, smiling at her friend, "I sure do too!"

Laurence stood in the doorway, his coat over one arm, hat and empty picnic basket in the other hand. "Shall we make a move, Sharon? Don't take this the wrong way, but however pleasurable your company undoubtedly shall be, I'd like to spend some time with Mary, too, on my day off."

Sharon pushed her empty tea cup aside and stood up. Tugging her short bottle-green coat down a little, she looked at her escort. "Ready when you are," and followed him from the room and out the front door.

No sooner had the door slammed shut than there was a very loud *quack* quickly followed by the front door bursting open, ushering in an openly shocked Sharon and Laurence, who was doing his best to appear not quite as flustered as his companion.

At another decibel-testing *quack*, everyone's eyes turned to Doris.

"Duck really is a sweety," she declared, getting to her feet and trudging into the hall. When no one replied, she tried one more time, her hand on the front door handle. "Honestly! Anyone want to come outside with

me?" Everyone vigorously shook their heads. "*Et tu,*
Walter? Then Doris falls!" she badly misquoted, before
throwing a salute and going out to pacify the mad fowl
of Hamble.

****

Left with a temporarily empty house that Sunday
morning, not even needing to take Bobby out for a
morning walk, Ruth decided to see if Ambrose was
around. As she walked toward the farm, she had time to
ponder and come to the conclusion that she hadn't
actually seen him around for a while now and, now she
came to think about it, she couldn't recall anyone she'd
come across mention they had any dealings with him
lately. To all intents and purposes, life around the farm
seemed to be plodding along as it ever had. Deliveries of
feed were accepted and the van from the slaughter house
came and went each week with its sad load of pigs.

Two questions immediately struck Ruth's
newspaper editor brain: Just who was working the farm?
Which led to the second: where was Ambrose?

Approaching the farm gate, Ruth automatically
tapped her thigh and when, after the normal few seconds
had passed and Bobby didn't appear at her side, her
fingers were halfway to her mouth to whistle him to her
before she remembered he wasn't there. Not normally a
nervous person, Ruth suddenly found herself gulping
and wondering if she shouldn't put off her visit until she
had some company?

"Get a grip, girl," she scolded herself, backing the
words up by sharply rapping herself around the back of
her head.

Taking a deep breath, she opened the gate, walked
through, and closed it. With a shake of her head, she

jutted out her chin and forced away thoughts of the stand-off with a mad gunman at Betty's cottage a few months back. Instead, she began to holler, "Ambrose!" at the top of her lungs.

Shoving away more thoughts about putting off the visit until she could at least have Bobby's company, she marched up to the front door of the farmhouse, raised a fist, and banged upon it a couple of times whilst again shouting out the farmer's name. Somewhat to her surprise, it was jerked open and the man in question appeared framed in the doorway. Before Ruth could find her voice, Ambrose jerked forward, as if propelled by an unseen force between his shoulder blades. Before Ruth could try to see what, or who, was behind him, the door slammed shut.

"Ambrose? What the hell's going on?" she blurted out and opened her mouth to say more, only words failed her when she actually looked at the man.

Normally as clean as it was possible for a busy farmer to be, his usual denim dungarees were hanging from one shoulder. Peering closer, she could see the loose strap wasn't simply undone, it had been slashed, roughly too, by the looks of it, certainly not something his late wife would have approved of. She'd have mended it, long before he had the chance to be seen out in public in such a state. Further scrutiny revealed holes in both knees and a nasty, half-healed cut poking out from beneath a rolled-up shirt sleeve. She was on the point of reaching out a finger toward the cut, when Ambrose became aware of where he was and hastily took a step back, so Ruth couldn't reach. Unfortunately, this took him back against the shut door and Ruth wasn't exactly a shrinking violet when she set her mind to

78

something.

"What the hell's going on?" she asked, feeling as if the question was on repeat lately. Not giving him time to reply, Ruth followed up with, "Where were you when I came up the other day?" and this time, managing to get a firm grip upon his wrist below the cut, she added, "Why haven't you cleaned that up? You know you could pick up an infection around here easily enough."

Instead of replying to his old friend, Ambrose kept looking around, as if expecting someone else to turn up, or something else to happen.

His actions so unnerved Ruth that she found herself also whipping her head around, just in case someone was indeed sneaking up behind her. Though no one else was in sight, she recognized the same feeling she'd had on her last visit—the feeling she was being watched. Seeing as it was only Ambrose's farm, she felt rather silly fighting the impulse to take flight.

Pulling his arm from his erstwhile friend's well-meaning grasp, Ambrose found his voice, though the tremor in his usually soft bass merely confirmed to her something was definitely not right. "What do you want, Ruth?" Plus, he'd never been short with her before, that she could remember. Yes, they'd had playful arguments when they bartered for each other's goods, but he'd never snapped at her before.

Nevertheless, she forced back a response in kind. "You've got the whole village worried," she decided to reveal at once. Perhaps a shock would work? Ambrose had always loved being part of Hamble, especially when his wife had been alive. Maybe knowing she wasn't the only one worried about him would get her some answers?

"Perhaps the village should learn to mind its own business," came back the sharp retort.

Whether it was his intention or not, Ruth found she'd taken an involuntary step back. However, circumstances notwithstanding, the unexpected statement made her more determined than ever to get to the bottom of what was going on. This was *not* her old friend. "There's no need for that, Ambrose. We've all known you pretty much all your life, so we've a right to be worried when one of our own starts behaving strangely."

Reaching behind himself, Ambrose pushed away from the door, not noticing that the meagre force it took was enough to reopen his wound. Ruth noticed, though, and whipping a handkerchief from her dress pocket, she pressed it to the cut before Ambrose could prevent her.

"Right, that's enough from you," she decided. "Let's get you cleaned up, and then you can fill me in on whatever's going on around here, because…" She paused for effect and reached behind him to push the door open—and it totally failed to move. Not put off at all and keeping hold of her friend's injured arm, she made to drag him around toward the rear of the house. Unfortunately, she hadn't accounted for the difference in their respective bulks. Though not the tallest of men, a life of hard work on the farm had made Ambrose not only strong but determined, and there was no way Ruth was able to make him budge an inch.

Instead, and with the slight belligerence he'd been displaying, he simply shook his head. Gently, he removed her hand from his arm, though keeping the now slightly bloody handkerchief in place. "If I promise to clean this up, will you please…just go away?" His eyes looked past her, toward the ground.

Ruth's jaw dropped open. "Go away? Go away! Can't a friend be worried about another friend these days?"

Ambrose's head drooped before he eventually told her, though he didn't look up, "Yes, they can, but this isn't the right moment." Grasping the door handle, he pushed it open enough so he could squeeze through. Only then did he look up. "Please, Ruth, for your sake, don't come back."

Quickly he said in a voice so quiet she had to hurriedly lean in so as to hear, "It's not safe at the moment." Straightening up and adding, in the voice of a rather bad actor, "All right! I'll do you a swap! Leave a couple of rabbits beside this flowerpot," he nudged the one to the left of the door, "in the morning. Two pats of butter will be there for you. Now, go away!" he said, a little louder before and with another seemingly unnecessary glance toward the ground behind Ruth, shutting the door.

For the next minute, at least, Ruth stood stock still, trying to make sense of what had just occurred, especially the last part of their interaction. Was he trying to tell her something? Well, obviously he was, but what? And what was the meaning of that last quick dip of his head? As if she should look down? But look down at what?

Feeling a little stupid, she glanced down at her feet. At first, there was only dirt but then, something glinted against the early morning sun.

There, about a foot or two from the toe of her left foot, was a piece of metal, tubular in shape and unmistakable to Ruth's keen eye. Picking it up, she brushed some dirt from it and weighed it in her palm. What was the bolt from a Lee-Enfield rifle doing cast aside on a pig farm?

Chapter Nine

"Does this feel strange to you?" Sharon asked Lawrence as they strolled hand in hand along the bank of the Solent.

These were the first words either had spoken since Lawrence had parked his car fifteen minutes ago. During the drive, the policeman had suggested they play the role of a courting couple and Sharon, unable to think of a reason why not, had agreed. Upon beginning their walk, the empty picnic basket had been left on the rear seat and both had swiftly found the situation…awkward. It wasn't as if either expected to run into anyone either knew, especially in Sharon's case, but each could feel the other fighting the urge to let go of the other's hand whenever anyone else came into view. Fortunately or not, as the case may be, this wasn't often.

After opening and closing her mouth a couple of times, Sharon eventually found her voice. "Very." She then coughed to clear her throat, waved hello to a couple coming in the opposite direction walking a dachshund, and suggested, "Perhaps we should have brought Bobby along?"

Lawrence nodded at the same couple. "Good point. We'll have to remember for next time."

"Next time," Sharon mimicked. "Yes, I suppose we'll have to do this again. Is Mary really bothered?"

The question made Lawrence chuckle before

shaking his head. "No. She was only pulling my leg."

Sharon let out a *phew* of relief, actually allowing a smile to come to her face. "That's very good to hear. I don't know them that well, but Penny's husband was fond of telling tales about the—what are they called?—Air Transport Auxiliary Mystery Club, and I get the feeling they're all very close." She waited for Lawrence to nod in confirmation before carrying on, with a slight shake of her head. "So you can understand why the last thing I want to do would be to upset one of them, especially as I'll be working with them."

"I don't think you'll have anything to worry about. You forget, you do know Penny quite well, at least, and you and the girls have been to a hangar dance with Clark Gable!"

It was her turn to laugh. "That's a bit of a push. I didn't get to dance with him."

Lawrence leaned in a little. "Nobody needs to know that." When she didn't reply straight away, he nudged her gently in the ribs. "I'm sure Stan will understand."

Sharon sniffed and nudged her companion back, a little harder. "Is being psychic normal for a copper?"

"Only this one," he quickly replied. "Seriously, I'm sure he'll understand, once this is all over," he tried to reassure her.

She pulled Lawrence to a stop and turned to face him, worry once again etching her pretty face. "And you're certain we had to break up? I still feel terrible and can't see any way he'll take me back."

"If it comes to it, I'll put him in an interrogation room and beat him around the head with a wet lettuce until he sees sense," he informed her.

Sharon's burst of laughter startled some birds from

the trees and set to barking the dog they'd just passed, his owners giving her curious glances. Once she'd calmed down, she gave his hand an affectionate squeeze. "Come on. Let's make ourselves seen. Mind you, I am a little surprised at how many people there are around," she remarked, and then pointed with her free hand toward some other couples doing the same thing a short way away. "I would have thought we wouldn't be able to get this near to the river."

Lawrence took a good look around before, a frown now creasing his forehead, said, "I can see what you mean. Obviously, I can't tell you some things I may have come to know, but you're right, it shouldn't be this accessible; not with what's going on across the way. We expect there to be the people we're after, but not this many. I'll have to have words about it."

Sharon followed his gaze to where she could quite clearly see huge blocks of concrete being constructed, already larger than either Betty's cottage or Ruth's. Indeed, as they watched, one was apparently finished and in the process of being launched into the Solent. Unable to tear their eyes away, the huge structure slid with incredible grace into the water, sending splashes of dirty water up to nearly the height of the structure itself. Somehow, through what method of science neither Sharon nor Lawrence could comprehend, it didn't sink, merely floating until a tug gently nudged it on its way.

"Quick!" Lawrence urged her. "Take my pen and pad," he took these out of a pocket and passed them to her, "and pretend to make some notes."

Nodding in understanding, Sharon even took a few steps closer to the river. Exaggerating her head movements, she watched the tug and whatever the huge block of concrete was called, before looking down at the pad and beginning to scribble.

Behind them, the couple with the dachshund shared satisfied looks and strolled off. Only once they'd disappeared out of sight did Lawrence allow himself a wry smile, being careful not to let Sharon see. To be on the safe side, he reassured himself that his revolver was still in his coat pocket.

****

Taking advantage of the warm mid-April afternoon, Betty's household was lying outside on various blankets, enjoying a rare, lazy day. Everything was peace, quiet, and contentment. Well, nearly.

"Now look, Gertrude," Penny was saying, her face hidden behind the book she was reading. "I know you were only joking about pulling rank the other day, to get your hands on this book, but lying next to me and trying to read over my shoulder isn't going to make me read it any faster or finish it any sooner. I like to savor my books..."

Betty loudly interrupted Penny's monologue, with a very loud cough, whilst Bobby *woofed* in his sleep, no doubt in agreement with his favorite provider of dog biscuits.

Penny didn't miss a beat. "As I was saying, I like to savor Betty's books, sometimes even reading the same page twice before moving along."

"I sympathize with Jane," Doris put in, laying down her copy of *Death on the Nile*. "I've nothing against old Hercule Poirot," she told them, tapping her book, "but until *The Moving Finger* comes out in June—and I know I won't be first, or even second to read it—I've been waiting to get my hands on what you're reading for long enough."

Penny waved a single finger in the air above the book. "Nagging won't make me read this any quicker."

"Nor let me read it any sooner," Jane muttered, flopping back onto her part of the rug she was sharing with Penny.

Penny took a hand away and patted her boss on the thigh. "Sorry about that."

Taking her cushion from beneath her head, Jane placed it over her face and let out a not-so-silent scream of frustration.

"Shh," Penny urged. "I'm getting to a good bit."

Jane raised the cushion up a little. "Care for a transfer to Scotland?"

"As long as I can take this book with me," she shrugged, "I'm fine."

"What about Tom?" Jane tried, mentioning Penny's husband.

Penny marked her page and leant up on an elbow. "I know we're not exactly the couple of the month at the moment, but we are working at our marriage. I don't actually think that's very funny," she finished, frowning down at her friend.

With a sigh, Jane swept the cushion off her face and hurriedly sat up. She took Penny's hand, "Oh, hell. I'm sorry, really sorry. I only meant that as a joke and certainly never wanted to hurt you." She gripped her friend's arm harder when Penny didn't meet her earnest, half-joking gaze. "You have to believe me!"

Taking her by surprise, Penny, in one swift movement, laid her precious book down and rolled on top of her friend to launch a ferocious tickle-attack.

This was how Ruth and her boyfriend, Matt Green,

found them when they appeared around the side of the house. On one hand, Betty was cheering on Jane, who'd managed to turn the tables on Penny who was now pinned underneath her boss's thighs and was roaring with laughter.

"What the…?" Matt said.

"I wouldn't worry," Ruth told him, pressing Bobby's lead into Matt's hand and rushing forward to take sides.

"I heard…" Walter shouted as he ran out the kitchen door, before coming to a halt beside his wife. "I don't know." He shook his head. "I try to have a little quiet time—*The Brains Trust* on the wireless, admittedly not the most thrilling of listening, but it was nice, mindless stuff—try to catch up on my sleep a little, and then it sounds like someone's trying to strangle an aria!" He looked down and began to laugh before joining his wife, cheering along to the tickle-fight at their feet.

However, his words had come during a lull, and he found he was the only one cheering, which rapidly tailed off.

"Sounds like someone trying to strangle an aria?" Penny looked up at Walter, before asking Jane, "I thought I had a nice voice. Don't I have a nice voice?"

"I think you've a lovely voice," Jane agreed, all pretend animosity between the pair forgot. "Doris. How…fit…is Walter?" she asked.

Doris took a step away from her husband, who twigged onto what her friends were up to as quickly as she had. Shrugging her apologies, she answered, "Well, as of last night, I'd say he's fully fit, no matter what the doctors will have you believe."

"Doris?" Walter slowly said, as his wife edged away

from him. "I haven't been declared medically fully fit yet," he tried to plead.

"Sorry, hon," she said as she continued to back away. "All's fair in love and war."

Belatedly, Walter tried to edge back in the direction of the kitchen, but in talking to his wife, he'd taken his eye off the other four. Turning, he found Betty and Ruth were blocking the doorway, whilst Penny and Jane were advancing, fingers and hands outstretched, and before he could beat a hasty retreat, he'd been pounced upon. The five fell to the floor in a melee of tangled limbs, and before too long, the roar of Walter's bass laughter was echoing around the garden.

"Steady, lad!" Penny's voice shouted, as Bobby decided to try and join in the fun. Her warning was too late as, before anyone could prevent it, the Cocker Spaniel had torn off one of Betty's shoes and was making a dash for the hole in the hedge which led to his owner's cottage.

Next thing anyone knew, the shoe's owner had disentangled herself from the still ongoing tickle-ball and was alternately hopping and running toward the hedge where she stopped, bent over and stuck her head through the hedge and yelled, "Bobby!" at the top of her voice.

When he failed to reappear, she turned back to find everyone had now stopped and were watching her with expressions of intense amusement.

"What?"

The other members of the ATA Mystery Club were all looking at each other, their faces, one by one, gaining the same expression of understanding, closely followed by everyone's eyebrows shooting up their brows. They all turned to look at where Betty was now stood with her bare foot upon her remaining shoe.

"What?" Betty repeated.

"Do you want to tell her?" Penny asked Doris, who shook her head.

"You can have the pleasure."

Betty hopped up toward them and collapsed onto a blanket. Looking up, still none the wiser, she demanded, "Tell her what?"

Penny knelt down beside her friend. "We think we've worked out what's happened to our missing clothing," she told her, resting a hand upon her shoulder.

Slowly, realization dawned on Betty's face, and her head began to flick back and forth between her friends and the hole through which Bobby had disappeared. Eventually, she threw her head back and laughed out loud. "The little tyke!" she managed to get out before her friends joined her, leaving poor Walter to recover from the unprovoked attack.

"I'll never understand women," could just be heard.

"You and me both," Mary agreed, leaning out of her bedroom window. Whilst everything had been going on around her, she'd been quietly dozing in her room. "Can you tell that lot to quieten down? Some of us are trying to have a snooze."

At hearing their friend, all the girls looked up and, as one, shouted, "Tickle-fight!" and rushed indoors. Now the shoe was on the other foot, Walter was happy to see the blood drain from Mary's face as she realized what she'd done.

Chapter Ten

Sharon slumped back in her chair and threw her best glare toward Lawrence. Her mood wasn't helped when her companion merely put the newspaper he'd been reading aside and cocked an eyebrow.

"Finished?" he asked, as he got up from his seat to take the paper from her.

"I hope so," she muttered half-turning her head to look at the three previous attempts, which lay crumpled beside Lawrence, having been deemed not up to scratch. They were there so he would be certain to take them away with him to be disposed of securely. Picking up her cup of tea, she took a sip, crinkled up her face in disgust, and put the stone-cold cup back down.

"Fresh cup, anyone?" Mavis asked.

"God, yes, please!" Sharon replied with feeling. Closing her eyes, she brought her fists up and rubbed her eyes. She'd been writing since she'd got back in from work, and her eyes were throbbing.

What she'd thought would be a quick exercise had turned into a major headache, literally. Never much of an academic, it had felt like being back at school. Her first attempt hadn't made it past the first line before Lawrence had tossed it to one side and told her, not asked, that she needed to change the first line. Apparently, "Dear Fred" wouldn't do. She'd pointed out the fabricated officer she was writing to was called Fred, and though Lawrence had agreed, he'd then told her to pretend she hadn't seen this Fred for over three years, and would you really begin a letter with simply, "Dear Fred"?

Her second attempt hadn't got much further, the third line, in fact. She'd allowed herself a metaphorical pat on the back when Lawrence had made it past her new salutation, 'My Dearest Fred,' but this had proven to be a false dawn. Who knew there was an art to writing a letter? Of course, she had a full page of notes which Lawrence wanted her to feed in, and so, before she'd started, she'd read the list through twice and only then had she begun. Lawrence being in the same room hadn't helped her concentration, and her third attempt had taken over an hour. Hence the cold tea.

Only when she realized Lawrence hadn't disposed of this one as quickly as the first two did she look up. Opening her mouth, she closed it as quickly. The policeman didn't need to know Mavis was reading the letter over his shoulder. Hoping her new landlady wouldn't spill boiling hot tea from the pot she was holding, she held her breath. The ATA girls had assured her he had a good sense of humor, but she doubted this would hold with an earful of scalding hot tea.

"Have you finished yet, Mavis?"

Mavis jumped back and, for a second, Sharon thought she really would drown Lawrence in tea, a very ignoble way for him to go. To her credit, she quickly recovered, "Thank you, yes," she told him and proceeded to ask, "Would you care for another cup too?"

He held up his empty cup. "I'm a policeman, never known to refuse."

"So?" Sharon couldn't hold it in any longer. "Is this one okay?"

"You know what a fox is?" he asked.

Sharon opened and closed her mouth before deciding he was serious, however cryptically. "Of course. I grew up in the country. Why?"

"I believe there's a saying which goes, 'as cunning as a fox.' "

"And?"

"And," he grinned back, "you've managed to turn the script we gave you into something a fox would be proud of."

"And that's good?" Sharon had to ask, stretching her arms above her head. "Mavis, does any of this make sense to you?"

After setting down the two cups of fresh tea, Mavis settled herself down in her rather worn yet favorite high-backed leather chair and reached down to pick up her knitting. She checked her needles and started where she'd left off the previous night before replying, "It's beginning to."

"Not you too!" Sharon declared, throwing her hands up.

"Don't start on me, young lady. I'm not supposed to know what's going on. However," she added, tapping the side of her nose, "I do watch what's going on around me."

Lawrence put down his cup and turned to face the elderly lady. "In that case, I assume I can trust you to keep quiet. I really don't want to have to throw you in jail."

"That makes two of us," Mavis agreed, treating him to a rare smile.

Shaking her head, Sharon turned her attention back to Lawrence. "Forget the fox. How about a plain answer?"

Picking up the letter from his lap, Lawrence came across to where Sharon sat, put it on the table, and pulled out a chair and sat. Placing a finger upon what she'd written, he gave her the same smile, only this time told her, plainly, "This reads exactly as we need. You've said what we saw at the weekend, and as that's easy enough for them to see from aerial reconnaissance, we're not telling them anything they don't already know. The way you've described other items…" Here, Lawrence paused and made certain Mavis saw the look he was shooting her way and didn't turn back to Sharon until he'd got a nod of acknowledgement from her, "…is perfect to whet their appetites. There's just enough truth in it, without giving away anything really helpful, that you'll have their intelligence bods foaming at the mouth with excitement."

Sharon reached out and turned the letter back around so it was facing her. "You mean, there really is something that does…"

"You don't need to know." Lawrence hurried to cut the girl off. "You certainly don't need to tell anyone else."

Seeing how serious he was, Sharon nodded. "I understand. Don't worry, I'll keep my lips sealed."

"Thank you," Lawrence said, reaching across and giving her hand a quick, tight squeeze. "Now, let's get this addressed and in the metaphorical post. Then we can relax for a while."

"What about replies?" Mavis suddenly piped up, causing Lawrence's head to jerk around.

"Mavis." Lawrence's tone held an obvious warning tone.

By reply, she zipped her fingers across her lips. "Within these four walls, Lawrence, within these four walls."

"As for replies," he began, getting to his feet and pulling his coat on, "the powers that be, shall be watching out for them. They'll let us know when they have one, and we'll go from there." With an exaggerated theatrical wink as he pocketed the letter, he suggested, "Let's enjoy a well-earned break from our labors," and he picked up his cup.

****

When she'd shouted out that she'd see the girls later as she'd climbed into the cockpit of the Typhoon, Betty didn't consider they could be the last words she'd ever exchange with her friends.

It was a beautiful late afternoon that Wednesday, with brushes of off-white clouds and nothing else in sight. If she'd had the time, it was the kind of day where she would normally spend as much time as she could watching the world pass by. However, what should have been a nice, hour-ish jaunt to RAF Manston was turning into a major headache.

As sod's law would decree, she was only around twenty minutes out from the airfield when she heard a muffled *bang* from somewhere around the rear of the fuselage. Instantly alert, she swiveled her head around as far as it would go to both sides, craning her neck in an effort to check for any visible damage. "Thank Christ for that," she muttered, when she saw the tail was still present, before cursing her stupidity. If the tail hadn't been present, she'd have spun in with little chance to bail out, even if she'd have been flying at ten thousand feet instead of her actual few thousand. When Penny told her that her last delivery of the day would be this particular type of fighter-bomber, she'd also drilled into her to take extra care due to this type's problems—its entire tail section being known to part company with the rest of the aircraft. It wasn't quite as bad as when it had first been produced, but she couldn't bring herself to entirely trust the metal fishplates that were riveted around the tail.

Satisfied the aircraft wasn't going to fall apart on her that instant, Betty took a few deep breaths to bring her heartbeat back under control. She prided herself on never panicking, no matter what the circumstances, whilst aloft. "Today's no different, Betty Palmer," she muttered, tightening her grip upon the control stick as she felt it begin to quiver in her hand.

"Oh, terrific," she mumbled. Glancing outside the cockpit, she assured herself she was still over *terra firma* and then did a quick instrument check. If she'd had a radio, she'd have made an emergency call. However, being a new aircraft, virtually straight off the production line, this plane didn't have one. Ignoring the usual thought regarding whose brilliant idea it had been to let them deliver aircraft and not include a basic piece of equipment such as a radio, Betty frowned at the starboard instrument board—specifically, the oil pressure gauge. Forcing herself to concentrate, she watched the needle carefully as her frown deepened. Now being forced to use her other hand on the control column, the judder having got worse, she could only nod her head and set her lips into a grim line of acceptance.

"Right. If that's how it's going to be..." she said. Taking a deep breath, she swiftly gripped the throttle and, fighting the urge to shove it fully forward, she eased it forward, at the same time pulling the control column back between her knees, praying she wasn't too late. As she coaxed as much power out of the dying engine as she could, she tried not to think of the bang she'd heard. "One problem at a time," she told herself from between gritted teeth. "Try to get some more height in case the tail does decide to drop off," she finished.

The vibration was now so bad she struggled to make out her true height on the altimeter. Another sharp bang from the rear of the aircraft made up her mind for her. Gripping the control column as best she could between her knees, Betty made sure her goggles were tightly on, fumbled a little as she tucked her silk scarf in, and, before she could change her mind, not that she had any other choice, yanked the cockpit hood back. The blast of freezing cold air took her breath away. Ducking her head back down out of the slipstream, Betty undid her harness and, not without some effort, rolled the dying airplane onto its back and allowed her body to tumble out of the cockpit and into the frigid early evening air.

Looking around, her sharp eyes quickly found her previous mode of transport. It resembled a sad, dark cross, and she watched as it begun to spin down toward the ground. Quicker and quicker it went until the tail broke off and began its own sad, languid journey to mother earth. "Bloody hell!" Betty swore.

Shaking her head to clear it, she forced her mind to concentrate on more urgent matters. She made a grab for her parachute D-ring. Missing it once, twice, she managed to snare it on the third go. As her chute opened, she experienced a massive tug, and the air whooshed out of her lungs. She sailed down toward the earth, her concentration gripped by the surreal sight of her right boot pinwheeling down about ten feet below her.

Chapter Eleven

Slowly, Doris lowered her binoculars and turned her frown upon the lowly pilot officer beside her. "What was that you said?" she demanded, turning fully around and stamping her foot in frustration.

Not sure how he should respond, no one having explained how the Air Transport Auxiliary rank structure related to that of the Royal Air Force, the spotty twenty-year-old pulled his collar away from his throat and stammered, "Nothing, miss. I didn't say anything."

Fully aware of his nervousness and not caring one jot, the American stared up his nostrils and took a reluctant step back, the better so he could see exactly how annoyed she was. "It's Third Officer Johnson," she snapped, "and yes, you did. But never mind that. Go back up the tower and find out if anyone's heard anything yet."

Taxi duty wasn't Doris's favorite task, and today's was onerous in the extreme. Most of the day's deliveries had been to the east and south of the British Isles and so, very unusually, it was just her and her trusty Avro Anson who'd landed ten minutes ago, expecting to pick up Betty and then swiftly take off for home. However, after waiting in her plane for fifteen minutes and there'd still been no sign of her friend, she'd made her way over to the control tower to see if she could find out where her friend was. As she'd got closer, she'd noticed the balcony full of men staring into the distance through their binoculars. That was when she'd broken into a run, as well as a cold sweat. The result of her yelling for attention had been the wee pilot officer, who'd informed her that Betty hadn't arrived yet. Apparently, she was now thirty minutes overdue.

Impatiently watching the second hand of her watch tick too slowly around, she was about to barge past the airman posted at the entrance to the tower, when the pilot officer reappeared. "Well?"

Whipping off his hat, he wiped a sleeve across his brow, obviously wishing he were anywhere but where he was. "I'm sorry, but we don't know where she is." He hastily added, when Doris looked like she was about to blow her top at him, "But we've been ringing around all the local stations, in case she came down at one of those by mistake."

"Betty doesn't make mistakes," Doris snapped, silently adding to herself that this little snot didn't need to know her friend used to make plenty.

"Yes, of course," he added, a little too smarmily for Doris's liking. "We've also tried to get hold of her on the radio, but she's not answering."

Somehow, Doris managed to make her single word reply extend for a full ten seconds, "Reeaallllyyy?" before stuffing her flying helmet inside her Sidcot flying suit. With an expression of thunder upon her face, Doris barged past both the guard and the officer before either had a chance to react. A swift kick from her booted foot nearly knocked the door off its hinges and Doris was taking the stairs two at a time before it stopped bouncing from the blow.

Bursting into the single room at the top of the stairs,

Doris picked up on the nervous energy permeating the atmosphere. All the telephones seemed to be in use, with various ranks all talking twenty to the dozen into the handsets. She could pick up a few words. "ATA" was spoken at least twice, and Betty's name three times, together with the word "missing," which Doris didn't like one bit.

Surprisingly, no one had noticed her appearance, so she made her way over to a sergeant on the radio and tapped him on the shoulder.

Without turning around, he told her, "Bugger off. I'm still trying to get hold of this girl."

Doris gripped the back of the man's chair and with all her strength, yanked him around to face her, no small effort, as the chair wasn't on wheels. She bent over until her nose was nearly touching his.

"Don't you lot know anything?" she began. "That Tiffy doesn't have a radio."

By the time she'd finished speaking, the man had recovered from his shock and, from his wide-open mouth, he'd been about to yell something (undoubtedly rude) at her, but he took in what she'd said and, instead, sprang to his feet, forcing Doris to jump backward. He gestured at a clearly very angry and worried Doris. "Is this officer right?"

Would anyone in the RAF ever work out what to call them? Shoving the thought to one side, Doris answered, "Of course I bloody well am! Now, who's in charge and can tell me what the hell's going on and where my friend is?"

A tall squadron leader peeled himself away from a telephone and came to stand before her. "I'm Squadron Leader Diamonde and…you are?"

Doris stuck out a hand and pumped the officer's once before letting go. "Third Officer Doris Johnson, and I want to know what's happened to my friend."

"Who is, I presume, the lady who was due to deliver the Typhoon we're expecting."

"Spot on," Doris replied. "Now, have you heard anything about her?"

Diamonde, a rather well-decorated pilot, she could now see, with an atypical handlebar mustache, glanced around and then pointed toward a corner somewhat less crowded than anywhere else. Hooking his other hand at Doris's elbow, he steered her there.

"Look, miss…Third Officer…Doris," he eventually settled upon, "I can appreciate how worried you must be, and believe me, I've done the same when a friend's been overdue, so I'll allow you those outbursts, but no more. Look around you—listen—everyone is doing their best to get to the bottom of what's happened. Your bouncing in here and ragging on everyone is only going to get on people's nerves." He took a step back, pasted on a sympathetic smile, and lowered his voice so only the American could hear. "I don't pretend to know how close you are to…Betty? But the best thing you can do right now is to let us do our job."

For one of the few times in her life, Doris bit her tongue so the first words which came to her mind didn't make it to her lips. He was right. Of course he was right. Letting out a sigh, she slowly nodded her head.

"Can I ask for two favors?" she began. "I'd like to telephone my boss, tell her what's going on." After he'd nodded his agreement, she then asked, after taking a quick look around the hectic room, "I want to stay. At least until there's some news!" she hurried to add, upon seeing that Diamonde's face had taken on a frown. "I'll stay outside and I won't be a bother to anyone. I only ask that as soon as you hear anything…" Doris swallowed before forcing her next words out. "And I do mean *anything*, you come and tell me right away."

This time, the squadron leader stuck out his hand. "You have my word. Come on, you can use my phone."

****

"Any sign of them?" Jane asked.

Penny didn't trouble turning her head from where she sat upon the steps of the ops hut. "Nothing. And…" She held up the arm upon which her wristwatch was strapped. "Yes, I'm perfectly aware they're fifteen minutes overdue."

There was a *clunk* as a mug was placed beside Penny, soon joined by another and then by Jane.

"Sorry," Jane told her friend, resting her head briefly upon Penny's shoulder. "We both know it's not like Doris to be late back."

"Especially since she was married," Penny added, picking up the mug and warming her hands.

"Especially since she was married," Jane agreed, with a somewhat mirthless laugh.

Penny kept her eyes glued toward the direction from which they were both expecting the Anson taxi to appear. "You know—and I wouldn't normally say this out loud, but what the heck—I worry about Walter. Have you noticed how, well, how tired he always seems to be now?"

Jane did a comically exaggerated scan around before saying, "See previous answer," and then adding, "As we're talking about marriages, can I ask how yours is? We haven't seen much of Tom lately."

For a few seconds, Penny allowed her head to droop, before forcing it back up to resume her vigil. "We're...okay."

"Okay." Jane put her mug down and turned to face her friend, who looked, if it were possible, more morose than ever. "You're going to have to do better than that."

"Better than that," Penny mumbled, taking a sip of tea. "Very well. I thought we were going to make a go of things, you know. He seemed very happy when I told him I was willing, but then, after the whole kidnap malarkey, he's always seemed busy, difficult to pin down for even a phone call. I can appreciate he's flying again, and I didn't like to say anything as I didn't want to sound, well, selfish."

"What about the other night? You know, after this whole Sharon thing began. I thought you'd spoken to him. You've seemed happy enough to me."

Penny shrugged. "Guess who should have taken up a career on stage."

Jane put an arm around her friend and drew her in. "You really have to stop being silly. We've had this conversation before. You can talk to me anytime you like, and I'm certain your other friends would say exactly the same."

It was a few minutes before Penny spoke, and when she did, Jane had to strain her ears a little to hear. "I know, I know. Despite everything, losing the baby and all that happened afterward, I still love him and know I always will."

"Well, in that case," Jane said, having come to a decision, "I think a spot of leave could be in order. Phone him when we get back, see what you can fix up which suits you both, and then tell me the dates."

Penny wiped a hand below her nose and Jane could actually see a small smile as she said, "You truly are a lovely person, Jane, you know that."

Jane opened her mouth to reply, but the ring of the telephone inside caused them to briefly stare at each other, before there was a frantic scramble, during which both mugs went flying, to get to the instrument.

"RAF Hamble, Flight Captain Howell." Penny perched on the edge of Jane's desk in support. Jane's head snapped up. "What's happened?" she simply asked.

The call didn't last long, though as Jane only nodded to whatever was being said, Penny could see her face grow more ashen by the second. Finally, with a toneless, "We'll let you know, and you do the same, and yes, you've my permission to stay there as long as you need." She replaced the receiver and slumped back into her seat, her mouth firmly closed and her head shaking from side to side.

When she could stand it no longer, Penny virtually shouted, "Well?" Was that a tear in her friend's eye? Penny wasn't given the chance to ask, as Jane, jolted out of wherever she'd been, jumped to her feet, sending her chair flying, and was around the other side of her desk before Penny could even register she'd moved.

"Come on!" Jane urged, matching actions to words by grabbing her friend by the arm and dragging her into the main part of the hut. Without speaking further, Jane grabbed a bunch of telephone directories from a shelf and threw them on Penny's desk. Just when Penny thought she may have to slap her, Jane looked up. Her face hadn't regained any of its color. If anything she was whiter than the deadest ghost!

"Jesus!" Penny swore. "Tel me what's going on

before I burst!"

Jane took a deep breath and, if she'd have been able to see herself, Penny's own normal healthy hue lost a few shades. "Betty's missing."

"Who was that?" Penny managed to get out on the second attempt.

"Doris," Jane answered. "She's at Manston and has just found out herself."

"What're they doing?" Penny demanded.

If sighs were currency, Jane mused, she'd be a very rich woman by now. "The control tower is full and everyone is phoning around, trying to find out what's happened. So far, nothing."

"No…crash, then, either," Penny couldn't help but say, instantly regretting the words. "Sorry, stupid thing to say. So, obviously, they're doing everything they can." She picked up one of the telephone books Jane had dumped. "I assume we're going to be doing the same from our end."

Jane gave a grim nod. "Too bloody right." She picked up a book. "Right, maps out, please. I need you to plot me a course, from the factory where she picked up that bloody Typhoon to Manston. No deviations, because Betty wouldn't, just straight to it. Then," she added, as Penny scrambled for the appropriate maps, making light of having full use of only one arm, "we need to mark out every police station, and we track them down and phone them. I know it's going to be difficult, Penny, but we have to be careful what we say. Introduce yourself and simply ask if they've seen any planes…crash," she finished, with some difficulty.

"And if they say yes?" Penny wanted to know, as she weighed down the edges of her maps.

"Then, and only then, you can ask if it was one of ours and explain why you're asking. Whilst you begin with those, I'll get onto the Observer Corps."

After noting down a telephone number, Penny, a pencil tucked behind an ear, looked up, "What about the others?"

"Others?" Jane echoed, a little confused, until she saw her friend jabbing at her chest with her free hand. "Oh! Right!" She looked around before asking, "Is Mary back yet?"

"She hasn't popped in to say goodbye," Penny replied, "so I imagine she's still in the flight line hut getting changed." When she saw that Jane was hesitating, she gently prompted, "She'd want to help, as will everyone else."

Letting out another pound's worth of sighs, Jane came to a decision. "Go and get her. No one else, mind!" she added. "No need for anyone else to worry, until they have to."

Chapter Twelve

Mary had taken the potentially grim news stoically. As Jane busied herself in tracking down and calling the Observer Corps, men and women who were trained to recognize aircraft and report upon every one they saw, Penny and Mary developed a methodology—whilst Penny cross-checked the towns and villages against the maps, Mary made the phone calls.

After the fourth straight negative result—not a totally bad thing, they all had to keep telling themselves—Mary suggested, "Would it help if we sent out an aircraft to go along the route Betty would have taken?"

Instead of answering, after a few seconds of staring at Mary, Jane stopped dialing, slammed her fingers down on the cradle to reset the phone, and dialed a different number. Despite the urgency of the situation, both Penny and Mary stopped what they were doing and unashamedly listened in.

"Hello? This is Flight Captain Jane Howell from RAF Hamble. Put me onto Squadron Leader Diamonde. …Interrupt him then, dammit!"

Penny and Mary exchanged knowing looks. Their boss had the bit between her teeth.

"Squadron Leader?" Jane said, "I know you're busy, but have you sent out any search aircraft? You know, to back-track her route." Jane's eyebrows shot up, and she was actually smiling when she shook her head this time. "I quite understand, and thank you for being so understanding too. No, the best of luck to us all." She put the receiver back down.

"Well?" both Penny and Mary asked at the same time.

"It appears Doris came up with the same idea as you, Mary, not two minutes ago. Typical of Forces types, they started bickering amongst themselves and, next thing they knew, and I quote here, Doris told them to, 'Stop acting like little boys! I'm going.' Before anyone could stop her, she'd jumped in the Anson and taken off!"

Time stood still for a few more seconds and then all three burst out laughing.

"Typical Doris," Penny was eventually able to say. "I hope she keeps an eye on her fuel, though," she added, wishing she hadn't.

"We'll just have to trust her," Jane replied. "Right, back to it, both of you! I'm going to give the mess a call and ask for some tea and biscuits. We're going to need something to keep us going."

Mary stopped dialing long enough to request, "Can you make sure Sharon makes it, if she's there? I think I'll be sick if I have to go back to Mavis's rubbish!"

How she did it, no one asked, but Sharon performed a minor miracle, and within ten minutes of Jane having asked, there came what sounded like someone trying to kick the hut's door off its hinges.

"Hang on! Hang on!" Penny shouted, dropping her pencil and rushing to open it.

"Sorry about that," Sharon apologized as she staggered into the hut.

Once she was in and the door once more closed,

everyone could understand why she'd had to kick instead of knock. How she'd managed it, they didn't stop to ask, but all were thankful for the girl's promptness and thoughtfulness. Somehow, she'd managed to cram onto the tray she balanced three mugs, a huge brown china tea urn, and a large plate of what would turn out to be jam sandwiches, together with the requested biscuits.

"With Mavis's compliments," Sharon began, once she'd put her load down upon a space Mary hurriedly cleared. "Oh, yes, I made the tea," she said, smirking as she noted the relieved expressions upon her new friends' faces, "and you've Mavis to thank for the sandwiches. She also told me to wish you the best of luck, though she admitted she didn't know what for. Here." She took over the teapot from Mary, who'd been looking at the size of the pot with great trepidation. "I'll be mother."

Once everyone had taken a rejuvenating sip of the nectar Sharon brewed, they all thanked her and, once she'd left, picked up their tasks where they'd left off. Soon, all that could be heard were the mechanical voices Jane and Mary were speaking in. After the end of every call, the other two looked up with identical expressions of hope on their faces, hope which grew harder to keep up as the number of negative phone calls increased.

"If I hear one more…" Mary began to say, when she was interrupted by Jane's phone ringing and making them all jump.

Quickly recovering her composure, Jane snatched up the receiver. It showed the stress she was under as, instead of introducing herself with her full rank and name, she merely said, "Hello, Jane here."

"Who is it?" Penny couldn't help but ask, to which Jane waved her into silence.

"Yes, yes, this is Flight Captain Jane Howell at RAF Hamble. Sergeant Vaizey? Oh, yes, I remember speaking to you. You've news?" Jane leant forward on her desk, as both Penny and Mary gave her their full attention from where they sat around Penny's desk. "Uh-huh, yes, yes. Okay, we'll wait to hear from you. Thank you!" she added, before replacing the receiver.

By this time, both her friends were nearly hanging off the desk.

"Well?" Penny got in first.

Jane looked across, with perhaps a little more color in her cheeks than previously. "That was one of the police stations you called, Mary," she began. "Well, they took a phone call from some Observers chaps. They witnessed what they told him was a Typhoon going down, in two pieces…" she had to stop as Penny and Mary had both gasped out loud at this, "about ten miles out from RAF Manston. They told the sergeant there were no other aircraft in the skies, and before they saw all this, they'd heard something flying over which sounded like it was having engine trouble."

Not waiting, Mary asked, "Did they see a chute?"

"Jane nodded, joining her friend in letting out a long breath.

"And now?" Penny wanted to know.

"And now, we carry on doing what we've been doing. We can't take it for granted that this is Betty. Plus, that policeman is going to call me back as soon as he has more news."

"What about Manston? Should we tell them? Just in case they don't know." Penny asked.

Jane picked up her receiver once again, "Good idea. I'll give them a call."

Five minutes and another phone call later, Jane poked her head out of her office. "Manston knows," she told them. "That sergeant was on the ball. Plus, Doris is back there. It turns out she didn't have much fuel and had to turn back when she was only five miles out. Apparently, she's giving the ground crew hell. She wants her plane refueled yesterday, so she can get back up. I asked Manston to pass on the news and insist she stays on the ground this time until I tell her otherwise. The Squadron Leader sounded quite pleased when he got this news. I left him musing about setting her under armed guard."

"I wouldn't give much for their chances if he did," Penny said, finishing off her cup of tea and gratefully accepting a refill from Mary.

Jane's phone rang again, and this time Jane remembered to answer correctly. However, once she'd finished nodding her head, she waved the other two back into her office to stand either side of her. Covering the mouthpiece with a hand, she quickly told them, "Observer Corps have just brought her into the station."

She waited until her friends had quietened their jubilant cries.

"She's apparently in one piece and they're just about to drive her to Manston. She insists upon that. Here she is!" she told them, and angled the phone away from the side of her head as much as she could, whilst still being able to speak and hear. "Betty! How wonderful to hear your voice! You're sure you're all right? Well, let's let our doctor check you out when we get you back. No, that's not open for discussion. Sorry, what was that? You've got to go? Well, Doris is waiting for you at Manston, but neither of you are coming back tonight. I'm going to call the Squadron Leader who's been in charge of searching for you from that end and get him to put the two of you up for the night. No arguments! We'll see you both in the morning. What was that?" Jane let out a belly laugh. "Don't worry about it. No, really. We'll see you tomorrow!" With that, she held out the receiver so the other two could send her their love before replacing it and slumping back into her chair, feeling quite worn.

Jane picked up her cup and peered at its now cold contents. "I wish we had something stronger to celebrate with."

"Me too," Penny agreed, before saying, "but let's wait until she's back home tomorrow, eh?"

"What was worrying her?" Mary asked.

"Hold that thought," Jane asked. "Let me give Manston a call. There's a good chance they've been told, but I'd like to make certain. Plus, I need to square away the overnight accommodation."

It didn't take long to make the call and the necessary arrangements. Jane had beaten the police and the Observer Corps, as when she'd finished giving them the good news, she had to hold the receiver away from her ear as the cheers were so loud. Doris, who hadn't been put under armed guard, had heard the commotion and Jane had been able to have a short word with her. She'd had to be firm, as Doris had been all for taking off and picking up Betty from the little village she was currently in. In the end, she thanked Jane for arranging accommodation—the squadron leader had told her they'd be put up in the officer's mess and Doris was already looking forward to a nice hot bath—and told her she was going to get someone to run her down to the guardroom to meet Betty when she arrived.

"So what was Betty worried about?" Mary asked again.

Through a now-happy smile, Jane told her, "Two schoolboys made off with her parachute. She said she had to cut it off, as it was very blowy and she was being dragged all over the place, and she was just getting to her feet to go and retrieve it when two lads on bicycles came out of nowhere and had it away before she could move."

"Good for them!" Penny let out, before she could stop herself.

After a moment's hesitation, Jane agreed. "Can't argue with that. We'll mark it down as a war loss. Either way, good to know she's still got her sense of humor, even if she doesn't realize it!"

Both Penny and Mary got up from their seats, did their best impressions of a cat stretching, and moved toward their coats and hats.

"And just where do you two think you're going?" Jane asked.

The girls exchanged confused glances. "Home?" Penny replied, though she didn't sound convinced.

Taking them by their arms, she sat each before a telephone. "Not yet. We need to phone every place we've called. Let them know they can call off any searches or any other activity they're doing because of what we told them. I don't want to be the cause of anyone being put out for us now the emergency is over."

Mary looked at the list of places she'd called, and Penny, now at Jane's desk, did the same; both groaned. "And where are you going?" Penny asked, seeing her boss pulling on her coat and hat.

"Me?" Jane asked, straightening her hat. "I'm going over to the mess. I need to tell Mavis and Sharon that everything's all right, and to thank her for the forethought of making us the sandwiches. I don't know if Mavis is psychic, but she knew something. For that, she deserves our thanks." As she opened the ops hut door, she turned around and clapped her hands together. "Come on! The sooner you finish those phone calls, the sooner we can all go home! Deliveries as usual tomorrow, remember?"

Chapter Thirteen

When it came time to leave RAF Manston early the next morning, Doris and Betty attracted quite the crowd. Squadron Leader Diamonde was creating merry-hell amongst the visiting flight ground crew—making certain the ladies' Anson was in tiptop condition, insisting everything that needed to be checked *was* checked at least three times—going by the muttering coming from the poor put-upon souls.

"Do you think they'll ever forgive him?" Betty nudged Doris lightly in the ribs.

"Bloody zob!" an aircraftsman swore as he stumbled past, a rag in one hand as he hurried to polish the plexiglass in the plane's door.

Doris shook her head and brought a hand up to hide her grin. "Not for a good while. It'd probably be for the best if we shot off as quickly as possible," she suggested, bending down to pick up her things.

"In a hurry to leave us?"

Neither had spotted their host as he appeared from the other side of the plane's tail.

Doris waved a hand to indicate the frantic activity around them. "For this lot's sake, it's probably for the best."

To his credit, the officer didn't argue but merely shrugged his shoulders. "I know. I'll make it up to them later, stand them a beer or two, maybe."

Doris fished in her handbag and handed him a ten shilling note. "Here." She pressed the note into his hand and closed it before he could protest. "Make sure they get some of the good stuff."

Beneath raised eyebrows, Diamonde shook his head.

"Don't even try to give it back," Doris warned him. "I'll be insulted, and you don't want to see me in a mood."

Betty laid a hand briefly on his arm. "You don't, really!"

Somewhat to Betty's surprise, Diamonde smiled and tucked the note into his trousers pocket. "You forget, Third Officer Doris Johnson, I've had a taster of your temper already and don't wish to go a second round."

"Doris?" Betty turned full attention upon her friend. "What exactly happened when you turned up here yesterday?"

Typical of Doris, she was totally unabashed as she told her, "Nothing out of the normal."

"That was normal?" the squadron leader asked, unable to keep a tone of surprise from his voice.

"Depends what she did," Betty supplied.

Taking off his hat, Diamonde absently ran a hand through his hair whilst smiling at Doris. "It was a bit like being caught in a storm," he began, before stumbling to a halt, his thought processes not helped by the soft laughter coming from the American. Then he rallied. "Well, she put us right about you lot not flying with a radio." He shook his head before continuing. "And once we'd told her you were missing and before we could inform her what we were doing about it, she tried to tell us what we should be doing."

"Sounds exactly like our Doris."

"She's quite a force of nature," the officer commented.

Betty leaned in and gave Doris a one-armed cuddle. "And we wouldn't change a thing."

"I'm very glad to hear that," Doris told them, just as a sergeant scurried up to them, coming to a halt and throwing a very smart salute their way.

"Everything's tiptop, sir. They're ready to go."

"Well done, Sergeant." As the girls watched, he took the banknote Doris had given him out of his pocket and handed it to the bemused man. "Here, courtesy of Third Officer Johnson."

Doris jumped in. "I know I was a bit…much, yesterday. I hope you can forgive me, only I was worried for my friend here."

Betty gave Doris another one-armed hug. "I imagine you all went through so much more than I did yesterday," she told him. "When Doris goes off on one, she's quite a sight! I sometimes think we should parachute her into Germany. She'd have Hitler sorted in a matter of a few days!"

Muttering his thanks, the sergeant did a swift about-turn and went over to his men, where they saw him show them the bank note. Swiftly, they all yelled over their thanks before he hurried them off in the direction of a hangar.

"You've made some friends there," Diamonde told them, adding, "not to mention, amongst those of us in the mess. You're both welcome back here at any time," he added.

Betty took him by surprise by going up on tiptoes and kissing his cheek. "Well, I don't know about Mrs.

Johnson here, but I'll see what I can do."

For a moment, the handsome pilot appeared to lose control of his voice, but eventually he recovered and, after a quick cough, turned a hundred-watt smile Betty's way. "Um, yes! That'd be lovely! Which reminds me, actually—you are aware, Betty, that you now qualify for membership in the Caterpillar Club?"

"The Caterpillar Club?" Doris asked, as she loaded their bags into their plane.

"May I?" Diamonde offered Betty his arm to escort her to the Anson's door, even though it was only a few yards away. She tried her best to ignore Doris, who was waggling her eyebrows in her direction.

"Certainly…?"

"It's Simon," he reminded her."

"Sorry," Betty apologized. "I may have had a few too many last night."

Treating her to a smile, he patted her hand as he helped her up into the plane. "After what you went through, believe me, it's quite understandable."

"I hope I didn't make a scene?" Betty asked.

"Not a jot," he assured her. "Though I think Doris has taught my bods a few songs they won't be able to sing before their mothers."

"They had a great time!" Doris shouted from the pilot's seat as she went through the pre-flight checks.

"I'm sure they did." Betty chuckled.

"Anyway," Simon said as Betty turned back, "find out the maker of your chute and get in contact with the company. Tell them what happened, and they'll send you a form to fill in. You'll get a lovely pin to wear. Everyone who has to make an emergency jump from a plane by parachute qualifies. Well, safe journeys to you both!" he shouted to be heard, as Doris started up the engines.

"What was all that, *Mrs. Johnson* about?" Doris asked ten minutes later, adding, as she turned her attention back to navigating them home, "And, aren't you engaged, by the way?"

****

One of the benefits of being the Editor/Owner of the *Hamble Gazette* at present was the free time Ruth had in which to do other things. Due to the shortage of paper and ink, the paper only came out on Fridays. So now, with plenty of time in which to get the small edition ready, she often used the time and good light in the office to catch up on her correspondence.

Pen clamped between her teeth, she pondered what her husband would think of the adventures she'd been involved with since becoming friends with the girls from RAF Hamble. "Probably think I'm making them up," she decided, flicking the end of the pen and frowning at being unable to share the stories in her paper. Both her nephew Lawrence and Jane had strongly impressed upon her that, thrilling though the escapades had undoubtedly been, it was in the best interests of National Security that they remain secret.

"Suppose I fictionalize them?" she'd suggested recently when Lawrence had been over for dinner.

When his aunt hadn't immediately elaborated upon the suggestion, Lawrence had laid down his knife and fork and, steepling his fingers before him, contemplated her words. "You're serious," he eventually decided, "aren't you?"

Pushing around her last few peas with her fork, Ruth took a while to reply, "Maybe."

"Why?" Lawrence simply asked and when he didn't

get an immediate answer, asked, "This hasn't got anything to do with the Mystery Club?"

Ruth began to shake her head and then changed her mind. "Well, for a start, it's lucky for you Mary and the others aren't here."

"I know," he nodded. "Why do you think I felt able to say that?" he added, mopping up the last of his gravy with a piece of bread. "Is it?" he pressed once more.

"I suppose their love for Miss Marple may have rubbed off a little," she agreed.

"And it's nothing to do with all the shenanigans which have gone on around them?"

"A...little, but," she began, "you can't blame me for thinking this way. I am a writer, after all."

"The paper's not enough? Sorry, I have to ask." He shrugged.

Her plate empty, Ruth drew her cup of juice toward her, Lawrence patiently waiting until she felt like speaking. "To be honest? Not really. I quite understand, I really do, why I can only publish once a week, but it leaves a lot of the week, well...empty." When Lawrence didn't reply straight away, Ruth reached across and prodded him with her fork. "Well, what're your thoughts?"

Snatching his hand back, he rubbed the back and peered closely to see if his aunt had actually left any damage. "As you asked so nicely..."

"Sorry about that," Ruth muttered, somewhat embarrassed.

Lawrence smiled at her to show there were no hard feelings. "Well...I suppose, if you really want to write a book, then you should give it a go. I honestly think you'd do a great job." Ruth beamed at his response, though this diminished somewhat as he went on to clarify, "Only, you'll have to be very careful, nor could you use our names."

"I am aware of that," she replied with a frown. "I'd just take some artistic license."

"Hmm," Lawrence replied. "Knowing what's gone on, you'll have to take an awful lot. Mind you, it will be fiction."

"Of course it'll be fiction!" Ruth told him, hoping he wouldn't spot that she'd swiftly placed her hands below the table. At least he wouldn't be able to spot her crossed-fingers!

Unfortunately, her nephew knew her very well. He leant across toward her and with both hands, took hold of her arms and pulled her hands back into view. "Now," he smiled, "shall we try that again?"

The sound of the door opening brought her back to the here and now, that and the feel of a soggy pair of paws upon her bare knees.

"Bobby! Down!" Walter tried to drag the excitable spaniel back whilst trying to take off his raincoat, not his best idea as Bobby merely proceeded to run around his legs and he had to hurriedly lean against Ruth's desk to avoid falling over. The only good thing to come out of it was that Bobby got himself so tangled up he could only move one front paw.

Kicking back her seat, Ruth hurried around to untangle the pair, getting pretty wet in the process. "You're soaked, so you hold him whilst I go and get his towel," she told Walter and shot out to the kitchen area before he could argue.

To the sounds of, "Urgh! Hurry up, Ruth!" she came back to find Walter flat on his back with Bobby standing on his chest, attempting to lick his face off!

Ruth knelt down beside the pair. "I don't think I'm going to ask how you two managed to get like this," she told them with a shake of her head. Leaning down, she swiftly wrapped Bobby in the towel and, clutching him to her chest, dried him as well as she could with the dog's unhelpful attempts to squirm and leap free. "Go and lie down," she instructed her troublesome four-legged friend, who promptly went and plopped himself down under his owner's desk. "And as for you," she told Walter, "dry your hair and tell me what they said at the hospital."

By way of a reply, he whipped off his hat and ran his right hand through his hair before rapping his skull with his fist, "All clear!"

Ruth beamed back, though she had to ask, "Really? Already? I thought it'd be a few weeks yet. Don't they need to see you again?"

"Nope! Maybe if we weren't at war…"

"So…no words of warning? You can carry on with the Home Guard, as before?"

Walter proceeded to appear a little sheepish.

"Walter?"

"All right!" he admitted. "I've got to be a little careful."

"Specifically?" Ruth prodded.

"Specifically? Well, try not to get knocked on the head, but that's good advice anyway."

"And?" Ruth wasn't going to let him get away with not telling her everything. "Don't think I won't be discussing this with Doris, either, so make sure you tell her the truth too!" she warned.

"Honestly, that's it. My hand's as well as can be, and

they've taken everything they could find out of my head."

"Including the brain!"

"Doris!" Walter exclaimed, jumping back in surprise and knocking his head against the wall. "How long have you been there?"

"You appear…puzzled?" his wife said, ignoring the question.

"But how…? I never heard you come in! Did you know she was here?" he asked Ruth, who nodded.

"Of course."

"But how?" he asked again.

Before she replied, Doris came up and pecked him on the cheek. "I'm a woman of many sneaky skills!"

"I'll say!" he agreed, shaking his head.

"So, you were saying?" Doris prompted.

Knowing she needed to know what he was saying was nothing but the truth, Walter took Doris's hands in his, "Honestly, my scary American darling, I'm as good as ever, ready for anything; even you!"

With a happy sigh, Ruth folded up the letter she'd been writing to her son. She could finish it later. Rummaging in her handbag, she took out the item she'd been carrying around for the last week since she'd last been up at Ambrose's farm. Turning it around, wrapped safely in a handkerchief, she laid it upon her desk, the resounding clunk it made piquing the pair's curiosity.

And what exactly it that?" Doris asked, poking it with a finger.

Ruth unwrapped it and sat back to allow Doris and Walter to take a closer look.

"Exactly where did you get the bolt from a Lee-Enfield rifle, Ruth?" Walter asked.

Chapter Fourteen

Well and truly fed up with the lack of co-operation from her wayward husband, Penny decided more drastic measures were called for by the time Friday trundled along. As it happened, lady luck was smiling upon her—though it may simply have been Jane being omnipotent once more—that morning she found a bunch of delivery chits on her desk, and it was all she could do not to let out a cry of triumph when she read the destination of the top one. Glancing around the ops hut, she was just in time to catch Jane smiling her way through her open office door before turning her attention back to her desk.

"What's made you so happy?" Doris asked, frowning down at her top chit. "Darn it! Hey, Penny, what did I do to upset you?"

First cup of tea of the day safely in hand, Penny glanced up at the American. "What's got your goat today?"

Doris pointed at a window. "What's got my goat? I'll tell you what's got my goat. In fact, my goat's about to munch up a whole field of nettles!"

Everyone had stopped what they were doing now. When Doris went off on one, it was usually worth paying attention as, though the subject of her ire wasn't usually too serious, it was always a good way of cheering one up; this one was par for the course. Even Jane's usually busy pen was poised in mid-air.

"It's hosing it down!"

When she didn't elaborate, Penny prodded, "And?"

"And? And you've got me down for delivering two Tiger Moths and a Vickers Wellesley. What the hell's one of those? About the only thing I *think* I know about it is that it's also got an open cockpit."

Noting Doris's still pointing finger, Penny nodded and sat back down, taking a long swig of her tea, courtesy of Sharon's now morning service to the group. She'd volunteered this after Jane had invited her to add her name to the signed sheet pinned up in the mess. The young girl had objected at first, pointing out that she'd been informed by Mavis that the names were all those of pilots. Jane had quashed this by stating, quite clearly, that the particular *job* she was involved in qualified as potentially just as dangerous as what her girls did, so she'd better sign it!

"Sorry, my darling, but it's your turn for some open cockpit work. It's not my fault it's raining."

Doris was silent for a few seconds and then shrugged her shoulders, her body language relaxed and everything forgiven. Everyone got on with what they were doing as Doris tucked her chits in a pocket and simply said, "Okay, just checking," before following the other pilots outside and toward the flight line hut.

"Every single time," Penny muttered to herself as she waited for everyone to file out before making her way over to Jane's office. "Got a second, Boss?"

Once again displaying her godlike omniscience, Jane sat up in her chair, attention riveted to her door as Penny spoke. "Of course. Take a seat."

Penny placed the delivery chits on the desk.

Jane echoed their American friend. "And?"

Slightly nonplussed, Penny ran a hand through her hair before stating the obvious. "I'm on ops today. Plus, there's the little matter of this sling," which she waggled for effect.

"Well done!" Jane merely replied.

"I didn't notice anyone missing. Are we short?"

Jane shook her head. "Nobody's missing, but we are actually short." At Penny's nod, Jane elaborated. "You've probably noticed there's been an upswing in how busy we've been since, well, since for a while now. I've tried to avoid it, but I'm going to need you to fly again a bit more; at least for a while, or until I can get another pilot in. You'll do your normal work as and when, otherwise, I'll be filling in."

Penny struggled to keep the grin from her face, and nearly succeeded. She'd been like a bear with a sore head since being wounded and losing the baby she'd been several months along in carrying. Grounded because of all that, she still was like every other pilot—there was nothing she loved more than to soar through the air.

"Don't hurt yourself," Jane told her friend, with a small chuckle. "I know you don't like the job I've got you doing."

These few words sobered Penny up and the grin slipped from her face. She was Jane's number two not only because of her previous medical condition but because her predecessor had been killed by the Nazis on a delivery flight. The promotion to Second Officer, which had come with the post, was scant consolation.

"You're right. Can I ask how long this state is likely to last?"

Jane spread her hands. "How long's a piece of string? Sorry, I wish I could tell you, but for the foreseeable future, I'll be needing you on deliveries every now and then, and also doing your normal job."

"Which brings me to…" She waggled her arm once more.

"Yes, well, I know you should be wearing that for another couple of weeks. However, I know you and I know if I asked if you feel you need it, you'd tell me 'no.' Strictly speaking, by the rules, I can't ask you to fly…"

Penny interrupted, struggling to keep the eagerness from her face as she whipped the sling off. "I'll see the doctor in the morning and charm the heck out of him. Can't see it being a problem."

Jane's return smile was as warm as a summer's day. "Thank you. Just remember, though, that you still won't be flying every day."

"I won't," Penny replied, massaging her shoulder. "About?" Penny began prodding the delivery chit.

Jane turned it around, though from the way she barely glanced at it, it was obvious she knew exactly what it was. "My, what a coincidence!"

When Jane didn't say anything else, Penny picked the chit back up, got to her feet and, leaning over the desktop, planted a quick kiss on Jane's forehead. "You're a good friend, thank you. Now, I'd better make tracks, or the Anson may try to go without me."

As Penny was about to open the ops hut door, Jane called out, "Don't tell anyone else yet, but that pilot I alluded to? With luck, it'll be Shirley Tuttle!"

****

"You called, I came," declared Lawrence as he opened the door to the offices of the *Hamble Gazette* with a flourish Errol Flynn would have been proud of.

"Good boy," Ruth told him, not looking up from her

typewriter. "Now, earn yourself another star and put the kettle on, eh?"

Shaking his head, Lawrence nevertheless set to the task his aunt had set him. Once the kettle was filled and boiling merrily away, he perched himself on the edge of her desk. "No Walter today?"

Still not looking up from what she was writing, Ruth told him, "He'll be in later. He's having a checkup at the hospital."

The policeman quickly asked, "Nothing wrong, I hope?"

Ruth straightened up and took off her glasses. Shaking her head, she said, "Not that he's said. I suppose when someone has operations on the head, they like to make sure everything is well."

"That's good to know," Lawrence agreed, getting up to switch off the kettle before it boiled over. With the tea served, he made himself at home on Walter's chair. Steepling his hands, he asked, "What's so important that you didn't want to tell me over the telephone?"

Ruth pulled open the top drawer on the left side of her desk and brought out something wrapped in a white handkerchief, which made a decent thudding sound when she placed it on her desk. She pushed it toward him. "Open that."

Getting up from his seat, he stared at it curiously for a few seconds before unwrapping it; then his eyebrows shot toward the ceiling.

"Christ, Aunty! Where on earth did this come from?"

Ruth went slightly red. "I found it up at Ambrose's farm last Sunday."

Lawrence picked up the bolt and turned it this way

and that before hopping up to sit on Walter's desk, putting the bolt down beside him and picking up his tea. Blowing into his cup to give himself a little thinking time, he didn't speak again until he'd forced half of it down. "You've waited nearly a week before revealing this?"

"Well…"

Letting out a big sigh, he verbalised his thoughts. "No, let me guess. The ATA Mystery Club already knows."

His aunt's silence spoke volumes. "If it helps, none of us have a clue what it could mean," she admitted. "Other than, we don't think it should be there. Farmers use shotguns, not a Lee-Enfield."

"You know what this is from, then?"

She nodded and took a sip of her tea to wet her dry throat. "Walter identified it for us."

"Walter knows too? Anyone else I should know about?" He couldn't keep a hint of sarcasm out of his voice, and Ruth let him know she'd picked up on it.

"No need for that, Herbert. You know we don't go around shooting our mouths off."

Suitably admonished, his aunt only ever called him by his detested first name when she was annoyed with him. Lawrence canted his head and smiled an apology her way.

"I'll put on my police head for a while then," he told her, going back behind Walter's desk and sitting down.

"That's why I called you. Go ahead," she said.

"First, what were you doing up at the farm?"

"Let's say I had the intention of doing a bit of bartering. I'm low on butter," she added, so there was no confusion.

"And you came across"—he prodded the rifle bolt with the end of a pencil—"this, how?"

Ruth settled back in her seat, her still steaming mug cupped in her hands. "It's a strange story. I hadn't been able to find him when I'd tried a few days before, so I'd gone back. This time, he was around, but he was acting…very strangely. He wouldn't let me in the farmhouse, though he did say he'd leave some butter outside for me the next morning…"

"Did he?" Lawrence interrupted.

"He did," Ruth confirmed. "As we were talking, he kept glancing down at the ground, which I thought odd, though I didn't do anything about it until he'd shut the door. Anyway, as I turned around, there, sticking slightly out of the ground, was that bolt. Like I said, Ambrose was behaving very strangely, so I hastily picked it up and, well, here we are."

Lawrence stroked his chin and once more picked up the bolt, as if it were capable of speech and could provide them with the answer to its mystery. Unfortunately, a miracle wasn't on the cards.

"Have you tried to speak to Ambrose again?"

She shook her head.

"Good. Please make sure it stays like that."

"But he's my source of extra butter and milk!" Ruth protested.

"Until this is sorted out, I don't want either yourself or any of your friends anywhere near that farm," he told her, the tone of his voice brooking no argument.

"There's one more thing I should tell you…don't be like that!" she half-snapped, seeing Lawrence raise both eyebrows. Honestly, she momentarily mused, how can the raise of an eyebrow or two cause humans to become so defensive? "Walter asked his sergeant in the Home Guard, Matthew Green, if any of his mob had *mislaid* a rifle bolt."

"And had they?" Lawrence asked.

"No such luck," Ruth admitted.

"Nice idea though, Aunty," Lawrence praised her. "I assume Walter knew not to tell Mr Green where the bolt came from?"

"Certainly," she assured him.

"Good, thank you. Now, if there's nothing else, I'd better get back to the station. I'll fill my sergeant in on everything you've told me, and we'll take it from here." At seeing the disappointed expression on her face, he came to stand beside her. "Aunty, I don't know exactly what's going on, at the moment. This could be something, this could be nothing, but if it's the tip of an iceberg, it could be major, and anything to do with guns is always serious. So," he bent and kissed her on the cheek, "by all means tell the girls what we've discussed, but also tell them to leave this to the police."

As he turned to leave, Lawrence noticed his aunt appeared to have a dejected look upon her face, so he hung in the doorway and pasted on his most winning smile.

"Hey! I'm not only saying this because I don't want any of you to come to any harm, but with your clear-up rate on major crime, you're making us look bad!"

The way his aunt's face lit up from ear to ear at his parting words made him glad he'd made the effort.

Chapter Fifteen

Penny let out a small growl as soon as RAF Marham sprang into view through a break in the clouds. She was about to venture into a hornet's nest of activity.

All she could see were swarms of Mosquitos starting up their engines everywhere she looked. Cursing that she hadn't taken the time to try and telephone Tom to let him know she was on her way, Penny at least satisfied herself there was nothing the control tower, or anyone else for that matter, could do to stop her landing. The runway was presently clear, they knew roughly what time she was due in, and she had no radio with which they could call her and tell her to stooge around whilst whatever was going on happened. Flying aircraft without radio was usually a curse, one every ferry pilot had to bear. However, only sometimes, mind you, it did come in handy.

Lining up on the main runway, she lowered the landing gear and flaps and went through the by-now-familiar multitude of other tasks landing such a powerful aircraft needed and was soon on the tarmac with barely a bounce. Now came the part where someone would very likely tell her off, probably by shouting in her face.

Instead of turning left off the runway toward where the aircraft was needed, she turned right onto the taxiway which led directly toward Tom's squadron. As swiftly yet as carefully as she could, she made her way toward the engineering hangar and a group of rather surprised-looking ground crew. Fortunately, a corporal appeared to understand that she wanted to park up and, using hand signals, directed her to follow him. Within two minutes, she was at the end of the hangar, its mighty doors wide open as if ready to swallow a whale. The quick-thinking chap had obviously been shouting instructions to airmen she couldn't hear, because as she came to a stop, two of them rushed up and placed chocks under her wheels.

Hurrying as much as she could through the shutdown procedures, acutely aware (as always) of the necessity for safety, Penny was soon kicking open the under-fuselage hatch and was on the ground clutching her flight bag.

The corporal was waiting for her.

"Ma'am…er, miss?"

If she hadn't been in such a hurry, Penny would have found his stuttering amusing. Every military type she ran into always had trouble with working out how to address a member of the Air Transport Auxiliary. "Never mind all that. Where's Wing Commander Alsop?"

The man opened his mouth as if to argue, only was smart enough to recognize the fire in the eyes of the woman before him and chose discretion over valor. Pointing a little to his right, he shouted, so as to be heard over the roar of the Merlin engines, "Second blast pen over there!"

Tearing off her flying helmet, she paused only to hand it to the man and instruct him, "Keep an eye on that, I'll be wanting it back!" before taking to her flying booted heels and heading in the direction he'd pointed as fast as her slightly cramped legs allowed.

Whatever was going on, though if she were a betting

girl she'd have a shilling on the squadron preparing for a sortie, seemed to pause when she rushed past. One poor member of the ground crew found himself being berated by an irate navigator after she'd passed, because he'd dropped the man's parachute whilst in the act of passing it to him.

As she swept around the leading edge of the blast pen the corporal had indicated, she ran smack bang into Flight Sergeant Stan Atkins. Being the smaller and lighter of the two, she promptly rebounded back and landed on her bottom. Fortunately, her Sidcot flying suit and the multiple layers of clothing she wore beneath prevented anything more than her pride being hurt, with, perhaps, a bruised bottom later on.

Recovering quickly from his surprise, Stan let his chute and flight bag fall to the ground and knelt to help Penny up, calling, "Boss!" as loudly as he could.

Now slightly deafened too, Penny allowed her friend to steady her before taking a step back. "Sorry about that, Stan!" she also shouted, though her attention was fixed upon her husband, who had a foot on the crew egress ladder under the fuselage of his Mosquito and had frozen at the unexpected sight before him.

Coming to his senses, he too dropped his chute and was by her side in an instant. So as not to be in the way, Stan picked up what he'd dropped and, to give them a semblance of privacy, went to stand by the ladder, though he was openly watching what now occurred.

"Penny!" He opened his arms to gather her into them and can't have helped but notice the slight hesitation from his wife before she accepted his hug. A few seconds later, he broke the embrace before taking her by the hand and pulling her forward. At first, she resisted and then, upon realizing what he was doing, jogged along with him until they were the other side of the blast pen and the thunder of the multiple engines was at a level where they could converse without having to shout at the top of their lungs.

"What are you doing here?" he asked, bending down to kiss her cheek.

Before replying, Penny looked up at her husband, the same husband who'd been confusing her emotions ever since she'd lost the baby. Jane's suggestion of a holiday together suddenly seemed a most peculiar thing. She knew people still took holidays these days, they'd had a honeymoon, but that was when she'd been certain they both loved each other, no doubt helped by the swiftness of their romance. Now? Now, things were no longer black and white, her doubts came flooding back, and when she opened her mouth, no words came out.

Swallowing, she tried again. "I thought we could do with having a face-to-face."

Tom laughed, though Penny didn't pull him up on it, as she recognized it was an ironic laugh. Sweeping his hands around, he then said, "Not great timing. We're about to get rather busy."

Briefly, Penny too looked around the airfield with its cacophony of noise and hectic yet orderly activity. "So I see."

"Please tell me you didn't pull the *I've got engine problems* routine?" he asked, though the face she wasn't sure she adored was grinning as he spoke.

She shook her head. "No, a genuine delivery, though," she admitted, "the kite is for a squadron the other side of the airfield, so they're going to be hacked off with me."

Tom looked around as someone called his name. Stan had poked his head around the edge of the blast pen and was making urgent *Come here* gestures. "Look, I'm sorry for not speaking with you before now, but as you can see, we're about to take off and I have to go. Can we talk later?"

Seeing there was nothing else she could do, Penny nodded and, acting purely on impulse, flung her arms around her husband's neck before letting him go and quickly kissing him. "You go and give them hell! I've got a suggestion of Jane's to put to you, so call me after six tonight. Promise?"

With a squeeze of her hands, which she could feel through the gloves she was wearing, he smiled and nodded. "I promise! Now, get going."

After giving her a last quick peck on the cheek, Tom disappeared back around the business side of the blast pen. Known as the *Wooden Wonder*, the Mosquito truly lived up to its nickname so, reluctant to leave, she settled onto the grass and waited until not only Tom's bomber, but the entire contingent taking part in the sortie had taken off and disappeared beyond the horizon.

Getting to her feet, Penny brushed off some grass and, with one last forlorn glance in the direction the fleet of bombers had disappeared, made her now weary way over to the Mosquito she'd unceremoniously abandoned. At least the corporal who'd helped her was still standing guard. Now she had to taxi it over to the other squadron and face the music. For once, not only did she know she didn't have a leg to stand on, but she didn't have any energy for trying to argue. She'd take whatever dressing down was coming her way.

****

"All aboard for the mystery tour!"

Her head through the door of the Anson, Penny stopped at the sound of the voice and took another, much more careful look at its owner. "Sorry, Mary," she told her friend, shaking her head, "but you sounded a lot like Doris."

Mary's bemused expression was priceless. "I'm sorry? You're saying I sound like our Yank!"

Hastening toward the cockpit, Penny sat down in the vacant co-pilot's seat and hurried to assure her friend who, to be truthful, looked more amused than insulted. "God, no! Thing is, it sounded very much like something our Doris *would* say."

"Hmm," Mary mused. "You know, I'm not sure if that's a good or a bad thing? I love Doris to death, but I think the world only has enough space in it for one of them!"

Penny didn't hear, though, as she stared out the cockpit windows.

Mary nudged her in the ribs. "Penny for them...Penny?" When she didn't get a response, she dug a little bit harder. "Hello? Come on, it wasn't that bad a joke!"

Penny turned to face her friend, though her eyes were glazed over and a single tear hung unshed at the corner of her right eye. Mary was nothing if not observant, as well as being a very, very good friend.

"Hey! What's the matter?" She looked around, and when Penny still didn't speak, Mary hopped out of her seat and rushed back down the fuselage and, to give them some privacy, closed the door Penny had left open. She hastened back to her distraught friend's side. "We're not going to be disturbed now, so please, tell me what's wrong? I'd like to help," she ended, her voice full of concern.

Instead of speaking, Penny merely turned her eyes so she was looking back from the front window; the tear, only one, slid down her face.

Mary took a semi-clean handkerchief from a pocket and dabbed her friend's cheek dry. "Shh. It's not that bad, surely? Tell me what's troubling you…please?"

With a visible effort, Penny took in two, shuddering breaths, joined by a third, before she gulped and opened her mouth. On the second try, it all came out in one long, barely comprehensible sentence. "I came here to talk to Tom; we've barely been speaking; Jane suggested a holiday together; I arrived too late; everyone was going on a sortie; he couldn't talk…" She took another deep gulp of air and then, looking Mary directly in the eye, confided what her major fear was. "And I made him promise to phone me tonight!"

Mary immediately understood and pulled her friend into a rather awkward hug, and though there were no more tears, from the tightness of her friend's arms around her, Penny really needed it. When she felt her friend was ready, Mary pulled away, keeping hold of Penny's waist. "He'll understand, I'm sure. He's a pilot. He knows it won't mean anything!"

"But what if I've put a curse on him?" Penny's voice cracked as she forced the words, her fear, out. "Never make anyone promise anything! It'll mean they won't be coming back to keep that promise!"

Mary took one hand away, put it behind her back and crossed her fingers, hoping her friend wouldn't notice. "Not this time. I'm sure he'll only have been saying it to agree with you. You'll see, he'll be fine and he won't phone."

Penny stared at her friend before bursting out with a peal of laughter. "You realize how many different ways I could take that, don't you?"

Wiping her own eyes, Mary told her, "For my sake, it looks like you've taken it the right way. Yes?"

Penny nodded. "Basically, try not to think about it. Not easy, but I'll try." She leant in for another quick hug. "Now, let's get out of here. I'm not very popular around this place at the moment."

Mary turned, strapped herself into her seat, and began the preflight checks. "Really? What did you do?"

After leaning out her window and telling the ground crew to remove the chocks from the wheels, Penny told her, "Well, first I landed without permission..."

"When will they learn we haven't got radio?" Mary broke in, stating the obvious.

Penny nodded before carrying on. "Very true. Then I taxied down the middle of Tom's squadron who were getting ready for takeoff, delayed it some more by grabbing hold of him for a quick chin-wag—which was a waste of time—and finally, when I was able to taxi the Mossie over to where it should have been, I was so distracted I nearly taxied it into the back of a fuel bowser!"

"So," Mary said after checking that they were clear to taxi, "all in all, a most successful day!"

Chapter Sixteen

"Whoops-a-daisy! Sorry, nearly didn't see you there, Penny," Betty apologized as she sidled around where the other girl sat upon the second bottom step of the stairs. "Actually, what are you waiting for?"

Mary popped her head around the door from where she was making tea that evening and spoke for her friend. "Can you come in here, please, Betty?"

Noticing the look of gratitude Penny shot Mary, Betty didn't question this and merely patted Penny on the head, went into the kitchen, and shut the door. "What's going on?"

Keeping her voice down, Mary filled her in on Penny's day and her wish that, despite her current vigil on the telephone, they have a normal evening. Opening the door, Betty asked the quintessential British question, "Cup of tea, Penny?"

"So long as Doris isn't making it, please," she replied.

"Hey," came the usual reply, this time from the lounge.

"Shouldn't you be at home with your husband?" Betty pretended to scold the American. "Is marriage that boring already?"

"Very funny," Doris retorted. "My dear Walter is on parade this evening, so I thought I'd come and see if I could have tea with my other family."

Betty and Mary exchanged knowing looks.

"Translation," began Mary, "Ruth isn't home yet and you're too hungry to wait for her."

Doris treated them to a very toothy grin. "You know me too well! And don't worry, I've left Ruth a note so she doesn't make me anything. Don't want to waste food, after all."

"Good girl," Betty told her, with a smile. "Now, whilst Mary's busy with the tea, you come and help me with the rest."

"Love to!"

"What's the time?" Penny suddenly asked out loud.

If anyone thought this was a strange question, being the girl was wearing a wristwatch, no one said so.

"Five to six, love," Mary let her know.

Around five minutes later, right as Doris was setting a cup of steaming hot tea down at Penny's feet, having reassured her that she hadn't made it, the phone rang. Narrowly missing knocking the cup over, Penny snatched up the receiver.

"Hello, Tom?"

Doris, never the most subtle of people, plonked herself down on Penny's step, unashamedly listening. "We're worried," she silently mouthed when Penny looked down at her. After a short pause, Penny nodded her head and sat back down next to her friend, holding the receiver a little away from her ear so Doris could hear.

"You were expecting someone else?" came Tom's voice.

Doris held her thumb up to Betty and Mary, who'd stuck their heads around the kitchen door. Both gave silent cheers, and, after unsuccessfully trying to coax the

American to join them, pointedly closed the door. Penny leant against her friend, who wrapped an arm around her waist in support, taking special care not to knock the arm which Penny had somehow managed to get the station doctor to certify was as fit as the rest of her, once she'd finished with her deliveries. From the way Penny winced as Doris accidently touched it, it was obvious she was still in pain.

"Before we say anything else, I'll have to find a way to get rid of Doris."

"Hi, Tom!" the American in question stage-whispered into the mouthpiece.

"That's the one," Penny said. "As I was saying, I will never ask you to make that promise again, I promise…oh, you know what I mean."

A soft chuckle came down the phone before Tom said, "It's all right, I know what you mean."

"You're okay, though, aren't you? And Stan?" she had to ask.

Tom's voice became a little more subdued, "We are."

Penny and Doris exchanged quick looks before both nodded. "Something happened, didn't it?"

From down the line, came the sound of something being poured and then the unmistakable sound of one glass being chinked against another. "That was Stan. We're having…a drink. Well, maybe it's our third. I can't go into details and, it goes without saying, none of what I'm about to say can get out…"

Doris crossed her heart.

"Go on," Penny urged.

"It was a bad one, love. We got jumped by a gaggle of Messers before we hit the target. I can only say that there are quite a few empty plates tonight."

"Oh, Christ! That bad?"

"That bad," Tom confirmed.

There was silence for around half a minute.

"Did you see any chutes?" Penny asked, clutching at straws.

It took a while for Tom to answer, and she could swear she heard him take at least two swallows of whatever he was drinking before he was able to find his voice. "I didn't see any, and we were so low I doubt if there was time to even get out."

At these words, Doris got to her feet and announced, loud enough for Tom to hear, "I'm going down the Victory for some Guinness. We'll toast those brave chaps later."

As Penny watched, her friend popped her head around the kitchen door, told the two briefly where she was going and why, and within a minute had grabbed her coat, hat, and purse and disappeared out the front door. Penny heard a brief, "Not now, Duck!" and then the only sound was that of a disappointed fiendish fowl as its favorite human ignored its calls for attention.

"Penny? Penny? Are you still there?"

She put the receiver back to her ear. "Sorry about that. Did you hear what Doris said?"

"I did. Thank her for us, will you?"

"She won't need it, but I will," Penny assured him.

"Before I forget, and I reckon she can't be living with you, can you tell Sharon that Stan misses her? Oh, shut up, mate, you know you do!" Penny heard him tell his navigator.

"I'll pass it on when I see her on Monday."

There was another gap of silence before Tom asked,

"So, what was it you came down for?"

Penny's first thought was, *If you don't know what it was, then why should I even bother?* However common sense prevailed, as knowing coming right out with such an inflammatory accusation was unfair, and that plus the trauma he'd been through earned him a little breathing room. She knew everything had to come out in the open, and soon, but now wasn't the time, and she told him so.

"We need a serious talk, you know we do, but not over the telephone. Look, do you have the weekend off?"

A weak laugh came down the line. "Definitely. We're in no state to try and hurt a fly as we are."

Gulping as the meaning of his words settled in, Penny did her best to keep her voice steady. "Right. If I can persuade Jane to let me test-fly a Magister, do you think you can book us a room at a pub?"

Hang on. What happened there? She'd meant to ask him to book her a room in the officer's mess, or suggest she kip with him in his rooms. It wasn't strictly allowed, but most everyone turned a blind eye. In the time it took him to reply, she pondered that perhaps her subconscious did want their marriage to survive. Then again, she scolded it, there's a big difference between surviving and flourishing.

"I could," he replied, then taking her by surprise, asked, "If that's what you want?"

"Why not?" her libido chipped in, using her mouth to convey its slightly treacherous message.

****

"Only me!" Walter called out as he opened and then shut behind him Betty's front door. As he expected, the owner of The Old Lockkeepers Cottage popped her head around the lounge door, nodded, and was back where

144

she'd come from by the time he'd hung up his forage cap.

"Grab yourself a bottle from the kitchen table, love!" wafted the dulcet tones of his wife as he strode toward where all the noise was coming from.

Detouring into the kitchen, Walter found the table heaving under a weight of Guinness bottles, a surprising number of which were empty. Undoubtedly, his wife had been busy. Finding one which had been missed, he looked around for the bottle opener, finally finding it on the floor. After taking a long, refreshing pull, he was about to join his wife when a thought struck him. His platoon had been marching across some boggy ground tonight, and though he'd cleaned the soles of his boots before leaving the church hall they used as their base, there was always the chance he'd picked up more dirt on the way home. Sitting down, he undid his bootlaces and left the boots to stand by the front door. Now ready, he retrieved his bottle and entered the lounge.

If he'd been expecting a party, then he was soon relieved of this notion. Even more empty bottles were spread around the lounge, but there was no music and everyone merely seemed to be sitting, or lying with their heads on cushions on the floor, and simply drinking. Whilst he was taking this in, Walter was surprised when Mary raised her bottle and the others immediately followed.

"To the Boys!" she declared, which was echoed by her friends, who all took long pulls from their bottles.

Doris glanced up at her bemused husband and patted a place on the floor next to where she was lying. "Take a pew and I'll explain."

Doing as he was told, Walter lowered himself to the floor where a slightly squiffy Doris draped one of her legs across his waist and laid her head upon his chest, effectively pinning him down. There were worse positions to be in, he decided, relaxing and doing his best not to spill any of the precious black liquid down his battle blouse, not easy when it became clear his wife was actually a bit more than the "slightly squiffy" he'd first thought.

"I haven't told you how much I love you today, have I!" she stated. This was quite a feat as, at the same time, she was trying to nibble his left earlobe, something he normally quite enjoyed. However, Walter had discovered the more Doris had to drink, the more…"enthusiastic" she became, and with the state she was currently in, he was in danger of losing an ear, not something he could easily explain away.

Turning his head, he kissed her just enough to cut short the cacophony of wolf whistles from her friends. "You always do, love. One of the many reasons I love you too."

Doris wasn't to be put off, though. Raising her bottle, she shouted, "To the Boys, and my wonderful husband!"

Once everyone had taken another drink, Doris shuffled around on the floor until she was able to wrap her other leg around her husband and then pull him up so he was all but sitting in her lap. Once she'd accomplished this and pretty much forced his head back so it was laid upon her shoulder, she at last appeared content.

Somewhat cautiously, Walter asked, "Would anyone care to tell me what's going on?"

As he glanced around, it appeared everyone else was in the same state as his wife, everyone except Jane, who put her bottle down, got to her feet, and helped untangle him so he was able to once more stand up. Taking his hand, she led him from the lounge, only pausing to ruffle Penny's hair.

Once the kitchen door was closed, Walter didn't give Jane a chance to speak. "Is Penny all right? Has that husband of hers upset her again?"

"Give me a hand making some tea, and a nice strong coffee for your wife," Jane asked. "They're flying first thing in the morning, so I'm going to need them sober. Oh, and be a dear and put the full bottles somewhere they won't be found."

Sensing something was up and Jane was probably building herself up to speaking about it, Walter nodded and added, "I'll get rid of the empties, too."

Once both the full and the empty bottles were cleared away, Walter reached up to pick a jar labelled "pickled onions" off a high shelf and, glancing around to make certain the kitchen door was still closed, brought down the small, plain jar. Untying the string, he removed the paper lid, brought it up to his nose for a cautious sniff, and instantly wished he hadn't. Setting it down, he waited a few moments, took the kettle from Jane, who'd just filled the teapot, refilled and set it to boil once more.

"I don't know why you always have to do that," Jane stated with a shake of her head. "You know you hate the smell."

Walter allowed himself a soft chuckle. "I suppose I'm hoping to at least put up with it. As I'm going to spend the rest of my life with Doris, I really should try and get used to the smell of coffee."

"Well, shovel a heaped spoonful in. This may be the time," Jane informed him. "This must be very confusing," she said stirring the tea around the pot. "A load of half-inebriated women, your wife included, lounging around and making strange toasts willy-nilly."

Walter waited for the kettle to boil before replying. Holding it over the cup into which he'd added the coffee, he held his breath, pouring as quickly as he could before putting the kettle to one side and breathing in safely once more. "You could say that."

Holding the tea-strainer over the first cup, Jane told him, "Yes, Penny's upset with Tom, but"—she quickly got it in before Walter could give forth his two-pennyworth—"this time, it's not his fault, or rather, it's for something out of his control."

Intrigued, Walter asked her to carry on.

"Well. As you're no doubt aware, things between them have recently had more ups and downs than a fishing boat in the North Sea."

"You could put it that way," he muttered, absently stirring his wife's coffee.

"So, the two of us were talking about it and I suggested they try and get some time away together. I *arranged*, shall we say, for Penny to fly a Mosquito to Tom's new base, as he'd not been answering her phone calls…and, before you say it, I shall: The silly bugger! The thing was, she arrived right when the place was about to set off on an all-up effort. She managed to speak to him, but only briefly."

Walter laid the spoon down, always a little worried it may dissolve in one of his wife's drinks.

"Anyway, they spoke on the telephone around six this evening. Don't worry," she hastened to say, seeing that Walter had opened his mouth and was about to ask the obvious, "he's okay, and so is Stan Atkins. I wish I could say the same for the rest of the lads who made the trip."

"Bad?" Walter managed to ask.

"Very," Jane confirmed, "though, please, don't tell anyone."

Walter took a few minutes to take in what he'd been told and then, a sad smile came to his lips and he shook his head. "Correct me if I'm wrong, but my caring, drunk wife went and bought as much Guinness as she could to toast the missing." They both noticed his avoidance of the rather more likely word, *dead*.

Jane finished placing the cups and pot on a tea tray, "Who else?"

With the coffee cup in one hand, he went to open the kitchen door for Jane. "Is it any wonder I love her so much?"

Chapter Seventeen

"Somebody's in a good mood this morning," Lawrence declared, finding he was nearly having to break into a brief jog to keep up with the young woman on his arm.

"Don't blame me!" Sharon puffed, before shouting for the umpteenth time since they'd got out of his car, "Bobby! Bloody well, heel!"

"I never knew you had it in you!"

"Had…what?" Sharon asked, as she finally managed to reel in one very enthusiastic, back to his normal self, Cocker Spaniel.

"Never knew you swore," Lawrence answered.

Rising from where she'd made certain Bobby's leash was secure, Sharon replied, "Usually only when something's out of my control."

The two set off back toward the riverfront once more. "In that case, I'm more than a little surprised you don't turn the air blue these days!" When she didn't reply straight away, he went on, "All this! Moving down here for who knows how long, hearing about your gran and what she's going through, pretending to be a spy. Living with Mavis, to top it all off!"

He'd been watching her face closely as he rattled off the list, and as one thing followed the other, he'd watched her get paler and paler and could tell it would only be a matter of time before she agreed with what he was saying. However, ending with the jocular dig about her landlady and well known purveyor of virtually undrinkable tea, she now had a big grin upon her face.

"When you put it that way…you'd think Mavis *would* have that effect upon me."

After walking in companionable silence until they reached the river, Lawrence asked, "I hope it wasn't too awkward, getting away this morning?"

Sharon shook her head and grimaced a little as Bobby made to dart after a duck he'd spooked out of the undergrowth. Fortunately, this duck did not possess the same temperament as Doris's Duck. "Not at all. Mavis said she needed only a skeleton crew in this Saturday morning. Nothing she couldn't spare me for."

Lawrence smiled. "She must be mellowing in her, um, older age."

It was Sharon's turn to smile as she told him her thoughts. "I doubt it's anything of the kind. I think she sees herself as involved in this business by proxy."

"You haven't told her anything, have you?" he quickly asked.

Briefly, she slipped her hand out of his to slap him lightly around the ear. "Of course not! And I know you had to ask, but you'll get more of the same, if you ask again." She went to retake his hand, but found herself instead distracted. Lawrence had a look of pain upon his face and was kneading at the ear she'd just slapped. "Hey, what's wrong? I didn't hit you that hard."

Instead of replying straight away, the policeman kept kneading away and it wasn't until a couple of minutes had elapsed that he stopped, a look of relief upon his features.

Concerned now, Sharon placed the same offending

hand upon his shoulder. "Are you all right? Seriously, I didn't think I'd hit you all that hard."

Retaking her hand, he began to walk again before replying, picking his words carefully. "You didn't. However, you did, quite accidently, hit me in exactly the right spot. Though I suppose I should call it the *wrong* spot."

Looking around, checking no one could overhear them, Sharon had picked up on the way he was speaking in low tones and keeping his head down. Obviously what he was about to share wasn't for general consumption. "Go on. I won't tell a soul! Hand over me heart!"

"You may have wondered why I'm not in the Forces?" As she went to open her mouth, he forestalled her. "It's all right, I couldn't blame you. I'm the right age, after all. You see, I'm deaf in that ear. Can't hear a sausage! They wouldn't take me."

Sharon's face fell and she looked mortified.

He hurried to reassure her. "It's all right! I've been like this since birth, so I don't know what I'm missing. It usually doesn't cause me any bother, excepct for that one spot where you caught me. It hurts like hell, but only for a few minutes. There's nothing I can do about it, so I try and avoid knocking myself there."

"And then I come along and give you a right old whack!" Sharon pulled the other two to a stop. "Please, forgive me? I had no idea."

Though his ear was still ringing, Lawrence forced a smile. "There's nothing to forgive. It was a complete accident, so do me a favor and put it out of your mind."

The look she gave him was full of skepticism, but eventually she agreed. "If you're sure…"

"Completely," he assured her. "Now, come on, let's

get on with our walk and think no more of it."

Ten minutes later, apart from Bobby having to be restrained from taking a flying leap into the Solent, the two were walking along and enjoying the relative peace and quiet of a Saturday by the sea. If it weren't for the pounding of hammers, jacks, and whatever other machinery coming their way from across the docks, it could almost have been called idyllic.

They stood watching a flight of swans alight upon the water in a flurry of spray and wings. "You know, you really should take Mary for a walk along here. I'm sure she'd love it," Sharon told him, once the swans had all stopped fighting amongst themselves, making a noise comparable to that coming from across the way.

Looking around, Lawrence could easily appreciate why Sharon had made the suggestion. "You're quite right, only I think I'd better wait until this is all over. Can you imagine what would be said if word got around that the local Police Inspector had been seen parading *two* beautiful women around? Let alone in the same spot! Plus, my boss doesn't know I'm part of this."

This was news to Sharon. "He doesn't?"

Lawrence shook his head. "Part of the deal I made with you-know-who, so he'd let me keep an eye on you."

"What, um, what would have happened if he hadn't let you?" Sharon asked, not certain she wanted to know the answer. What she got was exactly what she expected.

"You'd likely have been lumbered with someone who'd do a very good job, the job they'd been trained for, but they wouldn't have cared a jot about you."

Absently, Sharon looked around before speaking, and her eyes alighted upon a couple a hundred yards or so in front of them. It was difficult to tell, but even from the rear, they looked like they could be the same couple they'd seen on their first visit here. "You know, Inspector," she went up on tiptoe to whisper into his ear. "If I didn't know better, I'd say you're flirting with me."

Lawrence, on the other hand, didn't trouble to keep his voice down, not that he shouted. "Of course, or that's what it has to look like. However, being serious," he then said, "I've got to keep you safe so I can reunite you with your Stan, haven't I."

Sharon's step faltered slightly. "You think there's a chance he'll take me back?"

"Take you back? A national heroine, such as yourself? It's odds on!"

"Hardly," Sharon scoffed, only for Lawrence to squeeze her hand very firmly.

"You can stop all that right away, young lady," he began. "What you're doing is, I repeat, very brave, and I don't want to have to tell you again." He quickly looked around. "Would I be carrying this," he whipped open his jacket to show her the revolver in a shoulder holster, "if this didn't have the potential to turn serious?"

Coincidently, from the couple ahead, they both heard the woman clearly shout, "Hans! Stop Fritz from digging! He'll get all mucky."

In response, the man instantly flat-handed the woman across the back of the head, sending her stumbling forward, arms flailing. Barely in time, she stopped herself from falling.

Unable to prevent herself, Sharon yelled out, "Oi! Leave her alone!"

This prompted the man to half turn and stare back toward them. It was, indeed, the same man and woman! Before either Lawrence or Sharon could move, he'd picked up their dachshund, grabbed his wife by the elbow, and darted off, soon disappearing from view around a corner. At the same time, and without need to discuss it, Lawrence and Sharon both took off after them, Bobby *woofing* with the excitement of the chase. When they turned the same corner, the couple and their little dog were gone.

"That *is* interesting," Sharon declared.

****

"You're not serious!"

"Ssh!" Penny hissed at Doris, who was jumping up and down. "No one's supposed to know, and it's not set in stone yet anyway."

"But," Doris grunted, jumping once more as she helped heave Penny into her Sidcot suit in the now empty, except for themselves, flight line hut, "surely if Jane says so it's, well, all but set in stone, as you say."

"Oh, I wish I hadn't said anything," Penny muttered, sitting down and beginning to pull on her boots. "Look, you can't say anything to the others," she pleaded. "Jane will have my guts for garters!"

"She'll have your guts for what?" Doris asked, totally confused. "I assume this is some other cute English expression I haven't heard before?"

Standing up and stomping her feet up and down a few times, to make sure her socks weren't bunched up in her clumsy suit, Penny snatched up her flying helmet, grabbed her overnight bag, and turned to confront her friend. "Yes, and I'm quite serious, Doris. It's almost as if Jane said it in passing. I'm not denying it wouldn't be nice, more than nice, but until she hears something concrete, please, let's forget I said anything."

Seeing the serious way she was looking at her and

the earnestness in her voice, Doris agreed. "All right, you can trust me to keep my mouth shut." From the way Penny looked back at her, eyebrows burrowing under her fringe, Doris felt compelled to reiterate, "Truly! Don't worry, I won't say a word. The last thing I want is another day flying biplanes around the country."

"That, I believe!" Penny laughed. "Come on, then, walk with me to my Magister. The sooner I'm off, and all that." She handed her bag to her friend, asking, "Could you take this for me?"

"Arm's still hurting," Doris stated. "You're certain you're ready to fly again?"

Penny didn't reply straight away, and when she did, her answer wasn't quite what Doris was expecting. "I'm ready to fly at any time. My arm, though? Probably around ninety percent what it was, and I really can't see it getting any better."

"So that's why you're flying through the pain?"

"I believe it's something I'm going to have to get used to," Penny admitted. She stopped in front of her friend. "This stays between us, okay?"

Doris shrugged. "If you want. However, Jane isn't dumb, and neither are any of our friends. We'll all be keeping an eye on you. If it gets so you need to rest it, then tell us. Jane will understand and none of us want to see you in pain."

Penny held out a hand and Doris took it. "That seems fair. Thanks for looking out for me."

It wasn't often Doris blushed. "Hey, what are friends for!" They were now approaching the small, twin-seat trainer, so Doris asked, "You're sure you know the way? First time since his squadron moved from Marham, after all."

"Positive," Penny replied. "Got it all marked out on my map here." She patted the map sticking out of her trouser leg pocket.

"At least it's quite a way shorter to Little Staughton than to Marham, less chance of getting lost."

Penny had been ready for the remark and nudged her elbow into her friend's side, just enough so she knew about it.

Once Penny was safely strapped into the rear seat and her bags strapped into the front cockpit, Doris motioned to the ground crew to remove the chocks from before the wheels and stepped back as Penny went through the startup routine. The engine started, Penny began to taxi, and Doris waved her goodbye. Only when the plane was out of sight did Doris actually begin the walk back to Riverview Cottage.

It was strange, Doris mused, as she came up to Betty's The Old Lockkeepers Cottage, not to be living there anymore. It had been her first home in England, and she'd always have a very soft spot for it. The fact that most of her friends lived there meant she still was there often, when she wasn't doing something with Walter, of course. Something always seemed to be going on.

Riverview Cottage, in contrast, was sometimes disturbingly quiet. This wasn't Ruth's fault. She'd been nothing but welcoming to Doris since she first turned up in nineteen-forty-two with not a clue about anything on this side of "The Pond," as she still thought of the Atlantic Ocean.

Absently, she bent down to allow Duck to hop up into her arms and settle with a contented grunt, obviously having forgiven her for ignoring him the other day. Coming to a stop before the cottage's gate, she stroked

Duck's back as she pondered where these thoughts had come from. The only thing she could come up with was, whilst she'd been living in her home country, she'd lived alone for the majority of her adult life, and though she'd been thrown into sharing a, by the standards she'd grown up with, small dwelling, she'd rapidly found that with the right group of people it was more fun and rewarding than she'd believed could be possible.

"I miss Betty's," she sighed. Duck rewarded her with an understanding nip to the end of her nose. "Bless you, you understand."

Chapter Eighteen

Though it was 1943 and the war was still raging on all fronts with no sign of things slowing down, both the pub and the room Tom had secured for the weekend were of a surprisingly good standard. Considering the trouble Penny had in finding RAF Little Staughton, it was just as well its neighboring village of Greater Staughton, not even a couple of miles distant, had made an instant impression upon her—or perhaps it was the name of the pub in which they were staying?

Putting her small suitcase upon the bed, what she hoped was going to be a nice, comfortable four-poster, Penny opened the small, leaded window and a cooling breeze blew in. "Any idea where this place got its name from?"

" 'The Snooty Tavern'? Not a sausage!" he told her. "But what a name, eh?"

"Can't argue with that,' she agreed with a chuckle, flopping down next to her bag with a deep and satisfied sigh.

"Shall I call down for tea?" Tom asked, picking up the telephone from its small table beside the door.

Penny nodded approvingly. "Posh. Yes, that'll be nice."

Having made the call, Tom replaced the receiver, kicked off his shoes, and hopped up onto the bed. "They'll be up in about ten minutes."

Penny let an arm flop over her eyes. The trip over had given her a thumping headache, which was proving an irritation, and the trip from the airfield to the pub in Tom's newly acquired open-top car hadn't helped. "Pour me a glass of water, will you, Tom?" she asked. "My head's killing me."

Crossing over to the nightstand, Tom was back in a moment and, with a hand behind his wife's back, supported her as she hungrily drank the glass's contents down. "Shall I close the curtains?" he asked.

From where she once again lay, Penny cracked an eye and nodded. It was a lovely day, but her eyes couldn't take the sun's glare. "Please."

"Anything you want," he told her, leaning down to drop a kiss upon her forehead before drawing the cream curtains closed and climbing up onto the bed once more. Propping his pillows behind his back, Tom twiddled his fingers on his lap. "Not a great journey down, then?"

Penny snorted. "You could say that."

A little hesitantly, Tom touched the arm she'd been shot in. "How's the arm doing? Causing you any pain?"

Before answering, she shuffled herself up the bed, Tom swiftly plumping her pillows for her to lean back next to him. With her other hand, she absently prodded the spot on her arm where a Nazi bullet had hit her as it shot up the plane she rode in, causing Jane to crash land. If she was honest, the arm was still more than a little sore, though she was thinking that seemed to depend upon the weather and her mood. Right now, it was throbbing along with her headache, and she was looking forward to a soothing cup of tea. Wartime tea or not, there was still nothing like it.

"Nothing I can't handle," she told him. Undoubtedly

it was exactly the same answer Tom would reply with, if she asked him about his own wounds. The constraints of the war meant both were back on duty long before their bodies had fully healed, not that she'd admit anything of the sort, mainly because there'd be a risk Jane would hear about it and take her off flying duties once more. She was fully aware her boss was keeping a close eye upon her since she'd ditched her sling.

Tom began to say, "I'm so…" when there was a knock at the door, closely followed by a female voice calling, "Room service."

"I'll get it," Tom told his unprotesting wife and heaved himself off the bed to open the door.

Whilst Tom directed the maid in placing the tea tray, Penny heaved herself off the bed and padded in the direction of the bathroom, unzipping her Sidcot flying suit as she went. This unexpected sight nearly caused the startled maid's eyes to pop out of her head. She hadn't been the first, as Penny hadn't felt like changing when she landed. Tom wasn't known for being tight with his money, but his flying mates would have had words with him at the shilling he tipped the maid as she left the room.

"I don't think the poor girl knows what to make of you," Tom called as Penny threw her flying suit toward a chair.

"What do you mean?" she asked, as she padded out in her slip and stockings.

Tom's eyes nearly popped out of their sockets. "Never mind," he said, putting the teapot down at the alluring sight before him.

Penny held up both hands against her husband's chest, stopping him in his tracks, "Hold on," she told him as she went and retrieved a silk robe from her bag. "Pour the tea and then, before anything else *may*," she emphasized the word, "occur, we are going to talk."

Tom took a deep, steadying breath before obeying her instructions.

Over what turned out to be a halfway decent cup, they each took a chair at the table upon which the maid had placed the tray.

Feeling a little strange, Tom told her, "I can't thank you enough for coming over, Penny, so, please, let me start? I know things have been, well, up and down between us, and I know that's mainly down to me..." Seeing Penny open her mouth, he quickly amended that to, "Sorry. What I should say is it's entirely down to me. I reacted unforgivably when you lost the baby, our baby. In fact, ever since, I've been surprised you've wanted anything to do with me half the time. I'll never be able to say 'I'm sorry' enough, and I'll never stop trying to make up for my words and behavior that day. I know the main purpose of this weekend is to talk things over, see if we both want the same thing. Well, I want you. Sorry," he stammered, "I mean, I want to be with you, as a couple, and..." He trailed off, his hand running through his hair from nerves, so that it stuck up every which way.

All the while Tom had been talking, pouring his heart out as much as any man she'd ever heard, Penny had been determined to display the personification of calmness. Penny hadn't been certain, despite the few times they'd been able to meet up lately, that she wanted the same thing. They'd had some fun, shared a few kisses, and, on one memorable occasion, quite a bit more up against a secluded oak tree. She felt the tips of her ears heat up at the memory.

But was that enough? Tom was saying, in a rather

slapdash fashion, most of what she wanted to hear. So how was it making her feel? Did she once again feel the urgency of when they'd first met? Back then, she would have sworn the love she felt for the handsome flier literally took her breath away, hang the cliché. It was true, though, that whenever they were together was the only time she'd felt like she was whole. When he'd spat those words to her whilst she lay in the hospital bed, he'd shattered that feeling forever, and in spite of the ups and downs of how they were at present, there was enough of a spark left so that she was reluctant to finally sever their connection. Oh, it was all so very confusing!

When she finally looked up, her muddled brain took a moment to acknowledge that Tom was staring at her from beneath hooded eyebrows.

"Sorry," she stuttered to say, "got lost there for a bit."

"That's all right," he replied. "What do you think?"

It took Penny another few seconds to realize her husband was expecting an answer. To give herself some time to try and finish thinking things through, she decided to ask him the one thing she needed to know. Before she'd fallen pregnant, Penny hadn't given any thought to having children. The war and her part in it meant she didn't want to contemplate bringing a new life into the world when every day so many thousands lost theirs. It simply seemed…selfish. All that had changed after she'd gotten over the shock of finding out she was expecting. Tom had been over the moon, and when she'd lost the baby, to hear him blaming her had been like getting shot all over again. Now, however, and though it was a little like risking fate, she knew she had to ask how he felt about an idea which had been bobbing around her mind for a while. It was only because the fortunes of Great Britain were looking up—not that she'd say those words out loud—that she'd even utter the words.

"How would you feel about adoption?"

Tom's eyes shot wide open, such was his surprise at Penny's question. "I…I beg your pardon?"

Penny picked up and finished her cup, placing it down before repeating herself. "I said, 'How would you feel about adoption?' "

Tom's cup went up to and back down from his lips twice before he put it down untouched. He couldn't keep his hands from shaking slightly. "You mean, children?"

"I don't mean a poodle," Penny replied with a chuckle.

"Right…" He let the word lengthen out for much longer than it would normally need.

"And…"

It appeared her husband needed to pace before the window so as to formulate a reply.

"I, well, I can't say I've thought about that as an idea," he eventually came up with.

Reaching out a hand, Penny grabbed his arm as he made another pass and pulled him down so he sat beside her. "That's being honest. I don't know what you recall about that day?"

He could barely bring himself to look at her as her told her, "Unfortunately, I've a very good memory and can recall every spiteful word that came out of my mouth."

Determined to be strong and not give in to emotional blackmail, even inadvertently said, Penny told him, "Then you'll remember that I can't have children anymore."

She allowed Tom to take one of her hands, acknowledging both had need for contact. "I'll never forget."

"Then think about it. We both want children, but can't have our own. However, it's an unfortunate, undeniable truth that there are a lot of children out there who are now orphans and in need of a good home."

This time, when his eyebrows tried to hide amongst his hair, Tom had a smile on his face. "That's…that's a wonderful idea! Are you sure?"

Penny studied her husband's face for a long minute before answering. She needed to be as sure as she could be that he meant his words. Finally, when she could find nothing but earnest truth, she said, "I am. I never thought I wanted children until…well, you know, but I knew you did. Your reaction at the hospital proved that."

Tom moved ever-so slightly closer to his wife and then, gradually edged an arm around her until he had a firm grip upon her waist. Still slightly cautiously, he planted a tender kiss upon her cheek. "Darling, I shall forever be ashamed of my words and actions of that day, but if you'll give me one last chance, I shall do my utmost to be the best husband, and father, you could wish for."

With a contented sigh, Penny let her head drop onto Tom's shoulder. "You do understand that this won't happen right away? I don't feel it would be right for us to act upon this idea until after we've won this war. Plus, we really do need to get to know each other better, this damned war allowing. We've been up and down, together and apart, and I'm fed up with not knowing what's what. Now, are you all right with all that?"

She felt his jaw working on the top of her head as he

unhesitatingly replied, "That makes perfect sense."

Penny wriggled out from his grip, knelt before him, and let her robe slip from her shoulders. "Good. Now, two things. First, go and lock that door." She waited until Tom had done so and returned. Lying back, she looked up and whispered, "Now, make love to me."

Chapter Nineteen

Sergeant Terry Banks unfolded his willowy frame from the police car, placed both hands at the small of his back and stretched. Oh, for a decent-sized car again! Looking back at whatever was the tiny thing he'd been forced to use today, he kicked one of the front wheels in frustration and not a little pain. He sometimes thought he'd been born in the wrong century and, even though he didn't actually ride, felt his frame was more suited to riding a horse than driving a car.

Reaching into the passenger seat, Terry grabbed his hat and jammed it on his head. Feeling a little better now his uniform was complete, he worked out the last few kinks from his back, regretting the early hour he'd got up that Monday morning, straightened his tie, and made his way toward the front door of the farmhouse. Knocking sharply on the door twice, he stepped back to await the response. After a third round of his polite knock, Terry raised his fist and banged upon the door whilst yelling, "Mr. Foreman! Police!"

When there was still no reply, Terry huffed, turned on his heels and made his way around the side of the house and into a courtyard. Hands on his hips, he stared around. He was a city boy at heart and all this country stuff tended to throw him, even though he'd had to deal with plenty of crime outside of Portsmouth. Perhaps everything was too...green? It certainly smelled different, too, he thought as he followed his nose toward what turned out to be a pigsty and its porcine contents.

He pushed his hat back and whistled. "Now that'd be worth stealing!" Which was when he felt something hard jab against the small of his back.

"I wouldn't, if I were you." The words were snarled from behind him and the voice likely belonged to whoever was holding what he suspected to be a shotgun on him. "On your knees."

Willing his voice to remain calm and collected, Terry complied. "They were only words. I have no intention of stealing your pigs."

He felt another hard nudge in his back. "Reckon you'd say anything right about now."

"A very good point," Terry conceded. "Right. My name is Sergeant Terry Banks of the Portsmouth Police Force, and I'm going to reach into my pocket and show you my ID. All right?"

At the word "police," Terry felt the gun's barrel waver slightly and for a moment—one rather silly moment, he'd concede when thinking about the situation later—he considered making a grab for the barrel. Common sense prevailed, though. Instead, he took a deep breath and did exactly as he'd said he would, hoping whoever was holding the gun was reasonable. His warrant card in hand, he opened it up and held it up so the man could see it.

He felt the barrel being removed from his back, followed by someone taking a few steps back behind him. "All right," came a reluctant voice, "you can get up."

Hoping his legs wouldn't betray him, Terry got as smoothly to his feet as he could. Deliberately, he kept his back to his would-be assailant as he brushed the dirt and straw off his trousers. Turning slowly, it seeming better to be safe than blasted to hell, he found himself nearly belly to nose with a somewhat rotund farmer. Keeping his warrant card in view, Terry decided to make sure. "You believe I'm a policeman, and not some thick as thieves pig-rustler in broad daylight?"

Slightly surreally, the man bent backward to look up at the sky, as if he needed to check it was still daylight. This had the unfortunate effect of causing what was indeed a shotgun he was carrying under his arm to rise up and point toward Terry, who hurriedly scurried to one side.

"Do me a favor and crack open that shotgun?" Terry asked, using a non-too-steady finger to point at the shotgun.

"Hmm? Oh, right you are," the man said and matched words to action, also pocketing the two cartridges for good measure.

"Thank you," Terry said, fighting to stay polite. "Now, I presume you are the owner of this farm? A Mr. Ambrose Foreman?"

"Aye, that I am," came back the reply.

Terry noted that though it was unloaded, the farmer still had a tight grip on the shotgun. "For my peace of mind, do me a favor and put the shotgun down too?"

After a few moments of silent sparring, the farmer finally crossed toward what looked like the rear of the farmhouse and placed the still cracked open shotgun carefully against the wall. The policeman noticed Ambrose stayed where he was for a few seconds, not quite with his back turned to him, but enough, before acknowledging that he'd lost the second battle and made his way back to join him.

"What do you want?"

Biting down the retort on his lips as to why farmers were always grumpy these days, Terry put his hand into an inside pocket and brought out a handkerchief. Unfolding it, he showed the rifle bolt to him, whilst watching the man's face and demeanor carefully for any reaction. Deliberately, he kept his hand close to his own chest, forcing the older man to come closer to have a good look.

After a few seconds, he stepped back and glanced up at the policeman. "A Lee-Enfield rifle bolt, I'd say," he began. "What of it?"

Without thinking, Terry said the first thing that came to mind, "So you know what it is, then?"

He was rewarded with a withering look, such as one would reserve for something you'd scrape off the sole of your shoe. "I should bloody well think so. Two and a half years in the trenches in the first lot! Bally right I know what it is. What I'd like to know is, why are you showing it to me?"

Terry never had been one for small talk. "Because Ruth—you know Ruth Stone, of course, owner and editor of the *Hamble Gazette*—claims she found this half-buried outside your front door." He decided to prod the farmer a little, test if what Ruth had told him was correct. Leaning a little toward him, Terry added, "Ruth told me you kept turning your eyes to the ground, as if she should look down. She did as you hinted," he told the man, before rewrapping the bolt in its handkerchief and putting it back in his pocket.

If Terry was expecting this revelation to set the cats amongst the pigeons, he was half correct. Though no confession was forthcoming, he was rewarded by the sight of the farmer's eyes flicking back and forth, but what he was looking for wasn't obvious. He opened his mouth, but before any words got out, the door Terry still assumed was the kitchen flew open. What came forth appeared to be a caricature of what a farmer should dress like—flat cap, knotted scarf around a rolled-neck jumper, some blue overalls, and a pair of bottle-green wellington boots. Everything was spotlessly clean!

Taking the initiative, the sergeant strode past Ambrose, hand outstretched to the stranger, forcing him to choose between stepping back into the kitchen and accepting the handshake. Terry believed you could learn a lot from a handshake. The man chose the latter. Despite his appearance, there were calluses on both hands, though more prevalent on his right. So, right-handed, Terry assessed. His grip was also firm, but that didn't prove anything. However, despite the evidence of hard work, the man's hands were clean, as were his fingernails. Obviously, whatever else he was doing there, it wasn't farming. There was something about his demeanor, however, which sent Terry's senses into overdrive. He was built like a human oak tree, and Terry would bet everything he had that here was one chap who had regular dealings with the police, on the wrong side of the law.

"Sergeant Terry Banks," he introduced himself, "and you are?"

"Ambrose's second cousin," was all he replied, crossing his arms before the open door.

Deciding to let his ill manners slide, for the moment, Terry let his gaze slide around what he could see of the farm. "Bit quiet. No one else around? Don't you have any Land Girls?" he asked, curiosity piqued by the strange place. It wasn't like the sergeant had been around many farms lately, but he couldn't imagine Ambrose managing to keep even this small pig farm going on his own, and he couldn't see this "cousin" pitching in, without a great deal of effort. From the corner of his eye, he did his best to study the farmer's face. There were dark shadows under both eyes, which could mean anything, though when he glanced down at the man's hands, the left one had a tremble he didn't seem aware was present.

"Had to let them go," Ambrose uttered.

"Bunch of bloody thieves!" spat his companion.

Terry made a point of looking around him once more. From what he could see, unless someone wanted to smuggle a pig out under their jumper, there wasn't much worth stealing. Of course, the inside of the farmhouse could contain the Crown Jewels, for all he knew. Still, it was worth stirring the pot.

"Don't take this the wrong way, but I can't see anything out here anyone would want to steal. Saying so, why didn't you report any incidents to the police?"

Again the belligerent reply came from the cousin. "Would there have been any point?"

Terry fixed him with a stare and was secretly gratified to see him ever so slightly squirm. "Without any proof, probably not."

Without any other response other than a disgusted huff, the disagreeable chap turned his back, stomped back inside, and slammed the door shut. However, when he heard no further noise come from inside, the sergeant surmised that he was actually behind the door, endeavoring to listen to what was still to come.

"Friendly sort of chap," Terry declared, deliberately loud enough so if he was right, his words would be clearly heard inside. "Is he your only help around here?"

Ambrose whipped off his cap and wiped his brow with it. "You take what you can get these days." He shrugged. "Selwyn's all right."

"Selwyn?" Terry pounced, and this time there was no doubt he heard a distinct curse come from behind the door. "I've got to say, if he's your help, judging by his clothes, he doesn't like getting dirty."

"He does what he can," Ambrose replied after a pause. He'd obviously decided to think before he replied, having let slip the other's name, at least his first, when the man in question had avoided volunteering it. "Besides," he then said, moving toward Terry and lowering his voice so they couldn't be overheard, after having had what the policeman recognized as an internal battle with himself, "he's the least of my worries."

Terry matched the other man's low voice. "And what is?"

"Government's requisitioning some of my land, right at the end of Hamble's runway."

"Doubt if there's anything I can do about that," Terry replied. "War and all that."

"I need..." He stopped speaking as his voice was beginning to rise and tried again. "I need that land!"

His curiosity aroused, Terry asked, "But why? It's not even connected to your farm. Do you even use it?"

Looking now like he regretted his small outburst, Ambrose took a step back and, clearly choosing his words carefully, said, "Well, no, but it's been in the family for generations, and it's not nice to lose something and not have a say in it, is it?"

What sounded like a fist impacting the door came from the kitchen. Ambrose turned his head to look, and when he turned back, his expression could only be described as fearful.

Knowing he wasn't going to get anything else out of the farmer, yet more certain than ever that something much more than a single rifle bolt was amiss around here, Terry touched the brim of his hat. "Well, I won't take up any more of your day, Mr. Foreman. Sorry you couldn't shed any light on the bolt, but if you think of anything, feel free to telephone me. Here's my card," he added. Taking advantage of their privacy from spying eyes, Terry handed him one card, whilst quickly tucking another into the man's trouser pocket and winking.

Chapter Twenty

"There'll be bluebirds over the white cliffs of Dover, tomorrow, just you wait and…" Betty sang in a sweet, clear soprano.

It was one of those days where everything was going right. No putty had melted in the windows, each dropoff had gone ahead on schedule, and to top it all off, she had a letter from her fiancé, Major Jim Fredericks of the USAAF, tucked safely away in an inside pocket to read and savor as soon as she put back down at RAF Hamble. She could even laugh now at the memory of Jane ushering her out of her cottage, which she owned, before she was able to read it. Even being too busy to make five minutes didn't matter on such a day. Yes, this was turning out to be one fine Monday!

Glancing around the clear blue sky, she began her approach toward the airfield. Humming what should be the next verse, because she could never remember the words, she became aware of what sounded like a soft moan. Quickly, she pushed a finger into her flying helmet and pulled it away from an ear. Listening carefully, Betty couldn't hear anything and replaced her helmet.

The airfield in view, Betty stopped humming, did her best to ignore the machinery the other side of the fence at the end of the runway she was approaching, and settled in to bring the Anson in for a perfect landing.

Landings in front of their friends, and particularly Jane, were a matter of pride for everyone at Hamble. No one wanted jibes aimed at them about having filled up with kangaroo fuel! Satisfied she was on course for a smooth one, Betty reached for…there it was again! Only this time, it was much louder and getting closer. What on earth could it be?

Somewhat urgently, she looked out both side windows and both engines were turning over, the various dials on the control panel told her the same story; everything seemed fine. Puzzled, she looked back out the front, wondering quickly if she'd be best to go around, or to make as swift a landing as she could?

The choice was taken out of her control by the sudden and completely unexpected appearance of Ruth's Cocker Spaniel, Bobby, by her side. His ear-splitting whine surprised Betty so much her hands jerked on the control yoke, fortunately not hard enough to throw the plane out of control. "What the hell?" she swore, whilst wrestling with the controls before following the direction his entrance had veered her off on, and she began the long slow circuit of the airfield for another try.

As she straightened up, she had time to glance to her side, only to find Bobby had hopped up onto the co-pilot's seat and no amount of shooing movements or noises could persuade him to move. He was, however, quite amenable to allowing her to clip the seat restraints around him, whereupon he sat back on his haunches and proceeded to look around outside the aircraft.

"One of us is in trouble here, and I'm not sure who," Betty muttered to him as she brought the Anson around and lined up once more with the runway.

As soon as the words were out of her mouth, she

became aware of Jane's voice in her earphones. "I say again. Betty, what's wrong? Are you all right? Over."

"Here we go," she said to herself before clicking the radio transmitter to send and replying, "Lost Child replying. I'm all right, just something unexpected turned up in the airplane and I had to go around again. Over."

There was a short pause before Jane came back on. "Er, you did say, in the plane? Over."

"I did. Don't worry, everything's fine, though you may want to get Ruth over. There's something you both will want to see. I'm about to land now, so I'll be with you in a few minutes. Come over to the flight line, please. Over and out."

Taxiing up to the flight line hut, Betty could see she had a waiting committee of Jane, Penny, and the engineering SNCO. Once the ground crew had safely chocked the wheels, she went through the shutdown checklist and only then did she turn to unsecure Bobby from his seat.

"Come on, let's go and face the music," she told him. Taking a firm grip of the dog's collar, she began to lead him down the gangway, though she had to help him over the covering of the wing spar for some reason, and toward the door. "I know it's a little strange to say, but you look a little pale. You feeling all right, boy?"

As she went to open the door, a fraction before Penny, she caught a whiff of some foul odor. Looking around, it didn't take long to find the source. Dotted around the rear of the aircraft was evidence that Bobby had not only been airsick, multiple times, but had also had to go to the toilet! Quickly opening the door, she wasn't surprised at the looks upon her welcoming committee.

"Bobby!" both Jane and Penny exclaimed at the same time, whilst the SNCO simply shook his head in disbelief before trotting back into the hut.

"Yes, this is why I asked you to send for Ruth."

Crouching down, she kept hold of the dog, who was now very eager to get four paws back on terra firma. "Here you go," she said as Jane reached up to catch hold of Bobby around the middle.

As Jane put him down, the SNCO came back and handed her a piece of rope he'd acquired, a loop in one end. "Good thinking, thanks," she said, looping the end over Bobby's unprotesting head, whereupon he flopped down at her feet.

Penny had disappeared into the Anson as Jane asked, "Exactly what happened here?"

Kneeling down beside the airfield's mascot, Betty rubbed his ears, something he normally adored and would be guaranteed to send him into fits of joy, though this time he just lay there, barely acknowledging the fuss she was making of him. "I've not got a clue," she answered honestly. "I've not been back all day, you know that, so I have to assume he must have sneaked in whilst the plane was being prepped this morning and hidden himself away."

"He's kept himself busy, though," Penny announced, leaning out of the door.

"Why I didn't smell it, I've no idea," Betty replied with a shake of her head.

"At the risk of getting myself chucked out of your cottage," Jane said, though she was struggling to keep a straight face as she spoke, "I'm going to have to ask you to clean up the mess before handing the Anson back to the ground crew."

Looking around, Betty could see that everyone there had heard her words. The engineer must have had some kind of telepathic link with Jane, as one of his other ranks appeared at his side holding a mop and bucket, which he took and, with great reverence, handed to Betty. She noted he was struggling to keep a smile off his face.

****

Having kissed Walter goodbye and wishing him to keep safe as he went off for an evening with his Home Guard platoon, Doris hurried back into the lounge.

"You're still not ready? Come on, Ruth, they're expecting us!"

Ruth smiled up at her friend and lodger. You could never say life was boring when you lived with Doris Johnson, and incidentally, she'd get used to it not being Doris *Winter*, one of these years. Though the younger woman was clearly champing at the bit, Ruth patted the space on the sofa next to her. "Sit. I want to say something."

"We've not been too…loud, again?" Doris asked, blushing.

Ruth's face joined the American's. Stammering a little, she shook her head, saying, "Not this time." They both waited a silently but mutually agreed time for their complexions to return to normal. "No, I simply wanted to ask if you and Walter are happy. Staying here, with me, I mean," she added, upon seeing the curious expression on Doris's face.

"Of course we are," Doris assured her, bumping her shoulder in a friendly way against Ruth's. "Don't get me wrong, like any married couple, I'd love to have my own place, but it wouldn't be right, what with the war still ongoing. The country still needs all the housing it can get for those who've been bombed out. I dare say you wouldn't mind having the place to yourself, and with your Matt, either."

Ruth could feel her ear tips flush once more. Leaning down to tie her shoelace, she used the fact her face couldn't be seen to say, "There are times I forget you're a Yank."

However, Doris waited until the lace was tied and Ruth had straightened back up to reply, "I can remind you more often, if you like," she said, deadpan.

Ruth regarded Doris with friendly suspicion, before eventually shaking her head. "Nope, I'll never figure you out, and you know what? I think I'll stop trying."

Doris planted a kiss on her friend's cheek. "Good decision! But I've got to ask why you wanted to know." Ruth went to rise to her feet, only Doris wouldn't let her. "Come on, you can't ask a question like that without explaining why!"

"I feel such a fool now," Ruth replied, flopping back down. "All right, it's only that you spend a lot of time around Betty's, with your friends."

"You're my friend too," Doris told her.

Ruth gave her an understanding smile. "But they're your best friends."

Doris shrugged. "Honestly? Yes, they are, but—and maybe I'm strange like this—I've never really considered anyone to be a *best* friend. I suppose you could say so, as they're the ones I first met down here, but don't forget I met you the very next day." She considered Ruth's words again. "And yes, I know I still spend most of my time, when Walter's not here, around there, but I hadn't realized I'd upset you, Ruth." She took hold of her friend's hand. "I'm sorry. We'll…I'll stay in more."

"Heaven forbid!" Ruth exclaimed. "No, that's not what I meant at all!"

"It's not?" Doris asked, confusion painting her face.

Ruth's face dropped, causing Doris to cover her friend's hand in both of hers. "I'd never want to stop you spending as much time as you want over at Betty's. Heaven knows, with the war, you can never be sure when you'll next see your friends, can you. No, I only wanted to make sure you don't regret agreeing to live with me."

Doris let out a *Doris* laugh, and this did more to reassure her friend than any words could. Sidling in until she was all but sitting on the newspaper owner's lap, Doris locked eyes, "Of course I don't! Walter loves you to death, you know that, of course, and so do I. Now that nonsense is settled..." She waited a moment so Ruth could nod her agreement. "Don't you think it's time we did that interview you asked me to do?"

It took half a minute, whilst Doris patiently waited for Ruth to realize what she was talking about. When it finally hit her, you could almost see the lightbulb appear over her head.

"You thought I'd forgotten, didn't you?" Doris teased.

Hastily and totally unsuccessfully, Ruth shook her head before admitting, "Yes, yes, I had. Let's speak to Jane about it, just to be on the safe side, as there may be some authority she needs to speak with to get permission."

Doris bounded to her feet, pulling a rather surprised Ruth with her. "Just as well you've finally got your shoes on, then! Come on," and she all but pulled her out of the cottage, only allowing her time to prod Bobby awake.

On account of the balmy evening and the next-to-no distance, neither bothered picking up a coat. Arm in arm, the two made their way along the riverfront, stopping only once when a loud "Quack! Quack!" punctured the air.

"That's not, Duck?" Ruth cast her eyes around, she too had been a victim of Doris's feathered fiend's feistiness.

Pausing, Doris listened closely as another call penetrated the air, before shaking her head and smiling, "Nope. Only a duck."

Allowing herself to be pulled along, Ruth had just enough time to share a confused look with Bobby who, at being reassured he wasn't about to be chased, came out from behind his owner's legs. "I've said it before and I'll say it again, one of these days, I'll figure you out, Doris."

They'd reached the gates of Betty's cottage by now, which Doris held open for them both. "Good luck with that!" was all she replied, a sweet grin upon her face.

A few minutes later, Doris and Ruth were happily eating the stew Betty had put together by combining the leftovers she had been storing with those Ruth and Doris had brought over. Everyone who'd made the mistake of looking in the pot agreed it was best not to dwell on what they were eating or how it looked, but instead to simply try and enjoy. This was made considerably easier by the fact the stew tasted delicious, as everyone happily agreed. Everyone except one.

"Anyone else think it's strange for Bobby not to be trying to steal or beg a tidbit?" Penny asked, prodding him gently with her toe.

Ruth glanced over to where her faithful canine was

lying under Doris's outstretched feet.

Before anyone else could speak up, Betty, her spoon in midair, declared, "After what I had to clean up today, I doubt if he feels up to eating anything. I'll just say this—warm dog sick smells awful!"

"What I'd like to know is, how did he get into the plane?" Mary asked.

"And why didn't he make a sound until you came back to land at Hamble? Why not on any of your other stops?" Doris added.

Ruth shook her head. "All very good questions, and I guess we'll never know the answers. Perhaps he knew none of the other airfields were Hamble?" she mused. "It still doesn't answer why he never made a sound earlier, though. Maybe I should keep him at the office from now on?"

This suggestion was met with a cacophony of protests, with Doris reaching down and dragging the semi-comatose pooch up onto her lap. Picking up an unprotesting paw, Bobby's eyes were both somehow still closed, she waved it at Ruth. "No! Don't keep me locked up. I love roaming around the airfield!"

Frowning, Ruth reached over and took the wagging paw. "I don't know. Look how much trouble you got Betty into."

"I'll say!" Betty agreed.

"Don't listen to her!" Bobby pleaded in Doris's voice. "Look how cute I am. You can't keep me locked up! Please!"

"How do I know you won't pull the same trick?" Ruth found herself addressing the question directly to Bobby before she could stop herself. "We're very lucky you didn't hop out whilst the door was open. You could have ended up who knows where, and we'd never have known what happened to you. But if you will roam around, I'm a bit surprised this is the first time you've flown."

"Your mistress makes a very good point, Bobby. What do you have to say for yourself?" Jane asked.

Doris wagged the paw a little more vigorously, and Bobby cracked open one eyelid before closing it as though their antics were not worth his interest. "Please! No!"

"I guess it's down to you, Boss," Penny announced and promptly settled back to finish her stew.

Jane threw her a semi-annoyed look, "Remind me to find a biplane for your next week's tasks."

Penny held up her arm. "Can't fly open cockpit aircraft for the next four weeks. The condition the doc said. Remember?"

"Bloody doctors," Jane mumbled. "Fine, how does this sound to everyone? I'll have Penny here putting up notices around the station tomorrow, stating everyone is to watch out for Bobby, especially to make sure he doesn't climb into any more aircraft. I'll also make a couple of announcements over the PA to that effect. Short of banning him from the station, which I know wouldn't go down well, I don't see what else we can do. Sound good to you, Bobby?"

Doris held up Bobby's head and rubbed a rather wet nose against Jane's chin. Instantly, an even wetter tongue shot out and licked her on the end of her nose.

"Eww!" Jane let out, hastily scooting back in her seat.

Everyone else laughed, with Ruth adding, "I think that's a yes, Jane."

"Just as well," Jane said. "If I stopped him from coming on the airfield, I think I'd have a riot on my hands."

Her tea finished, Doris happily settled back with Bobby draped across her lap. For his part, the dog didn't look like he objected to the arrangement in the least. "I've figured it out, you know!" she suddenly announced.

Sensing something was afoot, Penny asked, "My turn to bite. So, Doris, what have you figured out?"

"The runway."

"What about it?" Penny asked after waiting for her friend to elaborate.

"The extension."

"Doris!"

"It's being done because Betty needs a longer one. I mean, she needed two goes around this last time!"

Right on cue, Bobby let out a soft *woof* in his sleep.

"See, Bobby agrees!"

"It's Bobby's bloody fault I had to go around, and well you know it, Doris!" Betty declared in no uncertain terms.

Doris blew her friend a kiss. "Oh, Betty, I love you to death, but sometimes you're so easy to wind up!"

Betty crumpled into her seat and shrugged her shoulders. "I know, I know. But that doesn't mean I won't smack your bottom again!"

"About the extension," Jane said, cutting into the well-rehearsed banter, "expect the work to start sometime next week. It shouldn't cause us too much trouble, but remember to call in when you're five minutes away. That'll give us plenty of time to have the workmen move any machinery out of the way. However, you'll all have to be extra careful on both takeoffs and landings."

Mary asked, "Exactly why are we having this extension done, Jane? Seriously, we've always had plenty of room. I don't see the need for it."

Jane looked carefully around the room before speaking, making certain she had everyone's full attention. Doris even stopped scratching Bobby's stomach. "Again, this goes no further than this room. I know you all know what's coming?" Everyone nodded, including Bobby, though that may have been Doris manipulating him. "We're being upgraded to act as an emergency landing field. We have to be able to take anything we've got, up to and including Lancasters, Halifaxs, Flying Fortresses—you get the picture."

As one, everyone's head turned in the direction of Hamble airfield, and when they turned back, there was a little less color in their faces. Even in this war, things could still get a little more…real.

Chapter Twenty-One

"Good morning, Jane! Mary, Penny, Betty, and…" Mavis actually hopped out from behind the servery, belying her advancing years, "our Doris! My goodness, what a mouthful! How are you all?"

After being subjected to an unexpected hug, their usually cantankerous mess manager retook her place to await her next customers. Unspoken, the girls all brought their cups of tea warily to their noses and sniffed.

"Smells fine," Penny announced, as everyone nodded.

Mary sniffed once again and, before anyone could stop her, took a tentative sip.

"A bit early for brave pills, isn't it?" Doris asked and they all watched in open-mouthed amazement as Mary supped back the rest of her tea before looking into the now empty cup. "Are you feeling well? You're not ill, are you?" Doris wanted to know, genuine amazement in her voice.

"Not only am I more than fine, I'm going back for seconds," Mary stunned her friends.

Being the first into the mess that Tuesday morning, there was only one person to ask about this strange turn of affairs. However, before this, potentially drastic measures needed to be taken. As one, the remaining girls brought their cups to their lips, matched Mary's sips, watched each other's eyebrows shoot up in surprise, and then they all downed their respective cups.

"Mavis," Jane began, as she stepped behind Mary, whose cup was indeed being refilled, "what exactly is...this?"

"Tea," she merely replied, hovering her large teapot over Jane's empty cup.

Jane raised her cup back up to her nose before saying what was on everyone's mind. "No, I mean yes, it's tea, but it's..."

"Drinkable?" Mavis ended for her and then, instead of the usual mood she got in when someone passed a comment on her brews, she once more smiled.

Jane had to physically stop herself from taking a step back at the unexpected sight, "Well, yes, of course, but the taste!"

"It's Sharon's brew," Mavis stated.

"That's it!" Penny announced, a little too loudly, as everyone turned to stare at her. "Sorry," she mumbled, before taking a place behind Jane for seconds.

"Go on, ask away," Mavis said. "I can see you're dying to."

"All right, I will," Doris agreed, when no one else immediately piped up. "Why, after all this time, are we being treated to a drinkable...'brew,' I believe is the right word?"

Mavis shook her head, yet she still had the same smile on her face. "This morning, of all mornings, Doris, nothing you say can get to me. You see this?" She reached into the pocket at the front of her apron and took out a slightly tatty envelope. "My son's coming home on leave for a whole week!"

A spontaneous cheer erupted from the group, and then they all stretched over the servery to pat whichever part of Mavis they could reach.

After the jumbled congratulations had died down—everyone knew how unhappy the mess manager had been without her boy—Jane called for quiet. "As you can tell, we're all very, very happy to hear this news. As soon as you know the dates, come and see me and we'll fix things up."

Doris tapped the side of her cup with a spoon. "I'd still like to know why the sudden change in the tea? I mean, for myself, it's still not a patch on a cup of joe in the morning, but at least I don't get it confused with engine oil now."

If there'd been anyone around who didn't know the history between the two women, they'd have been waiting to step in between a pair of fighting wildcats any minute now. However, the war-of-words between Mavis and Doris was simply a front the pair kept up, more out of habit now than anything else, as they were actually quite fond of each other. In fact, it was Doris who'd got out of Mavis that her son was a very late-in-life surprise arrival, though none the less wanted for that.

"Well, you can blame young Sharon for that. She's been slightly more tactful than you lot about my tea-making skills, but when I told her my news when the letter came this morning, she took a chance..."

"I expect it was," Doris couldn't resist chipping in, being rewarded with the flick of a tea towel toward her for her troubles.

"...and asked if she could show me *her* tea-making skills. Well, I was in such a good mood, and she didn't mean any malice when she offered, I took her up on the offer."

"And this is the result," Betty said, reaching for the

teapot and getting her knuckles rapped with a spoon by Mavis.

"And this is the result," Mavis agreed.

"Speaking of Sharon," Jane said, looking around the mess, "where is she?"

"I almost forgot!" Mavis snapped her fingers. "She sends her apologies, but Inspector Lawrence unexpectedly called around this morning. Said he needed her urgently and that he'd give you a telephone call later about it."

"Oh!" Mary let out before she could stop herself.

"Everything all right?" Betty asked her friend, noting the frown on Mary's face.

"I was just thinking it'd be nice if he called on me with such enthusiasm." She then put down her empty cup and left the mess.

Penny, having witnessed their friend's exit, tapped Betty on the shoulder. "What just happened?"

Betty thought for a minute before replying. Passing Penny her cup, she picked up both her flight bag and the one Mary had left. "I think Mary's having a little crisis with jealousy."

"I beg your pardon?"

"Never mind. We'll see you in the flight line hut," she told Penny, before dashing out.

"Where've those two gone?" Jane appeared at Penny's side, unable to keep a blissful expression from her face whenever she took a sip from her cup.

Penny shook her head, "I'm not quite certain, but I think Mary's feeling a little unloved."

Jane wasn't the boss for nothing, and it took her a mere moment to thread together the earlier conversation with Mary's actions. "Ah. Do you think Betty will sort her out?"

"I should think so," Penny told her. "However, to be on the safe side, I think we should speak with Lawrence, remind him on which side his bread's buttered; for his own good."

****

"Mary's quiet!" Penny yelled into Betty's ear an hour later.

That was the problem with their taxi aircraft as, though not the nosiest of aircraft, the Avro Anson still wasn't conversant with keeping the volume of a conversation at normal levels. True, if there was someone onboard whom you didn't wish to know what was being discussed, they didn't have a hope of hearing what was being said. Unfortunately, it was also impossible to keep any conversation secret.

Doris, despite not being able to hear what her friend said, was able to tell who the two were talking about and so unbuckled her harness and came to kneel behind the pair, tapping them on the shoulders so they knew she was there. "Any luck?" she too shouted, acutely aware the subject of conversation was watching them through the rearview mirror.

Before anyone could try to reply, the plane dropped like a stone for a few seconds, then pitched up and rolled slightly to port before Mary levelled it off.

"Sorry. Turbulence!" she shouted, as the abused plane continued on its way as if nothing untoward had happened.

By unspoken consent, the other three stopped talking and, especially in Doris's case, strapped themselves into their seats a little more tightly than they'd ordinarily have bothered to do. They all knew there was no chance of turbulence today, and didn't want to give their compatriot another chance to find some. Fortunately, it was only a short hop across to the Supermarine factory at Woolston, Southampton that morning, or what was normally an uncomfortable ride could have proved to be unbearable. To cover for cutting short their chat, the three took out their ATA pilot's notes and studied those of the Supermarine Walrus, a biplane none of them had flown before. An amphibian which looked like it was from a different era, it nonetheless always paid not to take chances in their line of work. If there were any quirks about a plane, it was always best to find out about them in advance.

When they were dropped off, instead of the usual hugs and wishes, their taxi driver merely watched over her shoulder as they disembarked, threw them a very quick wave, and then turned back to her controls. She didn't even acknowledge Doris's cheerful cry of, "See you later, me old duck!" Maybe that was because of the awful cockney accent she tried, though.

Within five minutes, the Anson was on its way, leaving a very bemused and slightly hurt threesome watching from the same spot where they'd been dropped off.

"Well, that settles it," Penny began, picking up her flight bag and lugging her parachute over a shoulder. "When we get back tonight, we need to pin her down and get her to talk. I don't suppose you got anything out of her back at Hamble, Betty?"

Betty shook her head. "Not a dickybird. When I did catch up, she was mumbling something along the lines of, 'Bloody Sharon,' over and over, but when I caught her elbow, she refused to speak to me. All I got out of her was that we needed to get going."

"Well, girls," Doris said, barging her way between the pair, "it's plain we really need to set her right, and the only way that's going to happen is if we can get her in the same room as Lawrence and Sharon. Come on, let's hand in our flight chits and get this day over with. Penny, I'm going to ask you to pull rank shortly." When asked what she had in mind, Doris told her, "Give Jane a phone and ask her to get hold of both Lawrence and Sharon and get them to come over to Betty's—no, make that Ruth's—this evening. Tell her why. No one mention this to Mary!"

****

"Give me a Spitfire any time!" Penny swore for about the fifth time since she'd clambered her way into the ungainly Walrus. Risking a nod of satisfaction, two minutes later she had the single engine idling and was waiting for the signal to release the brakes. Ahead of her, she watched as first Mary and then, a little more shakily, Doris took off and began the long, very slow climb away from Southampton.

Taking one more look at the notes she'd made on the course they'd all agreed to take to Royal Naval Air Station, St. Merryn, Penny shuffled around in her seat to see if she could make herself a little more comfortable. Reluctantly, she gave this up as a waste of time and resigned herself to a less than pleasant flight, all the way to Cornwall. At least this was one biplane which didn't have an open cockpit.

Satisfied she'd taken in the takeoff procedure, she released the brakes at the signal and began to taxi toward the runway.

"Flipping heck!" she shouted, as a strong wind

whipped the aircraft broadside on, just as she made her final turn. Kicking in the opposite rudder to counter, she straightened up and touched the brakes a spot to bring the large biplane to a brief stop. "Right," she uttered from between clenched teeth, "off we go."

So saying, she released the brakes, eased the throttles to full and the biplane began its graceless lollop down the runway. No sooner had she begun to roll than the same wind hit the side of the fuselage again and she was forced to apply the opposite rudder again to keep her nose headed in the right direction. However, Mother Nature had other ideas and another, even more violent gust hit her, and she felt the airplane begin to roll to her right. The left-hand side's wheel came off the ground, the right wing-tip hit and began to scrap along the runway, and the control wheel began to judder violently.

Penny had barely enough time to realize that the aircraft was now out of her control before a final gust flipped the other wing up and the Walrus tipped over. Only the tightness of her harness prevented her from being thrown out of her seat. Bringing her arms up to protect her face as best she could, Penny saw blue, then green, then blue, finally settling on green, before blackness mercifully engulfed her.

Chapter Twenty-Two

Jane sipped yet another of Mavis's marvelous new teas and pushed back the thought that if she kept up her current intake, she may have to think about moving her desk into the toilet block. Setting her cup down on her desk, she mused that being in command had its perks, but it could be a lonely job. That'd make a half-decent quote, she thought, as Penny's telephone interrupted her train of thought.

Pushing back her chair, she rushed around to answer it, actually feeling the copious amounts of tea she'd consumed slosh around in her stomach. With luck, she'd have Penny back to her non-flying duties for the rest of the week and she wouldn't have to keep this up. She snatched up the receiver. "RAF Hamble, ops hut, Flight Captain Howell."

If anyone else had been there, they'd have seen Jane jerk the receiver away from her ear, as the voice down the other end was in barely controlled hysterics.

"Jane! This is Betty!" she heard her friend say and then, before she could get a word in, "It's Penny! She's crashed!"

Jane felt her blood run ice cold, and she had to fight off an attack of lightheadedness. From somewhere she heard a voice say, "Wait! Slow down. What did you say?" eventually, recognizing it as her own. Hurriedly, she took a few calming breaths, fighting to get back in control. If what Betty was saying was true, and she had no reason to believe her friend would ever make up something so dreadful, then she desperately needed to keep as calm as she could.

"Jane? Are you still there?"

Wiping her brow, Jane hurried to answer. "Yes, I'm here. Now, slowly this time, Betty. Exactly what's happened?"

There was a momentary fight on the other end of the phone where Jane heard Betty telling Doris to leave her be, along with many more *choice* words. "Sorry, sorry. Right, Penny's Walrus crashed on takeoff," Betty started with, before she paused for a breath allowing Jane to do the same. "She was thrown clear before it burst into flames, and the rescue found her still strapped to her seat…"

Jane couldn't stop the question from blurting out, "Is she alive?"

"Yes," Betty simply replied, knowing, in spite of her own state of mind, this was the one fact her friend needed to hear without any elaboration.

"Thank Christ!" Jane exclaimed, briefly aware her legs had folded beneath her at some point and she was now sitting on the floor, though the handset was still glued to her ear. Not troubling to get up off the floor, as she wasn't certain her knees would handle her weight at the moment, she managed to ask, at the second attempt, "Is she injured?"

"She can't see you shake your head!" Jane heard Doris's voice say to Betty. "Give that here! Jane? It's me," the American announced. "We don't think so."

The relative calmness in Doris's voice did more to reassure her than Jane would have thought possible.

Doing her best to match her, she asked, "What do you mean, you don't think so?"

"What we mean," Doris stated, "is that by the time Betty and I had reached the plane, the crash crew were already putting out the fire and the meat wagon lot had Penny on a stretcher. We only had time to see that she was conscious and...well, no other way of putting it, that she had all her limbs, before they whisked her off."

"Bloody hell!" Jane said, before something struck her. "Was Mary still there?"

"No, she'd already left."

"So she doesn't know," Jane muttered.

"I think she's on her way back," Doris said. "Will you tell her?"

Jane nodded herself before saying, "Of course. Hang on, where are you two now? Shouldn't you be on your deliveries?"

Doris didn't reply, she merely gave her boss the time to think on what she'd just asked.

"Ah, you both saw the crash and landed back at Southampton."

"Of course we did!" Doris snapped. Jane didn't blame her, as she'd have reacted the same way. "We're both in the waiting room of the station medical center, waiting to hear about her."

Now back in a seat, Jane said, "Give me a minute," before covering the mouthpiece with a hand.

She had a few reasons for this. Firstly, she needed a little time to take in what had been said and had happened. Despite the danger of their job, crashes were mercifully few, but when they did occur, for there to be no injuries was exceptionally rare. Despite this, she also knew the job they were doing needed to carry on. She needed to persuade her two friends that they needed to get the remaining two Walruses delivered. However, she was realistic enough to realize that if she tried to order them to leave without knowing their friend was going to be fine, she would be told (especially as it was Doris she was talking with) exactly what she could do with that order.

"Jane?" It was Betty this time. "I know what you're going to say…"

Glad there was no one around to see her gaping-fish impression, Jane replied, "Go on."

"You're going to say we need to get on with the delivery…and you're right." Before Jane could say anything, Betty added, "We will, but only once we're both assured Penny's going to be all right."

"I would expect no less. Thank you both."

Before she could add anything, Betty exclaimed, "Hold on, Jane, the doc's coming out!"

Betty must have clamped a hand over the mouthpiece as Jane could only hear muffled words. It was very frustrating. After what seemed an eternity, Betty came back, and she sounded relieved.

"Betty! What happened? What did they say?" Jane demanded, before her friend had a chance to speak.

"Yes. Right. Sorry, Jane. Um, right, okay," Betty rambled.

"Betty, take a deep breath and try again," Jane gently suggested.

There was the sound of heavy breathing for a few seconds before Betty got her emotions back under control. "Sorry about that," she said, before filling her in on what they'd got out of the doctor. "Right. He said she appears to be uninjured, but he's sending her off to

Southampton General Hospital for a full checkup and a set of x-rays."

Jane took a few moments to process this information. "So he's playing safe," she surmised.

"Exactly what he said to us," Betty agreed.

"Has he let you speak to her?"

"We're just about to go in," Betty informed her.

Jane realized her heartbeat was returning to normal. "Give her my love, will you? I'm going to assume they'll be keeping her in for at least tonight, so could you also tell her we'll be along later to see how she is?"

"Will do. Oh! Look, he's calling us in, we've got to go. I'll give you a call as soon as we're done, to let you know, and then we'll get back on the job."

Acutely aware her two friends were about to take up two of the same kind of aircraft which had so nearly killed Penny, Jane had barely enough time to wish them a hasty, "God speed!" before the line went dead.

Tom. She needed to call him, she thought, staring at the lump of Bakelite in her hand.

****

At that particular moment, Wing Commander Tom Alsop was just waking from a rather enjoyable dream. For once, just for once, it hadn't been filled with exploding shells, jagged shards of white-hot metal piercing his aircraft and himself, nor nightmares of plunging into the ground at such a speed he couldn't get out of his disintegrating Mosquito. No, instead of a sheen of sweat, he woke with a beaming smile upon his face. It wasn't hard to know why.

"You know you've had a soppy grin on your face ever since your Penny left, don't you?" Stan told him, leaning around the open office door and catching his pilot and friend in the act of stretching. "And what's this kipping in the office? She's tired you out that much?"

Tom looked up into the weatherbeaten yet comfortable face of his navigator and shrugged before heaving himself to his feet. "What can I say?" He clapped a hand on his shorter friend's shoulder and indicated he should take the seat he'd just vacated. Never one to pass up comfort when it was offered, Stan sank down. "No one's going to begrudge me forty winks. Besides, I'm happy, Stan. As far as this bloody war will let any of us be, I'm happy."

"Wish I was," Stan muttered.

Seeing his friend was in need of a small pick-me-up, Tom locked the door to his office, then went around and pulled open the bottom drawer of his desk. Momentarily, he passed his friend a small glass of whiskey. "Get that down you."

With a quick salute, Stan did as ordered, before placing the once again empty glass on the table before him with a heavy *thunk*. "So, you and your Penny. Back on?"

Tom didn't hesitate to nod. "For real this time…I think," he found himself adding.

Never one to let rank get in the way, the flight sergeant told him, with a wag of a finger, "I hope so, for all our sakes. Don't make any more mistakes, Boss. That one's a keeper!"

"I'll do my best," Tom replied, raising and emptying his own glass in one move.

Looking a little uncomfortable, Stan looked up from under his eyebrows before forcing the question on his lips out, "Did Penny say anything about Sharon?"

Fighting the urge to tease him, Tom put him out of

his misery. "She did. I was surprised, and I think you will be as well, to hear that she believes Sharon is actually on a little job—her words, not mine," he hastily put in.

"A little *job*? What on earth can that mean?"

Tom's eyebrows disappeared. "Come on! Wake up a little, man. We've all done jobs we can't talk about, and from what Penny hinted, I don't think this will be much different, only without Mossies."

Having told him all he knew—he'd pressed Penny, but if she knew more, she refused to reveal it—he waited for Stan's mind to catch up. When it did, he whistled long and low, his own eyebrows matching his friends.

"Put two and two together..." Tom prompted.

Finally, after a metaphorical eternity, Stan seemed to do so. "She'll be back!" He looked up, beaming, and it was if the years he'd built up in the short time she'd been gone had dropped from his face.

Tom came around from his desk and lightly thumped his friend on the shoulder. "I kept telling you there wasn't anything to worry about."

As only two people who'd been through what the pair had, Stan immediately said, "You'll forgive me for not taking your word for it. Let's be honest, your track record hasn't been that great lately."

"Ouch!" Tom clutched his chest, pretending to be wounded, "Straight to the heart," though when Stan opened his mouth, undoubtedly to apologize, Tom stopped him, "And very true."

"Do you think I should phone her?" Stan asked, his very frame quivering in a state of nervous tension.

Tom shook his head. "I don't think so." When Stan went to protest, Tom explained, "Penny hinted she'd already said more than she should have."

Stan's face fell. "So I shouldn't do…anything?"

"No. It's hard—believe me, I know—but the best thing you can do right now is to let things play out as they need to."

"What if she gets into trouble?" Stan quickly asked back.

Tom settled on the edge of his desk. "I'll admit, with that lot—the Mystery Club," he amended, "—anything is possible. However, it looks like Inspector Lawrence is looking after her, and I think, after everything that's happened, we can trust him to look after Sharon, even with his life, if it comes to it."

The telephone chose that moment to ring, and upon answering it, it was Tom's turn for the blood to drain from his face.

Chapter Twenty-Three

"Come on, come on!"

"Urging her to land won't make things speed up any," Betty informed Doris, ignoring the fact that similar words had come out of her own mouth when the Anson had droned into view a few minutes ago.

Doris flopped down cross-legged onto the grass and toppled over when she half landed on her parachute, before recovering with her hands spread behind her for balance. "I know," she muttered, "but it doesn't do any harm to wish."

RNAS St. Merryn was stationed on the north-facing coast of Cornwall, about as near as it was possible to get to the USA without getting your feet wet. This meant that when the wind blew, you knew about it, and sitting out by the side of dispersal wasn't that great an idea. However, as they both urgently wanted to get back home to Hamble as soon as possible, they'd both ignored all offers of a seat inside whilst they waited, and so long as it didn't rain, they'd stay right where they were.

"What a dump!" Doris uttered, not bothering to look around in case she could be overheard.

A little more aware they were guests, Betty checked no one was about to jump on them from a great height in response to her friend's disparaging remarks. "Not sure I'd go that far, but I certainly wouldn't wish to be stationed here."

"And it's not as if they even thanked us for the two Walruses!" Doris added. "Kept going on about not getting the three they were expecting."

Betty patted her fuming friend on the arm. "I'm very impressed you didn't do more than chew out that pompous engineering officer after he complained for the third time. I know he couldn't have known about Penny, but if he'd have listened the first time, he wouldn't have been so embarrassed after you'd finished with him."

Doris nodded vigorously. "You're right. My first instinct was to punch his lights out."

"And I wouldn't have stopped you!" Betty had to raise her voice, as their Anson was now taxiing toward them. "To top it off, they weren't even expecting them! Said they didn't fly Walruses!"

"Good idea of yours to get him to call his boss, or we may have ended up flying the buggers back!" Doris shouted.

Betty had to lean in close to Doris's ear to be heard now. "They can do what they like with them, for all I care, and if I never have to fly one again, it'll be too soon!"

Mary's Anson had just about come to a stop now, a mere twenty yards from where the two, back on their feet, were waiting for it. Instead of rolling up next to them, their being plenty of room on the dispersal pan, the plane came to a halt when it was still ten yards away, causing the surprised ground crew to sprint up so they could place the chocks under its wheels. Sharing looks which made it clear they thought Mary was still in a mood, they shrugged, shouldered their parachutes, picked up their flight bags, and trotted over.

The engines were winding down by the time the two

reached the Anson, and they could see Mary making her way down the fuselage toward the door. Beating her to it, Doris jerked open the door and flung her gear inside, where it landed at Mary's feet, causing her to make an awkward half-jump backward.

"In a bit of a hurry, are we?" Mary asked, stepping over Doris's things and standing in the doorway, thus blocking their entry.

Betty placed a warning hand on Doris's shoulder and stepped before her. "Too bloody right we are!" she snapped.

She wasn't exactly known for her swearing, so whatever Mary had been about to say died upon her lips. Confusion then added to her emotions as she realized she only had two passengers. "Where's Penny?" she asked, her voice hesitant.

"By now...Southampton General Hospital," Doris snapped, making shooing motions at Mary so she could climb in past her.

It took a few seconds for Mary to register what she'd just been told. "Betty, what did Doris mean?"

Though about on the limit of her nerves, Betty made an effort to calm down before speaking this time. "What she means is, Penny's plane crashed on takeoff, and she's now in hospital. Didn't Jane tell you all this?"

Instead of answering, Mary stumbled back until she tripped over Doris's things and landed in a heap, staring into space. Her two friends hopped up into the fuselage and hurried to her aid.

"Mary! Are you all right?" Betty asked as the pair grabbed a hand each and hauled her to her feet.

Shaking her head, Mary then demanded, "Never mind me, what's all this about Penny?"

"She's all right," Betty immediately told her, knowing that would be what she'd want to know straight off.

"But you just said something about a hospital?" Mary asked, her eyes wide and her body beginning to shake.

Gently but firmly, Betty and Doris pushed her into a seat before leaning over her. "The doctor told us he couldn't find anything wrong with her, but he was sending her to the hospital to be on the safe side."

"And you've both seen her?"

"Briefly," Betty admitted. "A few cuts and bruises, from what we could tell."

Mary made an attempt to get to her feet, but the shock of the news was still being felt in her legs and they collapsed under her.

"You stay right where you are," Doris informed her in no uncertain manner. "I'll fly us back. Mary," she raised her voice as her friend's eyes had begun to wander, "how's the gas situation?"

"Sorry? The what?" Mary replied, her eyes flicking past the American and then back again.

"Do we need to refuel?" Betty translated.

Slowly, Mary shook her head. "The tank's half full," she told them. "Should be plenty to get us back to Hamble, if we take it easy."

"We'll see about that," Doris announced as she pushed past and made her way to the cockpit.

Whilst Doris was busy with the startup procedure, and it looked like she was going to break all records, Betty asked Mary, "Didn't Jane tell you what happened?"

"Hmm? Oh, the radio's on the blink."

Glancing toward the cockpit, Betty could see Doris speaking into the R/T. "Stay there," she commanded, pressing her friend's shoulder to emphasis her point, before quickly going and getting Doris's attention.

"What's up?" Doris asked. "Hang on, I'm just trying to get hold of Hamble."

"Don't bother," Betty instantly advised. "The set's busted Mary said."

"Bloody hell!" Sitting back momentarily, Doris stared ahead before exclaiming, "Right. We'd better get moving. Full speed to Hamble it is. Get Mary strapped in, please, Betty. I've got this!" Thus saying, she began to turn the Cheetah engines over.

Leaning past her, Betty sought out the fuel gauge and turned a frown upon her friend. "I know Mary said we had enough to get back, but"—she lightly tapped the gauge with her finger—"I'm not sure we've enough for anything other than a cruise back."

Not exactly looking at what she was doing, Doris tapped the same gauge, only much more firmly. It jumped, ever so slightly, more toward the full end. Sparing a glimpse, Doris gave a satisfied nod. "Nonsense, we've plenty. Now, go and keep Mary company, we're about to see what this crate can really do!"

Knowing there was no point in arguing, let alone trying to pull rank on the Yank when she was in this mood, together with the fact that in Doris's place she would do the same, Betty did as she was told.

As she felt the plane begin to roll, she raised her voice so Mary could hear her over the din of the engines. "Best to hold on! We're in the lap of the gods and Doris's flying skills!"

****

"What couldn't wait?" Sharon asked Lawrence straight away she sat down in his car. "You know you've got me into trouble with Mavis, don't you? And she's in such a good mood now she knows her son's on his way home."

Lawrence had been about to move off, but stopped when he heard this. "He is? That's marvelous news! Christ knows I think we're going to be needing bits of good news before too long."

As the car pulled away, Sharon asked him what he meant. "I thought we were winning now."

Making a noise in the back of his throat which could have been interpreted in any number of ways, Lawrence crunched another gear into place and didn't say a word until they turned onto the road which would lead them once more toward the Solent. In fact, he didn't speak again until he pulled over in what was becoming their usual spot. Getting out of the car, he hurried around to hold open Sharon's door before taking off his hat and clutching it to his chest.

"Please accept my apologies. I've been unforgivably rude."

"I don't think I'd call being quiet, rude, Lawrence," she assured him. "Was it something I said?"

Despite feeling quite comfortable in the policeman's presence now, Sharon couldn't help but feel a little awkward that afternoon, and it took her a few moments to realize the cause. They didn't have their doggy chaperone. Her mind flicked to Stan's face, with a bout of guilt hitting her once more at the way she'd left him. There had to be a way she could get back in touch. Offer him some reassurance, without going into details?

Lawrence had been very particular about her not doing anything of the sort, essentially, not giving in to guilt. It was getting harder and harder, though, as the two of them had been getting very close before her moonlight flit, and the distance and potential harm she could come to hadn't done anything to diminish her feelings for him.

"Could you slow down a little, please?" she asked. "My legs are shorter than yours."

"Oh, sorry," he told her, matching actions to words. "Look, it isn't anything you've said, or done," he hastened to add. "We, the police, had a briefing the other day. I can't go into details, but it's to do with what's happening around the area and what the end result of all the activity will likely entail. I suppose you could say I'm feeling guilty."

Hopping over a large fallen branch, Lawrence held Sharon's hand as she, a little more gingerly, stepped over. "What on earth do you have to feel guilty about?" she asked.

With his free hand, he slapped his ear. "Because of this."

Sharon understood what he meant straight away and promptly slapped him hard on the shoulder with her free hand. "You're a silly sausage! You know that." Upon seeing the slightly shocked expression upon his face, she promptly went on, "I'm sure Mary at least has already had this conversation with you." At seeing the tips of his ears redden, she knew she was on the right track. "You've absolutely nothing to feel guilty about. It's not your fault you're deaf in one ear, and from what the girls have told me, you do a wonderful job! Yes, I know what you're talking about, about what's going to happen, and there's nothing directly either one of us can do about it.

Except we are, aren't we? That's what all this malarkey's about, so please, get all those thoughts out of your head."

Lawrence regarded the confident young lady by his side. "You're no country bumpkin, are you," he told her and was promptly rewarded with another slap on the arm. "Ouch! What was that one for?"

"For only just coming to that conclusion!" she told him, a smug look on her face. "Now, are you finally going to tell me why we're here? There's no Bobby, so we can't be pretending to take him for a walk."

Lawrence brought them to a stop beneath a large oak tree, glanced around to make certain they weren't being watched and reached into his inside pocket. "We got a reply," he told her, brandishing a rather battered-looking envelope.

Sharon's eyes opened wide. Taking the nondescript envelope from his unprotesting hand, she turned it over and over before remarking, "That was quick."

He shrugged. "I can only say that there are ways to speed up the post, given the right circumstances, and these are those."

"Hmm, I wouldn't tell Ruth about this," she advised. "Isn't her son a POW?"

Nodding, Lawrence took the envelope back. "Good point."

"Forgive me for asking, but why did you bring me all the way out here to show me this? Surely we could have done this back at the house. Or, well, anywhere else."

"True, true," he agreed. "Except for the fact that the powers-that-be wanted to see if anything happened, if we were seen opening this, around here." He swept his arm around to encompass the waterfront where they'd stopped off. "There are other *people*," Sharon couldn't help but notice the emphasis he put on the word, "who've been watching over us and, like me, they know we're being watched, and this is the most likely place we could be observed."

Sharon couldn't help it. She gripped Lawrence's arm tightly as her head flicked back and forth, trying to see if they were being spied upon. Something cracked in the forest behind them, and there was a splashing noise from the river, both of which made her jump.

Lawrence placed a soothing hand over hers. "Ssh, I'm sure there's nothing to worry about. It's probably only a squirrel and some fish, or bird."

Taking a few deep breaths, Sharon agreed, "Not even a country bumpkin now, eh?"

"You're allowed to be a little on edge," he told her. "Look at what you're doing, after all. Anyway, come on. There's a nice fallen tree trunk over there. Let's sit down, and you can read what it says."

"Really?" Sharon's voice rose a few octaves. "I didn't think I'd be allowed to."

As they strolled over toward the trunk, Lawrence said, "I admit, I had to fight to get them to let you read it, but when I pointed out it'd help when you're writing out a reply, they saw sense, and it's not often you can say that about the higher-ups!" he added, getting the hoped-for laugh out of his companion.

Whilst Sharon slowly read through the letter, Lawrence watched her face for any reaction. Apart from slightly pursed lips, he was impressed at how calm she kept.

"Rather an arrogant lot, aren't they," she commented once she'd finished, causing Lawrence to burst out with laughter.

"Sorry," he told her once he'd got back under control, "but that wasn't what I was expecting to hear."

"Bloody master race, my foot!" Sharon muttered, getting to her feet and deliberately kicking a stone into the river. Turning around, she set her hands upon her hips. "Come on, let's go back to Mavis's. I think we need to reply to that," she pointed at the letter in Lawrence's fingers, "right away. If all that," she gestured behind her, where more huge concrete caissons of varying guises were taking shape, "is going to help Hitler pay for starting this war, anything we can do to help will be worth it. Nobody tries to use my Nanny Ada!"

Both were so set on their course of action neither's head turned when there was a small bark from down the riverbank and a dachshund trotted into view.

Chapter Twenty-Four

Betty decided that worrying they'd fall out of the sky due to Doris pushing the little Anson's engines to their limits (and probably a little past it) so they'd get back to Hamble as quickly as possible was pointless. Trying to hold a worthwhile conversation with Mary in the increased racket inside the fuselage was just as impossible, so she took out the letter she'd stashed in her pocket that morning. She'd been dying to read it ever since it landed on her hall mat, and her frustration at being unable to know what it said was just about at its limit. The inside of a noisy aircraft hardly matched the romantic location of lying under a tree in her garden as she'd envisaged. Still, if she didn't read it now, heaven knows when she'd get the next opportunity. She was certain Penny would understand if she took a few minutes off from worrying about her.

Casting a quick glance over the aisle assured her that Mary appeared to be staring out the window. Leaving her to whatever thoughts were occupying her, Betty took in the cream envelope, made of much better paper than anything available in Britain at the time, a simple reminder of the gulf there still was between what was possible for the two allies with war raging all around.

Carefully, Betty opened the letter and held the two pieces of crisp white paper it contained up to her nose, imagining she could smell the scent of the free air it was infused with. The two had talked about going to live together in the United States once they were married and the war was won. Suppressing the urge to sigh, this still seemed a long time off, despite how much more favorable things appeared than even a year ago. With one final glance at her companion to make certain she still had a semblance of privacy, she smoothed the pages on her knees. Looking down, she smiled as the letters and words jiggled around in time to the movements of the aircraft. Despite the difficulty, it now seemed the right place to read it.

My dearest Betty,

As always, I shall start by telling you how much I love you and that I bless the day you came into my life. Clark Gable's loss was my gain—don't think I didn't see him eyeing you up! Okay, maybe I didn't, but you were the most beautiful gal at that dance and I knew, there and then, I'd do anything to make you mine. I know we didn't have a normal courtship, but perhaps someday most relationships will start with a telephone call, though ours was more through necessity than anything else. I don't know about you, my darling, but I believe I got to know you all the better through all that time we spent talking before we were finally able to meet up properly.

So, where am I with my little scheme to wangle my way back to Blighty and your wonderful self? Not much further, I'm afraid to say. If there's one thing which is common in the armed forces of all countries, it's that nothing gets done in a hurry, when it can be made to wait; even in wartime. I keep bugging them—sorry, annoying them—but it doesn't seem to have helped. I guess I'll have to try being sneaky. What do you reckon? It's worth a try.

My folks send a humdinger of a hello to you and everyone in the Mystery Club. I'd already told them all about you in my letters before I got sent back, of course. Well, since then, I've taken to regaling them with stories about what you and the girls have wound up getting involved with. They seem to think you're all some kind of female Sherlock Holmes! I haven't dared tell them about what you used to do, not that I'm ashamed, you know that, but you should be the one to decide whether they should know or not. Personally, I think they'd be even prouder to have you in the family, if they knew. Wasn't there a film with David Niven, called Raffles? They'd want Hollywood to remake it, with you as the lead. Actually, that'd be some kind of wonderful!

How's life treating you? I can't help but worry though I know you told me not to, but I can't help it. Here I am, thousands of miles away, all safe and sound with no worries, the worst that can happen would be my steak and eggs turning up cold. I remember plenty of Brits who'd love even that right now, whereas we'd send it back without thinking. What a world, eh!

"What are you reading?"

"Hmm? Pardon?" Betty muttered, her concentration unexpectedly broken. Mary was watching her, the expression upon her face wouldn't have been amiss on an eagle as it stalked its prey.

"The letter," Mary nodded toward the missive in Betty's hand. "Who's it from?"

Reining in her annoyance at being disturbed, especially as it had taken this long to actually begin reading the thing, Betty carefully folded the pages before tucking them back into her pocket. Her friend didn't know it, of course, but the letters from Frank were her way of shutting out the war, albeit temporarily, and the spell had been broken. As she was now committed to attempting to hold a conversation over the drone of the engines, she knew there was no point in trying to recapture the moment once they were done. Still, it'd be very nice to lose herself in it again later, once she'd satisfied herself that Penny was all right.

She leant across the aisle and raised her voice. "It's from my Frank!"

Contrary to what she expected, half-heard enquires on what he was doing and the like, Mary instead slumped back into her seat, a look of thunder upon her face. It was only because she could read lips pretty well, a useful tool she'd picked up in her previous career as one of the country's best fences of stolen jewelry, that she knew what her friend had said.

"Lucky sod. Must be nice to have a man you can trust."

From the cockpit, Doris waved a hand to get their attention. Looking out the window, she saw they were indeed turning onto the approach path for RAF Hamble. She rolled up her sleeve and glanced at her watch. Just as she began to shake her head in disbelief at how quickly Doris had got them back home, the port engine began to cough, which broke Mary out of her mood.

"What was that?" she asked, her head turning this way and that.

"Strap in!" Betty told her. "We're coming in to land and I don't think we've much juice left!"

"Bugger!" Mary swore, though she did as she was bid, and as did Betty herself.

Leaning into the aisle as much as she could, Betty heard the starboard engine also begin to cough. At the same time, the port one gave out one final belch of smoke before it died, leaving the propeller to slow to a windmill as it cut through the air. Sitting back and gripping the seat all the tighter, she felt Doris correct for the lack of power on one side.

"You can do it, Doris," Betty coaxed her friend. "Don't let me die a few hundred yards from home!" she added, involuntarily ducking her head as a Mosquito recklessly flashed over the top of the fuselage before landing ahead of them.

Up front, Doris swore as she fought to stabilize the already underpowered Anson, before the view settled down and she brought the plane in to land slap-bang on the rogue Mosquito's tail.

****

It had turned into rush hour at Piccadilly Circus, Jane mused, shaking her head in despair and anger. She nipped back into her office, grabbed her hat, and jammed it on her head before slamming the ops hut door shut behind her and running over in the direction of the flight line hut where the Mosquito, which had nearly wiped out the Anson carrying her friends, was taxiing up. She'd had no need of hearing the call over the radio to know who was crewing it and, circumstances notwithstanding, she was going to chew the pilot out! When she'd phoned him, he'd told her he was on the way, only she hadn't expected such an entrance. Mind you, considering what she'd had to tell him, she might have suspected he wouldn't be catching the train. Still, some antics are unforgiveable.

As soon as the ground crew had chocked the light bomber's wheels and the propellers had spun to a halt, Jane was waiting for the crew as the first pair of legs appeared from the hatch below the fuselage. She barely had enough patience to let the two straighten up.

"What the flaming hell did you think you were doing?" adding, before either could formulate a reply, "You could have knocked my Anson out of the sky!" Jane held up a hand as the pilot opened his mouth. "Yes, I know how worried you are, as are we all. Penny's fine," she told him. "I spoke again with the hospital five minutes before you landed. They're keeping her in overnight." Another hand signal. "Yes, I know you couldn't have known that, but there's no excuse for that stunt."

Any further talk was deemed temporarily impossible as the Anson being discussed rapidly—or as rapidly as it was possible to do on just one engine—approached their location. Looking as if they were about to step into the middle of a minefield, the ground crew hurried forward as Doris brought the plane to a stop, bare feet behind the Mosquito, whereupon the final engine gave a last cough and ground to a halt as the fuel supply ran out.

Before her passengers had even had the chance to unbuckle themselves, Doris, obviously forsaking the post-flight checks, could be seen flinging open the fuselage door, eyes flaming and fixed upon the Mosquito pilot.

"Alsop!"

Before anyone could do anything, Doris jumped down and sprinted over to where Penny's husband Tom was standing, a mixture of sheepishness and shock upon his face from the chewing out Jane had been in the middle of giving him. His navigator and friend, Stan, had sidled off to the side, hoping to stay out of the firing line.

Tom opened his mouth, and that was when Doris drew back her arm, leapt into the air, and punched him on the nose with all the force at her command.

"Come on!" she yelled, leaning down to where he sat upon the concrete, blood streaming from his nose. "There's one each for Mary and Betty to follow!" So saying she actually grabbed him by the lapels of his flying suit and tried to haul him to his feet.

Jane stepped between them, trying to force Doris's fingers loose. "That's enough, Doris," she told her, trying her best soothing voice and then, when both failed to soothe their irate Yank, turned to Stan for help. This was pointless as the man was nearly wetting himself with laughter. The situation was saved by the appearance of Mary and Betty, who sauntered up, their lack of haste patently declaring whose side they were on.

"Need a hand?" Mary asked, though not moving as if to help.

Jane gritted her teeth. "If you both can spare it, yes, please."

Stepping forward, each girl took hold of one of Doris's hands, though by this time the adrenaline burst had run out and they had little trouble with releasing her hold. Jane didn't say anything when Betty *accidently* trod hard on one of Tom's hands as he tried to steady himself.

When he finally got to his feet, Jane stood right next to him and told him, in a voice that brooked no rebuke, "Do not make the mistake of thinking you're the only one who's concerned about Penny and, taking into account your past behavior toward her, you should count yourself lucky to have got off the hook with only Doris punching you. I haven't finished," she told him, when

Tom went to speak. "There will be no, I repeat, *no* comeback from you against Doris. No one here saw anything! If you don't believe me, then take a look around," she added, sweeping her arm around which showed the ground crew all had their backs to them. "You may speak now."

Having got himself under a modicum of control, Stan held out a hand and hauled his friend to his feet. "Hell of a punch, Boss!" he added, handing Tom a slightly clean handkerchief.

Pinching the bridge of his nose, which made him wince, Tom held the cloth to his nose. Firstly, he turned to address Doris. The girl herself looked as if she was totally drained, the events of the day finally catching up with her. He held out his free hand which, after a moment's hesitation, she took. "Doris, I'm sorry. That was an idiotic thing to do. Are we okay?"

"So long as you don't hurt my friend," Doris informed him, getting a nod in reply.

He then turned to address Jane, still holding out his hand. "Jane, I'm very, very sorry too. I wasn't thinking, with that landing, and I can't apologize enough to you and the girls."

Deciding the man had suffered enough for one day, Jane accepted his hand. "Let's leave things as they are, shall we? By the way, how did you wrangle using a Mosquito to come down?"

"The boss told engineering she needed a test flight," Stan announced, still with a huge grin on his face.

Betty actually laughed. "I'd love to hear you explain this one when you get back!"

Tom took the handkerchief away from his nose, dabbed his nostrils and then, upon finding he was still bleeding slightly, reapplied it. "Let me worry about that," he replied, before turning to say to Jane, "Penny's really going to be all right?"

Jane laid a hand upon the man's arm and nodded. "Honestly, she is. I really did finish speaking to the hospital about five minutes ago, and they're only keeping her in overnight to make sure nothing crops up. She's got some cuts, her fair share of bruises, and the odd minor burn, but," she quickly added, as Tom began to go white, "considering what happened, she got off lightly."

"Christ," Tom shook his head. "It's like she's half-cat! How many more lives can she go through?"

Chapter Twenty-Five

The group had reached the steps to the ops hut when Lawrence and Sharon hove into view, pulling up next to the hut. Hurrying around to do the gentlemanly thing and pulling open the passenger door for Sharon to get out, he studied the group.

To one side he was surprised to see Wing Commander Alsop, and even more surprised to see the state of his nose and what appeared to be the beginnings of a beautiful pair of black eyes. Standing next to him was Stan Atkins. Behind him, a gasp of indrawn breath told him Sharon had spotted him at the same time. Doris was on the far side of Jane and, unless he was much mistaken, Betty and Mary each had a good grip on her arms. The American herself seemed to be wringing her right hand. Well, that explained the nose. At seeing Lawrence turning up with Sharon, Mary came to a stop, causing her friends to stumble and nearly fall over.

Quickly, as he could see now what Sharon had been talking about in the way Mary was glaring at him, he asked Jane, "Anything I need to know about?"

"Tom?" Jane asked, a foot on the first step.

Though he was obviously in pain, Tom replied, "Nothing I know of. Good to see you, Inspector."

The two RAF chaps followed Jane up the steps and into the hut.

At the same time, Betty and Doris prodded Mary

222

toward where Lawrence was standing, a look of apprehension on his face. "Go on. Talk with him. Now!"

Sharon pushed him. "What they said!"

Skirting warily past Mary without greeting her as usual, Sharon skipped up the steps, shortly joined by Betty and Doris. Inside, they found Jane cleaning up Tom's face, with Stan providing unhelpful suggestions like, "It's no use straightening his nose. It matches his bent personality now."

"Very bloody fun...oww!" Tom howled as Jane unexpectedly cracked his nose back into place.

"Should have done that first," she muttered, handing him the handkerchief again. "Here, in case it begins bleeding again."

"Thanks...I think," he told her, once more dabbing at his nostrils, but no more blood seemed willing to flow.

At seeing Sharon and with no Lawrence around to interfere, the flight sergeant left his friend's side and cautiously approached the young lady he'd begun imagining spending the rest of his life with. Seeing her for the first time since her moonlight flit, everything he'd planned upon telling her immediately went out of his head. This wasn't unusual, as he'd never been able to figure out exactly what such a beautiful girl, with her long tresses of blonde hair now down past the small of her back, could see in someone so ordinary as himself. As ever, when he couldn't think of what to say, Sharon came to the rescue. All the same, considering how they had—or had not—parted, what she did next took his breath away; in more ways than one.

"Stan!" she cried, her voice breathless and as sweet to his ears as always, before throwing her arms around him.

After a few moments, she let him go, though only to immediately take hold of his right hand. When he looked up, it was to find she had tears in her eyes. Instinctively, he reached into his pocket, only to find he'd already loaned out his handkerchief. So instead, slowly, carefully, in case he'd misread the signs, he reached up to lovingly wipe away the first tear that had leaked from her eye. When she leaned into his rough hand, he felt his heart leap.

With his other hand, he gently cupped the other side of her face and asked the simple question, the only question he needed the answer to, "Why?"

Instead of replying with mere words, Sharon took his hands in hers and crushed her lips to his, conveying far more in the few moments they were as one than anything in the Oxford English Dictionary could define. Only when someone, neither was sure who, pointedly coughed, did they break apart.

Sharon looked around. "I know this is strange, but can we use your office for a moment, please, Jane?"

After briefly thinking over the request, Jane nodded. As Sharon took a slightly shell-shocked Stan's hand and led him away, Jane told them, "Leave the door open!"

Once inside, with the door half open, Sharon immediately told Stan, gripping his hand tighter than ever, "I'm sorry! I am so, so sorry, Stan."

Stan leant back against Jane's desk and replied, in a voice his squadron mates would have made fun of him for using, "It's all right. Everything will be okay. We're here together, and right now, that's all that matters."

Without warning, Sharon fell against him, her forehead thudding against his shoulder, though instead of a squeal of pain, she merely shook her head, or attempted to. "It's not all right! Look at what I did, how I left you!"

Stan plucked up his courage and stroked her hair, something he'd been wanting to do ever since this beautiful girl had agreed to step out with him. Truth be told, when she'd left, he'd first thought it had only been a bit longer in happening than he'd expected, but then Tom had put him right, over a few drinks. Only with the way things had been left, he was unable to do anything about it. It had nearly driven him mad and, though he hated to admit it, could have cost them both their lives on an operation or two.

Now, with her back in his arms, everything seemed right with the world again. The doubts plaguing him ever since they'd begun seeing each other, doubts which had only escalated because of recent events, were whisked away. If the world ended right at that minute, he couldn't have been any happier.

"None of that matters." He took a deep breath and, with all his newly found confidence on how he felt, spoke the words he'd never thought he would: "My love."

His choice of words pierced whatever was going through Sharon's mind, as her head jerked up so abruptly, Stan barely had the time to move his chin out of the way.

"What did you call me?" she asked. Her words were uttered so softly, it was as if they were wrapped in silk.

"None of why you did what you did matters. You, us, we," he stumbled over his words, "this, proves it. Oh, and yes, I do love you."

Sharon ignored the happy tears now coursing down her face. "I still can't tell you why I'm here, Stan. I can't tell you anything more than what you've guessed." She looked up into his eyes and told him, "And I love you too."

After a quick kiss, Stan pulled back, hastily informing his disappointed girl, "Well, I'm guessing it's something important and that it's something only you can do." He waited until she nodded before saying, "In that case, I won't pry any further. I ask only two things—make sure you take good care of yourself."

She rewarded him with another kiss. "And?"

"And make certain the inspector watches out for you. Like I said, I don't know exactly what you're up to, but I do know he's a big part of it."

"He will," was all Sharon said before she proceeded to try to glue their lips together.

After a few minutes, Jane shouted out, "Hey! Open that door a little wider and feel free to come up for air!"

****

"Mary!" Lawrence yelled, and then, when she showed no signs of halting, even louder, "Mary! Will you bloody well stop a second?"

Halfway around the ops huts for the third time, two things occurred to him. First, Mary was striding around for its own sake—she had no destination in mind. And secondly, if he simply perched on the steps, he could save himself a lot of effort. So, when his errant girlfriend continued along the same route for a fourth time, that was exactly what he did. When she next appeared around the corner of the building, he got to his feet and planted himself right in her way, and when she went to step to one side and then the other, he merely made sure he matched her motion. Eventually, she gave in and slumped down on the steps.

Somewhat warily, Lawrence sat down next to her. She promptly shuffled along to leave a gap between them, whereupon the policeman did the same until, inevitably, she found herself up against the handrail.

"Are you ready to talk?" he asked. "Because I really don't think I've done anything worthy of this treatment, but until we actually talk, then we can't fix this. I don't know about you," he steeled his nerves, nudged her lightly with his shoulder and, smiling, added, "but you're way too important to me to want to lose. So, please, talk to me?"

Lawrence didn't need to put on his detective hat to know that from the way Mary crossed her arms and legs, she was in a belligerent mood. He quickly decided it would be best to treat this situation as if he were interviewing a female victim of an assault. He'd listened to what Sharon had said to him in the car on their way back from the Solent. She'd been adamant that he needed to talk with Mary as soon as he could, before it was too late, which was why they'd agreed to putting off writing the letter and to come along to Hamble instead. They both knew nothing was going on between them, other than a blossoming and unlikely friendship, but all Mary could see was the pair of them spending a lot of time together, time which Mary would normally have expected him to spend with her. With their work consuming a considerable amount of their days for both of them, he now saw how Mary could have misconstrued appearances. Yes, she knew why Sharon was there and what they were doing, but human nature being what it is…

Without looking at him, Mary snapped, "Is there anything going on between you and Sharon?"

Lawrence fought hard to stop an immediate reply from leaving his lips, even though he knew the lack of one could be detrimental to his case. He opened his mouth to speak, just as Mary's head whipped around. "Other than the job we're doing, which you know about, no."

"But you spend so much time together!" Mary accused.

Fighting back his immediate thought that they didn't spend that much time together—he knew this would help no one—Lawrence again took a moment, eventually saying, "And it's all a façade. I'm sorry, very sorry, for not fully explaining to you what happens when we're out, and I realize that's a mistake. I totally understand how you'd come to believe as you're saying."

"So what does happen when you're with her?" Mary asked. At least she didn't snap this time.

Cautiously, encouraged by the more normal tone in her voice and that she'd uncrossed her arms, Lawrence reached out for and took hold of, very gently, her nearest hand. When she didn't pull it away, he gave her a shy smile. "Some of this," he began and then had to quickly keep hold of her hand as she went to snatch it away, "but with none of the love I have for you!" he quickly assured her, happy when he felt her relax. "We're playing the part of a couple, but that's all it is, an act." He let out a soft chuckle. "I'm not sure I'd believe us, if I saw us."

"That's…that's all it is, an act?" Mary asked, needing to hear him say the words again, as she turned her body so their knees were touching.

Hoping he was reading the situation right, Lawrence leaned his head toward her and was overjoyed to find Mary mirroring his action, neither stopping until they touched. "It's all an act. Do you believe me?"

After barely a few moments, and he couldn't blame her for taking some thinking time, Mary kissed him quickly on the cheek. He'd take it. "Yes, yes, I believe you. Have I been silly?" she then asked, turning her head ever so slightly down, slightly embarrassed for asking.

Lawrence raised her chin with one gentle finger, kissing the end of a nose he considered adorable. "Not at all. I'd been so wrapped up in this case that I hadn't realized what things looked like. Sharon pointed this out to me."

Mary looked a little sheepish. "I think that's what my friends have been trying to get through to me, too. I think I've a few people I need to apologize to."

"About bloody time!" Doris's announcement above them startled the pair so much they nearly fell off the steps.

"Flaming hell, Doris!" Lawrence said, as Doris's unexpected appearance had caused the two of them to jump apart. "How long have you been there?"

"And what did you hear?" Mary added.

Without waiting for an invite, Doris sat down between them and planted her elbows on her knees so she could rest her chin upon her palms. "Long enough. If you really want to apologize, you can get in the fish 'n' chips tonight."

Tom appeared above them, with Jane, Betty, Sharon and Stan beside him.

"I don't know what's just happened, and frankly, I don't want to. All I want is to get to the hospital and see how Penny is." He came down the steps and looked pointedly at Lawrence's car.

"Sorry." Lawrence shook his head. "I need to get

back to the office."

Jane tapped him on the shoulder. "You can use my Jeep."

"Yes!" Doris crowed. "I'll drive. Keys in the normal place, Jane?" she asked, bounding to her feet.

Not many people got to drive Jane's beloved Willys Jeep, a kind of present from an American she'd been seeing who'd been killed the previous year. However, she couldn't deny Tom wanting to see his wife, and it was the easiest answer to his transport problems. After a moment or two, she came to her decision.

"Very well, Doris, you can take her. Don't forget to give Penny my love and tell her I'll be phoning the ward in the morning. Now…" She turned to address everyone else whilst Doris nipped into Jane's office. "There's no point in everyone going, but…" She raised her voice to drown out the protests she knew were about to break over her. "As I know it's pointless to say that, Mary, Betty, Sharon, do you want to go?" Sharon shook her head, whilst Mary and Betty both jumped to their feet and took off without another word, Tom close behind, as Doris ran around the back of the ops hut to where Jane kept her Jeep.

"Poor sod," Jane muttered and then, at the quizzical look she got at this from Stan, informed him, "I'm a quick driver. Doris is a quicker one! I hope he's got a good stomach."

"He flies a Mosquito," Stan felt the need to point out.

"By the time Doris has got to Southampton, he's going to think going on a raid to Berlin is a milk run!"

Chapter Twenty-Six

"Never. Again," Tom declared as Doris brought the Jeep, tires screaming, into a parking spot at the hospital.

"We did warn you to hold on," Betty reminded the pilot as she helped Mary to unlock her fingers from the back of the passenger seat and the side of the vehicle.

Tom was holding onto the bonnet as he struggled to get his shaking legs under control. "I thought you were joking!"

Doris had hopped out from behind the wheel and clapped him on the back. "About what?"

He turned his head to the side and slapped his left leg until he had it under control. "You, Doris Winter…"

"Johnson, Doris Johnson," she reminded him, with a wide grin.

Tom waved her words away. "Whatever you're called, you're a menace!"

"Thank you!" Doris replied.

"That," he began, finally having managed to straighten up, "was not a compliment. Put you behind the wheel, and you're more dangerous than a squadron of Messerschmitts!"

"In that case, I thank you again and half-apologize for the punch."

Cautiously, he rubbed the end of his nose, immediately removing his finger before touching the skin around his eyes, with the same result. Already a pair

231

of black eyes were beginning to bloom.

"Only half?" Most of the color had come back to his face by now, and he managed a small smile.

Doris leaned in and nudged him none too gently in the ribs. "You did deserve it for nearly killing us," she pointed out. "Take it or leave it."

"I'd take it," Mary advised. "It's the best you deserve."

At seeing Betty nod, Tom agreed. "Fair enough. Now, as we got here in one piece…"

"Be careful what you say," Doris interrupted. "Don't forget, I'll be driving you back."

"…thanks to Doris's skill behind the wheel," Tom continued without missing a beat, "let's find where Penny is. I doubt the doctors will be very keen on visitors at this time of the evening, so let's be on our best behavior."

Betty linked her arm through the pilot's and steered the group toward the entrance. "Hey, speak for yourself. We all look very presentable." The girls had quickly changed out of their flying suits and into their uniforms before leaving Hamble—Betty's idea. "Whereas you, Wing Commander dear, look like you've gone ten rounds with Joe Louis!"

After seemingly being sent from pillar to post, the group eventually managed to track down the ward where Penny was supposed to have been admitted. Tom had insisted upon speaking to the Ward sister, quite rightly pointing out that he was her husband. Even Doris couldn't argue with this logic, not that she hadn't tried and was now standing between her friends, obviously frustrated.

"That's her!" Tom said, jabbing a finger at the list

the sister was holding. "Second Officer Penny Alsop of the Air Transport Auxiliary!"

The sister sounded and looked to be in her seventies, probably brought back into service for the duration of the war. Though she'd once undoubtedly been very efficient, and probably a bit of a looker in her day now, she was nearly bent double from age and, doubtless, a lifetime of hard work. Strangely, she sported a set of pince-nez perched upon her nose. It was obvious to all that she wanted to deny entrance to her ward, as they were outside of visiting hours. However, there was still nothing like the allure of a good uniform and, his current resemblance to a Giant Panda aside, Tom did carry off the RAF uniform very well.

"Well, it is highly irregular..."

Tom actually reached out and took the lady's free hand, brought it to his lips, and pressed a gentle kiss to its back. "Please. I'd...we'd be awfully grateful. We wouldn't take up much of your valuable time, only she *is* my wife and these ladies' best friend. We only want to say hello and satisfy ourselves that she's going to be fine."

"She is going to be all right, isn't she?" Betty had to ask.

The sister flapped a hand in Betty's general direction and then, with visible effort, straightened up and treated her to an intense stare, the kind she'd indubitably used upon all the nurses who'd been under her care. "Of course she is!" she told them, before adding in a kinder tone, "She's been a very lucky girl, mind. Not many come out of a plane crash with barely a scratch, relatively speaking, you know."

"I know," Tom muttered, remembering and feeling

his own injuries twinge.

"All being well, unless something turns up overnight, she should be all right to come out tomorrow."

"So, we can go in?" Tom asked.

The little sister stepped aside to allow the group to pass. "Five minutes only. I'll be watching the clock."

"Tom! What are you doing here? And you three! How?"

Her husband was lingering toward the rear of the group, so Doris gave him a helpful push forward. "We used the charm of the Brylcreem boys, or at least, one of them."

It was obvious to all that Tom was acutely aware of what had occurred the last time his wife had been in hospital and was singly ill at ease; it hadn't been his proudest moment and had been the source of all the awkwardness and tension between the pair from then until only recently. He'd had no excuse for storming out on your wife, who'd not only been wounded by enemy fire but as a consequence had lost the baby she'd been carrying.

His nerves were there for all to see as he stood awkwardly next to her bed, reaching out a hand and pulling it back a couple of times before finally taking one of Penny's in his slightly sweaty one. Everyone could also hear it in his voice as he told her, "Penny I'm…I'm so happy to see you. When Jane phoned and told me what happened…"

Seeing he'd temporarily lost the power of speech, her three friends filled the gap, all secretly pleased the pilot hadn't recoiled at the facial injuries his wife had suffered. None appeared to be disfiguring, but nevertheless, she wasn't looking her normal beautiful self. "Jane sends her love," Betty told Penny, leaning in and finding an uncut, unscratched spot on her left cheek for a brief kiss, "only there wasn't enough room in her Jeep and she said she'd be checking in with the hospital tomorrow morning, making sure you can escape."

By the time both Doris and Mary had also greeted their friend, Tom had recovered his voice. Perching on the bed beside his wife while her friends stood on the opposite side, he took in her appearance. Her left arm had bandages both below and above the elbow, whilst her right also sported one. Her face was bruised and puffy in places, though her hair seemed to have survived intact.

Noticing his glances, she gave his hand a quick squeeze and hurried to fill him in and reassure her friends too. "I know I look a bit like a mummy, but it's all superficial, I've been told. These"—she looked at the arm bandages—"cover a few minor burns and a couple of cuts they had to stitch. I've a few more on my legs, but that's it."

Tom let out a whistle. "I can't believe you've got off so lightly. Any concussion?"

She shook her head. "No. Even the headache I had has mostly gone. Speaking of which, what happened to you?" she asked, pointing at his somewhat battered face.

"That was me," Doris happily volunteered.

"Er, why?" Penny asked. "Did you deserve it?"

"Definitely," Tom quickly volunteered. "I was in such a hurry to land, I cut up Doris's Anson, quite badly."

Penny looked over at her friends, who all nodded. "So you punched him?"

"Quite right," Doris agreed.

"And I deserved no less," Tom reiterated.

Penny looked up at her husband. "I'd have done the same," to which Tom could only nod his head again in agreement.

"Someone was looking out for you, all right," Doris told her, breaking the silence which followed and, for once, being quite serious.

"Very true," Tom agreed. "Oh, bugger!" he said, spotting the sister hobbling their way. "Look, we're about to be chucked out, and I may be in trouble back at base. I told them I was just taking up my Mossie for a test flight," he explained, as Penny turned a quizzical look at him.

To his and everyone's surprise, Penny let out a burst of laughter, at which the sister speeded up.

"That's enough from you lot. You've had more than your five minutes, and now, before you disrupt my ward anymore, off you go," she told them, looking about as fierce as her age and size would allow.

Tom leant in to kiss his wife whilst everyone, except the sister, turned their heads to give them a semblance of privacy. "I'll see you soon, love, and come what may, I'll call you tomorrow. Hopefully you should be back at Betty's by then."

Her friends all said a hurried goodnight too, before they found themselves being ushered out of the ward.

"Hey! Who's driving?" Penny shouted after them.

Doris waved the Jeep's keys in the air. "Me!"

Penny's eyes widened and she yelled after them as the door to the ward opened, "I'll have them ready a bed next to me, Tom!" She was secretly pleased to see the color, not for the first time that day, drain from her husband's face.

****

"And none of the machinery's been touched? You're sure? They've only appeared in the area which is about to be dug up anyway, you say, and nothing appears to be missing either? That's what the foreman's told you, got it. Yes, yes, I agree, Jane, it's all very strange, and no, no reason comes to mind straight away to me either. None of the station guard saw or heard anything either? I'm sorry, but we won't be able to make it over for a while."

"What's happened at Hamble now, Boss?" Sergeant Terry Banks asked, taking off his glasses and wiping them on the sparkling clean handkerchief his wife always made sure he went off to work with. Looking at his watch, he commented, "It's barely half nine. A bit early for trouble, isn't it?"

Lawrence put down his pencil and took a long slurp from his now lukewarm tea, before replying to his colleague, "With that lot, nothing surprises me. Just a load of holes appeared overnight, where they're extending the runway. Tell me, Terry, before Penny, Mary, and especially Doris turned up, had you even heard of RAF Hamble?"

Terry nearly snorted his own tea out his nose. Wiping it with the same handkerchief, he replied, "Heard of, yes. Had any cause to deal with anyone from it? Definitely not. I bet Jane Howell rues the day that lot turned up."

"You know," Lawrence said after finishing his cup, "in one way, I expect so. We all like a quiet life, even if we don't actually say so. However, it's certainly made her job a lot more interesting than it must have been before."

"Interesting," Terry repeated. "An *interesting*

choice of words. I suppose if you consider kidnappings, shootings, and solving murder cases as interesting, it'd be the right word. Okay, I can see what you mean, but isn't it all a bit dangerous for a bunch of women?"

Lawrence admonished his sergeant with a wag of his finger. "Now, now, you should know better than to say that. You've only got to look at the work they do."

Looking suitably chastised, Terry put his cup down. "Point taken, and please don't tell any of them I ever intimated anything to the contrary. I've no wish to die just yet."

"Hey, I've only just sorted out things between Mary and me," Lawrence informed his sergeant, "so the last thing I want to do is to say or do something which could be misconstrued again."

"You do know that if you marry her, you're going to be in trouble every day, for the rest of your life?" Terry told him in a voice as pure as honey and twice as sweet.

Lawrence nearly replied straight away, only noticing the gleam in his sergeant's eye, telling him he was being made fun of, just in time. "Oh, very funny. Who says we're going to get married anyway?"

"These little gray cells are good for more than just rooting out criminals, you know."

"I had been wondering what they were for," Lawrence shot back.

"More than just a pretty face," Terry replied, waggling his thick glasses.

"Which it won't be if you don't change the subject," Lawrence shot back with a grin, so Terry knew he was only joking with him. "Anyway, two calls and we haven't even finished our first cups of tea!" Lawrence remarked.

"What is the world coming to," Terry replied, losing most of the biscuit he'd been dunking in his tea.

Noting this with a slightly self-satisfied smirk, Lawrence got to his feet. "And seeing as you took the last biscuit, I think you should go and take a nose around these holes Jane's just reported. It may be nothing, but people don't go digging holes, especially at night, for no reason. No, you mark my words, there's a lot more going on than we know at present. I'd bet good money on it. You know what those girls are like when there's a mystery around. I'd rather clear it up before they get themselves into trouble."

Gathering up his own and Lawrence's cups to wash up before heading out, Terry checked. "Before I forget, Ruth really didn't have an idea who this cousin chap was up at the farm?"

Lawrence shook his head. "Hadn't seen nor heard of him before in her life, even from this Ambrose Foreman."

Five minutes later, Terry came back into the room and placed the now clean and dry cups back next to their kettle. He looked up at the Inspector. "Sorry, but I have to ask. How long do we keep that in-house? You're probably thinking the same. This could be a bolt some erk or Home Guard chap's lost. Maybe it's as simple as that?"

Lawrence shook his head. "Sorry, I should have told you. Walter, that's Doris's husband, he's in the Home Guard, has already checked, and no one is missing such a part. As for how long can we keep this between ourselves? Not for long, so let's try and clear it up quick. It may be nothing, but my copper's instinct is ringing its head off!" He stopped to pull on his coat and hat before carrying on.

Matching his boss, Terry asked, as they made for the door, "Where are you off to?"

"I'm going over to Hamble too. Firstly, there's that *other* matter I still can't tell you about, and yes, I am sorry about that. Then, I'm going to take a walk up to the farm, have a nose around myself."

Chapter Twenty-Seven

Having left Betty in charge at the ops hut, Jane drove her beloved Jeep to Southampton hospital to pick up Penny. Getting into work early, she'd received confirmation over the telephone at around half seven that morning that Penny would be ready for discharge by the time she arrived. The almost-whispered, "Please hurry!" from the nurse whom she'd spoken to had her laughing out loud, and the phone was rather forcibly banged down at the other end. Obviously Penny hadn't been a well-behaved patient!

Having made her way up to the ward her friends had visited the night before, Jane went to push the doors open, only to have to take a hasty step back as a wheelchair containing a one-legged teenage girl crashed its way through. Her eyes flicked up from the sight of the poor girl, and she froze when she saw the wheelchair's driver. Jane always prided herself upon remembering names, but this one's eluded her. It was the man's face she recalled, a face she'd only seen once and not under the happiest of circumstances.

"Well, well, Flight Captain Jane Howell!" he said, a wide grin coming to what she had to admit was a handsome face under a mop of black hair.

Had it always been handsome? She couldn't remember. What she did know, though, was that he was now leaning on the handlebars of the chair, regarding her expectantly. Jane rather suspected she was doing a fair impression of a fish out of water. Fortunately her blushes were saved when he introduced, or rather re-introduced himself.

"Doctor Simon McNichol?" he told her, prodding his chest, not noticing the girl below him turn her head around and glare up at him. "I fixed up your wrist, just before last Christmas."

Jane did recall that, and though the name still didn't ring any bells, the face was becoming clearer. As she'd only been to this hospital that once, she decided to go with logic. She held out her hand. "Of course! So sorry. How's life keeping you, Doctor?"

Taking her hand, he shook it warmly, treating her to a smile which actually threatened to make her toes curl for the first time since Frank had died. *Well, that was unexpected*, she thought. "Busy, as always," he replied, "though I expect you'd say the same. Oh, don't let it bother you that you didn't remember my name, I'm hardly memorable."

Jane felt her body relax slightly at these words. "If memory serves, I think your wife at least would disagree." She grinned before adding, "Though I definitely remember your face."

"I expect she would have," he replied somewhat cryptically, before straightening up. "However, I'll certainly take that!"

Before either could take the conversation further, the wheelchair's passenger banged the side with the crutch she'd been cradling on her lap. "I'm sorry to interrupt, but my mum's waiting for me."

Jane immediately took a step back, as the words registered with the doctor and he came all the way through the doors.

"Sorry, Enid, that was very rude of me. Bear with me a few more seconds." He looked directly at Jane once more. "If you go through, I believe the patient you've come to spring is sitting beside the nurse's station. Sister will be very glad to see the back of her!" he told her in a voice designed to carry. "I'll be back in a few minutes."

"I didn't know Penny was your patient," Jane said to his receding back.

"She's not," he replied. "But I was passing and heard your name and wanted to see you. I don't forget a face or a name!" he teased as he disappeared around a corner.

Slightly flummoxed, Jane shook her head and opened the door, a little more carefully this time, and still shaking her head, spotted a well-bandaged Penny. Waving, she hurried over as Penny heaved herself to her feet so as to greet her friend with a big hug. Jane pretended to ignore the wince of pain her friend couldn't keep hidden.

Holding her at arm's length, Jane shook her head in wonder. "How the hell did you get out of that crash and still look so good?"

This brought an obviously painful smile to Penny's face, and the girl's eyes ranged over her bandaged arms. "I know. Believe me, I know. I'm pretty battered and bruised, but everything will heal, I've been assured."

Jane lifted a hand up to Penny's face and, warily, touched a couple of the plasters on her forehead and neck. "Any of these going to end your days as an *IT Girl*?" she teased.

Penny batted the fingers away. "God, I hope so!"

Though her words were flippant, Jane could see

from her friend's eyes that she wasn't serious. Penny had made the transition from pre-war magazine cover girl, in a very tasteful fashion, of course, to serious Air Transport Auxiliary pilot seem effortless. Nevertheless, she'd always been a very beautiful young lady, too, and Jane wasn't naive enough to think the facial injuries she'd suffered wouldn't affect her self-confidence. Plus, this was the second time within a year that she'd been nearly killed in an incident involving a plane. Yes, she'd have to keep a very close eye on her.

"We'll see," was all Jane could think of to say.

Penny tapped her boss on the shoulder before easing herself back down into her seat, "Look at it this way, no more reporters or photographers hiding in the bushes!"

With no other seat available, Jane leant against the desk, smiling at the nurse behind the desk, who frowned up at her. "That was fun, wasn't it? You know, for a minute, I thought they were going to wet themselves!" The nurse swallowed the tea she'd been drinking the wrong way at hearing this, so Jane went around and slapped her on the back, before apologizing. "Sorry. Don't worry, my friend and I'll be out of here shortly."

"What's the hold-up?" Penny asked, looking around. "I've got my discharge papers, so what are we waiting for?"

Jane often wished she didn't blush so readily; this was one of those times. "Did you recognize the doctor who was pushing that poor girl through the doors just now?" she asked.

Penny nodded. "Poor Enid. She lost that leg when she tripped whilst out in the blackout a few weeks back. Fell under a passing lorry."

"Christ!" Jane shook her head.

"Neither of us could sleep last night, so we spent the night talking. When she found out I was a pilot, you should have seen her face! She totally transformed. I spent the rest of the night regaling her with our various adventures."

"You did censor them?" Jane asked, though with little hope.

Her friend's answering grin told her it was, indeed, a forlorn hope. "Why do you think the nurses are so keen to get me out of here?"

"And she still wants to be a pilot? Even after all she's been through and what you spun for her?"

Penny nodded her head as eagerly as a puppy wagged its tail. "Even more so!"

Jane couldn't help turning her head in the direction the girl had gone and musing, "A one-legged girl pilot."

This time, Penny rapped her friend much more sharply on the thigh, "Hey! A one-legged pilot. Less emphasis on the *girl* part, okay? I don't see why not. We've a few pilots in the same predicament in the ATA, we've both run into them. Besides, it gave her something to think about, to focus on."

Turning her attention back to Penny, Jane asked, "How old is she?"

"Just turned fifteen," Penny replied. "Why?"

"Did you find out where she lives?" Jane asked, ignoring the question.

Penny frowned again, but told her, "Just down the road from us, actually. Netley. Why?" she once more asked.

"Well, though I obviously hope this war is long over before Enid can take any part, I think we may be able to do something to stoke a fire under her ambitions. What do you say?"

Not needing a moment to put things together, Penny shot to her feet, her aches and pains forgotten, and turned to the nurse. "Hi! You must have heard us talking," she began, barely waiting for the acknowledging nod, "so, how about helping us?"

"If it gets you out of here sooner," the nurse said, with a smile which spoke of longsuffering, "what do you need?"

Penny raised her eyebrows at her companion. "I shall let my superior dig a hole."

Jane bowed her head slightly. "So very kind," she said before turning her attention upon the nurse, who now looked like she wished she'd not spoken. "I imagine you've young Enid's address somewhere on your desk…"

"I may…" the nurse reluctantly admitted, sensing she was being backed into a corner.

"How about if you close your eyes for a minute and we'll see if that miraculously gets copied into this notebook of mine?" Jane took out a notebook from her uniform top pocket and laid it upon the desk before the nurse.

Before either pilot could say or do anything else, and hoping to speed up their exit, the nurse didn't hesitate or close her eyes. Instead, she flipped through a few files, selected one, opened it and swiftly copied down an address onto Jane's notebook, pushing it back toward her as soon as she'd finished. "Now, will you please leave the ward?"

Jane flipped open to the page before saying, "But Doctor McNichol wanted to speak to me."

The nurse pointed at the door, heavily suggesting,

"He can speak to you just as easily on the other side."

Knowing she'd pushed her luck as far as it would go, Jane held up a bag. "It is okay if my friend changes into these clothes first? You can see she's still in her hospital gown."

"I was wondering about that," Penny commented.

By the time Penny had changed, with a bit of a hand to get into her uniform trousers (Jane thought it would help her moral to walk out in uniform) and to tie her shoes, and the two had made it through the doors, held open by the nurse, they didn't have to find anywhere to wait, as the doctor in question was waving at them as he came down the corridor.

"He seems friendly," Penny remarked.

"Before he gets here," Jane said, ignoring the comment, "what's happening with you? What's the follow-up?"

"This time?" Penny replied, deadpan.

"This time," Jane agreed.

Penny let out a deep sigh, a sure sign that, so far as she was concerned, it wasn't good news. "I'm grounded for two weeks, with instructions to go to our local hospital every day to get my bandages changed and examined."

"There, that wasn't so hard, was it?" Jane patted her friend's hand. They both knew it had been, and after moving the hand she'd had at Penny's back, they both also knew that the instructions were right—Jane had to replace her hand swiftly, as her friend had begun to sway without its support. "Well, it's just as well we don't have our own medical officer at the moment. He picked the right time to go on leave, so he won't have to put up with one of his favorite patients."

"Very funny," Penny barely had time to say before the doctor reached them.

Seeing how tired her friend was, and trying to ignore the flight of butterflies which had taken wing in her stomach, Jane didn't waste time. "So, what can I do for you? You asked me to wait."

Instead of speaking, the doctor reached into his coat pocket and pulled out a knotted handkerchief. Holding it in a palm, he held it out toward Jane.

"What's that?" she asked.

Without speaking, he simply pulled at an end and the knot unraveled. Jane could swear her eyes popped out on stalks and, for a few moments, exactly who was holding up who was up for discussion. She knew she'd lost it at the same time Penny and herself had ended up at Southampton hospital after their crash landing, only it wasn't quite clear in her mind where or when it had disappeared. This was all moot now as, there before her, looking as good as the day she'd first seen it, was the treasured present from her American boyfriend Colonel Frank Lowlan, who'd died the previous year. Her beloved gold watch.

****

Even as the words left Lawrence's mouth that fine Wednesday morning, Ruth was striding along the country lane leading up to Ambrose's farm. Never one who'd had the patience of a saint, she'd woken up that morning determined to try and get to the bottom of things. Not only did she consider the farmer to be a good friend, he was also her source of illicit butter! So, as soon as Walter made his appearance in the kitchen, she'd jumped to her feet, told him of her plan, and then before he'd been able to open his mouth to protest, she'd dragged him out into the early morning sunshine and made him follow her on her quest.

"Explain to me, again, what we're doing?" Walter asked for the third time, hoping he'd get an answer this time, toward Ruth's back. "I thought we had a newspaper to get out," he added, with a yawn

Barely stopping to pick up a stick to throw for Bobby, who was now back to wild health once more and enjoying this nice, unexpected walk, Ruth didn't turn around as she replied, "We're nearly done, you know that. We'll easily finish it off in time for going to print when we get back. It's not my fault it's been a slow news week."

"There's the government banning everyone from travelling abroad. We could have led with that," Walter suggested, as he bent to pick up and throw another stick for Bobby, who promptly disappeared into the undergrowth before returning with what was definitely not the same stick!

Both the humans looked incredulously at each other, whilst Bobby merely sat down before his mistress and laid his prize at her feet. Carefully, Walter took a step toward the waiting dog, making certain to reach over and give the expectant dog a quick fuss between the ears. "Good boy," he gently said, before asking, "Ruth, do you have a hanky on you?" He took out his own and accepted the one Ruth offered him. "Could you put Bobby on his leash, too?"

Edging around the non-stick, Ruth didn't argue, though Bobby wasn't impressed at this development and whined in protest. "I see where you're going, Walter. You stand guard, and I'll run back to the office and call up Lawrence."

Looking around, Walter did his best to assess his situation as Ruth hared off as quickly as she could back toward Hamble. The lane was lined on both sides by shoulder-high hedges, and the spot where he stood was right in the middle of a bend. Not a great tactical situation. If anyone wanted to jump him, there were too many avenues of approach that offered great cover. He'd have to be careful.

Putting the handkerchief away, as he'd decided against picking up what Bobby had brought them, Walter decided his best bet would be to simply stand still whilst keeping his ears pricked for any strange noises. The crow of a cockerel took him by surprise, making him jump. Wiping his brow, he looked down and wondered once again how a Lee-Enfield rifle had ended up in a hedge.

Chapter Twenty-Eight

Terry scratched his head for the umpteenth time since he'd arrived at RAF Hamble and nudged a clod of mud so it tumbled back down into the hole it had come out of. Straightening up, he stared around once more at the building site. Dotting the ground were various holes, the only thing seeming consistent about most was the depth, each around a foot deep. There were two, however, which were nearly perfect rectangles and both were considerably deeper than the others. At each of those two, there were unmistakable marks to indicate something heavy had been dragged out.

"Any thoughts, Terry?" Jane asked from where she stood slightly behind him as he knelt down to make a closer inspection of one of these.

"Aside from the obvious?" he asked, interrupted by Jane stretching and letting out an enormous yawn.

"Sorry, sorry. It's been a mad morning. I've only just got back from picking up Penny from the hospital."

"She's all right?" Terry enquired.

"She will be," Jane replied. "Anyway, back to the holes. I assume it's not moles?"

"No, but something's been taken out of these two," he remarked, "something heavy, and long." He observed Jane with a shrewd eye. "Say I asked you if Ruth Stone had shown you and, perhaps, talked about a certain…item…" he left the sentence unfinished, adding a questioning eyebrow for good measure.

Jane played along by not catching the policeman's eye when she replied, "I, well, my friends and I, that is, we do know all about the rifle bolt Ruth found and passed to your inspector. So shall we assume we both know the same things and stop pussyfooting around?"

Terry straightened up and turned a wide smile Jane's way. "I can see why you're such a good boss," he announced. "You and Lawrence are pretty much alike."

"For heaven's sake, don't say anything like that when Mary's around!"

"Strange. Lawrence said much the same thing at the office earlier," Terry replied.

Even though the girl in question was out on deliveries, Jane still checked briefly around before speaking further. "Silly girl got a bee in her bonnet about Sharon and Lawrence. There was—and is—nothing going on between them, other than all this…other malarkey," she ended with, raising an eyebrow at the policeman.

"Well, he hasn't told me anything about that," Terry revealed. "I admit to being curious. I wouldn't be a copper if I wasn't, so it's probably best if you don't let anything out of the bag, no matter how much I want to know."

"I understand," Jane replied.

Mollified, Terry straightened up and took in the two deep holes. "You know, if I were a suspicious man—and I am—I'd swear these holes would be the perfect size to contain boxes for rifles." At seeing his companion's raised eyebrow, he went on, "And if I had spare cash, I'd put money on them being Lee-Enfields."

Jane nodded. "I'd take some of that bet. So the

question is, who's been burying rifles on my airfield?"

"And, when were they buried?" Terry put in. "For all we know, these things could have been here for years."

"So why dig them up now?" Jane asked and then snapped her fingers as she answered her own question. "Of course! The extension."

"Bang on," Terry agreed. "I reckon we've taken someone by surprise. Whoever did this was in a hurry. They didn't even attempt to fill in any of the holes, nor try to cover their tracks, so to speak."

"Well, I can't believe it's going to be anyone local," Jane stated, peering around with a frown. The workmen she'd sent away whilst Terry looked around had taken her literally and were nowhere in sight. In fact, the only other person around was their foreman, and he was sat in the open cab of a grubby lorry, smoking and reading a newspaper. She made a mental note to tell him to go and drag his men back to work once she was finished here. Returning her attention to the policeman, she said, "I know pretty much everyone in this village, and I don't believe any of them would be involved in anything like this. Oh, yes, there's plenty of trade going on in black market food stuff, but nothing like this." Jane then remembered exactly to whom she was talking. Blushing, she coughed. "I'd, um, appreciate it if you'd turn a deaf ear on what I just happened to say, Terry…please?"

Terry appeared to be busy inspecting his fingernails when he answered, "Sorry, went a little deaf there. Didn't hear anything after you said you didn't believe any of the villagers would be involved in something like this, or something like that," he finished.

Breathing a sigh of relief, Jane joined him by the

hole. "Putting two and two together, do we know of any newcomers to the village? Specifically, ones who've acted in a suspicious manner?"

Terry offered her his arm and the two began to walk back toward the ops hut. As they passed the lorry, Jane rapped on the open door. Treating the startled man to her best frown, she suggested he go find his men and get them back to work. He was so surprised to be spoken to in such a forceful way, and by a woman at that, that he half-fell out of the cab and tried to put the newspaper on his head instead of his flat cap as he ran off in the direction of the mess. Of course, Jane thought with a shake of her head. Free tea!

"That was very impressive!" he told her, slamming the lorry door shut as they passed. "I wonder if it'd work on my boss?"

"I'd have thought Lawrence was a good man to have as a superior," Jane told him. "You've no complaints, have you?"

Terry shook his head, with a small laugh. "Certainly not. Merely thinking out loud," he assured her. Regarding her sideways for a minute, he said, "I assume we're both thinking along the same lines?"

Further conversation was rendered moot, as they were interrupted by a loud barking that got rapidly closer by the second. Breaking apart, the two hurriedly scanned the sky for any signs of approaching danger, both having recognized the sound of Bobby, their air-raid-warning good-luck charm. As they got amongst the airfield's buildings, they saw that most everyone else had stopped work and were also warily eyeing the sky. Some were reaching for discarded helmets or checking how far they were from the nearest slit-trench they could dive into.

"Can you see anything?" Terry asked, as they came up on the steps to Jane's domain.

Jane turned back to him. "It's clear blue up there, plus, I can't hear anything either."

Bobby himself came haring around the corner and, upon spotting Jane, turned in her direction. At reaching her feet, he promptly flopped onto his back, offering his stomach for tickling.

"I don't think he's barking about an air raid," Jane surmised, as the soppy dog was looking up at them expectantly and had stopped his barking. Whilst Terry bent down to give the dog what he wanted, Jane cupped her hands around her mouth and shouted as loudly as she could, "Back to work, everyone! No air raid! Pass it on!" Once she was satisfied that everyone was doing as she ordered, she made to bend down and join Terry, only for Ruth to appear, all a-fluster and very out of breath.

****

Taxi duty wasn't the most exciting job, which was why the girls took it in turns. However, today it meant that Betty finally had time to finish off her letter from her Jim.

Still, with a bit of luck, and if I can persuade you to leave that sceptered isle—I think that's how Will Shakespeare put it—you'll be able to enjoy that little privilege. Saying that, who are we to say that things will return to how they were pre-war? Hell, if a beautiful Limey can fall in love with a stuffy Yank, anything is possible!

You know, I've one huge regret, apart from never learning to write properly that is, and that's not having bought you an engagement ring before I left. I feel terrible! Which is why I'm taking this opportunity to let you know that a small package should be winging its way to you shortly. When I say "winging" I mean that literally. I've a friend who's taking a trip over the Pond, as you love to say, and when he gets to England, he's going to put it in the post for me. He's a bit of a klutz, so it's just as well I dissuaded him from bringing it to you in person; he'd likely lose it a few miles from you, knowing him. Plus, he's much better looking than me, so I didn't want to take the chance of you falling for him instead of me.

"As if," Betty mumbled, turning over the last page.

Well, I'm real sorry I don't write longer letters, just know that you have my heart, now and for always. Keep yourself and your terrific friends safe, and I'll be back in your arms as soon as I can.

All my love,

Jim F

Sighing in contentment, Betty slumped back into the not-very-comfortable Anson's pilot seat. "You may not write long letters, my darling," she mumbled, carefully refolding the letter and placing it back in her flight bag for safety, "but you do know how to write the words that make my heart flutter."

"Whose heart's all a-flutter?"

"Doris!" Betty's annoyance at having her private moment interrupted nearly made her friend's name sound like a curse.

Completely unabashed, the American took the seat next to her and grinned like the Cheshire Cat, though without disappearing. "Hey, don't blame me. It's not my fault if you don't pick somewhere with some privacy to read your love letters!"

Feeling her skin prickle right to the tips of her ears,

Betty contented herself with glaring at her friend. However, she'd not considered with whom she was dealing. A glare to Doris was like water off a duck's back; it had no effect.

Her first delivery must have gone off well, though, as Doris didn't tease Betty too much. "Hey, I'm sorry," Doris told her. "You know what I'm like. Anyway, never mind me, how's old Jim keeping? Any news on him coming back yet?"

Perhaps it was the letter, or Doris's candor, but Betty found herself wiping a tear from her eye before she was able to answer. Doris noticed, though, and ignoring how awkward it must be, turned to sit sideways in her seat so she could look directly at her friend.

"Come on, we're not as bad as all that," she told Betty, treating her friend to a wide smile. "I know we're no substitute for your man, but we're all here for you."

Wiping another tear away, Betty took a steadying breath. "I know, I really do. You know what I think all this is?" she said, taking out a cleanish handkerchief, as her fingers were no longer sufficient to keep pace with the tears betraying her emotions.

Fortunately, though brash at times, Doris had proved time and again what a great friend she was and merely took her friend's free hand in one of hers and squeezed her encouragement before letting go and allowing Betty to find her voice in her own time.

"I think I'm getting all emotional because I never thought I'd be good enough for any man, and as the years have gone by, nothing happened to change that opinion."

"And then you lost your sister," Doris softly added.

Betty nodded, and it was a few seconds before she was able to regain her voice. "And then I lost Eleanor. I thought I was being punished for not being a nice person…"

"You're one of the nicest people I know!" Doris protested.

"You can't deny I didn't used to be," sniffed Betty, referring to her times as one of the best stolen jewelry fences in the business.

Doris waved her friend's words away with a flick of a hand. "All in the past."

"Well, perhaps," Betty reluctantly agreed. "Whatever, I thought my time had passed, but then along came Jim, when I wasn't even looking."

Glancing around as if to make certain they were indeed alone in the narrow cockpit, Doris leaned in. "That's the best way! Look at me. Lost one husband in the Spanish Civil War, and now I'm more happily married than ever! And don't tell him, but Walter's *not* the type I went for in the past."

"You fail to surprise me," Betty told her, trying to stifle a chuckle.

Doris held a finger up to her lips. "Our secret!"

Betty held out her hand and the two shook on it. "Deal."

"Now," Doris declared, "there's no one else around, and we don't have to take off for another ten minutes, spill the beans. I want to hear everything!"

Chapter Twenty-Nine

Lawrence had read and rejected Sharon's first three attempts at replying to their Nazi counterparts. Apparently, they were too confrontational, which they both found rather ironic, though she had to agree with him.

After picking up her pen for a fourth attempt, Sharon just as quickly threw it down. It bounced off the table onto the floor, and she crossed her arms in disgust. "I give in! I've copied what I was supposed to write, changed it around, done everything but throw it on the fire, but it still doesn't read right, despite what MI-whatever-they-are may think! You write what you think needs to be written, and I'll copy it!"

Retrieving the pen, Lawrence straightened up and motioned for the girl to vacate her seat. "I'll do you a trade," he offered whilst selecting a fresh piece of paper. "If you make me one of your world-famous cups of tea, I'll make a start. Deal?"

"Deal!" Sharon quickly disappeared into the kitchen.

Whilst mulling over how he should change the wording of the letter, Lawrence twirled the pen between his fingers and then asked a question which nearly caused Sharon to drop a mug. "Just as well we waited before replying," he muttered. "When this is all over, have you given any thought to permanently transferring onto Hamble's staff? I mean when this task is finished," he added, as Sharon stopped her mug-juggling routine.

As the kettle came to the boil, Sharon leant against the door frame and gave his question some consideration, finally settling upon, "You know, I hadn't thought about it before you asked, but it may not be a bad idea. What with Stan not being at Marham any longer, I've no reason to stay there."

"No family?" Lawrence enquired, with a challenging eyebrow.

Giving him a lopsided half-smile, Sharon turned back to take the kettle off the burner. "I reckon you already know the answer to that, but for the record and in case MI-whatever have bugged this place, there's only my granny and Aunt Mable. Oh, I almost forgot. I'm no longer welcome at my aunt's now."

This got the policeman's attention. "Really? Why on earth's that?"

"She says I'm a waste of time. Reckons I was using her, which was why I wanted to stay, after not seeing her for donkey's years—her words—only to drop her when I got a better offer." Sharon stopped talking whilst she poured boiling water into the pot and whisked a spoon around it with unnecessary force. Then, carrying on where she'd left off, she said, "Silly old bat! I mean, I'm not even sure what all that means. Mind you, I suppose there is some truth in what she said."

"Do you want me to have a word with her? After this is all over, of course," Lawrence offered. "It is much my fault, after all."

Sharon poured the tea through the strainer into two of Mavis's second-best cups, added a splash of Carnation evaporated milk, and brought them over to the table.

Placing his to his right, Sharon took a seat. "No, don't worry yourself. The brief chat we had was more than enough to make me realize why I hadn't been in touch with her. Plus, it's not your fault. I know you're here to keep me safe, so forget it."

"You're sure?"

"Very!" Sharon told him, bringing her cup to her lips and blowing on the surface.

"Good," Lawrence replied, wiping some pretend perspiration from his forehead. "Now things are good again with Mary, I don't want to talk to any more women than I have to at the moment."

"Hey!" Sharon declared, treating him to a glare a bear would be proud of.

Smiling, he ignored his companion and took up his pen again.

Taking the hint, Sharon took her cup, got to her feet, and went to look out into the back garden. The same as for many other ordinary people in wartime Britain, what may once have been a proud, green space with borders of colorful flowers of every genre that could take the climate was now much more utilitarian. There were rows of what she now knew to be potatoes, carrots, and peas, and a few others she couldn't recall off the top of her head. Mavis hadn't wasted any time in utilizing Sharon's much younger back, and though it wasn't time for any harvesting, it was surprising how quickly she'd begun to enjoy working on something she would be eating before too long. Her pleas to keep rabbits or chickens had fallen on deaf ears, though. Sharon suspected it was the look she'd been unable to keep from her eyes at the thought of keeping animals. She had to admit the older woman was probably correct; she didn't know if she'd have it in her to wring a rabbit's neck or chop the head off a chicken.

She must have been staring for longer than she'd been aware of, as when Lawrence coughed and announced, "There, all done," she jumped slightly before turning back and leaning over his shoulder to read what he'd written. For his part, Lawrence took a long pull at his tea, sighing in deep satisfaction.

Because they had their backs to the kitchen window, neither Lawrence nor Sharon was aware of two faces peering at them through the hedge at the end of the garden. Neither face could clearly be made out. However, what was noticeable, though you'd have to look very closely, was the small dachshund the woman was cradling in her arms, a hand clamped around its muzzle.

****

It was coming up to an hour since Ruth and Bobby had left, and so far, Walter had fended off two attacks from a blackbird who seemed to take offense whenever he passed by the hedge from which Bobby had dragged the rifle, and one from Duck. After being chased in circles for a minute, the fiendish fowl had grown bored and flown off. Now he'd got his breath back, Walter thanked small mercies there'd been no one around to witness the scene. He suspected someone would pay good money for a storyboard of the incident. Whether to tell his wife about it or not was another matter. Doris was the only human Duck would tolerate, and Walter was certain she'd take her aquatic friend's side, even over her husband.

He looked at his watch and frowned. Glancing down at the rifle for what seemed like the hundredth time since

Ruth and Bobby had left, he grunted and set off toward the bend in the road. Thinking, once again, it was a good thing it wasn't raining, as he didn't have his coat or hat with him, Walter meandered over, looked down the lane, a little more in hope than expectation, and turned to go back the way he'd come because the lane was as empty as ever.

"What on earth's she doing?" he muttered. Looking down at his feet, he kicked a stone which seemed to be lying there in a particularly malicious way. Looking back up, his eyes bulged in surprise. The stone should have ended up approximately where he'd been waiting, perhaps even rebounded off the rifle. Only…the rifle was no longer there to impede its progress. "Oh, hell!" he swore and took off at a run.

Arriving back where the rifle had been less than a minute ago, Walter looked around, desperately hoping his eyes were playing tricks upon him. Maybe it was delayed concussion from the grenade? Very, very delayed, he thought dismissively. Willing his breathing to steady, he looked around once more, only much more carefully this time. He accepted the rifle had gone, but perhaps something, some kind of clue was staring him in the face as to its whereabouts. Cursing himself for turning his back on it, Walter got down onto his hands and knees, then lowered his head until his eyes were a mere six inches from the gravelly surface. Scrunching his eyes up, he thought he could just about make out a slight scrape mark where he believed the rifle's butt had been.

He was in the process of clambering to his feet when he thought he heard a rustling sound. Not certain what it could be, he was hurrying to get to his feet when something hard struck him behind the ear and the world dissolved into an array of spinning stars before he lost consciousness.

****

No sooner had Bobby disappeared from view than he was back, albeit briefly. Ruth's faithful Cocker Spaniel stayed at the bend in the road only long enough to let out a flurry of what could only be urgent barks before turning back.

Ruth and Terry barely glanced at each other before they took off after him as fast as both could manage. Rounding the bend, Ruth let out a shout of surprise to see Bobby lying next to a prostrate Walter, one of his front paws nudging his face.

To her credit, she didn't let the sight slow her down, and she was actually at Walter's side slightly ahead of her police escort.

"Christ! What on earth's happened now?" Terry grumbled. As quickly as he could, whilst at the same time being careful not to touch Walter, he knelt onto one knee and, acutely aware of being under Ruth's scrutiny, he felt for a pulse on the side of the man's neck, letting out a sigh of relief at finding it.

He'd opened his mouth to tell Ruth this when Walter let out a groan.

"Walter!" Ruth hurried to support her friend as he began to stir. "Hold on! Take it easy," she told him, whilst hooking one of her arms beneath his armpits, with Terry mirroring her actions on the other side.

Together, they helped a rather dazed Walter into a sitting position, each with a hand supporting his back. Reaching up, Walter touched the back of his head, immediately pulling his hand away and wincing in pain.

"Show me your hand," Terry said. Ruth noted he used his best policeman's voice in order to get the injured man to obey him. Taking the palm in his free hand, Terry looked at it before showing it to Ruth.

"Well, that's something," she said, with a shake of her head.

Walter tried twice before managing to ask, "What's something?"

She showed him his hand. "That. No blood!"

"Good," Walter said and made an attempt to get to his feet, only succeeding in landing on his backside again.

Terry and Ruth pressed their hands onto his shoulders. "You're going nowhere just yet, young man."

"Exactly as Ruth says," Terry backed her up. "What happened here? And where's this rifle Ruth mentioned?"

Slightly befuddled fire shot from Walter's eyes. "That's what I'd like to know! One second it's there, so I took a walk down to the bend in the road, just to see if I could see you, Ruth, and when I turned back, it was gone."

"And...this?" Terry asked.

Walter took a few moments to think things over before saying, "I reckon someone was watching, waiting for me to let my guard down."

"And they got their chance," Ruth finished, before pushing Walter's head forward. "Stay like that," she instructed. "Just because your hand came away clean, it doesn't mean to say you're not bleeding. Now, where you were bashed?"

"Do as she says, lad," Terry advised once more, as Walter opened his mouth.

After putting up with a minute investigation of his

head, far more than he'd deem necessary, Walter was finally allowed to straighten up. "Well?"

Ruth showed him her clean hands. "I can't see any cuts, but I do reckon you're going to have a big bump coming up soon."

"In that case, help me to my feet," he asked, holding out his hands. "We've a rifle to find."

"You've nothing to find," Ruth told him, in no uncertain terms. She looked over at Terry and pointedly raised her eyebrows at him, as if to say that he'd better not argue with what she was about to say. "We're taking you to the cottage hospital. After the injuries you've only just got over, I want a doctor to take a look at you before anything else."

"She's dead right," Terry quickly said, when it looked like Walter was about to object. "Leave the looking for the rifles to the police."

Showing he was a lot more awake now, Walter jerked his head toward the policeman, "Rifles. You're saying there's more than one?"

Terry's face clearly conveyed his annoyance at himself for his slip. Knowing he couldn't take back the words, he instead firmly told him, "And that's nothing to do with you. Understand?" He waited until Walter gave a very reluctant nod. "Good. Now, let's get you to hospital."

With Bobby taking point and with Walter between Ruth and Terry, each having a hand hovering in case he wavered, the trio set off, back down the lane toward Hamble village.

"Heaven knows what Doris is going to say. I'm going to get the blame for this," Ruth muttered.

At hearing these words, Walter lost a little of the

color he'd regained. "Something tells me you won't get the worst of it," he assured her.

Chapter Thirty

Lawrence was made aware of the attack on Walter when he stopped off to update Jane on how things were with Sharon and their little game of spies—he knew he probably shouldn't, but he'd trust Jane with his life and he'd picked his words very carefully. He even shared his strong suspicion that Sharon was being watched, a near-assumption which, so far, he hadn't mentioned to the girl herself.

Lawrence spent an hour at the local hospital, talking to Walter at his bedside and taking his statement. Together with the mysterious holes Terry had investigated at the airfield and the conclusions his sergeant had come to, which Lawrence agreed were probably on the money, it presented a worrying state of affairs.

As was common with police forces around the country, manpower was at a premium and not of the same quality as pre-war. Most of the able-bodied, fit young men had either volunteered or were now being called up to serve with various branches of the services, so he'd quickly dismissed the idea of calling together an armed police raid on Ambrose Foreman's farm. However, it had given him an idea, and with time a factor, he was eager to follow up on it.

Tucking his notepad away in his inside coat pocket, Lawrence got to his feet and held out his hand for a most unhappy Walter to shake. "Very sorry to see you back here, Walter, but at least they're only keeping you in overnight."

His attempt to make light of the situation failed to illicit the hoped-for response, as Walter merely allowed himself to slide back down into the bed until the cover rested under his nose.

Appearing out of nowhere, a special power of nurses everywhere, Grace Baxter quickly inserted a hand beneath one of Walter's armpits and physically dragged him back up onto the pillows. With a laugh, she then told him, "It's no use hiding. I'm certain Doris will find you, even if you were to sneak down into the boiler room."

Looking, if it were possible, even more miserable, Walter reluctantly allowed her to re-tuck the sheets around him. Making sure there was no one around, like for instance the ward sister the nurse didn't get along with, Grace leant in to say, "If it makes you feel any better, Penny is an even worse patient than you. I can't believe she got out of that crash in one piece, for a start! Jane dropped in on their way back from the hospital. She wanted to make sure Penny knew she was to come in to have her bandages changed and that she was to take a few days off. Penny was even grumpier than you! I think she was hoping to go straight back on flying."

Lawrence shook his head. "Knowing Jane, there's no way that's going to happen yet."

"And quite rightly, too," Grace said. "Right. I've other patients to attend to, but I'm sure I'll see you before I knock off, Walter. Inspector." She nodded her head at the policeman before moving along to her next patient in need.

"I've got to be going as well," Lawrence said. "Do

me a favor? When your wife gets here, try not to let her kill you."

"Can't guarantee that," Walter muttered and closed his eyes.

Accepting the dismissal, Lawrence hurried out before anything else could distract him. Once in his car, he headed off toward the offices of his Aunt Ruth's *Hamble Gazette* newspaper. By the time he'd parked, Ruth was waiting in the open doorway, Bobby in her arms to prevent him jumping into the car. He'd got the taste for motor cars after hitching a lift in Jane's Jeep a while back and now associated every vehicle with Hamble's commanding officer's runabout.

"How's the wounded warrior?" Ruth asked, as Lawrence strode past her into the office.

"Dreading Doris finding out," he replied, grinning.

Ruth closed the door behind him, only then letting hold of her frustrated companion. "I know it's not funny, but I wouldn't mind seeing that reunion." She then turned serious. "So, nephew of mine, what's the next step?"

Lawrence perched on the edge of Walter's vacant desk. "I'm very glad you asked. I want to run by you an idea I've had. It's slightly unconventional and may need some hurried phone calls."

Ruth leaned toward him from behind her desk. "I'm intrigued. What do you have in mind?"

"How's your relationship with Matt Baines?" he stunned her by asking.

Ruth liked to think of herself as open-minded, but the question took her by surprise. "Why on earth would you want to know? What's he got to do with…" She didn't finish her sentence, as when Lawrence failed to react defensively, she realized he wasn't interested in knowing anything romantic-wise. "What do you need?" she hastily asked.

"Do you think he could get permission to support a hard-working…" He stopped to raise an eyebrow at his aunt until she stopped fluttering and muttering. "…a hard-working policeman with a raid?"

It took only a few moments for Ruth to fully understand the implications of what he was asking, and when she did, she immediately picked up the phone on her desk. Before long, she'd spoken to Matt. "He'll be over in five minutes."

Lawrence got up and went to the kettle. "Shall I be Mum?"

"Good idea, Matt loves a cup," Ruth informed him.

No sooner had the kettle boiled, and Lawrence was pouring the water into the teapot, than Matt himself appeared at the door. They both gave him a few seconds bent over to catch his breath—he had obviously run over from his builders' yard.

"You called? I came," he announced.

Ruth was waiting for him with a kiss for his cheek. "Thanks for coming over so quickly. Did we pull you away from anything urgent?"

Matt shook his head. "Nothing that can't wait."

Conversation ceased for the next minute whilst Lawrence finished making the tea. Once everyone had a cup, Lawrence outlined his idea. "Well?" he asked, once Matt's eyes had shrunk back down to normal size.

Matt took a deep breath and a long swig from his cup. "You're serious, aren't you?"

"Deadly serious," Lawrence instantly replied. "So, do you think your mob could help?"

Whistling, Matt set down his empty cup. "I'll need to ring my commanding officer, and he may need to phone his…"

Exasperated, Lawrence slapped a hand onto the desk, making the other two jump. "Christ! I was hoping to get things moving as quickly as possible. Who knows how long those arms will be around!"

Matt reached into the back pocket of his trousers and put his wallet on the desk, opened it, and laid a well-worn piece of paper before him. Taking up the handset before him, his finger hovered over the dial. "And you're a hundred percent certain these rifles will be up at this farm? We are talking Ambrose here, aren't we?"

"If it makes you feel better, I'm pretty sure Ambrose doesn't really have anything to do with this."

"Ruth," Matt asked, "what do you think? You've known Ambrose as long as I have. Have you ever known him to be involved in anything shady?"

"Well, taking a certain arrangement I have with him for certain, ahem, *items*, no, nothing like this. I've spoken with him a few times since all this began, and I'm sure he's tried to warn me off. For my own sake," she hastened to amend, as Matt began to frown. "Now, if you're going to call your CO, would you please telephone?"

"One last question," Matt said. "What about the station guards? Have you asked to use them?"

Lawrence appeared a little embarrassed, eventually saying, "I did contemplate asking Jane, but I know how the military mind works, and there'd be simply too many hoops to jump through."

Matt's finger was still hovering over the dial. "What makes you think I won't have as many?"

"I'm betting your boss will be as keen for a little action—though I hope it won't come to that—as you and everyone else in your platoon is," Lawrence admitted, with a hopeful grin.

Wasting no further time, Matt dialed and within a few seconds was through to George Ellis, the new publican who ran The Victory, causing both Ruth and Lawrence to share a look of complete surprise. Both held a silent conversation whilst Matt, in tones of increasing urgency, explained the situation to the chap who had to make the decision.

When he finished, he had time only to open his mouth before Ruth interrupted him with, "I never knew George was in charge of our Home Guard!"

Matt shook his head. "And you call yourself a newspaper editor, love!"

"Can't know everything that goes on around here," Ruth muttered, though she looked pleased at his tone of affection.

"A few weeks, that's all. The other chap was called away. Never mind that." He waved a hand. "The captain's all for it. In fact, he's ringing around as we speak, getting as many of the platoon together as he can. In his words, his senior officer can court-martial him if he wants, but he'll help one of our own any way he can."

"Walter's going to be so disappointed to miss this," Ruth put in.

"I think he'd rather this than facing up to his wife later," Lawrence agreed. "Right. How long before you reckon we'll be able to make a move?" he asked Matt.

"Give it an hour, to be on the safe side," Matt replied.

"An hour? But they could have carted everything

away by then!" Ruth stated.

Matt shrugged. "Best we can do," he began, before explaining. "We're not likely to get everyone, maybe half a dozen, and we know the time constraints; you heard me explain them to him."

Lawrence opened his mouth to say something but closed it upon further reflection. "And, I very much appreciate what you're all doing to help me."

"In that case, let's get down to the village hall. I've got to get the ammunition unlocked, and I'll have to go by my workshop. I need to pick up my rifle." He got to his feet, came around the desk and, going up to Ruth, gave her a peck upon the cheek before asking Lawrence, "Are you armed?"

In answer, the policeman pulled a Webley revolver out of his coat pocket. "I've reasons to be armed at the moment."

"Sharon?" Ruth asked, before she could stop herself.

Lawrence, putting away the revolver, fixed the home guard sergeant with a pointed stare. "Forget you know about that."

"Knew what?" he answered quickly, making his way to the door and holding it open. "Shall we?"

Suddenly left alone, Ruth sat down, then got to her feet, then repeated the process before making up her mind. Taking Bobby's leash from her desk drawer, she clipped it to his collar. "Come on. I can't sit here. Let's go for a walk."

Upon hearing the "w" word, Bobby jumped to his feet and pulled her toward the door.

"At least someone's happy," she murmured, before slapping her hand down hard upon the desktop, making pencils and pens jump. "To hell with waiting around!

He's my friend!" Closing and locking the office door behind her, she looked down into Bobby's intelligent eyes. "Come on, let's go and see what happens. Best behavior, mind!" she told him, wagging her finger.

Bobby gave her his best *woof* in reply, and the two set off with a determined stride.

****

Penny was bored, very bored, extremely bored. In fact, if anyone had had the nerve to ask her, she'd have bet she was the most bored person in the whole world. If she hadn't been so bored, she might have sat down and worked out the odds, only she was too bored.

In fact, she was annoyed to find she couldn't remember reading the last chapter of the Miss Marple she was reading. She'd better keep quiet about that, or Betty would refuse to allow her to borrow any more of her books. Carefully flicking back, she found where she'd picked up. *The Body in the Library* had been gripping her, and now she was not only bored but rather annoyed with herself for allowing anything to interrupt her enjoyment of one of Agatha's stories.

Bartlett's burnt-out car had just been found, in her current chapter, and Penny could feel her attention span kicking in, thankfully, when the sound of boots pounding along hammered through the window she had open in the lounge. Another set went by a few seconds later, and when what sounded like a few more thundered to join those, she scrambled off the sofa. Catching the burn on her left forearm and wincing, she peered out the window.

"Heck with it!" she exclaimed. Quickly, yet carefully, she marked her place in her book, put it down on the sofa, and hobbled, somewhat stiffly, to the front door.

Once outside, she was in time to see a couple of men in Home Guard uniform run past. Each was dressed, so far as could tell, in full battle dress. Well, each was carrying a rifle, had a steel helmet on, and wore a set of webbing around their bodies. Looking up the lane, she was just in time to see a pair of them catch up to what had to be other members of Hamble's Home Guard platoon.

Turning the other way, she spotted a man in a sergeant's tunic running up and, unhesitatingly, she stepped into his path. "What's going on, Matt?" she asked, as he skidded to a halt.

"Christ, Penny!" he half-shouted. "Watch what you're doing!"

Penny didn't let his obvious annoyance deter her and repeated her question. After he'd told her where he was going and why—she was rather surprised he caved so quickly, but he was obviously distracted—she took a step to the side and told him, "Right, hold on. I'll just get my shoes on and I'm coming with you."

"No, you're bloody well not!" Matt told her, his head shaking determinedly before he took to his heels once more. He just had time to shout out, "Stay there, if you know what's good for you!" before taking to his heels without looking back or checking that Penny was doing as he said.

A mistake, as it turned out.

Chapter Thirty-One

Wincing in pain, Penny pulled off the cardigan she'd pulled on against the chill wind which had sprung up the second she'd decided to set off after Matt and what seemed like at least half of Hamble's Home Guard platoon. She'd nearly been caught as Ruth and Terry sped past, half-carrying Walter between them. Doris's husband hadn't looked good, and it was only the fact he was in good hands, that she stuck to her original plan. The slight diversion meant she was now far enough behind the Home Guard that they wouldn't be able to hear her, so long as she was careful. Whether to try to move a little faster was taken out of her hands, as her burns had tightened up her skin, making it painful to run, so she was reduced to an inelegant lope. At least there was no one around to witness her discomfort.

"Oops!" she cried, slipping. She got her feet under control just before she crashed into one of the many large trees which lined the riverbank.

Unfortunately, Duck was around and, judging by the vicious *quack* he threw up at her, he wasn't in the best of moods. Penny had barely enough time to take to her heels, pushing her punished body as fast as she could bear, before the fiendish fowl ruffled his feathers and took off after her. It took a surprising amount of effort for her to keep ahead of him, and Duck didn't give up until she'd followed the bend in the lane, away from the river and toward Ambrose's farm. If she could understand duck language, Penny imagined her ears would be red with embarrassment. Something seemed to have riled him. Certainly, she'd be a lot more careful on her way back home!

Now no longer in danger, she stopped to catch her breath, carefully listening for any signs that the Home Guard had heard the commotion she'd caused with Duck. Satisfied her presence was still unsuspected, Penny put her hands on her hips and groaned. "What am I thinking?" she mumbled to herself, at the same time twisting her body around and slowly stretching her arms above her head, until her left arm, which had taken the worse battering of the two, reminded her it wasn't in the best of shapes by beginning to throb before a nasty pain, like she'd been stabbed, shot through her wrist.

Hugging her arm to her side, Penny waited until the pain had settled back to the throb once more before gingerly pushing the arm back into her cardigan. To her dismay, the nice, clean, white bandage Grace had so carefully applied was now not quite so white, nor totally in place. "Bugger." Glancing up the lane, she quickly decided that finding out what was going on was more important than her own comfort. Gritting her teeth, she hastily rewrapped the bandage and, not being able to locate the safety pin or tie a knot one-handed, tucked it through a loop before tying it off as best she could by using her teeth and other hand. It wouldn't last forever, but it should hold, so long as she didn't do anything more strenuous.

****

Betty pushed the disgusting cup to one side and made a face at Jane. "This is what comes of you allowing

278

both Mavis and Sharon the afternoon off!"

Finishing off the remains of her jam sandwich, Jane took a sip of water, having decided to play safe with her choice of beverage. Putting her glass down, she looked over her shoulder before replying, "Not entirely my fault. Sharon had to write a new letter for you-know-what, and Mavis asked if she could go home early as her son sent a telegram saying he'll be home sometime this afternoon or early evening. She takes so little time off it wouldn't have been fair to say no."

Somewhat mollified, Betty nevertheless commented, "You'd think she'd teach the rest of the mess staff how to make Sharon's tea first."

Jane took a pen and fumbled around her pockets until she found a piece of paper. "I'll make note of it."

"So does Doris know about Walter's latest accident?" Betty asked, pouring herself some water from the jug on the table.

Grimacing, Jane told her, "Let's put it like this—we should be happy we're not living in the same cottage."

"That bad?" Betty asked, the glass halfway to her lips.

Jane nodded. "I'm only guessing, but if I were him, I'd be tempted to ask a doctor to break my leg, so I could stay where I was for another week or so."

"And I don't expect it matters that it wasn't his fault?"

"She said that made it all the worse!" Jane replied.

"That sounds like our Doris," Betty remarked. "What's up? You've gone as white as a sheet!"

Unfortunately, as they were sat near the servery, both weren't paying attention to the comings and goings through the main door to the mess, and Betty had her back to it. Neither had seen the American in question entering, accompanied by Mary, until her hands clapped both on the shoulders and her head appeared over the empty seat between the two.

"Who's gone white as a what?" Doris asked, before pulling out a seat and sitting down next to Betty.

"Why didn't you warn me?" Betty hissed at Jane.

"Don't blame me," Jane replied, with a shake of her head. "One minute she wasn't there, and the next, well, it's Doris."

Swiftly swiping Betty's glass, Doris emptied it and got back to her feet. Smacking her hands together, she announced, "Now, if you'll both pardon me, I've a husband to kill!"

In unspoken unison, Jane and Betty both grabbed one of their friend's arms and pulled her back into the vacated seat, while Mary, still standing, helped keep her in place.

"Sit down and calm down," Jane advised. "That's not going to do anyone any good."

Sensing neither were going to let go of her, Doris relaxed a little. Stretching out her legs, she automatically reached for Betty's discarded cup of still steaming tea and, her eyes glinting, took a deep swig, before almost gagging. You could see the force of will it took for her to swallow. "That isn't coffee!" she declared, as long was her wont, before adding, "and it's certainly not Sharon's tea, either!" Swiftly refilling the glass, she downed a full glass of water in an effort to get rid of the foul taste. Glancing behind her, she asked, "Where are the pair, anyway?"

Betty looked up and ticked off on her fingers. "Sharon is off fighting her shady war with Lawrence and

Mavis discovered her son's due home anytime, well, now."

"Great news for Mavis, but I'm a little puzzled about Lawrence and Sharon, though I loved how you describe what those two are doing."

"Puzzled? Why?" Jane asked.

Retaking her seat, Doris told them, "I was turning into the landing circuit when I spotted what I thought was Lawrence's police car at the end of our lane. You know, where it bends around and up to Ambrose's farm. He didn't seem to be alone, and though I'm not sure since I didn't actually break off course to take a closer look, I'm pretty sure there were some soldiers around the car."

This quickly got her friend's attention. "Say that again?" Jane said before adding, "No, don't. I heard you."

"What on earth could he be up to?" Betty mused, though from the way she raised a knowing eyebrow, she had a good idea and proceeded to outline it. "I think that after what happened with Walter this morning, Lawrence is going to pay the farm a visit."

As one, a thought hit them. "Of course," Mary put their thoughts into words, "you know whose cottage they'll all have had to go by."

"And who doesn't seem to have a very good sense of self-preservation these days?"

"Oh, hell!" Betty swore, getting to her feet with a screech of metal chair legs. "Are we finished for the day, Jane?" Mary joined in the questioning look at their boss.

Jane coughed. "Well, I've some paperwork to finish and a phone call to make," she began, turning her head away as she spoke. "You, Doris, can finish up."

Doris didn't pick up on how Jane spoke. "In that

case, I'll get going, since socking my husband senseless will have to wait," Doris said, adding, "I've a bad feeling about this."

As soon as Doris opened the mess door, they were met by a cacophony of barking, which they all immediately recognized as coming from Bobby. Indeed, the owner of the racket sped through the open doors—he seemed to be getting younger, if his running was anything to go by—and leapt onto Jane's lap. Only just managing to stay in her seat, Jane patted his head and wrapped her other arm around his body to prevent the dog from jumping off and causing more mayhem.

"Where did you come from?" Mary asked.

Bobby opened his mouth and much to their surprise, they heard Ruth's voice!

"There you are!"

Before anyone could make fools of themselves, Ruth herself joined them, looking completely exhausted. Without preamble, she clipped the end of a leash to Bobby's collar and with a gentle pat of her hand on the wayward dog's bottom, encouraged him to jump off Jane's lap.

"Sorry about that," Ruth told them, once she'd finished catching her breath.

"That's all right," Jane replied, brushing dog hair off her lap. "What happened?"

Treating her dog to a mock evil stare, Ruth took Doris's vacated seat, looking around before replying, causing the other three to do the same. She leant forward. "I was on my way to find out how Lawrence and the Home Guard got along."

"I knew I saw something!" Doris said, before she was shushed into silence by Betty and Jane.

"As you heard," Jane said, treating her Yank to a real evil stare, "something's going on. You obviously know more than we do, so…?"

"The short version is, Lawrence has recruited some of the village Home Guard to help him search Ambrose's farm."

"What about the police? Where's his sergeant?" Doris asked.

"He hurried back to the police station after we'd taken Walter to the hospital," Ruth informed them.

"Probably not the best idea he's ever had," Betty remarked.

Ruth nodded. "Maybe, but I can't wait around any longer. Thanks for catching Bobby. I'm off after my nephew," she told Jane, before haring out the door without another word and not giving anyone a chance to try and stop her.

"Well, where does that leave us?" Doris wanted to know. "Are you sure you wouldn't like me to try and find Penny? My husband isn't going anywhere."

Jane thought for a moment before coming to a decision. "Doris, go see your husband, and try not to kill him. Penny's the opposite way to the hospital, after all. Leave her to us. Also, let us worry about Ruth's nephew. I'm afraid I have a last-minute job for you pair," she ended, looking at Mary and Betty.

Mary looked at her watch. "It's getting on a bit. Will we have time to get back?"

Shaking her head, Jane filled in the blanks. "I had an urgent phone call. They need an Albemarle at RAF Brize Norton, and no, I didn't get why. We never do. So I need the pair of you to get your overnight bags together, get in a Magister, and get to the Maintenance Unit. I know it's a type neither of you have flown before, so that's why I want the two of you on this job. I've a feeling it won't be the last, and the more of us who're familiar with the type, the better. Details and chit are on my desk."

"What are you going to do?" Betty asked, scooping up her bag, coat, and hat.

"Me? I'm going to finish up some damned paperwork. If I could leave it, believe me, I would, and then I'll be taking the Jeep down the lane and toward the farm as soon as possible. I'll pop into the cottage on the way, and if, as we all suspect, Penny's not in, I'll have the Jeep to take her back home."

After everyone left, Jane made herself another jam sandwich, then made her way back to the ops hut and her office. Opening the door, she heard the telephone ringing and hurried to pick it up. Much to her surprise, it was Detective Sergeant Terry Banks.

With very quick introductions out of the way, he wasted no time in asking if his boss was around.

"Sorry, Sergeant," Jane replied a little formally, "but, if it helps, I do have a good idea where he is."

"Which is?" Terry asked.

"Ruth, you know, Ruth Stone, the editor of the *Hamble Gazette*? Well, she just ran into the mess and told us he was about to launch a search on the farm." She held the handset away from her ear until Terry had calmed down. "No, not on his own."

"Who with then? I can't get back there in time to be of any use, so who's supporting him?" Terry wanted to know.

"Some members of the local Home Guard," she told him, going on to tell him what little Ruth had informed them before she shot off.

"Great timing!" Terry muttered, before telling her why he'd called. "I've just taken a phone call from Ambrose, though I'm not a hundred percent certain, as the voice was slurring. He said he needed to warn me, and then the line went dead."

Jane looked at her pile of paperwork and came to a decision. "You get to the farm as soon as you can," she told him. "I'm going to get to him as quickly as I can too."

Snatching up her uniform jacket, she jammed her hat onto her head, not hearing Terry's farewell warning to, "Be careful!" as she slammed the receiver down, the paperwork untouched.

Chapter Thirty-Two

After playing rock-paper-scissors to decide who would fly the Armstrong-Whitworth Albemarle, Mary had strapped herself into the pilot's seat with Betty doing the same in the co-pilot's next to her. Both had then spent about half an hour going through the pilot's notes they had on the type and a reasonably comfortable takeoff was duly performed, though Mary did complain about the poor surface of the runway at the Maintenance Unit. Both agreed that RAF Brize Norton's should be a lot better.

"Care for a sandwich?" Betty asked as they both settled in for the relatively short hop to their destination airfield in Oxfordshire.

"Depends. What are they?"

Betty lifted up the top slice of the national loaf. "Looks like raspberry jam." She dipped a finger and took a taste. "Or a fair impression," she amended. "It's a bit dry, too."

"Some things never change," Betty muttered and held out a hand. After making short work of the snack, she asked for a cup of tea to wash it down with.

"Be aware, it's not Sharon's or Mavis's," Betty warned her, as she poured.

Mary made a face. "Are we back to the bad old days, pre-Sharon, then?"

Nodding, Betty lifted the cup to her nose, took a

tentative sniff and swiftly recoiled. "Better think of England when you drink it," she advised.

"Eww!" Mary couldn't stop herself from commenting as she forced the liquid down. "We really need to persuade those girls to teach the rest of the mess staff how to brew their tea. That's only fit for killing moles!"

Betty nearly snorted hers down her nose at this comment.

With their sandwiches finished, more as fuel than for the enjoyment of eating, they settled into a companionable silence as they flew through the gathering dusk. Both found flying a mixture of relaxation and exhilaration, though admittedly more exciting in a single-engined fighter than the twin-engined transport they were currently piloting. At the moment, neither felt the need to fill the void with unnecessary conversation. That was until they were around ten minutes out from their destination.

"Do you have the same feeling as me?" Betty suddenly asked.

"What kind of feeling?" Mary replied.

"That we're missing something."

Mary glanced at her friend. "You got that too, huh?"

Betty nodded "What Doris said when she came into the mess... Then there was Jane saying she'd go and see about Penny..."

"I remember," Mary said. "Typical, isn't it? All the excitement's happening, and where are we? Stuck ferrying a transport!"

"You know," Betty mused, "before you and Doris and Penny came into my life, I was quite happy with my relatively boring life."

"Happy?" Even over the racket caused by the engines right beside the cockpit, Betty could hear the disbelief in Mary's voice. "I don't believe you. In a way, possibly," she allowed, going on before Betty had a chance to interrupt her. "However, you must have been missing the excitement of fencing all those jewels and baubles."

Betty was silent for a few minutes whilst she thought over Mary's words. "Maybe, but when my sister died, I wanted to leave that life behind me. There's plenty I've done that I'm not proud of, you know this."

"I'll allow you that," Mary agreed. "However, you've done plenty, especially since you came into Eleanor's money, that goes beyond being simply good. Look at what you gave to the orphans' fund! I'd love to have been a fly on the wall when your cheque arrived on their desk."

"I suppose," Betty replied, turning her head away from Mary, who suspected her friend was blushing.

"But, come on!" Mary persisted. "A little excitement in life, even in a war, and yes, I know that's quite a contradiction. Wouldn't you love to be there? See what happens? Get our teeth into the end of another mystery?"

She knew she was right when Betty didn't say anything for a few minutes, until, "Oh, all right! Yes, I'd love to find out what happens, maybe stop Penny doing something silly…again. Still, haven't we all done something silly lately? Don't answer that! What does it matter, though? We're here, they're there…"

"Getting up to heaven knows what excitement!" Mary supplied.

"Your definition of excitement and mine may be a

little…different," Betty explained, shifting in her seat in an effort to get more comfortable before giving it up, like in most RAF planes, as a waste of time. "Don't get me wrong. I still love a mystery, but I'm just not keen on being shot at."

At hearing this, Mary fell silent until it came time to line up for the approach to RAF Brize Norton. "You don't think that's happening, do you?" she asked, eyes firmly fixed ahead.

Judging there was time to speak before they touched down, Betty admitted, "I don't know, though I am worried, since Lawrence seemed to feel the need to have backup. This is Lawrence, though…" She continued in what she knew was a false-sounding, cheerful voice, hoping Mary wasn't worrying too much about her boyfriend, not that she'd blame her. "He's come through a lot worse. I'm sure he'll be fine," she finished at exactly the same moment the tires touched down.

After a few bumps, which Betty wasn't going to comment on, they'd slowed to taxiing speed. Unable to stop herself, she gawked out the windows as they passed row upon row of huge aircraft, only these had no engines.

"Have you ever seen the like?" Betty asked.

Though she was busy with following directions to where the transport needed to go, Mary couldn't help but notice how crowded the airfield was. "Just as well we've air superiority," she commented with a shake of her head. "What a juicy target!"

"Have you noticed they don't have propellers?" Mary asked, glancing out of the window on her left, as another of the strange giants slid past.

Betty had barely stopped shaking her head the whole time they were taxiing. "Idiot!" she told Mary fondly.

"I've never seen gliders this big before! What on earth could they be using these for?"

As she said the words, Mary touched the brakes as they approached a hard standing. The airman in front of their aircraft signaled for them to stop and, with another slight jerk, Mary brought the transport to a halt. Betty saw the airman wince as the aircraft shuddered to a halt, other chaps scurrying forward to place sturdy chocks under the main wheels before hurrying away.

"Don't know what their problem is," Mary uttered, also watching them, as she turned off the engines, unlocked the brakes, and the two pulled out their manuals and began the post-flight checks.

A short while later, the two climbed out of the aircraft, and both patted its nose as they made their way over toward a waiting car.

On the trip to 297 Squadron Engineering offices, the two girls leaned out the back and watched enthralled as a squad of men, each wearing a purple cap, drove a Jeep up to a ramp on the left-hand side of a glider.

"They're called Horsa's," the man in the front seat told them. "They're going to be in the fore…"

Betty squeezed his shoulder. "Perhaps you should stop there," she advised.

The man who'd begun to talk too much clamped his jaw shut, realizing how close he'd come to giving too much away. "You're right," he agreed, then turned back to face the front and didn't say a single word more.

As they watched, two of the soldiers climbed inside the glider and took up stations either side of the open door.

"Stop, please!" Mary asked. "I'd like to watch this."

At a nod from the blabbermouth, the driver slowed

to a stop. With great interest, the two girls watched as, guided by the men inside the glider, the driver inched the Jeep up the ramp, his head hanging over the side as he tried to watch both his wheels and the guiders at the same time.

"A shilling he drives off the edges," the driver offered.

Not bothering to look at him, Mary offered her hand. "You're on."

With greater interest than before, the foursome watched the exercise. At one point, one front wheel was on the verge of falling off, only for the driver to hit the brakes in the nick of time. Backing up slightly, he had another attempt and this time managed to get the front wheels into the glider. With much tugging and audible swearing, which their escort seemed a little embarrassed for their passengers to hear, the group managed to manhandle the Jeep into the fuselage.

Holding out her hand for her winnings, Mary asked, "How the hell do they get it out?"

Although he'd just lost a shilling, the RAF corporal burst into a laugh, telling them, "That's twice as much fun!"

Chapter Thirty-Three

"So, how long have you been engaged for?" Walter asked, letting out a whistle and dropping Nurse Grace's hand, the one with the minute diamond ring upon her engagement finger.

"Only about a week," the nurse answered, unable to stop herself from admiring her new ring up close.

"I thought you weren't supposed to wear jewelry at work," he commented, and only the fact that Grace saw the smile upon his lips made her aware he was only teasing her.

However, she did say, "We aren't, or rather, Sister says we shouldn't, but as she's not around this afternoon and you looked in need of cheering up, I thought it wouldn't do any harm."

"Well, you're spot on, you have cheered me up," he answered, and was rewarded for his words by a huge smile. "Does Betty know?"

Grace shook her head. "Around here, only you know."

Walter bobbed his head and then said through gritted teeth, as the sharp movement made his head hurt again, "I shall consider myself honored."

A distant door slammed shut and Grace shot to her feet. Sister present or not, most of the doctors didn't like to see any of the medical staff sitting around.

"I see I'm not the only one feeling jumpy," Walter

remarked.

Grace threw a look over her shoulder once more before retaking her seat. "I wouldn't put it past that witch to check up on me."

"And why would she do that?" Walter asked.

Raising an eyebrow, Grace replied, "Guilty by association is, I think, the expression. If she knew you were back on the ward, she very likely wouldn't have taken the day off."

"I'm assuming this is mostly to do with my good lady wife?" he ventured.

Nodding, Grace added, "As well as a certain Cocker Spaniel."

"Ah, well, so long as there's a good basis."

"Give me a good reason I shouldn't tell Doris what you've just said," Grace told him.

Walter gave a weary chuckle. "I don't think I could be in any more trouble than I am at this moment."

"We'll see," she told him.

"Let's change the subject back to your engagement rather than discussing my impending doom," Walter said. "Why haven't either you or Marcus, I believe, told Betty, then? He is her half-brother, and I don't think it's my place to tell her."

The smile faltered upon the nurse's lips. "The truth? Very well, I like Betty, really, I do…"

"But…?" Walter gently prodded.

"But I'm a little worried that if I get to know her and the rest of her gang too well, I'll get dragged into their various escapades."

"And that's not for you?" Walter asked.

"That's definitely not for me." She nodded vehemently.

Walter took a few moments to compose his reply. "I personally think the ATA Mystery Club has more than enough members, so I don't believe you'll have anything to worry about on that front," he said and then, when she'd just let out a breath of relief, added, "I think she believes you're perfectly cast in your current role anyway."

"Just what is my current role?" she enquired.

"You're the one who patches them up when they come back from their adventures, of course."

After appearing to give this statement some thought, she let out a short burst of laughter. "You're so right!" she told him, before sobering up. "Makes me wish even more they wouldn't get into so much bother!"

"To be fair, it's not as if they go looking for trouble," Walter tried to placate her.

"Usually. They don't *usually* go looking for trouble," Grace amended, to which Walter could only shrug his shoulders.

"I can't argue with that. I mean, I know I'm here this time because Ruth's stumbled upon something weird…"

"…and the previous time, you threw a grenade away to save other's lives, and came pretty close to losing yours as a result."

Walter shut his mouth which had remained open during and after Grace's words, there being nothing he could say to what she'd just said. Eventually he remarked, "I suppose. Though that wasn't anything to do with the club, so there's really no reason for you not to tell Betty, then, is there?"

It was now Grace's turn to do an impression of a fish out of water. "I've talked myself into a corner, haven't I?"

"Somewhat," he agreed. "So when shall I tell Betty to expect you? Is there any way Marcus could join you?"

Grace frowned in thought. "I'll sort it, but you'll have to give me some time. I'll need to get hold of him and work out when we can both come around."

"I'm sure she'd love to see you both, but if only you can make it…"

"Well, I am coming around to check on Penny later," Grace mentioned.

"Ideal!" he announced. "We'll see you…" Walter began to say, only to grind to a halt as he spotted the slight yet imposing figure of his wife bursting through the door. For a smallish American, she currently bore a striking resemblance to what you'd believe a Valkyrie warrior would look like.

"Walter Johnson!" she bellowed. Grace looked around, expecting cups and jugs to be bouncing off various tables. "What the bloody hell have you been up to now?"

Grace instantly got to her feet, swept her hands down her uniform and arranged what she hoped was a friendly smile upon her face. "And there's my cue to get back to work. Doris! How lovely to see you again," she said as she drew level with Walter's obviously furious wife. "We must get together for a proper chat soon. Walter, stay in bed, and remember, no strenuous movements, including escape attempts!" she couldn't resist telling him whilst trying to keep the smile from her face at the sight she was leaving. If Walter could bury himself any more into the bed, he'd turn into a caterpillar! "Doris, try to keep the noise down. If you can't, at least make it look like an accident."

Doris quickly leant in to kiss Grace on the cheek,

saying, "Thanks for everything," before flinging herself upon her husband, arms around his neck whilst carefully avoiding the bandage once more around his head, and kissing him soundly. At this, Walter relaxed, but it was the calm before the storm as, after she stepped back, Doris turned her ire upon her poor husband. "Start talking, and make it good!"

****

Penny had discovered that somewhere along the line her first-aid skills were not as good as they once had been when she was in the Girl Guides. Of course, it didn't help that she kept stumbling and catching her left arm against the waistband of her trousers. In normal circumstances, this wouldn't cause any harm. Now, she could see that repeated impacts had caused blood to begin to weep through the dressing. Stopping for a few moments, she did her best to tie it as tightly as she could, wincing against the pain that caused. However, this was nothing compared to the headache which had come on a few minutes ago.

"Stiff upper and all that rot," she chided herself, trying with dark humor to take her mind off the plight she'd got herself into, and also to take her mind off what she might be walking into. Not that her mind would allow her to shy away from her intentions. A sneeze around the bend in the lane caused her to halt, literally with one foot off the ground.

"Quiet, Jones!" sharply followed a voice, not taking notice of its own advice.

It took a second for Penny's slightly befuddled mind to process, but she eventually placed the second voice as belonging to Matt Baines, and so far as she knew, he was still the sergeant of the local Home Guard. She needed to be extra careful, as she didn't want to be caught. Moving closer to the side of the lane, Penny forced her previously anxious pace down to that of a snail.

Bent as low to the ground as she could get without her throbbing head causing her to fall over, Penny crept forward until she was able to peek around a hedge. It was just as well she was being careful, as she was nearly nose to beige battle-dressed bottom. Only a foot in front of her, fortunately with his back to her, was one of the Home Guard, quite possibly the one who had sneezed. Slowly and ever so carefully, she backed up a few steps and froze. To do anything else would have been foolish. Calming herself as much as she could, she tried to get her thumping heart under control and held the hand of her less-bad arm over her mouth and nose.

The local wildlife must have sensed something was going on, as Penny couldn't even hear any birdsong Concentrating, what she could hear were instructions being given out. By the sound of it, both Lawrence and Matt were in charge.

"Everyone got that?" came Lawrence's urgent voice.

"No," Penny irritably muttered under her breath.

"Say that last bit again, Sarge?" one of the soldier's stage-whispered. Penny nodded in satisfaction.

"I swear you'll be the death of me, Jones," came back from Matt, accompanied by the sound of heavy army boots scraping across the lane. Penny hastily moved farther back around the bend a few steps and then stopped as the sergeant said, "Listen closely, Jones! I'll say this only once. Firstly, no one is to shoot unless the order is given by either myself or the Inspector. Got that? Good. Secondly, we're only expecting there to be two men up at the farm, the owner, name of Ambrose, and a suspicious bloke called Selwyn, but be on your guard. You do know what we're looking for? That's something," she heard, assuming the man he was berating had nodded. "Now, the rest of you, keep your eyes and ears open and everything will be fine. Anyone else have any questions? Good," he said quickly, not giving anyone the chance to speak. "Right. Safety catches off, and let's move out."

It was fair to say that the Hamble branch of the Home Guard were no highly trained commando unit, judging by the relative racket they made moving up the lane. Certainly, Penny felt confident enough to follow them around, keeping as close to the hedge as she could, whilst hoping that Ambrose didn't give the game away if he heard the unit first. She didn't like to think what the other chap would do. Not having met him, she couldn't tell what he was like, but going on recent experiences, she didn't think this operation had much of a chance of going off without a hitch.

From the bend in the lane to the entrance to the farm was only about half a mile, and at least the six chaps in khaki, with Lawrence rather conspicuously at the head of the small column in a blue suit with matching hat, were doing their best to keep up against the hedges either side of the lane. Penny estimated she was keeping about a hundred or so yards behind them.

"Hurry up a bit," she urged, though she knew it wouldn't be for the best if they did. Trouble was, her headache was getting worse, her arms and legs were aching like heck, and she was doing her best to convince herself she wasn't seeing some stars before her eyes. Because she wasn't feeling on top form, her foot slipped on a large stone she'd normally have seen and avoided. Only the fact that a dog barking somewhere behind her prevented her from being discovered, plus the fact that she rolled into the shallow ditch under the hedge.

Once she'd got her breath back, she gingerly poked her head above the lip of the ditch, only to find that no one was now in sight. They must have decided to rush forward upon hearing the dog, under cover of the noise it was making.

"Hell's bells!" she swore and, as quickly as she could, scrambled out of the ditch. She was halfway to her feet when Bobby appeared from behind her, very likely the source of the barking which had caused her to fall. Nevertheless, she was glad to see him and took a moment to give him a fuss behind his ears.

"Bobby! Bobby!" came what was unmistakably Ruth's voice, rapidly followed by the lady herself.

Well, what with the shouting and the barking, there seemed little point in trying to keep hidden any longer, so Penny straightened up or tried to, as her legs had taken the opportunity from the brief respite in the ditch to seize up. When she tried to take a few steps toward Ruth, her gait was more akin to Frankenstein's monster, with a touch of the Mummy thrown in, than the young lady she was.

"Penny? Is that you?" Ruth asked, making a grab for Bobby's collar as he jumped up and down, pawing at Penny's now much-bedraggled trousers.

In spite of how she looked and felt, there was something about a bouncing, friendly dog that would bring a smile to the face of even the most unhappy of people. "It is," she replied, resisting the urge to kneel down beside Bobby, mainly because she wasn't certain she'd be able to get back up without assistance, "though not that you'd think I should be."

With Bobby once more under her control, Ruth used her free hand to brush the worst of the leaves and twigs from about Penny, though she stopped almost immediately as her friend let out an involuntary hiss of pain when she brushed against the wrist from which the bandage was once more flopping free. "Hell! So sorry!"

Clutching her injured arm to her chest, Penny did her best to hide how much pain she was really in, but she didn't fool Ruth for a second. Indeed, the woman looked mortified at causing her pain.

"I'm so, so sorry," she said again. An idea struck her, and she thrust Bobby's leash into Penny's other hand. "Here, you hold Bobby. Now, give me your arm," she told Penny, taking the other before Penny was able to raise it, "and let's see what we can do about this bandage. I don't suppose there's any point in asking what you're doing, is there? I'm guessing you were following Lawrence and the Home Guard."

Penny was doing her best to grit her teeth because of the pain. The thought struck her that Grace wasn't going to be best pleased with her later, when she popped around to inspect her dressings. Whilst she thought about the young nurse, it made her wonder why they hadn't seen her since Doris and Walter's wedding. Ah, well, one problem at a time, and at least she could leave that one to Betty. Upon opening her eyes, though, she knew Grace wasn't the only one who wasn't pleased with her.

Ruth didn't wait for a reply to her question. Instead, she simply told her, "You should be at home, resting."

Unfortunately, whether it was the pain or her inbuilt pig-headedness, Penny didn't react well to the well-placed suggestion, ripping her arm from Ruth's grip and nearly causing the newly re-wrapped bandage to come undone again. "Don't try to stop me, Ruth! I need to find out what's happening up at the farm."

Before she could reply, both the girls became aware of a low rumble coming from somewhere below their eyeline. They looked down and, sure enough, Bobby stood between his owner's legs, head canted up at a now very surprised Penny. His hackles were up, his lips were curled, and he was actually growling at Penny.

This brought her to her senses, and before Ruth could speak, Penny was swept by a wave of guilt at the way she'd reacted. Much more tentatively than she'd ever have thought would be needed, she held out her hand a few inches from Bobby's nose, inviting the agitated dog to sniff, hoping he'd realize she wasn't a threat. Gradually, the growls died away, his fur settled back down, and then, with both women watching his every move, he flicked out his tongue and licked her hand before plonking his bottom back down and wagging his tail at the two of them.

"It seems," Ruth said with a smile, "that Bobby's forgiven you for shouting at me." Penny's mirrored smile was cut short by Ruth's next words: "I'm not so quick to forgive."

Nodding, Penny lowered her head in shame. "I don't blame you."

"Just what do you think you're doing?" Ruth repeated. "You barely know Ambrose, so don't give me some rubbish about looking out for a friend, because that excuse won't wash."

Penny opened and closed her mouth a few times before finally nodding in agreement. "You're right, you're right! I don't know why I decided to follow them. Curiosity? Boredom?" she answered, with a shrug of her shoulders.

"How about, sheer plain stupidity?" Ruth ventured. Bobby huffed his agreement of his owner's assessment.

Throwing a glance up the lane toward the farmhouse, Penny thought she spied a flash of movement and had to force her legs to stay still rather than move toward it.

This didn't go unnoticed by Ruth. "Don't be silly or I *will* set Bobby on you, and being slobbered to death isn't a good way to go."

As was his wont, Bobby chose that moment to *woof* in agreement and followed it up with another lick of Penny's dangling hand.

Seeing she was being listened to, Ruth advised her, "I want you to take Bobby and go back home." Seeing a frown forming, she added, "Please, don't argue with me."

"What are you going to do?" Penny wanted to know, already pretty certain she knew the answer.

"I know I didn't put it nicely just now, but Ambrose *is* my friend, and I have to find out what's going on."

A gunshot shattered the conversation, causing both their heads to jerk in the direction of the farmhouse from which it had come. Another two shots closely followed, before men shouting replaced them. Ruth and Penny took cover, dragging and pushing Bobby into the same ditch Penny had occupied not so long ago.

When it seemed safe to traverse the lane again, Ruth thrust Bobby's leash into Penny's hand and shouted at the pair, "Go!"

Air-raid warning system or not, Bobby understood

his mission and immediately proceeded to tow Penny back down the lane toward home. As she reached the bend, she glanced over her shoulder. As Bobby obeyed his owner's wishes, Penny kept her eyes on Ruth. The newspaper editor made her way, quite impressively, to Penny's untrained eyes, along the hedge toward the farmhouse, not once looking back.

Chapter Thirty-Four

"What did I say about not shooting, Jones?"

Sergeant Matt Baines elbowed his lowly private hard enough in the ribs that he had to swiftly grab the man by his webbing to prevent him from rolling out from behind the water trough they'd both taken cover behind. Above and to their right, the kitchen door hung half off its hinges, blasted away by the shotgun which had nearly taken the pair's heads off their shoulders.

"I tripped, Sarge!" the hapless man protested.

Satisfied they weren't in imminent danger, Matt looked over at his sole companion. the rest of his platoon and Lawrence had gone to cover in and around the pigsty. He wasn't sure who was in the best place. The old military saying "If you know a better hole…" came to mind, only he had more than enough sense of self-preservation not to risk moving unless he really needed to. When he saw the young man clearly for the first time since the shooting had started, he was instantly struck by how young he was. Like most units of the Home Guard, they were a mixture of the too young to join up, the too old, and the not-fit-enough. Jones fitted firmly into the first category, and it showed. His eyes were wide in fear and his hands were gripping his rifle hard enough to nearly break it in half.

Matt bit back the impulse to tell him to make sure his safety catch was back on; the kid didn't need another telling off, not with the predicament they found themselves in. Instead, he reached across and flipped the boy's safety catch on for him.

"Leave that as it is."

"What if someone shoots at me?" the boy asked, a trace of panic in his voice.

Recognizing the signs of someone experiencing their first time under fire, Matt quickly shoved away his own memories, which were trying to take him back to his time on the first day of the Somme battle of nineteen-sixteen, and gripped his colleague's shoulder.

"If that happens, two things. Take down your enemy's name and address and report them to the police. Then, you have my permission to shoot back."

After a moment, Jones let out a soft chuckle, and Matt was relieved to see him break his death-grip on his rifle.

"Good lad. Now, get your tin-lid on and stick close to me," Matt told him, gathering his feet underneath him and taking a firmer grip on his rifle with his free hand.

"Baines! Jones! You two all right?" Lawrence's voice echoed across the courtyard.

"Both okay!" Matt shouted back before launching both himself and a fortunately compliant Private Jones across the open courtyard and toward the pigsty. Reflecting upon it later, it was the longest ten or so yards in his life, and considering he'd served in the trenches in the Great War, that was saying something. They were lucky, though, as no one took any more potshots at them. Shoving Jones to where the rest of the platoon was huddled, Matt planted himself down next to where Lawrence knelt, his revolver tightly clutched in his right hand.

After briefly looking his temporary number two up and down, presumably to check he wasn't leaking blood from anywhere, Lawrence grunted in satisfaction before shouting out, "You with the shotgun! This is Inspector Lawrence of the police! Throw the weapon away and come out with your hands up! You have one minute to obey!"

Once completely back under cover, Lawrence asked him, "Did you see where that shotgun blast came from?"

"I'm not totally sure," Matt began, "but judging by the remains of the kitchen door, I'd lay odds on it being from somewhere around the entrance to that barn." He pointed a finger in the direction of the barn opposite the farmhouse.

"Makes sense," Lawrence agreed.

Matt felt a tap on his elbow. Looking around, he was surprised to find Jones besides him. He couldn't help but glance at where the man's rifle was pointing and was relieved to find the muzzle was directed skyward. "What is it, Jones? Haven't you caused enough trouble already?"

Due credit went to the young man as, though he visibly swallowed, he persisted. "Whose van is that, Sarge?" He was pointing at the bonnet of a dark blue Bedford van just visible around the corner of the barn where they suspected the gunman was currently sheltered.

As is the automatic reaction of senior non-commissioned officers everywhere, Matt opened his mouth to tell him that when he wanted his input, he'd give it to him, when something about the boy's demeanor stopped him. There was an urgency in both his voice and his eyes. "Go on, lad," he instead urged.

Fair credit to the boy, he pressed on under the intense scrutiny of both his NCO and the policeman. "I don't recognize it. I know Ambrose, too, me and me mum, well…"

Lawrence smiled as he told him, "No need to elaborate, I'm not interested in that."

Jones returned the smile before carrying on, "Well, Ambrose's van's the same color, but this one's got a split windscreen."

"And Ambrose's one doesn't!" Lawrence quickly filled in. "Well spotted, lad!"

Matt too nodded approvingly. "Keep this up, I'll forget about you nearly getting our heads shot off!"

Lawrence looked at his wristwatch, then turned his head back toward the barn. "Well, I've not heard anything," he said. He addressed Matt once more. "I suggest you take half the men and work your way around the back of the barn. Immobilize that van, I don't care how. I'll take the remaining three and, in a minute, we'll edge our way toward the front of the barn. Do you agree?"

Glancing back at the men they'd managed to gather, half of which were around the same age as Jones whilst the other half had fought in the last war and maybe some wars before that as well, Matt could see a mixture of eagerness and nervousness. Fine, that's exactly how he felt. He didn't bother speaking, merely nodding before turning back and, after choosing his men, told them, "Heads down, safety catches off. That includes you, Jones, and follow me. You all heard what we need to do."

With no further ado, they were off. Lawrence turned his head back and shouted, "You've had your minute! What's your answer?"

The reply he received wasn't what he was hoping for, as there was another loud retort, and this time shotgun pellets pinged just above his head.

"Not very sensible," he mumbled, wishing he too had a tin-hat, in place of his best fedora.

He was about to lift his head up for a better look when one of the men Matt had left with him gripped him firmly by the arm. "Wait!" the sixty-something man urged. "That was only one barrel."

No sooner had the words escaped his lips than there was another blast, and the contents of the second barrel whisked through the air.

Hoping he'd remember to thank the man later, Lawrence got to his feet, unhindered this time, and took off toward the barn as fast as his feet could take him. Halfway there, the same man who'd possible saved his life just now, yelled, "Down!" Automatically, everyone did so, and a few seconds later there was a much louder discharge as both barrels were sent their way. Their adversary was quick to reload. For the second time in nearly as many seconds, Lawrence had reason to thank the Home Guard private. This time, a few pellets whisked through his hat, and he felt a brief searing pain as one or two skimmed off his scalp. Something hot and wet began to run down the side of his face.

Ignoring this, he clambered to his feet and took off after his men. Not one to let pride get in the way, Lawrence was ready to take his cues from the same private, and at the same moment they got to the open entrance to the barn, four nearly simultaneous shots resounded, and he saw the suspicious van lurch as all its tires were flattened in a most satisfactory manner. This caused a voice from just the other side of where he was pressed up against the barn wall to loudly swear.

The unexpected damage to what was likely this Selwyn chaps van caused him to make another mistake, his first being to open fire. The barrel of the shotgun he'd been firing poked its way around the open doors. Without thinking, Lawrence let go of his revolver and made a grab for the shotgun, letting out a yelp of pain from the hot barrel. He almost let go and actually may have done, if his private, as he was coming to think of him, hadn't dived through the door and tackled the man around the waist. As they fell, Lawrence gave an almighty tug and managed to pull the shotgun from the man's hands, sending it sliding into a dark corner of the barn. Within seconds, the rest of his men surrounded them, all with their rifles pointed at the head of their prey.

Blowing on his hands, Lawrence retrieved his revolver, inwardly cursing his stupidity at throwing it down. "You can let him go now…" he told his man.

"Ian Ledbetter," the private helpfully supplied.

Lawrence held out his free hand to help Ian to his feet, whilst one of his colleagues handed him back his rifle. "Good man," he commended.

There was the thunder of army boots, and they were joined by most of the other half of the platoon. "You've got the swine. Good!" grinned Matt, shouldering his rifle as he looked down at where their prisoner was scowling up at him.

As if reminded of something, Lawrence addressed his prisoner, whom his new friend Ian had made to lie down on his front with his hands crossed palm side up behind his back. "As for you, you're under arrest. Stupid bugger, where do you think you are? The Wild West? Taking shots at us like that!" To Matt, he addressed the question, "Did you find anything in the van?"

Matt's grin was feral. "Boxes of Lee Enfield rifles. They don't look new, but I reckon there's nothing wrong with them, either. My other men are guarding them."

Everyone nearly jumped out of their skins when a voice from behind them said, "Oh, good, you've got him!"

Lawrence and Matt turned their attention to the newspaper owner who'd suddenly appeared in their midst. "Ruth!" they both exclaimed.

"Not guilty," she beamed, before turning serious. "Where's Ambrose?"

Before anyone could stop him, Ian Ledbetter jammed the muzzle of his rifle into the prisoner's stomach, not violently, but certainly hard enough to knock the breath out of his lungs. "You heard the lady! Where's Ambrose?"

No one objected to Ian's questioning method, especially as it produced results. Once he'd got enough air back in his lungs, he told them Ambrose was tied up in a corner of the pigsty.

"The pigsty?" Matt asked, puzzled.

"Very useful, pigs," their prisoner spat out. "You can get rid of all manner of evidence with a pig."

Lawrence and Matt both saw a horrified look pass over Ian's face as, swiftly, he turned his rifle around and raised the butt above the grounded man's face, but his two superiors managed to grab an arm each and wrestle his rifle from him before he could do more damage.

"Stand down, Ledbetter!" Matt firmly ordered, and with one twist, he had the rifle out of his hands.

"Anyone else around?" Lawrence demanded, which got a shake of the head. "Matt, don't take any chances. I wouldn't trust this bugger as far as I could throw him. Go and check, but be careful."

"I'll go with him," Ruth stated, before trotting off toward the pigsty, leaving a swearing Matt running to catch up with his girlfriend.

He paused only long enough to shove the rifle back into Ledbetter's hands and deliver him a firm non-verbal warning to behave, with a further instruction of, "Ian, I need you and these other two men to do a sweep of the farm. Make sure there's no one else around. Be very careful!"

"You going to be all right with this one?" Ian asked, not bothering to keep an expression of hate from his face.

Lawrence patted his revolver, before turning it back so it was pointed at where their prisoner was still lying on the floor, ignoring the murderous looks shot his way. "We'll be fine," he assured him. "Be quick, but thorough."

Left alone, Lawrence pondered his next move. He didn't even know this man's last name and didn't have the luxury of utilizing Ian's interrogation methods, no matter how tempting that may have been. He couldn't tie him up on his own, and knocking him out was against his own, not to mention the police's, code. Still, a revolver had its uses. Kneeling down a short distance before the man's face, he made a show of casually waving it around as he asked, "Last name?"

"Pike," came the somewhat muffled reply.

Lawrence raised an eyebrow, though he merely commented, "Pike, eh. Right. So, Pike, slowly turn over and sit cross-legged, hands palms up underneath your ass." He knew they'd soon find out who this character really was once they could fingerprint him.

Before his thoughts could go further, the loud beep of a car's horn caused Lawrence to turn his head. Unfortunately, this was at the same time as Pike was doing as he'd instructed. Taking advantage of his captor's momentary inattention, the man launched himself at Lawrence and the two crashed backward to the floor, where Lawrence's head made a cracking sound and he slumped into immediate unconsciousness.

Far from beaten, Pike picked up the fallen revolver and, with the lack of caution of the desperate, found himself face to face with a Jeep and its occupants, Jane, Penny, and Bobby.

He pointed the gun to the sky and pulled the trigger once. "No one move!"

Chapter Thirty-Five

Having put the world to rights with her husband, Doris decided to pay a call on Mavis. She was curious as to what her son was like. Surely no one could be as crabby as his mother. Plus, she'd always wondered how old the man could be. She'd always assumed Mavis was in her sixties somewhere, never quite having plucked up the courage to ask, so she must have had her son quite late. Why she felt the need to make this visit, she didn't know, and so, with no one around to talk her out of her innate nosiness, she now found herself turning the corner into the road where Mavis lived.

"You don't see many dachshunds around these days," was her first thought at seeing the smartly dressed couple a few dozen steps ahead of her, who'd just stepped out of a small gray Humber car, closely followed by, "I've never seen this pair before," as they opened the gate and knocked on Mavis's front door. Little and large seemed to fit them. The man, wearing a typical wartime nondescript suit, was a good head and a half shorter than the female, who appeared to be quite sharply dressed, though the fox stole she wore around her neck looked out of place.

Instinct told Doris to step into the shadows afforded by a tree and to keep quiet. Carefully, she leant her head around until she could just see, with one eye, her friend's house and the strangers awaiting there. From the moment the door was opened, things happened in a blur. In fact, it wasn't until the door slammed shut and she had a few moments to think about it, that she was certain the man had indeed pulled a pistol on Sharon, and Sharon had raised her hands high, palms forward. Fortunately for Doris, they'd disappeared before she could act in haste, probably preventing her from being shot.

****

Sharon put her arms back down by her sides, despite having them raised being the only thing the pair who'd accosted her had told her to do so far. It felt rather silly to have your hands up in your own home, or as near to a home as she'd ever felt she had. Now she was forced to look at the pair, she openly studied them, though she had to admit defeat after a few moments, as she didn't recognize either face and told them so.

"However, I never forget a dog," she stated.

The dog in question merely looked up at her and stretched out, trying to lick her face. The woman, in whose arms it was held, tightened her grip and stepped back until she was against the front door, admonishing the dog with a quick, "Fritz!"

"Enough!" the man told her. Though she'd never been further than Blackpool in her short life, Sharon had seen enough newsreels to recognize a German accent when she heard one and couldn't stop the sharp intake of breath upon hearing his voice.

"Hans," said his companion, "you said I was to do the talking!"

The pistol flicked carelessly up, causing Sharon to involuntarily duck, before it settled back to pointing at a spot between Sharon's breasts. "What does it matter? I've changed my mind."

Before anyone could say anything further, there was a noise from upstairs and Mavis appeared at the top of the steps.

"Why do I hear Kraut voices?" she demanded, making her way down the stairs, though it was only as she got to the bottom few that she was able to see the unwelcome guests. "And who do we have here?"

The woman, at least, going by her Liverpudlian accent, was English and seemed to maintain enough of her native manners to automatically step forward and hold out her hand. "Mrs. Rosemary Headman, and this is my husband…"

"Rosemary!" her companion snapped, and the woman immediately shut her mouth, whilst the small dog whimpered and then growled at the man. "And as for you…" The man actually pointed his pistol at the dog's head.

"Don't you dare, Hans!" the woman told him, turning away so the gun could no longer point at the dachshund.

"Hans!" cried Mavis. "You are a Kraut!"

Before anyone could say anything else, Mavis, with agility which would shame a teenager, leapt at Hans, actually managing to fasten her arms around his burly neck. It was being stocky that gave him even more of an advantage than he'd ever need, as he brought up his free hand and wrenched Mavis from her grip, throwing her to the carpeted floor. Before she was able to even contemplate getting to her feet, Hans brought the hand with the pistol in it around in a long, low arc, right across the back of Mavis's head. With a grunt, she slumped forward unconscious.

Sharon automatically took a step forward to bend

down and attend to her friend, "Mavis!"

"Leave her!" Hans harshly ordered, taking Sharon under the arm and dragging her toward the lounge. For a small man, he was astonishingly strong, and Sharon had to trot along to avoid being dragged to the floor. Once they were in the room, Hans unceremoniously flung her onto the sofa, knocking the wind out her. Recovering, she went to get up with the intention of helping Mavis, only to find herself staring down the barrel of the pistol.

"Let me help her," she pleaded, consciously avoiding calling him a rude name.

"Leave her," he repeated.

His wife appeared to be more humane. Coming up behind him, she placed a tentative hand upon his shoulder. "Hans, I'm not a murderer, let Sharon help her."

"How did you know my name?" Sharon asked, unable to stop her curiosity from showing.

Hans turned his full attention upon her, and Sharon couldn't help but instinctively shrink back into the sofa before she remembered that she was likely face to face with her country's enemy for the first time. Squaring her shoulders, Sharon moved forward until she was on the edge of the sofa, from where she could see Mavis. The sight both distressed her and strengthened her resolve. Fixing him with her most determined glare, she put away for the moment the question of how he knew her name—Mavis was her priority.

"Listen to your wife, Hans." She couldn't stop the slight sneer from creeping into her voice as she uttered his name. "Whatever's going on, surely you don't want the blood of an old woman on your hands." Sharon was glad Mavis couldn't hear her describe her as an old woman.

The man seemed somewhat in a quandary and began waving his pistol this way and that, almost as if he'd forgotten he had it in his hand. It took his wife turning a glare upon him and snapping, "Hans!" to bring him back to his senses.

"Ach, very well!" His German accent seemed a little more pronounced.

Not waiting for him to change his mind, Sharon rushed to Mavis's side. Kneeling, she placed two fingers against her neck and was relieved to find a strong pulse. Whilst her captors conducted a silent argument, Sharon did a quick check of the older woman's head, relieved to find only a small cut. By the looks of things, the pistol swipe had barely touched her, though obviously it had been enough to knock her out, probably due to her age. Assuming they got out of this predicament alive, Mavis wouldn't be happy to hear it had taken so little to knock her out. She prided herself on being a strong woman, age be blowed!

Whilst Sharon was pondering if she should simply drag Mavis over to the sofa, Rosemary came over, tucked the unhappy-looking dachshund under one arm, and bent down to take a firm hold of one of Mavis's arms with the other. Resisting the natural impulse to smile in gratitude, Sharon took hold of the other and between the two of them, they managed to place Mavis on the sofa.

"Happy?" Hans snapped.

This time, Sharon did speak before thinking. "Of course I'm not bloody happy! Now, let me get a damp flannel for her head."

Hans and Rosemary exchanged glances at this statement. It was Hans who recovered his wits first this time. "*Nein!*" he said, slipping into his native language, though he seemed to quail a little under the furious glare Sharon gave him and told her, "Get a tea towel. Use that instead."

After a moment, Sharon decided it probably wouldn't be a good idea to try his patience too far. It already seemed to be on a knife-edge. Nodding, she left her friend's side and, with Rosemary following her, went into the kitchen, pulled out a drawer to get a clean tea towel and quickly ran it under the tap. Hurrying back to Mavis's side, she perched on the edge of the sofa and carefully applied it to Mavis's forehead, making sure to cover the wound too.

"Are we done?"

"Good sarcasm," Sharon told him, her mouth once more operating before her brain engaged gear.

This time, it looked like she'd gone too far, as Hans was by her side in an instant. Grabbing her roughly by the arm, he tugged her to her feet and placed the barrel of the pistol under her chin. "Anymore backtalk from you, and I might forget why I'm here. Understand?"

"Why *are* you here, and how do you know my name?" Sharon demanded somewhat awkwardly, as the gun had forced her chin up so it was a little difficult to speak. Still, she was determined not to make things easy for whoever this couple were. Well, pretty obviously they were some kind of spies, she thought, before Hans brought her attention back to him and her situation.

"You seem a bright girl," he began, turning on a smile that likely owed a lot to dental surgery. He stepped back to stand by his wife's side. "Why don't you tell me what you think?"

As she'd been given carte blanche, Sharon decided

she may as well voice her thoughts; she was pretty certain she'd be right on the nose. "Very well," she replied, sitting down but being careful not to disturb Mavis. "As you know my name and you're a Nazi…" She broke off as Hans raised the hand with the pistol in it once more, but when Rosemary forced his arm down, Sharon raised her chin on her own accord this time, in defiance. "What's the problem? That's what you call yourselves, isn't it? How does it feel to be married to a Nazi, Rosemary?" Sharon asked, hoping the brave pills she seemed to have taken wouldn't wind up getting her killed.

"I'm not…" the other woman got as far as saying before her husband turned the pistol, with seeming nonchalance, on her instead.

"I think it's best if you keep quiet from now on." Once he was satisfied his wife would obey his instruction, he turned back to Sharon with, "Carry on."

With the curious exchange safely filed away in her mind, Sharon, a little more carefully this time, as this Hans really seemed to enjoy playing with his pistol, she continued, "As I was about to say, I would lay a bet you're spies, put here to keep an eye on me, to make sure I'm doing as instructed. How does that sound?"

Hans nodded. "Proceed."

"Not before I know how my Nan is," Sharon replied, jutting out her chin once more in defiance.

She noticed the pistol begin to slowly swing her way again, before he appeared to think twice. "Ah, yes, the formidable Ada Coates."

"You've met her?" Sharon couldn't help but ask, leaning a little toward him.

He shook his head. "Not myself, but my superiors

have, shall we say, had words with her."

Sharon gulped. She'd heard stories about what these Nazis were capable of and didn't like to think of her grandmother in their clutches. Taking a deep breath, she tried to calm down, as imagining the worst wouldn't help her. Somewhat to her surprise, Rosemary snapped at her husband.

"Don't be cruel, Hans! Tell her what you told me."

After a moment's thought, he said, "Very well, it can't make any difference now. Your grandmother is getting better. I was able to persuade my superiors, as a show of our good faith, that we should give her the first dose of medicine."

Not for the first time, Sharon was pleased she was good at poker, as her real reaction to these words didn't show upon her face. She knew her aged relation was dying. Her grandmother had told her that again in the last letter she'd read from her, and that, together with her telling her not to believe a word she might hear from any German she may encounter, was enough to firm up Sharon's belief that this toad before her was lying through his teeth. A vision of laughing on the beach with her nan in happier pre-war days flashed before her eyes. Reluctantly, she mentally shook the image away. If she, and Mavis, were to get out of this predicament alive, she didn't need any distractions, no matter how pleasant.

"That's…good of you," Sharon stuttered out, hoping they'd put her hesitation down to nerves, rather than trying to channel her best Vivian Leigh. "Thank you," she added, hoping her voice was just the right timbre to be believed.

The only reaction she could see was a slight raising of one eyebrow by Rosemary, though it was so brief

Sharon didn't know if it had actually occurred. Hans, by contrast, appeared to only have two emotions, angry or maddeningly calm. Sharon wasn't sure which she preferred. At least when he was angry she knew enough to be a hundred percent on her guard.

He waved away her thanks, making her wish he'd stop waving the damn pistol around. By the increasing frown upon his wife's face, she'd be in agreement. A small growl issued from the dachshund, so the poor animal didn't like it either.

"It is not measure…trouble," he amended. "We are always happy when we can help."

Sharon bit her lip from the effort of holding back what she wanted to say. He thought he was blackmailing her into helping his country, and it was to her benefit that he should continue to believe that was the case.

"So, what do you want? I've done everything you ordered!" She was quite happy with her choice of words. Being a military man from a dictatorship, they were designed to flatter. Looking directly at him, she could see they'd had the right effect, as he looked, if anything, smug. And he'd also let the pistol lie on his lap.

To her surprise, Rosemary asked him much the same thing. "Yes, Hans, what else does Berlin want from her? You said yourself that the information she sent was of great use."

The sneer which came to his lips sent a shudder through Sharon's body. "That is true, my wife. However," and here he turned up the fear factor in both his voice and his facial expression, "I am sure that if she wishes her dear, dear grandmother to continue to receive treatment, then she will continue to be of…use."

Despite knowing there was nothing which could be

done to save her nan's life and hoping she wasn't suffering, nor would suffer because of what she had to say, Sharon again prayed to the goddess in the form of Vivian Leigh. "That's…heartless." She added a shudder and then had to suppress a grin when his wife echoed her and the sneer morphed into a smirk. He believed he had her!

Getting to his feet, he reached down and pulled his wife, whom Sharon was beginning to have sympathies for, to her feet. "Come. It's time we left. Miss Sharon Coates has some thinking to do."

Without a backward glance, the odious man tucked his pistol back inside his jacket and began to stride out of the room. Sharon wasn't certain, but she thought she saw Rosemary mouth the word "Sorry" as she passed.

No sooner had the front door slammed than Sharon was leaning over Mavis, who chose that moment to let out a low moan. There was a sharp rap on the front door, and Sharon couldn't help but wonder if the pair were back. However, there then came the sound of two car engines revving, one after the other, before both pulled away, one a few seconds after the other, in a squeal of rubber, closely followed by someone pounding on the front door and a deep male voice yelling, "Ma!"

Chapter Thirty-Six

Ruth and Matt had, after a very dirty, smelly, and altogether disgusting search, unearthed a very much worse for wear Ambrose. Dried blood matted his hair and had left rust-colored rivulets down one side of his cheek. By the looks of it, he'd been knocked unconscious—by something heavy and blunt, Ruth's newspaper mind couldn't help but fill in—then dragged to the darkest corner of the pigsty, where who knew what had been shoveled over him until all that was sticking out was the top half of his head and one hand. This was far from being simply tied up. Who knew why the swine Lawrence had under arrest hadn't finished him off, though for this small mercy, Ruth was thankful.

Using what was almost certainly the same shovel as had been used to cover him up, Matt, carefully, had dug out their friend. After a frantic five minutes, they had him leaning up against the outside of the fence surrounding the pigsty.

"His breathing and pulse seem to be sound," Ruth told Matt, looking up from where she'd been checking. Taking out her handkerchief, she wiped pig excrement and mud from around Ambrose's mouth and nose. When there was still work to be done, Matt handed over his, and when she still wasn't happy, Ruth ripped the bottom few inches from the hem of her second-best dress, though now it was covered in things she'd rather not

323

think about and was only good for rags anyway.

"Why bury him in the pigsty?" she asked as she worked.

"I've an idea, but I don't like even thinking it, let alone saying it out loud," Matt told her, after a pause.

Ruth was a woman of the world and after allowing herself to swear profusely, she paused in her ministrations and looked up at where her boyfriend was standing guard. She could tell by the way his fingertips had gone white, how he felt about what they'd discovered. "Let's not talk about it right now."

"Your nephew should know that we found him," Matt stated.

Ruth looked up, her eyes as hard and sharp as flint. "Oh don't worry, he will."

Seemingly satisfied they weren't going to be disturbed by anyone else who shouldn't be there, Matt bent down and took a good close look at Ambrose. "By God, he stinks!"

Grimacing at the mess they both were in, she couldn't help but smile. "I doubt if we smell of roses either."

For the first time, Matt looked at the state of his own clothes. "Hmm, I don't think I'd pass inspection like this."

Further conversation was interrupted by Ambrose letting out a groan, as he began to stir. His rescuers immediately turned their full attention upon him, with Ruth moving to kneel directly before him, her hands cupping either side of his face.

"Ambrose," she began, her voice firm, her attention resolute. "Ambrose! Can you hear me? Squeeze my fingers if you can," she added, taking his incredibly mucky ones in hers, which were very nearly as dirty. "Ambrose!"

After a few heart-stopping seconds, she could feel him grip her fingers. It wasn't hard, but he also didn't let go.

Matt glanced down at the same moment Ambrose's eyes briefly flickered open. "You rest, mate. Help'll be here soon," he told him. "Ruth, can you stay with him? I'm going to get some water and more rags."

"Don't forget to telephone for an ambulance," she told him as he sped off, her full attention still on the farmer.

Rounding the corner, Matt raised his hand and was about to shout out a greeting when the sight before him brought him up short. Why and how was their former captive shouting at a Jeep full of Matt's friends?

"Get out of the Jeep!" Pike shouted, brandishing a revolver toward Jane and Penny. Penny was leaning over the passenger seat, her arms wrapped around Bobby to prevent him from attacking. The Cocker Spaniel's hackles were raised, and he was making noises that sent shivers up Matt's backbone, and he'd heard sounds in the trenches which still gave him nightmares. Just poking out of the barn's open door was a hand, and he was certain it belonged to Lawrence, though whether the man was dead or alive was impossible to tell.

He was about to edge back into the shadows, hoping he hadn't been seen, when the revolver moved in his direction.

"Freeze!" Pike told him. "Take another step toward me, and one of these ladies gets it!"

Taking a gamble he hoped they'd understand, Matt quickly stepped back the way he'd come, and before Pike could say another word, he was out of view.

"Very clever!" Pike yelled, so Matt could hear. "Stay where you are, but," he paused for undoubted effect, "if anyone else decides to be clever, I will shoot. Say *yes*, if you understand?"

Not doubting this was directed at him, Matt shouted out his agreement. He'd made his move, as he didn't want to risk giving his rifle to this piece of work. In his opinion, Pike was a few planks short of a pier, as he hadn't tried to get him to give up his rifle. He hoped the thought wouldn't occur to him now. It looked like what would happen to Jane and Penny, but also the rest of his platoon, was very much up to him now. He may not have heard Pike, assuming he was already shouting whilst they were dealing with Ambrose, but he couldn't imagine that none of them wouldn't react to that last warning.

It was time for his second gamble in as many minutes. Crouching down, he edged as close to the corner of the barn as he could and shouted at the top of his lungs, "Platoon! Do nothing until I say so!"

He held his breath and when, after ten or so seconds, there was no gunfire, he let it out. It appeared that both his men and Pike had taken notice of his words, as the next thing Pike did was to shout once more. Deciding it was worth the risk, Matt tentatively poked his head around the corner until he was able to witness what was happening. Until the end of his days, he'd keep replaying it over and over, never quite able to believe his eyes.

By risking another inch, he could just make out a few rifles poking around the other end of the barn, which had to be his other men. Lawrence's hand was still lying there, not moving. Fighting the urge to act on his instincts, he steadied his breath and waited.

"You two, out!" Pike was shouting.

"Fine!" Jane shouted back. "If you'd put the gun down, that'd be a nice start. I really wish you hadn't persuaded me to come up here instead of taking you home, Penny," she then muttered. "Maybe I should have just run you over."

"Shut up and do what I say, now!" Pike merely shouted back. Matt could swear he could detect a subtle Irish accent there.

And that's when all hell broke loose…

Ruth chose that moment to come around the corner. How she was upright, Matt didn't know. She had an arm around Ambrose's waist, whilst the gentleman himself appeared to be shuffling along by sheer muscle memory. His eyes were barely half open, and Matt didn't believe he had any real idea where he was or what was going on.

"Where's that water, Matt?" Ruth yelled as she came into view.

Pike began to turn his head toward the new voice, his upper body naturally following suit. It was all the opening Bobby had been waiting for. Like a furry torpedo, the cunning canine launched himself out of Penny's arms, and in a thrice, he'd clamped his jaws shut around the wrist holding the revolver! Pike let out a howl of pain and surprise, and the revolver clattered to the ground.

Before he even knew what he was doing, Matt was scrambling along the ground on all fours, his rifle banging against the ground as he went, determined to scoop up the revolver before Pike could recover. When it came down to it, this was a full grown man of some fifteen or sixteen stone against a twenty-odd-pound dog.

As soon as Pike got over his surprise, this brave act would likely be the last thing Bobby ever did. He didn't get halfway there before it was scooped up by Jane, who jammed the muzzle under Pike's chin.

"Stop moving, or I may forget I don't know how to fire this thing."

There was something in the tone of voice in which she uttered the words, and Matt had to force himself not to lay down his rifle in response. Pike opened his mouth, only for Bobby to clamp his jaws down a little harder, and all the man's fight dissipated before their eyes. Next to him, Ruth ordered Bobby, "Drop!" To Matt's amazement, Bobby let go and moved to sit next to his mistress, looking up at her, tail wagging and Pike's blood dripping from his mouth. 'Good boy," Ruth praised him.

Gathering his senses, Matt got fully to his feet and was by Jane's side, his finger on the trigger of his rifle, an instant later. Watching the prisoner closely, he asked, "You two all right?"

"We're fine," Jane assured him, and he believed her. The hands which held the heavy revolver betrayed not a trace of shaking.

"Good," Matt said. "Penny, if you're up to it," he began, spotting the bandages around her arms, "could you go and see how Lawrence is? I think this bugger must have knocked him unconscious when he tried to escape. As for you, take that ugly leer off your face or I'll let Bobby, there, chew on your other wrist."

"I'm on it, Matt," Penny told him, and she struggled out of the rear of the Jeep and hobbled over to where a groan indicated Lawrence was waking up.

"Can you give me a hand with Ambrose here?" Ruth asked Jane.

Instead, Jane asked Matt to tell some of his men to help with Ambrose. She still had the revolver and her eyes levelled at Pike, though she'd taken a few steps back.

"Jones! Bell! Get yourselves over here, at the double!"

"Yes, Sarge?" Jones said, as the two came to a halt before him, warily eyeing Pike, who was still under the armed care of both Jane and the sergeant. His nose twitched, but he'd learned when to keep his mouth shut.

Bell hadn't. "What the hell's that smell?"

To his obvious disgust, Ruth clomped the few steps over to the pair before telling them, "Shoulder your rifles." Once they'd done so, she proceeded to ask them both to hold out a hand.

Jones did as he was asked, allowing himself a sigh of resignation. Bell still needed to learn his lesson. "My uniform, Sarge!"

"Do as you're told and stop moaning, Bell," he snapped. "I'll give you all of tomorrow to get cleaned up."

"Well said, darling," Ruth praised him. "Come on, you two, let's get Ambrose inside. I need to get an ambulance out here for him."

"Wait for us!" Penny cried, as she staggered out of the barn, a rather groggy Lawrence leaning on her shoulder, her own face scrunched up in pain with the effort.

Jane saw this and asked, "Matt, do you have anyone else who can come and guard this bugger? Penny's nearly dead on her feet."

"Sorry, no. I need to keep my last pair guarding the rifles this one was trying to make off with. However," he quickly added, sensing an imminent protest, "nip into the barn for a minute. I'll be very surprised if you don't find some rope."

"You'll be okay?" she asked.

"Just let Pike here try something," Matt told her, making certain Pike heard every word.

"Hey, I'm bleeding here!" Pike protested, holding up a slightly mangled wrist.

"What of it?" Jane got in before Matt could speak. "If you run out of blood, then I may be interested. In the meantime, get your hands on your head and shut your trap."

"Do what she says," Matt reinforced her order and watched as the man placed his hands upon his head, doing his best to ignore the slow dripping of his own blood down the side of his face.

Once she was satisfied, Jane handed the revolver over to Penny, who levelled it with some difficulty but plenty of determination at Pike. Less than a minute after disappearing into the barn, Jane was back, a blackened length of rope in her hands. She advanced upon Pike until she was a few steps behind him. Matt moved until he was off to her side, leaving himself a clear field of fire.

"Know how to tie a knot?" he asked.

Jane snapped the rope, saying, "Oh, yes. You just cover me. I assume you're okay to leave him on the ground?"

"Fine by me," he replied. "Pike, believe me, you don't want to give me an excuse. Understand?"

A few minutes later, Pike was bound. None too gently, Jane also wrapped a rag she'd found around his injured wrist.

Satisfied, Matt allowed his grip on his rifle to relax a little.

"Right," Jane said. "Penny, if you can keep hold of the revolver?"

"I'd rather have it," Lawrence said, doing his best not to put too much of his weight on Penny.

Jane quickly looked him over before deciding, "I'll take it. Neither of you are in the best of health." She then matched words to action, also taking most of Lawrence's weight from Penny on his other side. "Now, come on, you lot, let's get this pair inside and taken care of. Matt, you going to be okay standing guard over this piece of rubbish?"

"Just let him try something," Matt replied.

"I should call my lot in," Lawrence added, as Jane took some of his weight.

"Terry should be here soon," Jane told him, making sure Lawrence, Penny, and herself were in front of Ruth and her charges. "I spoke with him right before I left to get here." She then added, "Uh, don't take this the wrong way, Ruth, but do you mind if we go in front of you? As Bell so succinctly put it, you do both smell something awful!"

Chapter Thirty-Seven

"I still think you should go to the hospital," Ned repeated to his mother for the fourth time in nearly as many minutes.

Mavis removed the new wet flannel Sharon had applied to her head, glanced at it, and held it up for them both to see. "No point," she stated, in a very Mavis voice. "Look, I've stopped bleeding. No point in wasting their time, when there's nothing they can do. I'll put my feet up for a bit, maybe have a kip, and I'll be right as rain."

"Ma…" The gentle giant of a man began to speak again but was waved into silence, and this time he took notice.

Sharon marveled again how someone so small could have produced someone so large! The thought made her think again about the possibility of having children, and she couldn't help the slight shudder that went through her. Maybe having children wasn't for her.

However… "I'm with your son, Mavis. You did get hit around the head with a pistol, after all."

"I do know what happened, young lady," Mavis told her, reaching up and touching the bump coming up. "It's not something I'm likely to forget."

"Then surely you can see the sense!" Sharon tried once again, with Ned vigorously nodding his large shaven head behind her.

"Please?" he tried, turning on what could only be

described as puppy eyes on his mother.

"No, and that's the last I want to hear about it." Mavis crossed her arms, daring the other two to speak up.

Sharon had grown up a lot in the last few weeks, and she had one more card to play. "All right, no more talk about going to the hospital." Mavis nodded, slowly, at this, and then begun to frown when Sharon suggested, "How about if we can get Betty's nurse friend to come over and check you out later? I've heard her talking at work about a Grace somebody or other—I can't remember her last name."

"Grace Baxter? Yes, the name does ring a bell," Mavis told her.

Seizing the moment before Mavis could change her mind, Sharon stood up. "Good. I'll pop down to the phone box and see if I can get hold of Betty. Ned, keep an eye on her, please. I'll be right back."

Mavis leaned forward. "You be careful! If those two are still about…" She left the sentence unfinished.

"I could go with Sharon?" Ned offered, though from the way he was looking concernedly at his mother, she didn't think his mind would be wholly on the job of guard.

Sharon laid a kindly hand upon his elbow; she couldn't reach his shoulder. "I appreciate the offer, Ned, but it's only about thirty yards down the road. Look"— she pointed—"you can see it from here. Plus, I'm certain they drove off."

"What did I miss?" Doris's voice demanded, the kitchen door banging shut behind her.

Ned turned from where he'd taken up vigil before the lounge window. "Sharon's gone to phone Betty," he informed her, before asking, "You found the outhouse then."

"Which reminds me, I need to cut up some fresh newspaper. Where d'you keep them, Mavis?"

"Cupboard under the sink," Mavis informed her, "but that can wait. Tell me again what you saw when those Krauts left. I want to make sure I didn't miss anything."

Distracted, Doris sniffed her fingers, recoiled slightly, hoping neither of the others had seen her less than ladylike action, and rushed back into the kitchen. Against the sound of running water, she repeated what she'd seen. Ned had hidden himself around the side of the house, under strict orders not to interfere, when Mavis's attackers had left. She'd seen the anger on his face and completely sympathized with his feelings even though, at the time, neither of them knew his mother had been attacked. Nevertheless, she'd implored him to trust her and to let them go. Though she didn't know everything with which Sharon was involved, her expression had been enough to convince him she'd been in earnest.

"Thanks again for trusting me, Ned," she shouted. "You've no idea how sorry I am that Mavis got hurt," she added in her normal voice, coming back into the lounge whilst drying her hands on a tea towel.

"Ha!" Mavis snorted. "Don't pretend you haven't dreamed of doing something similar!"

Ned opened his mouth, undoubtedly to protest, but Doris laid a newly clean hand upon his arm and shook her head.

"She's right, son," Mavis assured him. "It's only our banter." She shuffled her feet out of the way so Doris could sit down and allow Mavis to stretch her feet over her lap.

Ned, satisfied that the two were telling the truth, took up his vigil at the window once again, though not before he shook his head. "I'm still trying to get all this right in my head. I'm only a gunner, and we don't like having to think all that much. Little Sharon there, involved in some spy stuff!"

"And you can't tell anyone," Mavis reminded her son.

"I know, Ma. Trust me, I won't."

Not needing to check twice, Mavis dug one of her heels into Doris's shin. "You were saying?"

"I was, though I may be the one in need of a doctor now. That's the same leg I broke the other year!" she moaned, reaching down to move Mavis's foot and give her own leg a swift rub.

"Pish!" Mavis waved Doris's protests away. "We both know that leg's stronger than ever now. So stop with your moaning and get on with it."

"All right, all right," Doris grumbled, shuffling her legs so her sore one wasn't directly under Mavis's. "Well, those two came out squabbling away like a pair of hens. Neither Ned nor myself were what you could call well hidden, but I don't think they'd have seen us if we'd had billboards around our necks saying *Nazi Rally This Way*! Fortunately, they didn't see this Rover 10 pull out a few seconds after they'd driven off. What?"

"Sorry," Mavis said, though not actually feeling it one jot. "I didn't know you knew anything about cars."

Doris shrugged. "It's got an engine and looks nice, well, for a British automobile, I guess."

"Go and buy one, then," Mavis suggested.

"I just may," Doris replied, sticking out her tongue for good measure. "As I was saying, this Rover pulled out, and there were two guys in it. Nice suits, hats pulled down over their eyes a bit…hope they don't crash. Anyway, I think there's a very good chance they've been watching Sharon and Lawrence in case, you know, something like this happens!" Doris couldn't keep the excitement from her voice, and only when Mavis grimaced did she refrain from bouncing up and down.

The door opened and slammed shut.

"Only me!" Sharon shouted out.

"In here!" Ned called, going over to open the door for her.

"Did I hear my name as I came up the path?" she wanted to know.

Doris frowned. "How the heck did you hear that? You were outside!"

Sharon blushed a little, nevertheless, she replied, "Your voice does…carry a little."

"Translated…you've a big mouth!" Mavis added, chortling.

"Not much wrong with you," Doris then said, lightly pinching the elder lady's foot.

"Exactly what I've been saying all along!"

"A bit late for that," Sharon replied before she could stop herself.

"Careful, you'll cut yourself with a wit that sharp," Doris immediately teased her back.

"Look who's getting all British!" Mavis put in.

"Time out!" Doris cried. "There's no need to turn nasty." In spite of the words, there was a smile on her lips.

Ned had stood there the whole time, and all he could

do was shake his head. Now there was a temporary lull, he took the opportunity to ask, "Are you lot always like this?"

All three women exchanged knowing looks before Doris replied, "Pretty much."

"And I thought I was coming home for a bit of rest," Ned finally said, before settling down in an overstuffed and much-loved armchair.

Sharon reported, "I couldn't get through to Betty, nor anyone, come to that, which is quite worrying. I ended up speaking to the guard commander and he was able to confirm the nurse's name. So I called the hospital, and they quickly tracked her down. She's going to pop around to see you tonight after she's finished her shift. Oh, and Doris, she told me that Walter wants you to know he loves you very much and he's very, very sorry," she finished, her face flushed at the words she'd just spoken. "I didn't know he was back inside."

"That makes him sound like a convict!" Doris laughed.

"But I thought his head was all better now?" Sharon persisted.

"It was…until someone else bashed him," Doris supplied, much more seriously.

"Is he going to be all right?" Mavis asked.

"Sure, so long as he doesn't do it again. Then I may just have to strap him down to stop him going out of the house."

Doris looked at her watch and her eyes widened in surprise. "I never realized what the time is! Nearly seven. Right." She heaved herself out from under Mavis's legs and got to her feet. "Lovely as this has not been, I must be getting home. Ned"—she held out her hand and shook the one he extended in response—"I hope you have a lovely rest of your leave. Look after this one." She slapped Mavis lightly on the knee. "She's one of a kind."

Chapter Thirty-Eight

Sergeant Terry Banks turned up in a squeal of rubber at the exact moment all the excitement died down. He took in the sight of Jane and Penny taking Lawrence's weight upon themselves and struggling toward the farmhouse.

"Boss! Lawrence!" He hurried out of his car, leaving the door ajar. To get to his boss, the quickest way was right by the limping Ambrose, held up by Ruth and Bell, the latter doing his best to touch as little of the poor farmer as he could. As he drew level, he automatically swerved as his body reacted to the sudden assault on his olfactory senses. "What the…sweet Jesus!"

"Sorry about that," Ruth apologized, with a tentative smile. "One guess where we found this poor chap."

Terry had reached her side by now and, with one last wrinkle of his nose, he went to ease Ruth's arm from around the farmer. Ruth shook her head.

"I appreciate the offer, but there's no sense in more of us getting mucky."

"He could take my place?" Bell offered, a hopeful look on his face.

Ruth looked around a barely conscious Ambrose. "Not a chance, boy! See my last statement. Now, you, Mr. Policeman, go and give Jane a hand."

Nodding, Terry strode over and clapped his boss on the back, nearly causing the threesome to stumble.

"Oops, sorry about that."

"Take over from Penny, and I'll think about forgiving you," Jane told him.

"Has anyone called for an ambulance?" Terry asked, hefting Lawrence's other arm over his shoulder, much to Penny's visible relief.

"I was about to when it all went pear-shaped again," Ruth told him.

"Again?" Terry said, immediately picking up on her word.

"We'll tell you later," Lawrence muttered. "Can we get inside? My head's killing me!"

Once inside, with a very slightly more awake Ambrose settled in his favorite seat, Bell having gathered some newspaper from the kitchen to try to cover the seat and the sofa, Ruth hurried off into the hall, returning a few minutes later to announce, "The hospital's sending an ambulance, but it'll be about half an hour. Whilst we're waiting, let's get a bowl of water and some disinfectant, and clean this pair up. Jane, can you handle Lawrence and Penny? I think Terry should go back outside with Matt," Ruth said. "Bell and I will see what we can do for Ambrose, here. Ambrose," she said gently, kneeling before him, "Where's your disinfectant?"

It took him two goes to get the words out, and when he did, he barely lifted his head, so she had to lean in to hear what he said. "Under the sink. There're a couple of bowls under there too," he added before letting his head slump back from the effort. "Sorry, sorry, so tired…"

"Ambrose! Stay with me!" Ruth told her friend, clutching his hand. "Don't make me slap you! Believe me, you really don't want to know what's on my hand."

At hearing this, Ambrose managed to crank open his

eyes and raise one of his own up to his face. "I don't think you would make much of a difference," he said back, though when he finished speaking this time, he was able to keep his eyes open.

This was enough to satisfy Ruth, who hurried into the kitchen and, after much banging and scraping, followed by the running of water, soon reappeared. She placed one bowl and some towels she'd found next to Jane, who immediately began to run a wet cloth through Lawrence's hair, saying, "Don't move, Penny, you're next."

Ruth went back to retrieve her own bowl and towels once she'd seen Penny obeying Jane's instruction. "Now, let's make you presentable," she told Ambrose, settling in to her task. Bell made as if to leave, only for Ruth to grab him by the hand. "Oh, no, you don't. I need you to hold Ambrose steady, as this is going to hurt."

To the farmer's credit, Ambrose barely winced as she applied the disinfectant to what were now visible head wounds. Throwing aside first one and then a second towel, Ruth finally wound the last one she had around Ambrose's head and placed one of Bell's hands—after it had been rubbed semi-clean,—upon the top. She told Bell, "Don't move an inch," and went over to where Lawrence sat holding a damp towel to the back of his head. "Do you need a hand?" she asked Jane.

Jane looked up at Ruth and shook her head. "No, thanks. Lawrence there was very lucky. His scalp was nicked by a few shotgun pellets, fortunately without doing that much damage. The bleeding's stopped, and he's all cleaned up now. I'm just finishing up with Penny here. She's all right, just a little tired."

"And feeling rather foolish too," Penny admitted.

Indeed, she did look rather sheepish and couldn't look Ruth in the eye.

"I thought I told you to get home," Ruth said. "And to take Bobby with you," she added, before looking around. "Speaking of which, where is he? Bobby!" she cried.

There was an answering bark from outside, and Ruth rushed back through the kitchen until she was once more in the courtyard. Greeting her were Matt and Terry, both standing guard over Pike, who was lying on his side a few feet from the Home Guard sergeant. At his head, staring down at him with doggy malice, was Bobby. At the sight of his mistress, he looked up, wagged his tail, and then resumed his guard duty.

"Remind me to buy this chap a big bone, Ruth," Matt said.

Before replying, Ruth bent down to give her dog a quick examination and, upon finding nothing wrong with him, though she did her best to wipe some of Pike's blood from around his muzzle, stood up.

"I'm sorry," Penny said, from where she was leaning against the door frame. "I know you told me to go home, but when Jane came along, well, I'm afraid I was able to talk her into bringing me here."

Ruth didn't bother looking around, instead shouting over her shoulder, "Jane! Get out here."

A moment later, Jane appeared. "You hollered?"

"You've got some explaining to do. What did you think you were doing, bringing Penny here?"

Jane had the honesty to look uncomfortable. "To be fair, she can be very persuasive, and we didn't know what we were going to find."

"That's the whole point." No one had noticed they'd

been joined by Lawrence. Looking a little more like his old self, albeit a little soggy after Jane's ministrations, the policeman came and stood next to Matt and Terry. "None of you should be here. If it wasn't for a bit of luck, more than one of you could have been shot."

A little unexpectedly, Terry came out in the girl's defense. "Steady on, there, Boss. None of us knew what was going to happen today, how things would go down. You could—and probably should—have waited for me; you're the one who got shot, remember." Terry apparently felt the need to point that out. "No matter how we think it over, that's the end of things. We'll get this piece of filth back to the station, interview him, and get to the bottom of what's gone on here."

"I won't tell you a thing!" Pike spat from the ground.

In response, Bobby pressed his muzzle against the man's face and treated him to a full-throated growl. Pike immediately shut up.

"I suppose…well…" Lawrence began to speak a couple of times before whipping the towel around and wringing it out. "You know? I honestly don't know what to say. I never do, with you lot. No matter what, you always manage to get yourselves into trouble. Please, try to remember what happened today, and let's say no more about it."

Penny opened her mouth, only for both Jane and Terry to shake their heads. She wasn't given the chance to change her mind, as the clanging of an ambulance's bell could now be heard coming along the lane.

"Bet you're glad Doris wasn't here!" Jane said, looking directly at Lawrence, being rewarded with seeing his Adam's apple bob up and down as if upon a trampoline.

****

"Well, she's a tough old bird, that Mavis, and no mistake!" Grace remarked, settling on the sofa and holding out her hands for the cup of tea Jane handed her. "Her son Ned seems a nice chap. We spent half the time trying to convince her not to go back to work until she's really ready." She made sure she'd caught Jane's eye when she spoke. Blowing on her cup, she took a swift sip, wincing at the heat but glad of it, nevertheless. "So sorry to only just be calling around," she added, glancing at the clock on the mantelpiece, which stated it was just past ten at night. She looked around at the surprisingly empty room. "I was hoping to speak to Betty, actually."

"Sorry," Jane said as she took her place next to the nurse. "Betty and Mary are away for the night. I had to get them to take on a late job, so they're staying over."

"And Doris?"

"I don't suppose you'd be aware, but she's now living at Ruth's with her husband," Penny supplied. She was sitting, both stockinged feet tucked under her bottom, on the seat opposite the others, her eyes closed and obviously on the verge of falling asleep.

"I'd forgot," Grace answered, leaning down and placing her cup on the floor. "Now, let's take a look at you, Penny. You look like you've had a busy day since I last saw you."

"Maybe a little," Penny said, her words beginning to slur.

Grace deliberately took hold of Penny's left forearm a little harder than needed, and saw her wince.

"If the purpose of that was to wake me up…" Penny accused her, glaring.

Grace was busy unwrapping the bandage but took a

moment to reply, "It was," before carrying on with her task as if nothing had happened.

"I'm so happy you're on our side," Penny told her through gritted teeth. "Ouch!"

"Glad to hear it," Grace replied, looking into Penny's face, "or I might be worried about hurting you."

"I'd shut up, if I were you," Jane advised Penny.

"And that's why she's the boss!" Grace said, beginning to rewrap Penny's arm.

Ten minutes later, Penny had been poked, prodded, and was beginning to feel a real kinship with Egyptian mummies. Finally, satisfied that Penny was coming along well, Grace added, "Despite your determination to do yourself more damage." She went back to the sofa, picked up her cup, and finished off her tea. Smacking her lips, she fixed Penny with a serious expression. "Look at me and listen, Penny. You got lucky in that crash, very, very lucky. From what you and your friends told me, you should never have walked away as you did, with just a few burns and cuts. However, unless you stop playing silly games, you could easily get those burns infected, and then you'd be in for a long hospital stay. Is that what you want?"

Penny gulped. This serious side to their friendly nurse was new to her, and judging by the wide-eyed look on Jane's face, it was new to her as well.

When Penny failed to find her voice, Jane spoke for her. "Don't you worry, Grace. I'll make sure she does as you say."

"I'm going to be bored stiff, stuck here all day for the next two weeks!" Penny couldn't help but protest.

"No, you won't," Jane immediately said. "I can't go into details yet, as nothing's been set in stone. However, until then, you'll be coming in to work as normal. I know you've been told to take two weeks' sick leave, but we both know there's no point in your staying here, you've said so yourself, so I'll see you in the hut tomorrow morning. There are provisos, though, and if you break even one, I'll personally tie you to your bed and get Doris to force-feed you a cup of her coffee."

"There's no need to be nasty, Boss," Penny replied, unable to suppress a shudder. Everyone knew how much she hated coffee. "What are the terms?"

"Nothing too difficult to remember. You stay in the hut, and you do your job. That's it."

Penny frowned, suspicious. "That's it?"

Jane shrugged. "That's it. I simply don't want you to do anything silly. When things are slow, you concentrate on those exercises Grace just showed you."

The nurse nodded. "Not that you asked for my opinion, but I think that's an excellent idea. Especially the exercises. They'll make certain your muscles get the movement they need."

"You mentioned you wanted to talk with Betty," Penny asked.

"Ignoring the rather obvious effort to deflect the conversation!" Grace laughed. "Yes, I did."

"And?"

"And…God, you lot are nosey, even when there's only the pair of you!" Grace smiled. "And I wanted to let her know that Marcus and me, we're engaged."

Jane and Penny had only just jumped—in Penny's case heaved—to their feet when the lounge door flew open and Doris stood in the frame, with Ruth and Matt close behind her.

"You've told her!" She then stopped and looked

around, settling on Jane to say, "Oh, they didn't make it back."

"Afraid not," Penny said with a shake of her head, as she and Jane pulled Grace to her feet and enveloped her in a hug.

"Ah, well, never mind," Doris decided, stepping aside to allow her companions to enter the room. "Tell me, has anyone had time to eat yet?" They all shook their heads, not an easy task as Grace was now surrounded by the other four and none could move very easily. "Right, leave this to me," Doris told them, turning to leave. "Fish 'n' chips all around it is!"

Chapter Thirty-Nine

Betty and Mary stepped off the train next morning, stretched and groaned, then stretched again.

"What time's the bus?" Betty asked, not troubling to hide her yawn.

Mary looked at her wristwatch, then down the road, before sitting down on the bench at the bus stop. "It'll be along in about another three or four minutes."

"Thank God for that," Betty said, yawning again. "I don't know about you, but I didn't get a wink of sleep all night. Those beds in the mess were lumpy as heck!"

"Mine was fine," Mary told her.

"Well, lucky you," Betty moaned, too tired to feel gracious.

After a few moments' silence, Mary pondered, "I wonder what the others got up to yesterday?"

The sound of an engine caught their attention, and they both looked up in time to see what was unmistakably Jane's Jeep barreling toward them, with the lady herself behind the wheel. Picking up their bags, both looked at each other, thinking the same thing.

Mary put their thoughts into words. "Something definitely happened yesterday."

"And I don't think we're going to like it," Betty added.

From the passenger seat, Bobby barked his own hello as the Jeep screeched to a halt beside them.

"Get in," Jane ordered without preamble. "We had a hell of a day after you two left yesterday, and I'm afraid I need you both on duty right away, so I hope you managed to get a good night's sleep. I'll fill you in on the way back to the station."

By the time they arrived back at RAF Hamble and pulled up at the ops hut, Mary and Betty were in stunned silence. It had been a lot to take in.

"And you're sure Ambrose will be all right?" Betty asked, negotiating her way around Bobby, who was jumping from his passenger seat into the back and then back again. "Down, Bobby!" she tried to tell the overexcited dog for the third time. He kept sitting on her overnight bag between jumps. Mary came and picked him up, giving Betty the chance to get out of the Jeep. "Thanks, Mary," she said with some relief.

"Not even time for a wash and brush-up?" Mary asked Jane as they trooped up the steps.

Jane pushed open the door. "Sorry, girls, I really am. Best I can do is a couple of thermos flasks of Sharon's prize tea, a packet of jam sandwiches each, and my eternal thanks."

Betty looked at Jane through half-closed eyes and between yawns told her, "If you weren't such a good friend, I'd suggest what you can do with those."

"But…" Jane said, playing safe and moving into her office and behind her desk.

"But," said Betty, leaning against the door frame, "so long as Mary will fly us where we need to go, I'm sure some of Sharon's tea will soon restore me."

Doris, already clad in her Sidcot flying suit, met them both with a hug before going over to a large brown teapot on the end of Penny's desk and coming back with

349

two cups of the promised nectar. "There you go. Just what the doctor ordered."

"You are a blessing." Betty smiled, accepting her cup and taking a sip. A look of near ecstasy upon her face, she glanced around the room, taking in a rather battered-looking Penny leaning back in her chair. "You, Doris Johnson, are forgiven for all the trouble you've gotten me into."

"Aw, gee, isn't that sweet of you." Doris put her best drawl into the statement before she half turned away, a cloud drifting over her face.

Betty grasped Doris's arm. "I didn't mean anything by that. I was only playing around."

They all heard the deep intake of breath the American took before she turned back to them. Her normal smile was upon her face, though everyone could see it didn't reach her eyes. "I know," she told Betty. "I know you didn't mean anything by it. I'm just, and don't any of you dare tell him, a little worried about my Walter. That's two head injuries in a short time. Bad news comes in threes, I believe. He's coming home this morning, and I can't be with him. I wish I could," she swiftly swiveled her eyes toward Jane and just as quickly averted them.

Jane looked slightly abashed. "I wish I could spare you today, I really do."

Doris held up a hand. "It's okay, I understand." Then when Jane looked on the point of speaking again, she said, "I do. I understand how things are. He'll be waiting for me when I get back tonight."

To move things along from this rather awkward moment, Betty leant over Penny and carefully moved her hair aside to give her a quick kiss on the forehead, explaining, "That looked like one of the few places which wouldn't hurt," getting a smile in return for her thoughtfulness. She turned her attention back to Jane. "Before we go, you never answered me. Will Ambrose be all right?"

At least Jane had the good grace not to try sugarcoating her reply. "The doctors believe so. They're checking him out for various diseases, but please don't ask me to repeat the names. I've only just got my tongue back into shape, though they do say that considering what had been done to him, he's in good shape."

"I can't believe anyone would do that to another person!" Mary muttered, shaking her head. "Burying someone in pig sh…"

"People can be nasty," Betty hastened to interrupt. "You've only got to think of Hitler…"

"I'd rather not," Mary said in return.

"Do you really think this Pike character meant for the pigs to eat him?" Betty asked Jane, who shrugged.

"Who knows? But from what Lawrence said, it seems likely."

Mary leant on the desk, looming toward Jane. "And they released Lawrence last night? He's really okay?"

Jane nodded vigorously. "Just a bump. He refused pointblank to stay overnight. It wouldn't surprise me if he's back at work this morning," she added.

Mary looked longingly at the telephone.

Going back around, Jane squeezed Mary's shoulder as she took Betty's arm and eased her out of the room. "Help yourself. Five minutes."

Closing the door behind them, Jane, Doris, and Betty took up station outside the door, unashamedly listening in. Penny looked like she was thinking about joining them, only to decide the effort to move was too much at present, so she settled down to the paperwork strewn all over her desk. Once she got put through, Mary's voice was initially at a pitch a professional singer would be proud of. However, Lawrence must have quickly reassured her, as her audience was soon straining to hear.

"Let's move away," Betty suggested, after a few minutes. "It sounds like we may hear things we don't wish to. Plus, I've been meaning to ask you, who's looking after his farm whilst Ambrose is in hospital? I'm assuming they won't be letting him out for at least a few days."

"More like a week, I'd think," Jane said. "That's the interesting bit! Bell and Ledbetter, from the farm next door, are going to take care of it until he's well enough to come back. He's even agreed to getting some Land Girls in to help out once he gets back."

"Miracles will never cease," Betty barely managed to get out before Mary flung the door open, a huge grin on her face.

"I take it that went well?" Jane asked, folding her arms and winking.

All three could see their friend was fighting off the urge to hug herself. "I feel I could flap my arms and fly off!"

"Let's stick to the Anson, eh?" Jane teased, before going over to Penny's desk, where Penny handed her a couple of bits of paper. Turning back, she passed the girls each a chit for their next delivery. "Time to get airborne—in the conventional way, I'm afraid. It's only a couple of Mossies, but RAF Little Staughton needs them."

Betty shook her head. She knew that not all the

aircraft they delivered were for new units. Indeed, most were to replace losses, which meant more young men had been killed, wounded, or were missing in action, and not many of those were expected to turn up alive. She tried not to think that they were going to where Penny's husband Tom was stationed. Still, it was a job they were all proud to do, and both Betty and Mary accepted the chits and made their way to the door.

Mary displayed a feral grin. Jane should have known better than to ask, "What's up with you?"

"Lawrence had a message for you, from the hospital." Betty and Doris stopped where they were and waited, while Jane looked embarrassed. "A doctor McNichol spoke to him as he was leaving and asked if he could have your telephone number." Jane could only cough and wait for Mary to finish. "I just gave it to Lawrence, who's going to pass it on. We assume this is all right?"

The girls noticed Jane was fiddling with her watch, and Betty went over, gently took Jane's wrist, and brought it closer to her eyes. She looked up into Jane's eyes, pulled out her handkerchief, and gave it to her friend, who dabbed the tears from her eyes.

"That's the same watch Frank gave you, isn't it?"

Jane nodded, unable to find words.

"He'd want you to find happiness," Betty softly told her, receiving a single nod in return.

With a supreme effort, Jane gathered herself together before sniffing and saying, just as softly, "I know, I know. Now, get yourselves away. I've things to do."

Without waiting, Jane turned on her heel and marched back to her office, closing the door behind her.

The three remaining girls exchanged concerned looks, and none were surprised to hear a stifled sob escape through the door. Knowing their friend would want them to get on with the delivery and would prefer to be alone, they shouldered their kit and made for the door. Penny would be there if she were needed, and knowing that made it a little easier to leave.

As they left, they heard Penny quickly shout, "If you get the chance, tell Tom I'm doing fine and give him my love!"

****

"You've got the crowbar, Terry?"

The sergeant held the shaped iron bar out but refused to hand it over. "Let me, Boss," he told Lawrence politely, yet firmly. "I'm not even sure you should have been at the interview this morning, let alone out here."

Lawrence had to smile, though his hand did snake up of its own accord to rub where he'd been felled by Pike the previous day. A headache of monumental proportions was building, and he needed to get some fresh air. From the hollow sound the floorboard had made when Terry rapped his knuckles against it just now, he had high hopes they were in the right place. Heaven help Pike if he was lying. That aside, it was certainly the room Pike had occupied during his stay at Ambrose's farm. There were empty whiskey and brandy bottles lining the skirting boards, almost certainly black market, which would explain the man's breath and pallor.

When they were interviewing him that morning, the man had had a bad case of the sweats and shakes. His cup had rattled so much when he'd put it down on the interview table that half the contents had sloshed over the side. It had quickly become obvious the man relied

354

heavily upon alcohol to maintain a resemblance of control. Much, much quicker than either of the policemen could have hoped for, right after they'd told him he'd be breaking rocks for the rest of his life if he didn't talk, he'd cracked. It had taken all of Terry's concentration to take down what he told them, as the man's accent also became more and more pronounced as he rambled. Neither policeman could pinpoint exactly where, but both were in no doubt the man came from Ireland.

The rifles had been part of a cache stolen from an arms arsenal a week before the war had broken out. Unable to smuggle them out of the country due to heightened security, the team sitting on them had decided to bury them. At being asked why that location was chosen, he merely shrugged and told them it had looked like just an unkempt bit of ground at the time. When it was discovered that the airfield was being extended and the rifles would almost certainly be discovered, he'd been dispatched by his superiors to recover them. Terry had commented that it all seemed a bit amateur, and asked, why do it on his own? With another shrug, Pike had merely mumbled something about inciting an insurrection for the cause and didn't elaborate. He'd chosen Ambrose because he lived alone and so the operation was unlikely to be disturbed, though Ruth had put paid to that, and because he was known to own the land upon which the rifles were buried.

That was the last coherent thing they'd got out of him. Flinging him back into a cell, they decided to give him time to think things over and, perhaps, sober up. They'd get a full statement out of him tomorrow.

Kicking aside a well-worn copy of the *Irish Times*,

Terry dug the crowbar into an edge that bore signs of similar usage, and with a swift downward motion, had the floorboard out. Getting down on his knees, he shone a torch around the hole and then, very slowly and carefully, felt with his fingers for any booby traps. Taking out a small mirror from his inside pocket, he edged it into the hole and angled it around. Satisfied, he then felt around the sides of the single large, brown envelope which was all it seemed to contain. Taking a deep breath, he slowly took it out, keeping it as level as he could.

"Nice job," Lawrence praised him, as Terry laid it upon the bed, sweeping aside numerous empty cigarette packets.

"Right, let's see what we've got," Terry said, upending the envelope.

It was a veritable treasure trove! Spread over the rather dirty blanket were a number of passports, currency in quite a number of different denominations, including pounds and dollars, and an ordinance survey map of the area with, of all things, a large X marking the end of RAF Hamble runway.

Lawrence clapped his colleague on the back, "Bingo!"

Chapter Forty

"What do you make of that?"

Having left Jane and Penny in the ops hut, Betty, Doris, and Mary began pulling on their flying clothes, ready for a busy morning. "Are you complaining?" Mary asked, from somewhere within the depths of her off-white woolen pullover. "After the last few days, it'll be nice to have a long weekend. Heaven knows we've had few enough relaxing days over the last week!"

"That," grunted Doris pulling on one of her boots, "is an understatement. I still can't believe I missed all that at the farm!"

"By what we've heard, I'd hardly call it a bunch of fun," Betty advised. "I'd say everyone, including poor Ambrose, got off lucky to come away without getting hurt worse."

Doris paused, her remaining boot dangling. "That wasn't what I meant, and you know it."

Wagging a finger, the only appendage she'd managed to get out of her pullover, Mary felt the need to point out to Doris, "I hope you haven't forgotten how close you came to being shot too? Again!"

Doris's mouth opened and closed a couple of times before she settled down and pulled on her remaining boot. Once she'd had time to think, she could only agree, in a way. "I…suppose. Not that I think they even knew I was there."

"Didn't stop them attacking poor Mavis, though, did it," Betty stated.

"Didn't Grace tell Penny she'd persuaded her to come into hospital today and get herself checked out?"

Betty nodded. "I heard that too."

"Good for her." Mary nodded approvingly.

"Come on," Doris prompted. "The sooner we get these deliveries over with, the sooner we can enjoy our long weekend. Walter's coming out of the hospital this afternoon…"

"Again," Mary couldn't stop herself from saying.

Doris nodded. "Again…and I want to be around to welcome him home. I've managed to get some Guinness in, and it's my intention to feed him up. Either that or make sure he goes everywhere wearing a helmet."

"If he drinks as much of the black stuff as you usually get in, Doris, he's going to need that helmet!" Betty helpfully told her friend.

"Oh, very funny. Ha-ha!"

The door of the flight line hut opened, admitting Penny, who slumped down next to Doris, leaning her head against a locker.

"You look like hell, Penny," Doris remarked, draping an arm around her.

Penny cracked open an eye. "Just tired, that's all. It helps to get out from under Jane's gaze, too."

"Keeping a close eye on you, is she?" Betty asked, getting to her feet and heaving her flight bag up.

Letting out a chuckle, Penny replied, "You could say that. I'd just got rid of that sling, and then all this happens!"

"Well, to be fair, you've not got the best record of doing what you're supposed to," Mary said.

"You mean, like all of us?"

"Exactly. Like all of you."

Everyone's head whipped around to find Penny had been followed by Jane.

"Uh, hi, Boss," Penny said, struggling slightly to get to her feet before giving up and staying where she was. "Just making sure this lot don't spend all day talking instead of walking."

"Is that what you were doing?" Jane asked, allowing a small smile to creep onto her face.

Betty came and stood next to Jane and lightly nudged her with her shoulder. "Naturally. What did it look like?"

"Like you were talking all day, instead of getting out on deliveries."

"Well, I guess we've been caught, girls. Come on, sooner we get out, the sooner we can enjoy the time off Jane's so graciously arranged," Doris suggested.

Jane accompanied them out to the waiting Anson, letting a hand trail along the tail of the plane until she stood by the open door. "Make this a good one, girls. I want everyone back safe and sound. You all know it's been one hell of a week—well, a few days, at least. We've never had anything like it, and with you lot, that's saying something!"

****

"You didn't tell her, then?"

Jane shook her head at Penny, as they watched the Anson take off. "Not the right time. I want Doris focused on the here and now. I don't want her speculating on what may happen in the near future."

"So, it's going to happen?" Penny asked, as Jane opened the door to the mess for her. "Thank you."

"Sharon. How's Mavis doing?" Jane instead asked, as they stood before the girl, who began to pour them each a cup of tea.

"All things considered," she replied, handing the first to Jane and beginning the second, "pretty good. Her son's taking her to the hospital today, and I'm sure him simply being here has been a great help to how she feels."

"And how does she feel?" Penny asked, nodding her thanks for her tea.

Sharon gave the question due consideration. "Like I said, she says she's doing okay, and I haven't seen anything to persuade me otherwise."

"I don't need to ask you to keep an eye on her, do I," Jane stated, not troubling to wait for a response. "Doris said her son, Ned, is a good guy."

"Looks like a sweet bear of a man, so I'd agree."

"Good. Let us know if we can do anything, please, Sharon. Also, she should take the week off, no matter what the hospital says."

"What do you reckon?" Penny asked a few seconds later, as she and Jane stood admiring the sheet with theirs and the visiting aircrews' signatures adorning the wall. "I vote we allow Mavis to sign the sheet."

Jane appeared to consider Penny's suggestion. "Well, it is only supposed to be for pilots…"

"Couldn't we stretch that rule, for Mavis, the once?"

"I like the idea," Jane said, after some thought. "How about we take her up in a Tiger Moth? Say it's a little get-better treat, and then ask her to sign the wall?"

"That's a great idea!" Sharon crowed, appearing unexpectedly behind them.

"Jesus! Sharon!" Penny said, as she had nearly

jumped out of her skin. "Has Lawrence been teaching you how to creep up on people?"

At the mention of his name, Sharon frowned. "No, but I would like to know what's happening with those German spies. I've been expecting to hear from them at any time. It's got me on edge."

Jane took the girl's arm and steered her toward a chair. "Are you and Mavis going to be all right? You know, living at her place, seeing as those people know where you live?"

It took a moment before Sharon replied. The face she turned on the pair was pure determination and defiance, in spite of what she'd just said. "I love living with Mavis, and no Nazi is going to drive me out of what I consider to be my home."

"Good girl!" Penny told her, putting down her cup. "Shall we get back to work, Jane?"

"You let me, or any of the girls, know if there's anything you need or something we can do. You've got that?" Jane asked, making sure she locked eyes with Sharon as she spoke. "Oh, and..." Jane turned back to say, "I take it you're coming over tonight? Lawrence wants to speak with us at Betty's."

"I'll be there," Sharon assured the pair.

"Any idea what that's all about?" Penny asked, as they left the mess.

"Not really, though I've a few things to tell everyone later too," Jane finished and refused to be drawn into elaborating.

Chapter Forty-One

Betty flopped down onto her sofa and let out a deeply contented sigh.

"That sounded like it came from the heart," Jane commented as she came into the room, proceeding to do the same, narrowly avoiding landing on her friend's knee.

From behind closed eyes, Betty told her, "Oh, it is. You've done wonders for the station's morale by getting us this long weekend. You know that."

Jane's hand snaked out and briefly took hold of Betty's. "I'm so glad. You don't want to know how many phone calls I had to make to get permission for this."

"I must admit, I'm surprised and so's everyone else. We're not blind. We know what's going to be happening—is happening—which is a big part of why we've been so busy lately."

"Make the most of it. We're going to be extra busy next week because of it."

"Who's going to be extra busy?" Mary asked, coming into the room with Penny close behind.

"You lot are," Penny supplied, before Jane could answer. "I could always muck in, if you need an extra pair of hands, Jane?"

Jane and Betty both cracked an eye open, while Betty let out a chuckle and shook her head. "Nice try, but no, thanks. If needs come to it, I'll fly a few. You're

362

grounded until the doctors tell me otherwise and, knowing you, I think I should ask for that permission to be written in blood—yours—and in triplicate."

Mary looked at where Penny was eyeing Jane, her face aghast and not sure whether she should take her seriously or not. Taking pity, she led her friend to a seat, though she was unable to resist saying, "I'd behave if I were you, or Jane may carry out her threat."

Jane raised her head and took pity on Penny. "I suppose now may be as good a time as any."

"For what?" Betty asked.

"To tell you all this…"

"Wait for me!" Doris's voice was rapidly accompanied into the lounge by the lady herself, hand firmly gripping Walter.

Her husband had another bandage wrapped around his head, though he appeared more embarrassed than in pain from his latest run-in. If you had to ask, he'd accomplished the perfect longsuffering-husband expression. However, he also didn't look like he'd be letting go of his wife's hand any time soon, either.

Jane got up off the sofa and guided Walter toward it. "Come on, space for a wounded warrior next to Betty."

Head injury or not, Doris pushed him down, placing herself at his feet even before he knew what had happened. "What did we miss?"

Jane looked out the window and then asked, sounding a little grumpy, "Are we likely to have any more visitors?"

"Lawrence is bringing Sharon over later," Mary mentioned, though she gave no indication she was going to elaborate.

"And Ruth is out for a walk with Matt," Doris

supplied, leaning on one of Walter's knees.

From where she stood, Jane leant back against the window shelf. "I've been trying to tell you lot that we're going to have some more help in a few weeks." This announcement got everyone's attention. "Shirley Tuttle will be finishing her training a little early. I've asked for her to be posted to us, and the powers that be have agreed she can come and join our little group!"

Doris, who'd been especially supportive of Shirley, broke into a huge grin. "Great! She's not having her old room back, though."

"My old place in Ruth's attic should do her fine," Walter said. "She'll only be sleeping up there, after all."

"Ruth could do with being here," Betty mused.

"Speaking of Shirley," Mary said. "Has anyone seen any more letters from her husband? Apart from the first few weeks, I don't remember seeing any."

Jane answered, as she'd been the one forwarding the mail. "I'd thought it a bit strange too, but what with everything as it's been, I'm ashamed to say I'd forgot."

"I suppose we could ask her when we see her now," Doris suggested.

"Do you think Ruth will be all right with her moving back in?" Penny asked Doris.

"I don't see why not," she replied.

"Well, you do spend most of your time around here," Betty pointed out.

"Trying to get me back?" Doris asked, with a pretend pout.

"Well, you are a tad boring, now you're married," Betty teased.

"Speaking of moving back in," Penny interjected, pulling out a letter from her trouser pocket. "I've heard from Celia, and she's going to be finishing school in about three weeks' time."

"Hold on, hold on, hold on," Betty said, turning her head toward Penny. "If memory serves me right, didn't I agree that your sister could move in once she finished school?"

"You...may have said something along those lines," Penny agreed, not quite meeting her friend's gaze.

"Hmm, I think we really need to get together with Ruth and work things out," Betty stated again.

"If you think I'm moving out of Doris's old room, you can think again," Jane stated.

Betty held up a hand for peace. "No one's suggesting anything of the like. We've still got plenty of time."

"Though I'd think about putting up a name plaque on your room's door, if I were you," Mary advised.

****

After a rather splendid tea of chicken stew, the girls settled in around Betty's kitchen table.

Mary raised her bottle of Guinness to her lips and asked, "You know, with everything that's happened over the last few days, we never did go and look for all our missing clothes."

"Bobby!" Jane cried, putting down the copy of *The Body in the Library* she'd finally managed to get her hands on. "I'd completely forgotten you'd found out what had happened to all your clothes. Has anyone missed anything since?"

Everyone shook their heads.

"It is rather strange he's never tried to steal anything from his own home," Doris commented, popping the lid off her Guinness.

The back door opened and in strode Ruth, Matt, and the dog in question.

"Speak of the devil," Mary said, kneeling down and giving him an ear scratch.

"What's he done now?" Ruth asked, accepting a bottle of stout and passing another on to Matt, who opened them both before pulling out a chair for her. "Such a gentleman, thank you."

Betty waited until both their guests were settled and had taken a drink and put down their bottles. "Now there's no danger of either of you coating my table, we've uncovered what's been happening to our clothes which were going missing. Yon culprit has just come into the room."

"Matt! I never knew!" Ruth jokingly accused her boyfriend. "What do you have to say for yourself?"

Matt began to go red, but Doris saved his blushes. "As amusing as that would be, Bobby is definitely the culprit."

"What happened?" Ruth asked.

"I saw him disappearing through the hedge with my shoe," Betty said.

"What do you reckon he's done with everything?" Matt asked.

"Well, to be honest, we've only just remembered seeing him," Mary answered, "though I'd place a bet on him hiding them away in his dog house."

Ruth gave this some thought before replying, "That'd make sense. I honestly can't tell you the last time I took a look in there. There's no reason, as he always sleeps indoors. I suppose I really should give it a clean out. Heaven only knows what state it's in!"

Jane sat back to contemplate developments before

saying, "Let's check out his kennel in the morning. I don't think anything's going to go, if you'll pardon the expression, walkies tonight."

Shortly after, there came a knock on the front door.

"I'll get it," Ruth said. "It can only be Lawrence. He's the only one of us who bothers to knock instead of coming straight in."

As Ruth went to answer the door, Jane tapped Penny on the shoulder. "Can I borrow you for a minute?"

"Of course," she replied and followed Jane into the lounge. Jane shut the door behind them. "What's the problem?"

Jane turned and faced her friend. "I don't anticipate there being one," she said, a little enigmatically.

"Which means?" Penny asked, rather puzzled.

"It means," Jane told her, "that the inquiry into that crash you had in the Typhoon begins next week. The delegation's coming around to talk with everyone."

"Should I, er, should I be worried?"

Jane took a step closer and placed her hands on Penny's shoulders, and shook her head. "I don't see why. We all know what happened."

"Right, if you say so," Penny replied, but began to nervously rub the bandages on her left arm as she spoke.

Jane removed her hands. "Really, there's nothing you should worry about."

It took a few moments, but eventually Penny stopped trying to scratch at her burns and nodded.

"Have you two finished?" Doris asked, from the other side of the door. "I've left Walter with a Guinness, and he's enjoying it too much."

With one more nod of encouragement, Jane stepped to one side, opened the door, and allowed Penny to leave before her. "Tell everyone we'll be there in a minute," she told Penny. "A word, please?" she said to Doris.

"Whatever it was, I didn't do it," Doris said, as Jane closed the door.

"I'm sure you did," Jane retorted, clapping her friend briefly on the shoulder before sitting on the sofa. "Come and sit down."

"Okay," Doris replied, unable to keep the questioning tone out of her voice. "What's up?"

"I've had a request for a pilot," Jane began, swiftly elaborating when Doris merely raised an eyebrow. "The bigwigs want an ATA pilot to ferry around a general for a couple of weeks, as he does a tour of various military units around the country."

Doris was silent for a minute, eventually asking, "Why does he want one of us? Why not a military pilot?"

"I wish I could give you an official answer, but truth be told, I think they can't spare an operational pilot," Jane admitted.

Doris scoffed, "And we can? Don't they know how busy we are?"

Jane sighed. "Believe me, I reckon they do, but when the military mind gets an idea in its head, it takes an awful lot to sway it. I think that's where we are now."

"But we're so short! Why not another unit?" Doris tried again.

Jane could only shrug again. "Believe me, I've asked all these questions, and more. I'm sorry in more than one way, Doris, but they want you. Maybe it's because you're a Yank, or simply that you're one of our best pilots. Whichever way you look at it, however we argue it, there's no getting out of it. You're going to be a general's personal pilot for two weeks, starting Monday week."

"Will Shirley be here by the time I have to go?" Doris asked.

Jane smiled approvingly. "Excellent question. Hopefully, the timing will work out fine." She got to her feet. "Come on, let's not hold up Lawrence any longer. We'll talk more of this in the coming week."

By the time they went back to the kitchen, it was to find it rather crowded.

"Take my seat, love," Walter told his wife, making to get to his feet. He didn't get far before his good wife pushed him back down and sat upon his lap, draping her arms around his neck.

"You're going to need a bigger kitchen!" Jane commented, much to everyone's amusement.

"Everyone make yourselves as comfortable as you can. Lawrence wants a word with us all. Sharon! You all right there by the door?" Betty called.

"I've turned the key, so no one can knock me over!"

"Well, we're not expecting anyone else," Betty muttered, before saying to Lawrence, "We're all yours."

Lawrence cleared his throat, then nearly jumped as he felt a hand take his. Looking down, he followed the hand up its arm until he found he was looking into the welcoming face of his girlfriend.

"I won't tell anyone the big, brave policeman jumped, just because I took his hand," she told him, with a smile.

"We will, though!" Naturally, this was spoken by Doris.

Walter was heard to say, "Let the man speak, love. It's getting a bit on the warm side in here."

"Fair enough. Are you up for a walk after?"

His reply made the room laugh—"Only if you promise to protect me from Duck."

"Are we done yet, Doris?" Lawrence asked, semi-seriously annoyed. "Right. Thank you all for coming, and yes, I will keep it as short as I can, as I quite agree with Walter that a walk in the cool evening air with my girlfriend would be an excellent way to end the day."

Mary interrupted him by going up on tiptoes and kissing his cheek. "Good boy. You're learning."

"Well, right…" He stopped, regaining his composure before finally beginning, "I'm sure you can all guess why I want to speak to you. You've all heard about what happened at Mavis's home, and I'm very glad to say that she doesn't appear to have suffered any lasting injury. Sharon tells me she'll be back at work a week on Monday and that she wants no fuss made or she'll forget how to make Sharon's tea." This led to mutterings amongst the crowded room, which quickly died down when he held up his hands for quiet.

"You've been warned." He smiled. "Now, more seriously, you all know, or have a good idea, of what Sharon and I have been up to. Unbeknownst to even myself, Special Branch were watching us, not only to protect us—yes, I've heard they actually feel bad about what happened to Mavis—but to find out who the Germans' contact was over here. When they drove off after they left Sharon, they were followed. Unfortunately, the tail lost them after only a few miles, and they haven't been able to find them since."

"Do you expect them to contact Sharon again?" Penny asked.

Lawrence nodded. "We believe so, or, at the very least, we have to work on the premise that they'll carry on with their plan. We don't believe they actually knew they were being followed, though they managed to get over a train crossing before the Special Branch car could." He squeezed Mary's hand and looked down at her as he said, "So, Sharon and I will still be getting together to work on this conundrum occasionally. Needless to say, nothing of what I've said tonight can be discussed with anyone who isn't in this room. I'd get into real trouble if any of this gets out, as it is, so I'd appreciate it if you'd keep this quiet. And it goes without saying, watch your backs."

As Mary treated her boyfriend to a quick kiss, Jane banged her bottle of Guinness on the table for attention.

"Before we all have too much to drink, I want you all to listen and take in what I have to say. I want you to all be on your guard. This isn't over, by a long way!"

A word about the author...

Mick is a hopeless romantic who was born in England and spent fifteen years roaming around the world in the pay of HM Queen Elisabeth II in the Royal Air Force before putting down roots and realizing how much he missed the travel. This, he's replaced somewhat with his writing, including reviewing books and supporting fellow saga and romance authors in promoting their novels.

He's the proud keeper of two cats bent on world domination, is mad on the music of the Beach Boys and enjoys the theatre and humoring his Manchester-United-supporting wife. Finally, and most importantly, Mick is a full member of the Romantic Novelists Association.

His previous books published with The Wild Rose Press include *A Wing and a Prayer*, *Wild Blue Yonder*, *I'll Be Home for Christmas*, and *In the Mood*, all part of his Broken Wings series on the ATA of WW2, and *The Lumberjills*, beginning a series of another group of WW2 women who "did their part." He is very proud to be in The Rose Garden.

Thank you for purchasing
this publication of The Wild Rose Press, Inc.

For questions or more information
contact us at
info@thewildrosepress.com.

The Wild Rose Press, Inc.